Reviews

"The Secret"

"Standridge introduces Morgan O'Connell, a woman clawing her way out of grief to rebuild both her life and a sanctuary for others. Harmony Hills is more than a horse facility—it's the heart of Morgan's recovery. Standridge ties Morgan's emotional recovery to the daily work of restoring trust, both in herself and in others. Though the story's suspense heightens the stakes, it's Morgan's self-discovery and the authenticity of her connections that give it real depth." ~ **Prairies Book Review**

"Morgan picks up the shell of her life and moves to Arizona where she builds a new horse ranch called Harmony Hills... This book was such a page turner. Morgan is a flawed but strong character, and it was great to see how she grew in terms of emotional and even physical resilience." ~ **Amazon Review**

"...A truly heartwarming story of strength, resilience, and second chances. Morgan O'Connell's journey after a personal tragedy is inspiring...It's a beautiful tale of love, trust, and finding peace after hardship. A truly enjoyable read!" ~ **Amazon Review**

"...Absolutely phenomenal. I started reading it and couldn't put it down. It encompasses strength, bravery, passion, courage, and mystery..." ~ **Amazon Review**

"This book is fire! The characters will draw you in and make you feel like you're there. It is so good, I even read it in the bath tub! Must read!!!!" ~ **Amazon Review**

"This novel really resonated with me in ways I didn't expect... I appreciated that her healing wasn't rushed—she guarded her story, like many of us do. The romance with Josh was tender, but what stood out most was Morgan choosing herself, her peace, and her future. It's emotional, reflective, and quietly empowering in a way that lingers."
~ Amazon Review

"Jordan has a gift for bringing characters to life. Her writing is passionate, vivid, and flawless in my eyes. I could imagine everything so clearly... The emotional depth felt real... Highly recommend!" **~ ARC Reader/ Amazon Review**

"Jordan is really great at making the reader attached to the characters. You can feel the soul behind them. She brought every character to life with the passion she's invoked!

"The humor has been amazing as well! I haven't laughed out loud reading a book in a long time. And I'm a stone, so to actually cry while reading it was amazing. This one book really was able to touch all of my emotions and made me tap into them as a reader. Reading certain chapters definitely had me on the edge of my seat. I feel such an attachment to the characters and I need more! I'm hooked!" **~ ARC Reader**

"[*The*] *Secret* was such an amazing book, it kept me in suspense from one chapter to the next. I am not an avid reader, but could not put the book down until I had it read. Such courage by the main character Morgan, that it would give anyone hope and courage to move on with your life. The love that grew between Morgan and Josh was so real and very uplifting... You will not be disappointed in buying and reading this book. I look forward to more books by this author." **~ Amazon Review**

"Just finished *The Secret*. Loved it. Jordan writes so you can relate to the characters. You can feel their ups and downs. You felt what they were going through, and the courage they had to reinvent their lives and move on. The book completely held your interest so that you did not want to put it down but to keep reading to see what happened next. There was a surprise twist at the end that I didn't see coming. When reading the book, you actually feel what the characters feel. Can't wait for her next one. So far loving what I've read from her." **~ Goodreads Review**

"The Witness"

"*The Witness* shifts gears into high-stakes suspense. Raina, whose act of selfless courage turns her into a target, is thrust into a nightmare of trauma and pursuit. What follows is an emotionally gripping narrative where action and tenderness coexist in perfect balance. The pacing remains taut, the stakes high, but Standridge never lets the heart of the story fade. Through Detective Channion Scott's devotion and his growing feelings for Raina, the novel becomes less about survival alone and more about endurance and human connection.

"Standridge's prose is vivid yet unpretentious, the dialogue authentic, and the pacing perfectly tuned...She brings both the ache of grief and the promise of healing to life with quiet emotional precision." ~ **Prairies Book Review**

"Great mystery (Police FBI). Best 'free book' ever! Words to describe: RIVETING, PAGE TURNER, CLEAN, SUSPENSEFUL, GREAT CHARACTER DEVELOPMENT, WELL WRITTEN AND MORE!... WILL BE READING MORE of this author's books, and they don't have to be free!" ~ **Goodreads Review**

"Raina is a vivid presence throughout *The Witness,* filled with urgency from the very first page. Author Jordan Standridge does a very good job of convincing the reader that this woman is the sort who would instinctively intervene to save someone's life. Her recovery from her injuries and developing relationship with Channion as he strives to protect her both emotionally and physically are compelling and authentic... The sense of danger as Raina slowly recovers her memories and the police close in on the criminals is convincing...*The Witness* is buoyed by its core character relationship. Channion and Raina's burgeoning romance set against the backdrop of danger is consistently interesting and engaging." ~ **IndieReader Review**

"HEA!!! Wow. A page turner for sure. Just about the time you think you know where the story is going, there is a twist and turn I was so not expecting. It's impossible to stop reading once you start." ~ **Amazon Review**

"Fantastic book! Best book I have read all year. It has it all...courage, strength, laughter, romance, suspense, friends, and family." ~ **Amazon Review**

"...If you enjoy a strong female protagonist, thrilling action and a sprinkling of romance, then this is an excellent choice of book. The author balances the internal emotions and external action of the plot well and creates likeable, believable characters..."
~ Amazon Review

"I'm a huge fan. This book has incredible character development, making it easy to get attached to everyone. [Jordan's] attention to detail truly brings the story to life, immersing you in the world they've created. It's a fun journey to go on with the characters, and you can't help but feel invested in their adventures." **~ ARC Reader**

"The book is full of suspense from one page to the next. Just when I would go to put it down, something else would happen, and I would have to keep reading to see what happened next. The book held [my] complete interest from beginning to end.

"The main character fights hard for her life, her loved ones, and for what she believes in. She never gives up, but holds on to her values along the way. Can't wait to see more from this author. Well done!!" **~ ARC Reader**

"The Rescues"

"*The Rescues* brings the series full circle, returning to Harmony Hills with a story that hums with quiet strength. Ripley Capilano's chance arrival at the ranch and her bond with a traumatized horse set the stage for one of the series' most emotionally nuanced romances. Her relationship with the guarded and steadfast Ty Stanton unfolds with slow-burning depth. Their journey from cautious strangers to soul-deep partners mirrors the horse's recovery—pain yielding to trust, and fear to faith."
~ Prairies Book Review

"*The Rescues* is a heartfelt exploration of love found through healing rather than perfection. As Ripley helps restore a traumatized horse's trust, she and Ty slowly confront their own fears and past wounds. Standridge's writing is immersive and compassionate, blending emotional growth and quiet romance into a cozy yet powerful story about learning to begin again." **~ NewInBooks.com Review**

"For some years now, I've been looking for stories that have meaning, that are captivating but also offer a lesson. In *The Rescues,* I found everything I was looking for in a novel: a strong and determined protagonist, a gripping plot, and compelling characters...This is undoubtedly a story to fall in love with, to return to what we left forgotten, and to relive."
~ Amazon Review

"It left me feeling like I had actually been to Harmony Hills, breathing in hay, silence, and second chances. Seeing Ripley heal an injured horse while, almost without meaning to, letting Ty get close to her own emotional wounds, feels genuine, tender, and not at all forced. It's one of those romances where the process of learning to trust again is almost more enjoyable than the inevitable." **~ Amazon Review**

"This captivating story had me glued to every page. I found the use of a horse as both a connection and a mirror to be absolutely brilliant; it reflected exactly what the protagonists needed to face in their lives things they had been avoiding until that moment. This book taught me that coincidences are sometimes 'causalities,' and that destiny knows how to place us at the perfect moment, shining a spotlight on the call to face our traumas and fears. It's a journey that helps you not only discover the true reasons behind your actions but also work through them to lighten the emotional load.

"I highly recommend this book to anyone looking for a story full of hope, where the great quest to find true strength and courage within oneself is at the heart of a beautiful narrative." **~ Amazon Review**

"This story is tender, emotional, and full of quiet strength. It beautifully blends healing, romance, and personal growth in a way that feels sincere and uplifting... This book left me feeling calm and encouraged. It is a heartfelt addition to the series, and a beautiful reminder that love often arrives when we least expect it." **~ Amazon Review**

"...An inspiring story of resilience in the face of extraordinary challenges. *The Rescues* weaves together the lives of women bound by compassion and conviction as they fight to protect others and find healing themselves...Both moving and empowering, this book is a tribute to women whose courage sparks hope, even in life's darkest moments." **~ Amazon Review**

"The Guardian"

"...This volume succeeds as both a suspenseful conclusion to a larger mystery and a heartfelt exploration of what it means to truly love someone through uncertainty, loss, and change. A thriller fueled as much by emotion as mystery." ~ **The Prairies Book Review**

"The Women of Strength, Courage, and Hope" Series

"Standridge's heartfelt trilogy traces the intertwined journeys of three women overcoming loss and danger, each uncovering that the path to healing runs through connection as much as endurance.

"Rooted in the heart of Arizona, the stories feel authentic and alive. The expanse of the desert and the quiet pulse of ranch life anchor the emotional intensity of each story. Read together, the three novels form an emotionally cohesive trilogy that celebrates endurance, compassion, and second chances. Standridge's prose is vivid yet unpretentious, the dialogue authentic, and the pacing perfectly tuned to the rhythm of each story's emotional stakes. She brings the ache of grief and the promise of healing to life with quiet emotional precision. Harmony Hills feels real and lived in; a refuge where pain meets possibility and where the land itself seems to mirror the characters' longing for peace. Fans of Debbie Macomber's *Cedar Coves series* and Nicholas Sparks' *The Rescue* and *Safe Haven* will find much to admire. A page-turning, emotionally charged trilogy that blends suspense, romance, and redemption in equal measure." ~ **Prairies Book Review**

"Jordan's work has genuinely inspired us. Each narrative resonates deeply, exploring profound themes of faith, resilience, and the transformative power of the human-animal bond. Her storytelling captures universal messages of hope and personal growth, making her work truly special.

"Jordan's work is captivating with its emotionally resonant themes and interconnected narratives. The layered storytelling not only keeps readers engaged but builds anticipation between books. Her stories on faith, resilience, and hope also make them ideal for book clubs and online discussions.

"She has a genuine, emotional storytelling that distinguishes her." ~ **ARC Reader**

Also by Jordan Standridge

<u>The Women of Strength, Courage, and Hope Series</u>

The Secret *

The Secret, Large Print

The Witness **

The Rescues

The Guardian

The Guardian, Large Print

*2025 *Global Book Awards Gold Winner- Women's Fiction*

2025 *Global Book Awards Silver Winner- Romance Suspense **as well as*

**2026 *Next Generation Indie Book Awards -Gold x2- Suspense & Second Novel*

The Secret

Book One

The Women of Strength, Courage, and Hope Series

Jordan Standridge

HAPPY TRAILS PRESS

The Secret

The Secret

ISBN: 978-1-967457-00-7 (KDP ebook)

ISBN: 978-1-967457-01-4 (KDP paperback)

ISBN: 978-1-967457-12-0 (KDP Large Print paperback)

ISBN: 978-1-967457-07-6 (non-KDP ebook)

ISBN: 978-1-967457-06-9 (non-KDP paperback)

www.JordanStandridge.com

Happy Trails Press

Cover Design by Damonza

Formatting Software: Atticus

To the hundreds of horses and other animals and pets I've loved...so far.

To my mom Sharon for instilling in me the virtues of loving animals, hard work, having dreams and goals, and having the tenacity and sheer will of not giving up. I wish you were still here to see how far I've come. Mom, I did it.

Prologue

SHE KNEW HOW TO be patient because she'd had years of practice. It didn't mean it was easy.

Being married to a handsome, loving, and wonderful man wasn't easy, but this was only because he was hardly ever home. She knew this before she married him, but that didn't make it any easier now.

When he *wasn't* home, she worried deep down inside that one day, he wouldn't be *able* to come home. She always pushed that terrifying thought aside, which was far from easy.

When he *was* home, it reminded her how truly amazing he really was. They never took what they had, or each other, for granted. Their love was deep, strong, and true. Both knowing he'd have to leave again at some point was anything but easy for either of them.

While much of her marriage to her love wasn't easy, loving him body, mind, and soul was.

IT WAS AT NIGHT when she got the call telling her he was gone. The news almost killed her. In a manner of speaking, it did.

In an instant, the life she knew was over. And in the next, a new one began.

Chapter 1

January

SHE AWOKE TO THE distant sounds of horses nickering and a running tractor. Opening her eyes, she slowly surveyed the darkened room that was lit up only slightly from the little nightlights. Quietly, she lay there listening to the sounds in the background, getting her bearings.

Untangling her arms from the blankets, she reached over and tilted the clock to check the time. Turning off the alarm before it blasted the peaceful silence, she turned on the bedside light, squinting her eyes until they adjusted. Finally, she crawled out of bed, made it up neatly before turning off the bedside light and making her way to the bathroom. She flipped on the little television in her room to a movie channel so she could listen to it as she got ready for her day.

Eating her breakfast in her quiet living room, she returned to her spacious kitchen to wash her dishes, and then turned off the lights. At her front door, she pulled on her well-worn boots, jacket, and hat before she headed out into the morning chill after re-setting her house alarm. There was barely enough light to see the puffs of warm breath she exhaled into the cool air as she walked. Following the lighted path from her house down the small rise to the barns, she heard the familiar and comforting sounds that came from living at an equestrian facility.

Reaching the main office building that doubled as the barn for the trail rides, her best friend and unofficial partner, Ty Stanton, opened the office door for her when he saw her through the window as he was walking by.

"Good morning, Morgan! Chilly out again, isn't it?"

"Yeah, but it feels great! It sure makes it hard to leave my warm house *knowing* it's chilly out though. I could just stay up there all day."

He nodded in agreement as he removed a mug of fresh, hot coffee from the coffee maker. She enjoyed the comforting, homey, and familiar scent of mornings when Ty beat her to the office. While she couldn't stand drinking coffee, she loved the smell of it.

She said, "But I knew we'd be busy not just for today but all week. If the weather holds, we should start this year off in a fantastic way!"

"The weather should be good all week long." At her questioning look, he explained, "I caught the news this morning before I left home."

"*You?* Watching the early news? Don't you say there's no reason to start your day off on such profound negativity?"

"It was an accident." He grinned at her before blowing on his hot coffee and taking a small, testing sip.

She picked up the messages he'd taken from voicemail, listed in order of priority. There were some they'd need to call right away since they were for late morning and early afternoon rides for that day.

Morgan smiled in delight. "Wow! Business *is* going to be good today. Let's have extra horses pulled early in case something else comes along. I'd rather be prepared than not. All hands will need to be on deck for these larger rides this afternoon. Of course, I don't need to tell you that. You know what you're doing." She teased, "At least you should by now."

"Sometimes I just get lucky." He grinned before sighing and saying what he knew she hated to hear. "Ivy may be showing signs of colic again. Bo let me know earlier. He said she just wasn't looking right to him. He's walking her right now."

Morgan felt her heart seize. She'd had Ivy for years. The pony was the best babysitter for kids, but she had a tendency to colic no matter what they did to prevent it. "Again? Maybe I should have one of the vets back out for tests. I'll go see her in a minute."

Reading the employee roster for the day, she tapped her index finger on the countertop as she mentally planned the busier day. "Alexis was looking for extra money, so she could maybe do an all-day shift. I'm not sure if she has classes later on though. Did she give us her new class schedule yet?"

"No. Last I heard she was trying to get in one more class. She didn't want us to get confused with which schedule was the right one. I told her to just wait, and give us the one that we needed to work from. I'll ask her about that when I see her."

"Be sure you do." Morgan shot him a quick grin and took another look at the roster. "We should be fine if she can stay. If not, one of us may need to head out with the big rides."

She leaned back and stretched before she said, "I ran into Kat last night on her way out. Lessons are going well at Quail Run. She said they're pretty full today. With our show coming up in three weeks, she and Mel should be busy because of that alone. I'll probably need to run over there later to check in with them. Maybe help with any details they may need guidance on."

"Shouldn't be a problem." Ty grabbed the portable phone, glancing at the clock. "It's eight now, so we're officially open. I'll take the phone for now." He clipped on the two-way radio she handed him, checking the channel first. As she headed for the door, he added, "Ivy's in Grand View."

"Thanks. I'll go check on her, and see what the old girl is up to this morning." She tried to keep the worry from her voice, but she knew Ty could hear it.

She crossed the large gravel lot on her way to Grand View, their largest building. This was the location for small to mid-size local shows and get-togethers. She also leased it out as a horse motel to those needing a place to put their horses on long road trips.

Stepping through the wide, lighted doorway, she made her way to the large indoor arena. Looking over to the side, she saw Ben Owens, whom they nicknamed Bo, hand-walking Ivy. The little sorrel mare was now fifteen years old but didn't look it, or act like it.

Concerned about the sometimes steep and rocky mountain trails, they'd tried to retire the elderly mare, but each time they had the same result. The first day or two Ivy would seem fine. However, the longer she watched the other horses head out with riders on their backs, she'd eventually throw an equine tantrum worthy of any two-year old human. She'd get so upset when she saw the other horses leave while she had to stay behind, Morgan and Ty decided to let her work on a part-time basis. They also tried to keep her on the lower, flatter trails.

They figured Ivy just wanted to be needed. Like any human, she needed a purpose and attention. And like many an aging human, she also had her bouts with health matters. But unlike a human, since horses can't vomit, she'd colic instead. And colic could be fatal.

"Morning, Bo. How's Miss Ivy this morning?" The little mare recognized Morgan's voice and turned her head, pricking her cute reddish-brown ears in Morgan's direction.

"Morning, Morgan. She seems better. I was just thinking about putting her back up soon. Maybe put her in the red round pen so we could keep an eye on her in case something happens." Scratching behind Ivy's ear after he stopped walking, he mused, "Honestly, I think she could be faking it. She seems awfully perky to me now, but before she really didn't. I think she likes the attention she gets when we think she's sick."

"I wouldn't be surprised at all to hear she's got us trained!"

Bo moved out of the way so Morgan could check Ivy's vital signs. She leaned her ear against Ivy's side, listening for stomach rumblings. Hearing some was a relief. Lifting up Ivy's top lip, she pushed against the pony's gums and timed how fast the white spot disappeared. Color was good, so she wasn't dehydrated, and Ivy's eyes were alert.

"Her manure?" Morgan asked as she pet Ivy.

"She had some, and what I saw looked fine. She drank most of her water too."

Morgan had taught her staff one of the best and quickest ways to determine a horse's health was checking their manure. It was second nature to them all now to look anytime they went in a stall or by a pen. They knew what to look for when they did see it. How much? Too dry? Too moist? Diarrhea? Since it was a daily occurrence, manure mattered.

She leaned down and kissed the little mare's nose and smiled at the warm pony breath Ivy breathed back at her. "You're a good girl, Ivy. Yes, you are..." Morgan cooed to her as she stroked the pony's warm neck a few times before wiping her hands on her jeans.

"It could be she *was* feeling poorly, but maybe walking her did the trick. You did the right thing. Go ahead, and put her in the red pen. She seems just fine, but we'll keep an eye on her." She ran her hand down the pony's head and straightened out her forelock. "I'm going to go make the rounds."

Bo nodded as Morgan made her way toward Quail Run. This barn was where her boarders were, and where the riding lessons took place. One of her two riding instructors, Katherine Hatfield—or as she was called, Kat—basically ran this barn to gain the experience.

So far Kat was doing a great job, but Morgan still kept a close eye on it all. Nothing was ever done without Morgan knowing about it and giving her approval or denial. She knew Kat wanted to open her own stable someday, or just manage someone else's, so Morgan was giving her as much of the responsibility as she felt Kat could handle to better prepare her. She'd gradually added responsibilities over the past year for Kat to learn in phases. With her work ethic, horse sense, and people skills, Morgan was certain Kat would succeed. Of course, Morgan would prefer she didn't leave Harmony Hills at all.

Morgan was all about empowering other women simply because women still had to work harder and longer than men. She reasoned since she was in a position that could help another work toward her dreams, who was she to not do all she could to help her? But as others would attest to, Morgan also did what she could for any man too. To Morgan, a person was a person. If they were willing to work at it, she'd teach them and pass on her knowledge and experience.

Morgan's most recent test of Kat's developing skills was allowing her to plan their upcoming annual horse show called "Shamrocks and Dreams." Morgan was guiding her to avoid issues as planning a horse show was *not* for the un-organized... or the fainthearted. Morgan gave Kat permission to have her other riding instructor help her.

Melinda Wilder—or Mel— was a couple of years younger than Kat at a mature twenty-three and would learn at the same time. An eager beaver, Mel was always volunteering to learn more. Her bubbly personality was a nice contrast to Kat's more serious one. Thankfully, the two women got along wonderfully.

Morgan still gave riding lessons herself on occasion. When she could, she'd have a professional rider or trainer come in, hold clinics, and give lessons to them all to refresh their knowledge, sharpen their skills, or hopefully learn new ones. Considering her schedule that included running the trail rides, giving the occasional lesson, hosting or judging horse shows, assisting at clinics, and simply running the business end of it all, Morgan just didn't have a lot of free time.

She'd been blessed by finding and hiring reliable staff like Ty, Kat, and Mel to share the overall daily workload with. Her other staff members were just as super, but those three shared the managerial duties more. It'd taken her years to build Harmony Hills Equestrian Center, and it was her whole life now. She didn't take any of it for granted at any time, and she still worked long hours to keep it running smoothly. She knew how quickly everything could just disappear and be gone forever.

Now, years later, she had a lot of people and horses depending on her to succeed. *She* was their security, and she was determined to never let them down.

Kat was coming over from letting out some horses while Rory Jenkins, one of her part-timers, slowly drove the tractor and manure wagon up the aisle. Stopping for a minute, Morgan smiled as the herd of horses kicked up their heels at their early morning freedom. Their little smoke-colored puffs of warm breath in the cooler air made them look like happy hairy dragons. A pair of bays bucked and nipped at each other in elated freedom in the cooler air, swinging their elegant necks as they played.

This was one of the best times of the day for Morgan. She loved the smell of grain and hay, the sounds of horses eating, the chirping birds, and listening to the conversations between her staff.

Of course, it didn't *always* run smoothly. No place of business did. But for the most part, they all worked well as a team. She'd chosen her staff carefully, looking for certain traits to make this more of a reality than a mere possibility. Gossiping, drama, sexual harassment, drugs of any kind, and profane language were also never tolerated at her place, whether from staff or a client, and this made for a much more pleasant place to work or visit.

When Morgan turned to enter the barn, she saw Alexis closing a stall door. Morgan's longest employee, Alexis Carter was now a tall, slim, blonde-haired young woman who'd recently turned twenty years old. She'd been working part-time at the Center since she was in junior high school. Her original barn rat was now taking college courses. This realization sometimes made Morgan feel old. Ty and Morgan sometimes jokingly referred to Alexis as their kid. She, in turn, referred to them as her second set of parents.

Morgan called out, "There's my girl!"

"Yep, here I be!" Alexis smiled. "I saw Bo walking Ivy. Is she okay?"

Morgan nodded. "She seemed fine when I checked her, but we'll keep an eye on her."

The Darrells, her German Shepherds, spotted her coming down the aisle and came bounding toward her, tongues out and eyes dancing in excitement. Morgan had named them both "Darrell" after the two brothers in the TV show *Newhart*. Morgan thought it'd be funny to do. But with the sibling dogs, one was a male and the other a female, so she added a "B" and a "G" to their names. Those designating letters (for 'boy' and 'girl') were really only used when the dogs went to the vet for paperwork purposes. Otherwise, one could tell them apart by the color of their collars—blue and pink, respectively. And it turned out to be really handy that when the dogs needed to be called a person just yelled "Darrell," and they *both* came running.

Still young at barely three years old, they were quick to learn. They'd recently graduated from rattlesnake training classes, and she was confident they'd make the Center even safer. Reaching down to scratch their ears and rub their sides as they leaned against her, Morgan braced her legs so they wouldn't knock her over.

"Are you still looking for extra hours?" At Alexis' nod, Morgan said, "If you don't have classes this afternoon and evening, we could really use your help on the trail rides. We look like we're going to be swamped today, and we may still have walk-ins coming in. Can you work?"

"Sure. I only have two classes to study for tomorrow, but they're later in the day. Do you want me to hang out up there, or just listen on the two-way?"

"Either, but you may just want to stay at Sunset Ridge. Once you're done down here, head up there. We're all right for the next couple of hours. Any hours you want this week, you can probably have them all. We look to be really busy all week long. There's a convention in town, and I think we're getting some of them. I wish they'd have booked group rides to make sure we're ready for them, if so. Either way, though, we'll take 'em!"

Alexis grinned. "Of course we will! Any help you need, just let me know. I could really use the extra work and money for the lab work that's coming up."

"Sure will. Make sure you get me and Ty your class schedule as soon as you can so we can work you in later on, okay?"

"You bet. I don't think that one class I wanted to get in will work out, so those I have now are the ones for this semester. My counselor said it's a popular class that already had a waitlist to get in. It's probably for the best as I don't want to over-extend myself."

"I agree. Just pace yourself because there's no rush. If you take on too much too quickly, you'll just burn yourself out. Enjoy your youth!"

"That's pretty much what Mom told me just last night. I'll get my schedule to you or Ty later today."

"You'd better," Morgan teased as Alexis made her way to clean stalls with Rory.

Knowing feed was running low the other day, she thought she'd better check on the situation and made her way toward Red Rock, the feed barn. She'd placed large orders and wanted to make sure they were ready for the amount of grain and hay coming in later that day. She figured Ty, awesome and dependable Ty, had it under control already, but figured she'd check anyway.

Opening the door, she was getting ready to turn on the lights but turned around instead at the sound of footsteps. She saw the lone figure walking toward her.

"I just knew I'd find you over here," Ty said, joining her in the doorway as she turned on the lights. "The guys got together and moved it all over last night while you were giving your lessons. It should be ready in here for the new feed."

She nodded in approval. "It looks ready. Rotation should be a breeze seeing how low we are."

"Perfect rotation." He looked around before saying, "The feed store called just a bit ago. They should be here within two hours. The hay truck is still supposed to be here later today."

Morgan nodded as she turned off the lights, slid the door closed and latched it. She said, "Oh, I already spoke with Alexis. She's available and wants the extra hours. If she's not over there in Sunset Ridge, just radio her. I told her to just stay up there, though, once she's done down here."

"Okay. That'll definitely help having her up there." He paused. "Her schedule?"

"By end of today."

They headed toward the office at Sunset Ridge as the wranglers were leading the last horses over to the hitching rails to get them saddled for the day's rides. She tugged on her jacket as a sudden burst of cool wind blew it open. "And if it doesn't warm up soon, I'm not leaving the office!"

Ty laughed. "I thought you liked it cool?"

"Cool, yes. Freezing, no. Sometimes that wind is too chilly, at least when it blows like that."

"This is nothing like back East."

"Yeah, well, I think my tough Eastern blood has thinned. It finally happened—I'm turning into a wimp. *Dang* it!"

He laughed again because he knew exactly what she was saying. Living in southern Arizona for years now, he knew she spoke the truth. His own body had acclimated to the normally-hot temperatures as well. Sometimes when that cool came, it was felt a bit more acutely. And at night and in the mountains, the air often felt colder anyway.

He teased her, "Maybe you're just getting old."

She laughed. "Can't get any younger. Besides, you're older than I am, so what about you?"

Smiling, he put his arm around his longtime friend and pulled her closer. "C'mon, darlin'. I'll make you some hot chocolate."

"With marshmallows?"

"They only last about twenty seconds before they melt. Why does it matter?"

"It just does."

He glanced at his friend. "If there *aren't* any marshmallows, don't forget *you're* the one who bought the last box."

"Don't start using your man logic on me." She grinned at him. "And what a way to shift the blame!"

"Well, even my man logic knows *you* went to the store last."

They were laughing when they walked into the office. After Ty prepped a cup of hot chocolate (with marshmallows) for her, they got down to business. As they waited for the water to get hot, they went over the updated schedule since he'd called back the messages from earlier.

Signing waivers, getting payments, fitting helmets, matching people with horses, and guiding them on trails in the mountains had yet to become old and routine for her. She didn't often go out on the actual rides now since she'd expanded the business, but every now and then she would just for the varying routine. She also needed to see how the trails were holding up, as she didn't want them to get worn down and erode away. Some of the land they rode on was leased land, and she had a responsibility to keep it in good condition.

Building Harmony Hills Equestrian Center had taken years of hard work, business savvy, sweat, blood, worry, and tears. And it was born from more heartbreak than anyone could realize. She'd made more mistakes than she'd care to admit to, but it was all in the process of building one of the best businesses around.

She'd named her barns after what she'd felt and saw when she came out to look at the property again when she was seriously considering buying it. It'd been a little run-down at the time, which helped her negotiate the price lower, but she'd *felt* the potential when she'd walked the ground. The wide open space was welcome while the different access routes were mandatory.

But it was also the feeling of harmony in nature that sold her. Here, she felt at peace. Here, she felt safe.

She'd taken out a couple of small loans in the beginning to make friends and contacts with local businesses, and worked until her hands bled and her feet were too sore to walk on. Now Harmony Hills was a well-known, established horse facility that catered to both the many tourists that came year-round as well as to the locals.

With Ty at her side now, she had someone to share it with, bounce ideas off, and had a supporter when she needed one. Although they both knew they had a strong chemistry, neither was willing to risk what they had to take their deep friendship further. They also knew everyone and their brother wondered about them being a couple. But they'd settled into a friendship and working partnership that meant the world to them both. Years of working side by side had made them true friends that trusted the other but rarely anyone else.

And they each had their private reasons why.

Ty handed her the phone so he could go out and help the wranglers saddle the last horses. Seeing the cars pulling into her parking lot, Morgan finished making her hot chocolate, enjoying this last moment of peacefulness before her first customers walked through her door.

Morgan was adding up the daily totals at her desk when Bo walked in later that evening. Holding up a finger to signal him to wait a minute before interrupting her, she continued counting. He put his two-way radio in the charger for the night before he walked over to the stool and took a seat. When she'd recorded the total, she looked up. "Hey, Bo. Is Ivy okay? I checked on her a couple hours ago, and she seemed fine. Any changes since then?"

"Nope. Like I said this morning, I think she just wants the attention. Nearly every time I walked by the round pen today, there was someone there giving her attention. She was in heaven. Alexis and I went ahead and put her to bed like usual."

Morgan smiled at his choice of words. "We'll use her for the pony rides tomorrow so she stops hogging our time looking for attention. I love a horse with a personality, but I prefer one that doesn't make us worry about them!"

Ty walked in to replace his two-way radio on the charger. "I noticed Ivy was in like usual. She must be feeling better?"

With a smile, Bo stood up to leave. "Well, unless we ignore her again, she should be just fine. See you guys in the morning."

"Night, Bo. Drive safely!" she said. Looking at Ty, she asked, "Is everyone else gone? I know a couple came in to do their timesheets while I was counting, but they used the side door."

He nodded. "Yep. It's just us old folks burning the midnight oil."

As she finished the paperwork, Ty stocked the counter, swept the floor, and emptied the trash. He then walked the building to make sure all doors were closed and locked. They had a routine, and either could do the other's roles. Since she was almost done, he skimmed through the reservation book for the rest of the week, mentally listing which horses to use. Their number one rule was to take care of the horses, so they did their best to rotate through their herd to prevent burnout. But sometimes when they were consistently busy, they had no choice.

Tapping the papers in front of her now that she was done calculating, she said with a smile, "It was a fantastic day. I could stand having this kind more often!"

She handed him the daily report and leaned back in her chair while he read through it. It felt so nice to be off her feet for a few minutes. It *had* been a long day, but it'd gone by quickly. She considered that one of the perks for being so busy.

Ty looked at the totals. "It *was* a very good day. And tomorrow looks just like it." They both smiled at the prospect. As she gathered up the rest of the papers and slid them into a file, he mentioned, "Just so you know, the feed and hay are in, put away, and all is locked up."

She nodded. "Thanks." As she stood up, she said, "We can just do the bank deposit tomorrow with the other errands to save you the trip tonight. Cool?"

"You're the boss."

"Yep. And a pretty considerate one too," she joked back.

"Well, I can't argue with that. You *are* kinda pretty," he said, a twinkle in his eyes.

Morgan laughed as his teasing.

He filed the paperwork as she gathered the money to put it in the lockable, zippered bank bag. She opened the safe, tossed in the money bag, and locked it again.

After she pulled on her jacket and hat, she headed for the door. She turned off the lights as Ty set the alarm, locked the door, and pulled it shut behind them. The automatic outdoor lights shone brightly around the office as they walked toward the darkness.

"Goodnight, Ty. See you in the morning. Drive safely, okay?"

"Always. See ya in the morning, Morgan."

Ty watched her walk toward her house, her dogs seemingly materializing out of nowhere. He walked to his truck, pulling his keys from his coat pocket. Climbing inside, he started the engine before he scanned through the radio stations until he found a good song playing. He glanced over one more time before turning on his lights and heading home himself.

In the darkness, he could barely see her making her way up the rise. The pathway lights illuminated just the bottom halves of her legs, but he saw them moving. The lights showed The Darrells—one leading the way as point while the other was her rear guard.

Satisfied she was protected and safe, he drove away.

Chapter 2

February

MORGAN PULLED OPEN THE screen door that connected the tack room to the main office. She'd just spent the past couple of hours inspecting her tack and equipment. Since she kept herself on a tight budget, she bought the majority of her tack and supplies as lightly-used instead of brand-new. She taught all the wranglers how to look for weak spots like thinning leather or loose rivets, but she had a routine set up so she herself could look it over. Sometimes Ty would do it for her, but more often than not, she did it herself.

She took full responsibility for every aspect of her business, and the tack being in safe condition was basic and crucial. How would she explain a probably preventable accident with a customer if a cinch or something just happened to snap or break on a ride, potentially causing them to fall off, and even get seriously injured? Sometimes accidents just happen, but a lawsuit handled by a glory-hound lawyer could possibly shut her down. Or cause her insurance company to drop her or cause her premiums to skyrocket. She did her best, keeping meticulous records on everything. Safe tack and detailed records: Both were aspects she was teaching Kat and Mel too.

She'd been busy the past couple of weeks, working elsewhere than at the Center. One weekend she was in New Mexico judging a show, and she returned just yesterday from assisting with a clinic in southwestern Colorado. Now and then, she yawned from lack of sleep. Although she could've slept in and even hung out at her house today, she didn't want her staff, mainly Ty, doing more than they needed to.

Carrying her clipboard into the office, she laid it on the counter. Reaching underneath for her thermos bottle, she unscrewed the cap and drank a few swallows of the iced tea she'd made last night while waiting for her laundry to finish. Looking out the office window at her mountain views, she soaked up the sun's rays that shown through the clean glass while country music played over the speakers.

It was a warm, early February day, and it was already eleven in the morning. She knew they had three trail rides out at the moment, one of which was due back at the barn in about another fifteen minutes.

Moving to sit in her large, padded chair behind her desk, she glanced at her clipboard that listed the few repairs needed on her tack. She drummed her fingers on the desktop as she thought to herself. Mainly they were easy repairs, just switching out the worn-out latigo straps for new ones. There were a couple of bridles that needed re-stitched, but nothing was in dire shape. She may need to buy more leather straps to finish off this list of repairs and still have some more in stock. She grabbed her notebook and made a list of what she'd need.

As she stood up to return to her project, she noticed the first ride coming in. It was a small one with just a few customers on it. Toby Abernathy was an experienced wrangler and he could handle it, but she headed out to lend a hand. Toby had been with her for the past couple of years, coming back in the autumn to work through the early spring for her. He liked to travel the country, so in the late spring and summer months, he was normally up in Wyoming, Idaho, or Montana working on the dude ranches there. This year, his third season with Morgan, he'd pleased her by asking if he could stay on longer. Morgan really liked his work and fun personality, so she was more than happy to have him stick around longer than usual.

She laid the clipboard on her desk and walked out to meet them. She smiled and greeted the riders as they approached the area for dismounting the horses. Toby rode ahead so he could dismount and tie up his horse before coming back to help the customers down safely. He'd already instructed everyone to stop their horses in a line, and to stay on until he was there to help them down. On a good day, people actually listened. This looked like a good day.

After helping down the excited young girl named Erica, Morgan waited for another of the last two horses as Toby helped down her parents. Tying up the horses with a safety release knot, she walked back toward Erica and her parents.

Smiling, she took pity on the parents who looked like they'd been paddled but good. "If you want to keep from getting really sore, don't sit down right away. As a matter of fact, I'd just keep on walking for a good ten or fifteen minutes. Don't sit. Just walk. Stay hydrated too."

At their pained expressions, Morgan laughed. "Trust me. You need to limber up your muscles a bit so they don't tighten up on you. You don't want to be saddle sore the rest of the day, do you? You can walk around and pet the horses over the fences if you want. Just please don't go to any that are tied up, okay? Feel free to wander around. See the place for as long as you want to. It seems like Erica would really like that."

Morgan pointed to the office building. "There are a couple vending machines near the bathrooms up here, but if you want more than that, there's a food truck over there," she said as she pointed in the general direction. "They serve really good food at reasonable prices."

The mom smiled. "Thank you for the advice and the ride. I can't believe how sore I am already! I rode all the time as a kid. I guess I'm getting older more quickly than I thought." Turning her head quickly to her husband, she added, "No comment from you, Ian!"

"Babe, you don't look a day over what you were when I first met you. And you're just as beautiful as the day I married you." Ian grinned at his wife.

"And comments like that are one reason I *did* marry you!" She smiled broadly as Morgan laughed. She continued, "We had a wonderful ride. You have a great place out here, and your trails have such beautiful views! And Toby has the patience of Job. He was so sweet about stopping and taking lots of pictures of not just Erica on her first ride, but of all of us. We really appreciate him taking the time to do that. I hope we can come back here sooner than later!"

She lowered her voice even though Erica was now out of hearing distance and talking up a storm again with Toby. "Bless Erica's heart, she means well. But even as a mother, I have to admit, it was nice being able to tune her out for just a little while. Just let someone else answer her endless questions!" Smiling at her daughter, who was now heading toward them, she gave Ian a look and tilted her head toward Toby. He was in the process of answering yet another question Erica had posed.

"I got it right here. Hey, Erica, honey! Leave that poor man alone. He's going to go deaf listening to you chatter all the time!" Ian smiled when his young daughter laughed at him.

"Daddy, you've been saying that forever. And *you* can still hear just fine!"

"Huh? Did someone say something to me? I can't hear," he teased.

Giggling, Erica thanked Toby before she skipped over to her mom and Morgan as Ian was walking toward Toby.

Morgan thanked them for coming, asking them for an online review since they were so pleased. She was heading back toward the office when she saw Ian slip some money into Toby's hand. He said a few words that had them both laughing before he headed off to join his wife and daughter. Morgan was satisfied knowing her wrangler made tips. She hated it when her wranglers didn't get tipped, especially when they really earned it.

Wranglers lived and worked for tips, but some people were too stingy to care. When making reservations, she'd added the line *Prices don't include tips* as a heads-up for those who didn't already know. She'd also put up humorous signs and posters about tipping the wranglers all over the office area, and even on the return trail right before reaching the barn area. No one could say they didn't know they were *supposed* to tip them. If they didn't have cash on them, she could add the tip on their debit or credit cards and pass it along to the wrangler later. She preferred they didn't use any type of cash apps as she wanted her employees' contact information and names unknown for safety reasons, especially the females.

She'd worked for tips before herself so she knew firsthand how important they were. Although she paid her wranglers by the day to help them have a decent, livable wage, the rest of their income came from the generosity of her guests. She did whatever she could do to help out her employees.

Morgan was picking up her clipboard in the office when Toby walked in. She teased, "Got hired as a babysitter, did you? They seemed like a really nice family though."

Toby held out a ten-dollar bill toward her. "Here."

Looking at it for a second, she asked, confused, "What's this? Sharing your tips? You know better, Toby. It's *your* money. You earned it, not me."

Toby was grinning when he reached out for Morgan's hand, laid the bill in her palm and gently closed her fingers over it. Shaking his head when she opened her mouth to protest, he continued, "No, Morgan. This one is just for you. Ian said so. My tip's separate."

Morgan graciously nodded her head as she stuffed the bill in the front pocket of her jeans. "Well, you had your chance!" She grinned. "What woman in her right mind turns away free money? I'll take it!"

The wrangler smiled as he adjusted his hat. "They were a really nice family, pretty easy-going. Erica really wasn't all that bad, but then I had her for only an hour or so. Living with her would probably be another story! But she listened to me and did what I said to do the first time. She really paid attention. She was having the time of her life out there! She just likes to talk a lot."

Toby noticed the clipboard in her hand. "What've you been up to this morning?" Looking at the top page, he nodded. "Ah, your project. Are there many to do?"

"No, just a few. But I also want to go through my stock to make sure we don't run completely out. There's a big tack and horse auction in a couple of months up near Phoenix I'd like to go to. Maybe I can find some good tack there and get it cheap. When's your next ride?"

"Not until one. Unless you need some help, I'll just go get my lunch now." He looked at her questioningly.

"No, I got it covered up here. Go ahead and eat. Thanks for the offer... and for the money. Not many bosses get paid by their workers. I'm so glad you're sticking around longer!" She grinned at him.

He smiled back. "Well, you got the best set-up here, you know. The other stables in this area don't run nearly as well as yours does. I know, since I've been to most of them," he said sincerely. "Some I couldn't even stay a week because they were so bad. You enforce your rules, so it's safer for everyone. Your priority is always the horse. Many places, they're just animals to use, practically abuse. You have boundaries here and for good reasons.

"You also take care of your employees, safety-wise as well as paying better than the other places. And it's always clean and organized here. You're also way more selective on who you hire, meaning attitude and that. You don't just hire someone because they have a pulse. You like to make sure our personalities will fit so we can work better together. It all makes a difference."

He hesitated before he admitted, "Honestly, I've realized over the years that I sleep better when I work for you. I know that might sound corny, but I never stress over having to go to work the next day when I'm here. I'm not wondering what could possibly go wrong, if the horses are sound, if I'll actually get paid. There are a couple of ranches up north that aren't too bad, but your place is better and year-round. Anyway, I really do appreciate you for letting me stay on."

Sincerely touched, Morgan replied, "Thank you for the compliments, Toby. It's really nice to hear from someone who actually notices the efforts I put into my place, especially from someone who's been around to compare. I try to make it the best, but it's certainly a team effort. And I'm more than happy to have you stay longer this year. You can stay year-round, if you'd like. You're a great worker, so thank you for helping *me* out!"

"You're welcome."

With a smile, Morgan shooed him out the door. "Now get out of here, you brown-noser!"

With a quirky grin, Toby turned and scooted out the door toward the food truck on the other side of Grand View. A couple of years earlier, Morgan had the idea of getting a food truck not just for her horse shows, but for her employees, boarders, and any visitors. She hired a family who also ran a nice café in town to run it all. As long as they didn't use generators because of safety and noise issues, Morgan was fine with them being here. Her lawyer just wrote up an agreement, and all was still running smoothly.

As Toby left to get his lunch, she returned to the tack room and headed toward the separate back room where she kept extra tack supplies. She was looking through the third large tote box that held leather in it when she heard Maya and Alexis instructing the customers on a returning ride to stay on their horses. She peeked around the corner of the doorway and saw Toby coming over to help. This was a bigger ride with two wranglers working it, but with Toby helping, they'd be fine.

As she worked, she listened to the country station on the radio that played through the speakers. She heard voices talking and laughing outside. Looking up, she saw Maya and Toby walking the horses over to the water tanks to let them drink. She always felt good when she saw how well her horses were cared for. She'd been to some places where the horses were thought of simply as tools and commodities, as Toby had said. It was sad to see the shape some of them were in. Knowing so many horses weren't cared for like hers always made her heart break and her blood boil. One of her cardinal rules was that the horses came first. Without them, they'd be out of a job. Not to mention, her horses were her heart.

She looked up at the sound of the ringing phone. After the second ring, she heard Alexis' chipper voice answer it. Morgan listened for a moment. It sounded like a reservation was being made for later that day. She returned to her work as she listened to Alexis laugh and talk to their new customer.

Hearing the sounds of returning horses from the last ride currently out, she briefly looked up then continued working, knowing there were more than enough wranglers available to help everyone down. One thing she stressed was everyone should pitch in. Healthy horses, fair rates, great customer service, and teamwork were the backbone of her business.

Bo was now greeting the next riders going out on just the hour ride. She absentmindedly listened to Bo and Alexis signing them in as she worked.

She finished working on the saddles and turned next to the bridles. She pulled out her leather sewing kit and stitched them up where needed. She didn't really like to do the stitching part of the repairs, but she figured she knew how so she might as well do them. Smiling to herself, she realized she *could* just delegate it to one of the wranglers. She *was* the boss after all.

"It makes a man curious when he sees a woman all by herself smiling. What's got you so happy? Or is it something I don't want to know about?"

Morgan looked up at the sound of Ty's voice. Grinning, she replied, "Oh, nothing much really. I was thinking about how much I just *love* to do this. And then it hit me that *I* don't have to do this. I could just order one of my wranglers to do it for me. I mean, I *am* the boss, right?"

Ty cringed. "I knew I was right to be nervous instead of curious." He looked over his shoulder. "Who'd you like me to round up for you? Not Bo, please. Remember that time when he stuck himself? He's not very good at seeing blood, as I recall." He tried to hold back his grin but failed miserably.

Morgan agreed with him. Grinning herself, she laughed softly at the memory of Bo almost passing out once when he stuck himself with a needle by accident. They rarely teased him about it because it really wasn't a funny situation, but yet it was still entertaining to think about sometimes.

"At least not his own! He's about to take out that ride anyway. I've actually about got it all done. Your timing is still perfect, I see." She saw his smirk as she worked on the last piece. "You get all the errands done in town? Kat handling it all okay?"

"You bet. I let her do everything on the list you made her write up." He grinned when she caught his little jab about her penchant for making lists and smiled. He continued, "I was just more or less her chauffeur. I even dropped her off right at the door to Quail Run. She was rude, though, and didn't even tip me. You need to talk to her about that."

Looking up into his dark brown eyes filled with humor, she laughed. "Will do. The first chance I get."

Ty paused as he watched her push the needle through the tough leather. "As I was driving through town, I saw something that reminded me of you. I bought you something."

Not believing him, Morgan looked over at him with a quick glance. "You were awfully busy to be thinking of me." She paused. "Really? You're not just teasing me?" Ty shook his head. Excitedly she asked, "Did you buy me a *pony?*"

"No, I didn't buy you a pony. You have enough toys, young lady!" He grinned at her teasing and her laughter. "You need to come to the office to see it. Wash your hands first because you won't want to get it all dirty and grimy. Come on."

She snipped off the end of the stitch with her clippers. "Well, I think I'm done here anyway. So, what'd you get me?" She stood up, stretched her back. "Are you sure I'll like it? Most men don't know what would really make a woman happy, Ty."

He squeezed her neck affectionately with his hand. "You women don't even know. Besides, I'm not most men... You know that. Go wash your hands. I'll meet you in the office."

She stopped off in the bathroom and got cleaned up. Opening the office door, she rushed in, playfully shoving Ty out of her way. "Food! And it's still hot?"

"I ran all the red lights just so it would be," he deadpanned as he leaned against the desk. As she scarfed down an onion ring, he asked, "Well? Did I make you happy?"

Morgan looked at him, chewing the onion ring quickly and swallowing it. Nodding her head, she praised her friend, "You're the best! Thank you. Do I owe you?" She unwrapped her favorite burger and grabbed her banana shake for a quick taste. "I love this shake!"

He reached for his own double cheeseburger as he shook his head. "Nope. Just think of me someday, and we'll be square."

Smiling, she bit into her cheeseburger. "Deal."

Chapter 3

March

"AGAIN? NO." JOSHUA WRIGHT scowled as he held his cellphone up to his ear. Listening, he began drumming his fingers in agitation. Breaking in, he repeated, "No. You need to *stop* this, and I mean now. I'm going to hang up on you." He listened to the voice on the other end of the line. "I don't really care, you know that? I just don't."

He pushed back in his oversized chair, needed for his six foot even frame. Letting out a deep sigh, he continued to listen. He knew they were a necessity in modern life, but he often thought that phones rarely brought good news. This was a case in point. "Okay, fine. I will look into it and get back to you. But don't bet on this happening."

As he hung up his phone without any warning to his unwanted caller, his gaze wondered around his office. His mind was already focused on the task he had before him, a frown showing his distaste for it.

His frown turned into a wide smile, though, when he saw his best friend walking across his parking lot. A minute later, he heard Damien greeting his receptionist before he walked into Josh's office. Damien wondered at the look on his friend's face. Standing there in the doorway, he saw a mixture of relief and agitation.

"Damien, I need to ask you for a favor. First, shut the door, will you? Thanks." Josh stood up and walked around his desk, leaning against it. "What are you doing this Saturday? Do you have plans already?"

"Hello to you too. Nice to see you. How've you been?" He smiled at his childhood friend as he walked to a chair and sat down.

"Hello. It's nice to see you. You look fine. I'm glad to see things are probably going well for you. Saturday?"

Damien stretched out his legs, casually crossed his ankles. "Are you asking me out on a date? Don't you think my wife will mind?" At his pal's exasperated look, he conceded. "Okay, okay. Day or night?"

Taking a deep breath, and hoping to sound nonchalant about it, Josh replied, "It's probably going to be a night job, but I'm not sure yet. Are you free?"

"Could be. I guess it'd depend on the situation. Is it important for me to help you?"

Josh nodded.

"Is it something you really don't want to do?"

Again, Josh nodded.

"Seriously? Who is she *this* time?"

Josh walked back around his desk and sat down. "How should I know? Can't you control your own demented cousin from setting me up on all of these blind dates? Elise has once again, apparently, found the perfect woman for me and told her I'd meet her for dinner and who knows what else this Saturday. *Why* does she keep doing this to me? This is getting so old!" Scowling at Damien, who was laughing, he demanded, "Okay, how many times have I told Elise no more blind dates? I'm not in the market for a relationship. She puts me in the position of looking and feeling like a jerk if I try to back out. What else am I supposed to do here? Move?"

Damien smiled at his friend. He really could sympathize with him. Elise, bless her meddling and matchmaking soul, really was on the edge of harassing Josh with all of her blind date set-ups. At least this time she warned him about it first. Not like that time she said she'd meet Josh for dinner to catch up on what was going on with him, and then promptly left him with a stranger who was expecting dinner and a movie.

Inwardly he cringed just remembering that fiasco. But Josh pulled it off so well that the poor unsuspecting woman never knew Josh didn't know about her. Josh had avoided Elise for a good two months after that. Childhood friends or not, Josh about lost his patience with her that time. Maybe he really should have. Damien shook his head, feeling bad for his buddy. He again wondered how these women felt in regards to Elise afterwards, not to mention Josh. Couldn't they see the pattern?

Josh was looking at him expectantly. Damien relented, but still had to point out an important fact. "First off, you *are* in the market for a relationship. You're single, in case you forgot." Josh glared at him. "Okay, so you didn't forget. I'll see about calling either Elise or her mom or dad. Maybe all three. I don't know if Aunt Mary knows this is going on. Uncle Mike did, but he may have thought it was over after that one date when you got really pissed at her."

He saw his friend nod, knowing which time he was referring to. "I agree she's getting extremely annoying. I feel for you, man. I really do. I know it goes against the grain to just not show up, but maybe that's what you need to do. I'll call Mike and Mary again to see if they can stop their daughter. Maybe *you* need to call them too? They might think I'm exaggerating or something."

"Maybe. You try first, okay? I'd appreciate the help." Josh tapped his fingers on his desk, thinking. "Elise and I need to have another talk. And soon. I've had enough of this! If I want a date, I'll be a man and go find one on my own. I don't need a matchmaker. I'm already short on time with everything going on here, and I seriously don't need this right now."

Josh blew out a breath, trying to rein in his temper. He frowned as he swiveled his chair around and looked out his window. "My name is out there already thanks to Elise and her database of women seeking an eligible man. And if they all think I won't be around for a second or third date, if I ever *did* want a date, I'd never get one. At least, not around here."

"Possibly. Women chatter. Word spreads."

"On the other hand, I feel like I've already been set-up with all the locals by now. I'm going to have a horrible reputation with the ladies if Elise doesn't back off!"

"Unless, or until, you marry one of them and remove yourself from the market. It's not your fault, you know."

"I know," Josh sighed wearily.

"It's your mom's."

"What?"

"Sure. The way I see it, if Annabelle had raised you with no respect for women and all that, Elise wouldn't be hassling you with these dates. Elise is just making sure all that discipline and those lessons in manners weren't given for nothing. That's all."

Josh ran his long fingers through his thick, brown hair. "I'll try to think of it that way. Your cousin is a real thorn in my side, Damien."

"I know, and I'm sorry for ever introducing you two when we were kids. Who knew she'd end up doing this though? And who would've *ever* thought the three of us would end up living in the same area as adults? That was just a fluke, man. I had no part in it, and you know that for fact!" He shook his head at life's little coincidences.

Even as a pre-teen Elise was into everyone else's business, but at least she had to go home at some point. It was just pure, dumb luck she got a job in the same area he and Josh had moved to years ago. They probably would've moved except they both had thriving businesses there already.

Laura, Damien's wife, thought these two grown men were exaggerating Elise's nosiness—until *she* met her in person. "The woman can't have that many friends, not with her plowing headfirst into everyone else's affairs! If she's like this at her job, I can't figure out how she hasn't been fired!" Laura had exclaimed soon after meeting his cousin. "I'm so sorry I didn't believe you guys!"

Now, the two men sat there in silence, both thinking about this latest set-up by Elise. Glancing at his friend, Josh said, "Listen, be a pal. Why don't you bring Laura? We could just make it a double date. Maybe the girls would hit it off, and they could entertain each other. It's just for one day, less than, really."

"My wife doesn't like feeling, or being, used. You'd owe her one, you know." His friend nodded and shrugged his shoulders. "Well, let's go get lunch and work out a game plan. Laura really likes you so I'm sure she'll go along with it. Maybe we can come up with something actually fun to do. Mini golfing? Hey, we could go tubing down the Salt River. We haven't done that in a couple of years now."

Josh shook his head. "Not for this. Tubing is more fun with people who you like and really know already. It's too cold right now anyway. The mini golfing idea isn't bad, though, unless there are tons of kids there. They tend to get in the way, and it takes the fun out of it. Remember that last time we went? We stood there forever before we could take a single shot! And you complained that the place would close before we could finish?"

Damien winced. "Oh, right. I'd forgotten about that. That was the biggest birthday party for a six-year-old kid I've ever seen. *I* don't even have that many friends. Strike the mini golf idea. And yeah, you're right about the tubing thing too."

Josh just looked at his friend for a moment. "It's a good thing you're already married because you suck at dating ideas."

Damien laughed heartily, not offended in the least.

They sat there, considering ideas for a few more minutes before Damien asked, "Well, are you free to go to lunch now? I hope so because I'm starving."

"Yeah. I can take an hour or so. You drive this time."

Standing up, Damien walked toward the office door with his friend. "So, where are we going?"

Sending an exasperated look at him, Josh asked sarcastically, "When? Now or Satur-day?"

Chapter 4

A COUPLE OF DAYS later, Josh was writing up a work bid when his phone buzzed on his hip. He paused to look at the text. It was from Damien. It could wait until he was finished making an estimate on some construction work in one of the town's fitness centers.

One of the gym's business partners noticed he'd received a call. She called out, "Josh, if you need to answer that, you know you can."

He looked over his shoulder at the woman in wonder. "How on earth did you hear my cell from way over there? All it did was vibrate!"

She smiled. "I'm a wife and mother. I have huge ears, so my kids say. According to them, I hear everything. My husband claims I hear too much. But to ease your mind, I didn't hear it. I saw you look down at it, and I just assumed the rest."

"Oh. I guess that was a pretty logical deduction. It isn't important. It's just a friend letting me know he has some information for me." Josh felt comfortable talking to Leslie Travis. They'd known each other ever since he became the fitness center's remodeler and all-around guru, as Leslie called him. He figured he'd been their all-around guru for about four years now.

Leslie enjoyed talking to Josh as he was a smart and decent person. Watching him for a moment, she got up and walked closer to him so they didn't have to talk so loud. "Is it important information for you to know?"

Thinking of the upcoming blind date, Josh answered dryly, "Not overly. But I guess it'd really depend on who you are."

Smelling a story here, she leaned forward over the counter. It was just the two of them in this part of the office so she felt safe prying. "Okay, Josh. Spill it. I'm a mother, and I can tell you're hiding something from me." Watching his handsome face blush ever so slightly, she knew she was correct.

Josh continued writing for a moment longer. Thinking about this upcoming date had him almost desperate for help. He'd had another talk with Elise, his unofficial and unwanted personal matchmaker. He didn't want to hurt this woman he was supposed to meet, so he'd told Elise this was to be the absolute last set-up *ever*. He'd had enough of her meddling. Any more of her blind dates or meddling would end their friendship. He'd been so firm with her, she'd left in tears.

And having that attitude made him feel like the lowest layer of scum. But a couple years of these dates were wearing down his patience. Nothing he and Damien had tried, said, or did had made one iota of difference to Elise. This was the last straw. He was putting his foot down and hard. It helped lessen his guilt when both Damien and Laura backed him up one hundred percent.

Looking at Leslie's expectant expression, Josh took a chance and decided to explain his predicament. "Well, it's like this... I've been set up once again on a blind date by a friend's relative." Josh scowled. "She's taken it upon herself to match me up with every single woman she runs into for a couple of years now. I get to meet yet one more of these women this Saturday, and Damien—my best friend as well as her cousin—is helping me out. He was trying to find out what this woman likes to eat and do."

Her eyes went wide. She sounded surprised when she said, "Wait! You're *that* Josh?" At his stricken facial expression, she burst out laughing. She confessed after she got control of herself, "I'm just teasing you!" She giggled again.

Josh's relief was obvious. He'd actually never thought about his clients ever hearing about his dating entrapments, and what they'd think! Hearing about a limitless number of dates could portray him in a bad light. It turned his stomach thinking how that could affect his business reputation in a highly-competitive field.

He ran his hand through his hair as he looked at the smiling woman and said firmly, "Don't expect any type of loyalty discount, Leslie. Not now. As a matter of fact, I regret to inform you I've recently had to raise my rates."

Leslie laughed gaily again. With compassion and understanding in her voice, she said, "She's a meddling matchmaker. Is that what you're telling me?"

Disgust sounded in Josh's voice as he answered, "That's *exactly* what she is."

Leslie was preparing to answer him when her phone rang. After she was finished with the call, she got up to walk around the counter to stand closer to Josh. Nodding her head in understanding, she patted his arm in sympathy. "Have you talked to her about stopping her set-ups?"

"I have. And more times than I can count. Damien has threatened her, but it didn't do any good. We've even spoken with her parents! I put my foot down with her just the other day. Again."

"So, let's be practical and work this out, shall we? Okay, now that you have this blind date in a few more days, what do you plan on doing? Take her out to eat, to a movie, or to a zoo? To a marriage counselor?" She laughed again.

Listening to her husky laughter made Josh's heart feel a bit lighter. He was even able to genuinely smile. "Don't you have work to do?"

"Nothing pressing at the moment," she replied cheerfully. "It can wait. So, where to, Lover Boy?"

"You know, I heard a rumor that new Fitness & Physique Center was planning to remodel their entire facility. I think I'll head over there and see..."

Leslie laughed. "Okay, okay. Maybe I can help if you'd like to use me as a sounding board. Where are you taking her? Do you know yet?"

"That's the information Damien was getting for me. If you don't know somebody at all, how do you know where you're supposed to take them? He was doing me a favor and trying to find out through Elise what this woman's tastes are."

Seeing her expression, he forced a frown. "Now, Mrs. Travis, don't read more into it than there is. I'm just trying to make sure I don't take a diehard vegetarian to an all-the-steak-you-can-eat joint."

Smothering her smile, she nodded. "I think you're wonderfully sweet, thoughtful, and kindhearted. And quite patient, it sounds like, with this matchmaker person. All of that tells me even more about you. Oh, thanks."

She carefully read the bid he handed her, and then signed it. She knew his work was solid and trusted him, and his reasonable pricing was worth every penny. Handing it back to him so he could separate their copies, she said, "This looks fine with me. Check your calendar, and let me know when."

"Probably next week, if that works for you. Wednesday would be best. Is the morning good? It's a small job, so it shouldn't take us too long to do."

"Sure, and I can have that section cleared out for you by then with no problem."

"You'd better," Josh teased. He jotted down the date and time since they agreed on it so quickly, tore off her copy and gave it to her.

Placing her copy of the bid on her desk, she continued on without breaking her stride regarding his upcoming date, "So the question is where do you take her? You want my opinion?"

At the relieved expression on his face, she smiled. "Forget dinner if you can. It's usually too formal, too intimate. Both of you will be trying to make sure you don't slurp up the spaghetti noodles without flipping marinara sauce all over the place."

"That's why you never eat something like that on a first date." He nodded, smiled boyishly as he added mock seriously, "My mom taught me that."

"Good grief, Josh. You're too dang cute to be single!" Leslie shook her head. "And she's exactly right." She tapped her finger on her chin, studying him. "Let's see here... You're a big outdoorsy person, right?" At his nod, she went on. "In order for her to see you as you are, make it a day outing instead of at night. There's also less pressure that way. And do something outdoors."

"What if she has allergies?"

"That's her problem. And whoever it was who set you up since she should know better than to hook up an outdoors man with a girl who can't *go* outdoors. I bet she's already thought of that though." A sudden thought popped into her mind. "Take her horseback riding!"

"What?" Josh would hardly have chosen that as a first date idea. What if she was scared of them or got bucked off? Never mind *he* loved horses and had grown up with them all of his life. It was right up his alley, but how was he supposed to know if it was up hers?

"Sure! You'd be outdoors together but not alone. If you hit it off, you'll have made a great memory. If you don't hit it off, then you'll have lived up to your end of the bargain you so graciously accepted. You'll be together, but yet not required to be sitting next to each other trying to make small talk. And it's safer because you won't be alone in case she ends up being a psycho. Unless you are, in which case, it's now safer for her."

Josh laughed.

Leslie nodded as she went on, saying with enthusiasm, "Let nature take its course, so to speak. The trail guide will be talking to both of you, so that's enough to eliminate any pressure." Slapping her hand down on the countertop, she exclaimed, "Yes, that's it! Call and make reservations for a ride in the foothills. I can even recommend a couple of places."

Warming to the idea, Josh nodded. "Just in the foothills and not the mountains in case she gets too saddle sore. Or in case she's a bit scared of horses. Mountains are a longer ride, so we should do something more short and sweet."

He thought about it for another moment. "That's a great idea, Leslie! It may be the perfect idea, assuming she isn't allergic to them, falls off, or something." He filed his copy of the bid inside his clipboard before he shoved it into the side pocket of the bag he carried that contained his smaller hand tools and measuring tapes.

"If she does get bucked off or something, take advantage of it. If you like her, I mean. You know, some mouth-to-mouth and that kind of thing!"

"I'll keep that in mind." Josh laughed good-naturedly.

"Hang on a sec..." Leslie wrote out some information for him and handed the piece of paper to him. "These are a couple of fairly local places I've been to. The top one's the better one."

"Thanks."

He was walking to the door when she called out to him.

Looking him directly in the eyes when he turned around, she confided, "It might be interesting for you to know that my husband and I met on a blind date about eighteen years ago."

"Seriously? I never knew that. What'd you guys do on yours?"

She adjusted the angle of a potted plant on the counter as she answered, "We went horseback riding." At his skeptical look, she added, "Seriously. That's where we met. I mean, not here in Arizona, but it *was* a riding stable. Ask *him* if you don't believe me!"

"I don't even know him."

"I'll introduce you. When's a good time?"

He smiled broadly. "And I suppose you fell off your horse and had to have some of that mouth-to-mouth too?"

She laughed, shook her head. "No, that didn't happen. But I wouldn't have been opposed to it!"

"I think I'm just gonna go now. See you next week, Leslie!"

Leslie winked at him as he walked out the doors, shaking his head but smiling.

Chapter 5

WHEN MORGAN'S ALARM CLOCK sounded near her ear, she automatically reached over to hit the snooze button, gaining nine more minutes of sleep. When it popped back on, the country music station she had it set to began playing a song as soon as the DJ finished his announcement that the weather report would follow afterward.

It took only a few seconds for her sleepy mind to recognize the song. When she did, it snapped her wide awake. It was a song she knew by heart. Memories suddenly flooded her, and she gasped at the ache in her heart as they hit her like a tsunami.

She couldn't move. All she could do was lie there until the song ended and the clamps on her heart eased up. Slowly sitting up, she rubbed the heel of her hand against her chest as if that would help make it easier to breathe. The sharp pains and the aches had her almost gasping for air. Blindly reaching over, she turned off the radio. She needed silence. It took her another moment to realize there were warm tears streaming down her cheeks. She tasted the salt of them when they reached her lips.

She could do no more than simply sit there in her bed as memories from years past washed over her in waves. She was stunned they could feel so real, especially after all this time. She took a deep breath, then another, trying to focus on something, *anything*, else. But the deep breaths weren't helping this time. Before she could stop them, or herself, the tears just fell more quickly. Soon she was engulfed in tormented sobs as she remembered what used to be, what could've been, what *should've* been. She curled herself into a ball on her bed and just cried and cried until she had nothing left.

ALL AROUND GRAND VIEW, the atmosphere was already full of excitement by the time Morgan began to make her way down from her house. Normally she looked forward to a show day at her facility, and today should've been no different. But it already was. Trying to focus on what she needed to do, she adjusted her hat more firmly on her head as she walked down the path to the barns.

This was the fourth year of what she hoped would be an annual show for years to come. She'd named it "Shamrocks and Dreams" because she felt that title simply encompassed a lot of what the riders and trainers were wishing on and working toward. She thought it had a nice catchy ring to it too. And having it in March was purely a coincidence when she first did it. Now it was tradition.

Morgan pushed her sunglasses up a little higher on her nose as she walked. The sun was already bright with promise for a gorgeous day.

Looking around, she studied the small sea of trucks and horse trailers already parked in the far lots. Others were pulling in the driveway from the highway that bordered one side of the Center. On show days, she left the trail-riding aspect of the business completely in Ty's capable hands to spend all of her time at the show itself. She was sometimes one of the judges, like today, but she was never the Head Judge. She figured that way no one could accuse her of favoritism in the event one rider from her place beat out another who wasn't. She always hired outside, neutral judges for her shows. The third judge she'd wanted for today wasn't able to make it, so she was filling in for him.

Her plan was to go straight to Grand View and greet the participants as she ran into them. She spotted one of the sheriff's deputies by his car and saw the ambulance was already parked nearby in case of an accident. She waved to the deputy when he turned in her direction. He waved back and smiled. Morgan made her way over to him to check in.

She spoke with Deputy Matt Harvey for a few minutes and made sure everything she needed to comply with was done to his satisfaction. Being from a ranching family himself, his own daughters rode their horses in the shows held there. When he could, he volunteered for duty, both for the extra money and to be able to share in the day with his kids and wife at the same time.

As Morgan turned away to head to the barns, she saw Ty walking over from the office. Her step faltered. In her present state of mind, she didn't feel as confident as usual. Knowing Ty, he'd pick up on it immediately. She'd been hoping she wouldn't run into him until later, if at all. Or at least until she wasn't feeling so emotionally exposed from her morning wake-up call. She was afraid his questions and concern would unplug all she had dammed up in the past hour or two.

Ty saw Morgan's hesitation in her step, and because she didn't greet him as she always did, he knew immediately something was off. One thought after another raced through his mind as he got closer to her. If it was the show, she wouldn't be acting like nothing was wrong. She'd have been on her way to fix whatever needed fixing. It wasn't talking with the deputy. She'd seemed relaxed when talking to Matt before walking away. She hesitated when she saw *him*. Taking a breath, he slapped a smile on his face as he reached her.

"Good morning! I was heading over to get some snacks before the mad show rush came. In case you're wondering, Maya put The Darrells in the kennel run already. She made sure they had food, toys, and water. It's locked and secured." He casually glanced around. "It looks like a great turnout for it already."

He'd taken note of her sunglasses. She didn't normally wear them this early in the day because she liked to make eye contact with people to be more personal and open. He knew something was off kilter with her for sure now.

"Hey back. It's probably a good idea to grab some sort of food now as I'd hate to have my own people starving. If you get in a pinch, feel free to rob my fridge. Be sure to turn off my alarm first to save Matt from running up there." She offered a small smile but then looked away, acting interested in the trailers pulling in.

Ty was still suspicious. Morgan was a direct person, but she seemed preoccupied this morning. Maybe it was just the show, and her hoping all would go well. He knew she had a lot riding on its success, and that it was Kat's first time organizing it. He couldn't think of anything that could've been missed between her, Kat, and Mel. "You're not nervous about the show, are you? Between you and the girls, I don't think anything has been missed."

"No, I'm not nervous about the show. I had a meeting with them yesterday, and it looks like they have it all covered. I told them I think they did a wonderful job getting it set up. Why?" She ran her damp palms down the sides of her nice black slacks she wore when judging shows.

Ty noticed the gesture. Trying to see through her sunglasses, he was focused intently on her. Morgan sensed he knew she wasn't quite herself. Well, she'd known *that* would happen, didn't she? He could read her like a book.

When he still didn't answer, Morgan looked at him quizzically. "You okay, Ty? You seem distracted or something."

Instead of answering her, he gently took her elbow and began steering her away from the barn and people, heading toward the little group of mesquite trees for some privacy. She had no choice but to go with him. He finally stopped and looked at her.

"What's wrong, Morgan? Don't try to deny it. I know *something* is wrong. Is it anything you'd like my help with?"

When she didn't immediately answer, he reached over and gently removed her sunglasses. She'd carefully applied her make-up, but he saw through it. Someone who didn't know her well probably wouldn't be able to tell unless they really studied her. Ty knew immediately though. Morgan had been crying. His heart skipped a beat. Strong women don't normally cry, but when they did? There had to be a really good reason for it. And Morgan was one of the strongest women he'd ever met, if not *the* strongest. He was instantly concerned about his best friend.

Wordlessly, she reached over and took back her sunglasses. He was quick, she'd give him that. She'd read the instant concern in his eyes. She slipped her sunglasses back in place.

Ty spoke softly, "Morgan? Tell me what's wrong." Although he assumed he already knew, that didn't mean he was right. It'd be better if she told him.

Her heart squeezed like a vice was clamped around it, just as she knew it would if she talked to her best friend before she was prepared for it. Her bottom lip quivered slightly. She couldn't deal with kindness right now. She gave a little smile and patted his arm. The best thing to do was meet it head on.

"I knew you'd notice. No one but you would. Really, I'm fine. Or will be," she added at his raised eyebrow. "In a nutshell, it's just been a rough morning. All few hours of it. But it won't be one of those mornings that'll last all day, so don't worry about me. Okay?"

She looked away for a moment and took a slow, deep breath. She could feel more tears backing up in her eyes. How could there be any left? She explained quietly, "Some old memories were triggered. They were unexpected, and I just wasn't prepared for them. And I really don't want to go into it any more right now, okay? I can't." She looked at her friend as he silently nodded his understanding.

Looking toward the lot again, she saw people either tacking up or walking horses, hanging up hay bags, or carrying water buckets. It was always a hectic, yet somehow organized, scene on show days. It was a nice, familiar routine. And she needed the comforting distractions desperately right now.

She felt Ty run his strong and comforting hand up and down her right arm. Briefly, she closed her eyes. She turned back to him and gave another small smile.

"You're the absolute best friend I could ever have in this whole screwed-up world, Ty. And I mean that from the bottom of my heart, whatever condition it happens to be in at any given moment. It means a great deal to me to know I can knock on your door anytime, and you'd be there for me." She reached over and patted his arm.

Up until now, Ty hadn't spoken another word. He was afraid to say anything that would have her defenses walling up. Growing up with three sisters, he'd picked up some valuable input from the female mind. It didn't always work in his favor, but he felt he got points for trying. But his guess had been correct. And this certainly *wasn't* the time or place to discuss it further. He also had to respect her not wanting to.

He nodded again, saying just as softly, "You know the same goes for me, Morgan. It really does."

He knew the last thing she needed was sympathy, and that's why he rarely gave it to her. He'd empathize but rarely sympathize with her. She didn't need that from him. Morgan relied on his strength and steadiness.

Knowing not to push because it'd be pointless and insensitive, he replied, "Well, I'm going to go get some food." Trying his best to get her back on normal footing, he looked at her. "Why don't you get to work? I've been told there's a show here today that needs to be run, and I've got rides going out soon. We simply don't have time to stand here lolly-gagging in the shade." Leaning down, he kissed her cheek and said softly, "Good luck with the show, Morgan."

Realizing she felt better, she gave him a smile. She held his hand, squeezed it hard in hers. "Thank you, Ty. For everything."

Chapter 6

Josh looked down at his cellphone when it began playing a familiar ringtone. Answering it, he asked bluntly, "You're not chickening out on me, are you?" He heard his best friend start laughing then start talking to someone near him. "Is that Laura? Let me talk to her."

Damien's wife spoke into her husband's phone. She sounded irritated when she scolded, "Joshua Wright, you just cost me ten bucks!" He heard her scolding her husband who was still laughing in the background.

"Why? What bet did you make with Damien? You should know better than to do that after being married to him all these years, Laura."

"He bet you'd think we weren't joining you today. And *I* was positive you'd have more trust in us—in *me* anyway. And what's the very first thing you ask? You should know better than to do that after knowing me all these years, Josh!"

He could hear the smile in her scolding voice so he wasn't worried about her being truly upset with him. "Well, see, it's just that I've known Damien longer than you. No offense, Laura. I wouldn't put it past him to give support until the last second and then skip out. He and Elise *are* related, you know. Save time here, and just admit I'm right."

She laughed. "He wasn't *seriously* going to leave you, but just act like it." Laura sounded like her normally-happy self as she continued, "Anyway, we're all set in our most comfortable cowboy gear. We'll meet you and your date at the stables." When he didn't respond she asked, "Josh, are you still there?"

"Yeah, I'm here. There's no other place I really want to be either. And I mean that literally."

Laura laughed at the resigned tone of his voice. "It won't be all *that* bad, Josh. You've got at least me to be a buffer, if needed. Heck, *she's* the one who's going to be all alone amongst strangers so give her a break. She's probably nervous. Who knows? You might actually like her.

"We'll meet you guys at the main office. The trail-riding stable is next door to the show arena. I've been there before. I think it's called Sunset Ridge or something like that. Look for the trail-riding signs as it's all marked really well." She paused to take a breath. "You good?"

"Yeah, I'm good. We got a beautiful afternoon for this, if nothing else. Thanks again for going along with us, Laura. I'm sorry about the ten bucks you lost. Let me make it up to you, okay? I'll buy you lunch, but just you. Don't forget your husband when you leave." He heard Laura laughing as he hung up his phone.

Looking around to make sure he had everything turned off, Josh shoved his wallet into his pocket and grabbed his truck keys. His cat, Freeway, ran along in front of him, suddenly stopping so he had to jump over her to avoid stepping on her. His elbow hit the wall as he lost his balance. She ducked down.

"*Cat!*" he growled at her while still bending down and stroking her soft fur before gently shoving her aside to open the door. "I'll be back later to tell you how it all went, all right? Wish me luck!"

Freeway's bright green eyes followed him as he walked out the door. She romped to the living room, landing on the couch from an effortless leap and watched him through the window.

As he opened his truck door, Josh hoped nothing went wrong today. He just wanted a nice, easy-going, relaxing day. No surprises. No scenes. Just a nice day spent outdoors around horses and friends.

Here goes nothing, he thought as he pulled out of his driveway.

Chapter 7

Ty ADJUSTED THE SADDLE stirrups for the last person going out on this ride. He'd been kept pretty busy with rides going out and coming in, signing in everybody, fitting helmets on those who wanted them, assisting the loading and unloading of riders, and answering the phone to make more reservations, or to answer questions about the show. It was all in a day's work, and he loved it. Of course, the wranglers were great, each doing their fair share of the work. As Morgan said, everyone was to pitch in and not wait to be asked. Horses first, customers second. A fussy, unhappy horse was more important to her than a finicky human.

"All right, mister! You're all set. Remember how to steer and stop?" At the young teen's nod, Ty nodded back. "Just leave about a horse-length of space in-between you and the horse in front of you, all right?" The teenager nodded again. "Smile, partner! You're going to have a great time on Domino here. You'll have Eric here right behind you should you need help. Just enjoy the experience and the beautiful views!"

Ty gestured discreetly to Eric who was just mounting up. Eric, a part-time wrangler who just helped when the Center was really busy, saw the hand signal and nodded back. "All set in the back! Let's get moving!" Ty yelled up toward the front where Maya was waiting to start off. "Maya, you've got eleven riders on this one! Make sure you bring 'em all back this time!" He smiled at the riders who laughed at him.

Ty watched them leave for a moment, satisfied all was well. He looked at his waterproof watch as he walked back into the office. The next riders should be arriving within the next half-hour or so. Looking at the rest of the day's scheduled rides, he made sure he had everything covered. He figured he could water the horses that were tied up while he had the time. He put the cordless phone in his back pocket before he headed out the door again.

Reaching the shaded hitching rails, he pulled the safety-release knots of four of the horses and led them to the long metal water trough. He listened to them slurp up the water and watched as they splashed their muzzles in the cool water or playfully bit at each other. He gently pulled on Dusty's rope to keep him from grabbing hold of Ace's bridle. Full of personality, Dusty liked to grab onto another horse's halter or bridle and try to lead them around himself. It was entertaining to watch, but Ty had too much to do to let him begin playing right now. Norman nuzzled his arm, dribbling water and saliva on Ty's shirt sleeve. Not minding in the least, he ran his hand down the sorrel's sleek neck. Norman tilted his neck a bit toward him so Ty would rub behind his ears. Ty obliged the horse and scratched behind his ear for a moment.

He led the horses back to the hitching rail, re-tied them and took the next four over. After they drank their fill, and had also obligingly dripped water all over his shirtfront and arms, he led them back to the hitching rail to join the others. Glancing at his watch as the last five were watered, he saw a car pull up and park in the adjoining lot.

He was tying up the last horse when he saw the couple walking toward the office. "I'll be with you in just a minute!" he called out. They waved back in acknowledgement and looked around, talking and laughing about something he couldn't hear. He straightened Doolittle's forelock as he passed by the gray gelding on his way toward them.

He greeted them with his friendly, "Hi! You're here for the two o'clock ride?" He smiled as they nodded their heads. "It's a perfect day for a ride, isn't it? Let's get you signed in."

Damien and Laura followed him into the well-kept office. Since Laura had been there before a few times to go riding with her friends, she'd immediately recognized Ty when she saw him by the horses. It was pretty easy to remember the tall, tanned, black-haired, and muscular man. His friendly smile and demeanor contrasted with his air of authority and maturity. She'd always sensed a certain wise aura about him. All of that had always given her a good impression of him.

When she told him their last name to sign in, he looked up. "Hinton?" Ty looked at her and said thoughtfully, "You've been here before a number of times, haven't you?"

At her smile and nod, he said, "I thought I recognized your face. Let me think... You usually ride..." He paused for a moment, searching his memory. "Don't tell me, okay?" He thought for another minute before he snapped his fingers. "It's Bandit, right? I think I remember you requested him last time? He's actually on a two-hour ride right now, so he's not here for you this time. Sorry about that, Laura."

"*How* can you remember that?" Laura exclaimed in true surprise. "It's been months since I've been here, and you must get hundreds of people!" She looked at Damien, who looked impressed himself. Gently jabbing her husband in the ribs, she joked, "I bet *he* wouldn't conveniently forget to take out the garbage, and leave it for me to do!"

Damien winced in mock pain. "I swear to you, honey, I *did* forget. It wasn't on purpose." Looking at the tall man who was smiling at them, he asked, "You married? No? Good, because I'll tell you what. You forget *one* little thing, just once, and it comes back to haunt you even a couple of *years* down the road. Women never forget. They're like elephants, I swear!"

Laura gasped at being referred to as an elephant, but she knew he was only teasing. He gave her his wide grin, one of the things she fell in love with years ago when they'd met in college. Besides, as far as she knew, elephants were genuinely cool, social creatures.

"I have sisters though. And my best friend is a woman. Does that count?" Ty asked, playing along.

"Almost." Damien put on a serious face and leaned against the counter as if to impart with a great secret. "See, sisters aren't quite the same as a wife. You know with your sisters that sooner or later, one or all of you are going to move out of the house, right? You all go your separate ways. Not so with a wife because you're just stuck with *her*. Do you know what happens if you try to move away? She moves *with* you!"

They were laughing when the door opened and another couple walked in.

"Look what the cat dragged in! Good to see you, Josh. And who's this?" Damien smiled as he watched them walk through the door. His gaze took in the woman who had her thick, blonde hair pulled back into a low ponytail, with soft curls around the sides of her face. Her jeans looked worn and comfortable, as were her tennis shoes. She wore a lavender-colored sleeveless top that hugged her curves. She had a nice face and a bright smile. Dang, Damien thought to himself, Elise picked a nice-looking one this time. Of course, she was probably just running out of choices by now.

Laura stepped around her husband, holding out her hand to the woman standing beside Josh. With her mega-watt Julia Roberts smile turned on, she made the introductions, "Hello, I'm Laura. This is my soon-to-be-ex-husband, Damien. The man behind the counter is Ty. Don't tell him *anything* you don't want to be remembered!"

Josh introduced his date to them. He felt it only proper as she was being thrown into a situation where the only person she knew was herself. "This is Abigail Sloan. Again, we have my friends Laura and Damien," and smiling at the man behind the counter whom he'd never met before, "and Ty."

His date smiled at them, saying, "Just call me Abby. It's nice to meet you all finally because Elise has told me all about you guys. It's nice to put the faces to the names. I should probably admit to you guys that I don't ride horses normally, as in I've never. We didn't have any around where I grew up in Florida.

"But I'm looking forward to going riding! Being out here in Arizona it almost seems a crime to not go horseback riding, doesn't it? All Westerns have horses in them, so how can someone be out here and not go riding? It's like a requirement! When I heard we were going riding today, I thought it was a great idea. It's not really something I would've wanted to do on my own, and I haven't met anyone else out here that does it."

"Amen!" Laura said as she made room for them at the counter to sign in. "It drives me nuts when tourists come out here from somewhere else, but then insist on going to the movies. They can do *that* back home. If you're somewhere new, you need to experience what people *do* there! Taste the local flavor of the area, see the sites. Isn't that why you came here in the first place? You know what I'm talking about?"

Everyone nodded in agreement. Josh asked, "It's like when they go to Europe and eat at the local McDonald's, right?"

"Yes! *Why* do people do that?" Laura exclaimed.

Damien reasoned, "Honey, it's probably because they feel comfortable with what they know and recognize. They feel safe eating there."

"*Safe?*" Laura joked. "Babe, it's fast food!"

"I didn't say it was healthy!"

Smiling, Ty signed them in as he explained the process to them. Ty told them where the water fountain and restrooms were located. "If you get lost, just ask Laura!" he joked. He was rewarded with their smiles and laughs.

They had about fifteen more minutes before the ride was due to go out. Looking out the back window, Ty saw the two wranglers for this ride, Bo and Drew, come back from their break. He could hear Bo talking as they checked the cinches on their saddles. Legally, only one wrangler was required to go for this ride, but earlier both had decided to take it out. Returning to the desk, Ty could see the four people at the picnic tables as well as hear the sounds coming from the show area.

He heard some of the trail horses whinny. Jasper and Norman, Ty figured. After a short time, horses were seen almost as humans. And it didn't take too long for the real humans to learn not only their individual behaviors and personalities, but also their nickers, snorts, and whinnies. It was their vocalization, how they communicated. Humans just had to take the time to listen to understand them. Only then could they learn to tell the horses apart without even having to look.

Bo poked his head around the door. "Both of us still good to go?"

Ty nodded. "Yeah, we're still covered on the next rides. You guys ready?"

"Yeah. We'll go ahead and start to load them up now."

TY WATCHED AS DREW had them all stand up and asked the standard questions about if they'd ridden before, if at all, and their general experience level. He listened through the open window to their answers.

When the one named Josh answered he had lots of experience, he thought he'd just carefully observe him. Some people think they knew more about horses and riding than they really did. Generally, they're the most annoying—and often the most dangerous—people on a ride. Damien answered he had experience too. Clipping the office phone to his belt, he walked outside to watch and assist, if needed.

As Bo walked up with the first horse, Laura was already volunteering to get on. Ty wasn't surprised since that was her personality.

"What's this guy's name?" she asked, petting the Appaloosa's soft coat. She traced the small black spots with her fingertip, marveling at how the black hairs just stopped before going to white.

"This is Blackjack. He's got some spunk so I think you'll like him. He's more of a leader than a follower, so he's a good one to have up front."

"Cool." Laura patiently waited while Bo checked the cinch before signaling her to swing up.

As Bo adjusted the stirrups for the personable Laura, Ty watched as Drew got Damien mounted up and adjusted his stirrups and reins. "Cooper here will be good for you," Drew said to Damien. "But he can go between mellow and feisty, depending on his mood. He doesn't always warn you, but he's always nice about it."

"I can handle it. I've got lots of practice with mood swings."

"Honey, you'd better stop while you can!" Laura teasingly admonished him, knowing her husband was referring to her.

Grinning broadly, Damien said, "See what I mean?"

They all laughed as Laura inadvertently proved him correct.

Still smiling, Drew wrapped the lead rope around the saddle horn and then turned to go get another horse. Ty watched and listened as Josh reassured Abby about riding and horses in general. Listening to him, Ty was mildly surprised to realize he sounded like he really knew what he was talking about.

He had good people skills, Ty thought, as he saw the light and easy way he handled her. Abby seemed slightly timid but not scared. She nodded as Josh talked to her, answered her questions.

Drew led a calm buckskin gelding with a white diamond-shaped star on his forehead over to the mounting steps and had Abby step up. She swung in the saddle and landed just a little heavily. Just hard enough to make Ty and Drew wince inside a little in sympathy for Diamond's back. Drew walked the horse forward so he could get her situated.

"This is Diamond, and he's really good with beginner riders. Go ahead and pet his neck. Let him feel your touch. And don't be shy talking to Diamond. Horses are great listeners." Drew talked casually to Abby as he adjusted her stirrups.

Bo was on his way to get Josh a horse when Ty glanced at Laura, who was at the head of the line waiting as the others were being mounted up. Ty grinned at what he saw.

"Whoa there... Hey, Laura! Your horse has overheated and has sprung a *leak!*" Ty called out as Blackjack stretched out to relieve himself of his apparently full bladder.

"Oh! What do I do?"

"Just stand up in the stirrups to get off his back and kidneys," he called back, grinning at her facial expressions while she stood up, balancing herself by holding onto the saddle horn and sinking her feet into the wide stirrups.

Grinning, Josh looked over at Ty. "Sprung a leak, huh?"

Ty grinned back. "Yep. It happens sometimes when they get overheated like that. You should see what happens when it's *really* hot out!"

Josh laughed as he waited for his horse to be brought over. Bo had apparently decided to switch horses and was now leading over a tall gray.

Damien was joking with his wife as they waited for her horse to stop urinating. She grinned back good-naturedly then busted out laughing when Cooper did the same thing. Damien immediately stood up in his stirrups, joking if they all did this *he'd* have to go too. "It's like hearing a waterfall or running water."

Abby retorted, "Well, I'm no horse expert, but I'd say that's *exactly* what that is!"

Laura and Abby laughed again when Abby's horse decided to follow suit.

Damien looked over at Ty. "What the...? Just *what* kind of malfunctioning horses do you guys keep here?"

Ty laughed, enjoying this group's sense of humor.

Josh smiled at his friend. "It's just a chain reaction, really. When one goes, they all go! Our horses did the same thing, Damien." Looking at Laura, he quipped, "I guess Blackjack *is* the leader here since they're all following his lead!"

His comments drew laughs as Diamond continued to relieve himself.

Drew grinned up at Abby, standing well out of the way of the splash of liquid hitting the hard, sandy ground. "Our theory is it's the scent, but your friend could be right. Maybe it's just the sound of running water!"

Bo warned his boss, "Ty, you'd better see about plugging up all these leaks! The boss lady might not like hearing all the horses over here are leaking!"

Ty laughed at him as he glanced at his watch, wiping away some horse slobber (probably Dolly's) so he could read the digits. He noticed the man named Josh wasn't making any effort to get in the saddle when Bo stopped a tall, sturdy, gray horse in front of him.

Although Josh had seen Bo check the cinch and motion for him to mount up, he just stood there, his hands tucked into his back pockets. After a moment, Ty glanced at Bo, who shrugged.

When a puzzled look from the wrangler holding his horse was shot in his direction, Josh shrugged his shoulders. With a straight face he said, "I thought I'd just wait a minute or two..."

Sure enough, the last horse spread out his legs to relieve himself too. Josh casually moved out of the splash range. Grinning, Damien said, "Show off. You think you're so smart!"

"There's no *thinking* about it, Damien!" he replied cheerfully as he waited for his horse to finish.

Bo led the gray horse to drier ground so the man could mount up without having to walk in the now smelly mud. But in this sun, those wet, foamy puddles would be just dry, dark stains in the ground by the time they returned from their ride.

Impressed, Abby said, "Wow. It takes a really confident male to pee in public like that, doesn't it?"

Laura smiled at her as they waited patiently for Josh to get mounted up. Turning her attention to her husband, she called back, "Honey, don't get any ideas!"

Damien grinned back at her, shrugging his shoulders. "Aw, sweetheart, you're too late. Me and Josh here, we've been there, done that already!"

Josh laughed as he took hold of the leather reins. With a tinge of humor, he warned his friend, "*Damien...*"

"Well, we did! Many times, as I recall. Remember that time we wondered what it'd be like to pee on that electric fence your dad put up for the cattle that one summer?"

Everyone laughed, knowing the situation couldn't have ended on a good note. Josh was grinning broadly as he put his foot in the stirrup before swinging himself up, easily landing in the saddle. "Yeah, I'll never forget that! Back then, we weren't told '*Don't do this at home, kids!*' because we were apparently naturally smarter back then. And we were way younger then."

Laura grinned back at him, interjecting, "But probably still old enough! What did you *think* would happen?"

Josh said, "We didn't know... That's *why* we did it! We got lucky is all I can say! As an adult, I can say it's actually a bit on the dangerous side to pee on active electric fences. That's all I'm going to say about it."

Damien looked at his friend before looking back at his wife. "Well, in our defense, it just shows that we *were* paying attention in our science class. Our teacher always encouraged us to be willing to try new things, and to experiment to get accurate and true results. She must've said that at least a thousand times. Didn't she, Josh?"

Everyone laughed again. Ty was thoroughly enjoying this group of riders. He'd watched closely when Josh easily swung into the saddle, landing lightly and squarely in the Western saddle. Even with the length of the stirrups off a bit, his cowboy boots slipped unerringly into them without his needing to even look for them. He appeared to be a natural in the saddle, almost as if he were born there.

Ty saw Bo's surprised look and smiled. It wasn't often they had real horse people on their rides, at least not on this hour-long one. Experienced horse people liked the adventure and the challenge of the longer rides and normally booked those instead. Still, it was too early to tell with this guy. After all, he was just sitting there. But Ty was pretty sure Josh knew what he was doing. He saw Josh lean down, stroking the gray's neck as he smiled in genuine pleasure.

As Bo looped the lead rope around the saddle horn, he said, "This is Wish. You being so tall, I figured you'd like a taller horse."

"Yeah, I do. Thanks!" Josh continued to pet the horse, loving the familiar feel and scent of a horse.

Drew mounted Newton, a dun gelding, and trotted to the front of the line. With a wave, he moved them out. Bo rode alongside Josh, talking to him as they headed toward the trail.

Ty stood there and watched them head out. A nice bunch of people, he thought, as he continued to watch them turn around the bend on the hill and finally go out of his sight. Satisfied all was well, he turned and watched the activity at the show for a while, wondering again how Morgan was doing.

Chapter 8

JOSH AND DAMIEN LISTENED to the women talking up ahead as they rode along. Josh figured Laura would just take over, and that was fine with him as he was looking at the beautiful scenery. He couldn't believe he'd never even heard of this horse-riding place before talking to Leslie Travis that day. He'd have to thank her again for the recommendation. Of the two places she wrote down for him, she said this one was the better choice, so Harmony Hills is the one he'd called.

Bo had been watching Josh for about twenty minutes by now and came to the conclusion he really did seem to have the experience he'd spoken about back at the barn. Of course, all they'd been doing was walking, but Bo recognized the easy, natural way he sat in the saddle and his light hands on the reins. Horse people tended to recognize other horse people.

Knowing talking in a single file line wasn't the easiest thing to do, Bo decided to let Josh walk his horse beside Damien's. Normally this wasn't allowed, but he felt confident Josh could handle it if anything happened. Besides, he was right beside them.

Bo waited for a break in their conversation and raised his voice, "Josh, if you want to ride beside Damien's horse, you can. Just through this part here because up ahead there's not enough room to ride side by side. You'll know what I mean when you see it. After that section, you can go back to riding by his side though."

Josh slightly turned in his saddle to answer Bo. "Thanks, I appreciate it!" Josh eased Wish up beside Cooper.

Bo signaled Drew, who was riding twisted so he could answer a question from Laura, letting him know that it was fine for Josh to move out of line. Drew nodded and answered Laura.

When the trail began to get narrow, Josh automatically eased Wish back into line behind Diamond, so he was now riding right behind Abby. He was enjoying talking to her, but it was more like just some friends out on a nice ride. And he was fine with that.

It was all part of having a social life, after all. It wasn't always all about romance and love. Some dates were just for fun and the company.

Part of him felt bad because he knew he wasn't feeling that spark he was looking for in a relationship, but the other part of him felt immensely relieved because if he ever *did* fall for one of Elise's set-ups, there'd be no living with her. And he was really thankful for Leslie's suggestion to go for a ride. Although he was pretty sure taking a ride in the foothills on horseback wasn't going to end with a wedding ceremony like hers, he was glad he came.

Ty was sitting on the picnic table enjoying the sunny weather and the light breeze when he saw the group of six returning to the barn. He'd just sent out another ride and was taking a break. He heard the four customers and his two wranglers laughing as they rode up.

Ty watched as Bo and Drew helped them all down with no problems at all. Abby seemed fine although her legs were a bit wobbly. She had to hold on to the saddle for a moment until she was sure she wouldn't fall flat on her face. Josh stood close to her for a moment, making Ty wonder if they were a couple who recently got together or a long-term one. He was betting on a new one.

As the women made their way to the restroom, Abby walking a bit stiff-legged and Laura good-naturedly making fun of her, Josh and Damien stayed to talk with Ty as Drew and Bo tied up the horses. Conversationally, Ty asked Josh about his horse knowledge as his experience was evident.

Josh answered with a sentimental smile, "We had horses and cattle on our farm in Kentucky. My mom was a show rider when she was younger. She still competed for years after she married my dad but stopped when we kids came along. We also did horse rescues on the side.

"When Mom saw that I shared a love for them, I became her focus and new project." Josh thought back. "I was probably about five or six when she noticed me riding one of our horses bareback out in the field. I felt like we were running with the wind, like they do in the movies, you know?

"All the horse had on were a halter and a lead rope I had looped over for some makeshift reins. I had to climb on the wooden fence rails to even get on him. All I knew was I loved running through the fields on that horse! Gem was just what his name said."

Damien grinned because he knew this story by heart.

With his own grin, Josh explained, "What I *didn't* know at the time, though, was Mom was watching me. She'd run down to the fence apparently yelling at me to stop but, of course, I couldn't hear her with the wind in my ears. Finally, we slowed down and eventually stopped.

"I was all excited, smiling ear to ear probably. I turned Gem around to head back to the barns, and *that's* when I noticed Mom yelling at me. After she got her stopped heart pumping again... Well, the first thing she did when I got off was to make sure I couldn't sit on my butt for at least a week!"

Damien and Ty laughed along with him, picturing it.

"Yeah, she wasn't too impressed with my riding abilities for a good five minutes. But after that, she and I were out riding pretty much every single day. She later told me she felt really bad for spanking me and apologized for it. It was just that I really scared her, she said."

A bit surprised, Ty asked, "She apologized to her little son? She sounds like an honest and unconventional mom!"

Damien agreed before Josh could. "Annabelle is. She bucked conventional parenting wisdom because she was ahead of the times. I can say I don't think I've ever heard of another parent ever actually apologizing to their kid, except maybe them getting hurt by falling down or something. Even *my* mom didn't, that I recall. But I still love her!"

Josh smiled in agreement. "I know that I lucked out big time in the parenting category! I have the best parents. And your mom is a really good one, too, Damien." He then continued, "Mom taught me how to care for horses, ride them, train them, and even how to clean tack. Everything she could think of that had to do with a horse, she passed on to me.

"My two sisters liked our horses, but they just didn't have the same bug I had when it came to them." Shrugging his shoulder again, Josh said, "It probably broke Mom's heart when I didn't become a show rider like her. I don't even own a horse right now, which I think about doing more often than not. I really miss not having one, but I *do* have a cool cat!"

Damien joined in, "But Annabelle is still so proud of her son. Josh here is the apple of her eye although sometimes I wonder why." He laughed when Josh gave him a friendly shove.

Liking their easy camaraderie, Ty commented, "It sounds to me like he's the reason his dad put up an electric fence instead of more plank. His young son sure wasn't going to climb up to the top wire to get on a horse!"

Josh and Damien laughed at the thought. Damien joked, "No, but then it gave us something to pee on!"

They all laughed again.

Ty leaned against the table, asking, "So what *do* you do?"

Josh watched a couple horses chase each other in the paddock nearby. Smiling at their antics, he turned back to answer Ty. "I went into construction like one of my uncles. He taught me a lot as a teen and young adult, and now I have my own company. It's a mixture of new construction, remodeling, renovations, and carpentry. Anything to keep us busy, productive, and in the black with the bank. I like working with my hands, you know?

"And I'm not a person who can sit behind a desk for long. I need to be active. I belong outdoors more than indoors."

Lifting up his chin at Damien, he added, "And Damien here, well, he just follows in my shadow. He's been doing that since we were kids. Somewhere along the line I figured he wasn't going to leave, so I let him hang around more and more and stopped chasing him away. I figured he needed attention, love, and food like those rescues Mom brought home. The thing is, once we fed him, he never left! Dang strays."

Damien sheepishly shrugged his shoulders.

Ty figured there must've been an element of truth to the story. Smiling, he asked, "So what, then, he's a rescue too? But he just became a permanent fixture?"

Chuckling, Damien looked at his friend. "Yeah, whatever. Although, I have to admit he's right when he said I hung around there a lot. His mom and dad are great people. Seriously, like some of the best people ever. I even like his sisters, Angie and Val. In the end, because I was over there so much, they all just decided to basically adopt me."

With a straight face, Josh said, "Yeah. He became the little brother I never knew I didn't want."

They all laughed.

Damien was still smiling as he said, "But I didn't go into construction like he did. I had a talent with computers, which I fell in love with in high school. I went to college, met Laura, got a degree. When I moved out here, following Laura who took a job offer, I started my own computer business.

"My big brother here became one of my customers once he decided to give it a try out here too. It seems like he just couldn't live without me since he followed me clear across the continent!" He smiled as he teased his friend. "I had a small business going by the time he came out here, but he also helped me out later on by getting me more clients."

Ty didn't miss that Damien followed Josh as a kid, and then followed Laura as an adult. He wondered about this, just as a natural train of thought.

Bo and Drew had walked up to them while they were talking, leaning against the picnic table beside Ty. Having a lull in the conversation at that moment, Josh and Damien handed over their tips. They thanked Ty, Bo, and Drew for the ride and the entertainment. Still waiting on Laura and Abby, they decided they'd better go find them.

Just as they were getting ready to leave to go looking for them, they returned on their own accord. They'd been watching the show activities and came back to collect the guys so they could all go over. Laura and Abby thanked Ty, Drew, and Bo themselves before walking away with Damien and Josh.

As they walked away, Laura asked her husband, "You guys tipped them, right?"

"Yeah. We both did."

"Okay. I just wanted to make sure. Ty'd never forget if you didn't!" she teased.

Ty had directed them to the food trucks on the other side of Grand View in case they wanted a bite to eat as they watched the show. He told them they could buy their tickets at the little table stationed by the driveway leading to the barn. Since they'd get their hands stamped, they could then wander around the entire property and return to the show if they wanted to do that.

Josh and Abby walked behind Damien and Laura. As they walked, Laura took hold of her husband's hand.

Deep down inside, Josh wished he had somebody special like Damien had Laura, but he had yet to meet that woman he was looking for. Even with all of the women Elise had set in front of him, he hadn't felt that punch to the gut. That sizzle he insisted on feeling.

Maybe he was passing up on a woman who could grow on him. Someone who could make that feeling come later. Maybe he was asking and looking for too much, but he just couldn't settle for less. He couldn't settle for less in an area of his life that was so extremely important.

He wanted a woman who had the same manners, the same inner strength, humor, and values of his mother. If Mom knew that, she'd probably cry for a week, Josh thought. So until or unless that happened, he'd just be content as he was.

For now, he just walked beside Abby and made small talk with her as they followed his friends, bought their tickets, got their hands stamped, and walked toward the large show barn.

One day, he thought as he looked at the busy scenes around them, my patience will pay off.

His mom had always told him he was more like the rest of the males on his father's side of the family than her own. She'd repeatedly told her only son that he seemed to be the type when he met that special woman, she'd simply come out of nowhere when he least expected it. His mom said it'd just hit him, and leave him baffled at the suddenness of it all.

But, she'd stressed, the point was, he would know.

Chapter 9

MORGAN WAS STARVING. SHE'D been judging classes, handing out ribbons, and answering questions for hours on end now. This next class preparing to enter the ring would be the last before she got a break.

Having lost her appetite and not eating that morning due to it being a rough one, she wasn't sure she could last through one more class. She was already feeling a little nauseous, which for her wasn't a good sign. Just another fifteen or twenty minutes, she told herself.

She and the other two judges had confessed a couple of classes back that they were getting hungry. Unfortunately, their admissions just served to make them seem hungrier. One had to love the sheer power of suggestion, Morgan thought ruefully. She glanced over and caught the eye of Renae Lancaster, one of her judges. They smiled at each other, knowing they were thinking the same thing.

They moved apart so they could get good views of the horses and riders as they rode around the arena. Tracy Conley, the Head Judge, was standing in the middle of the arena already.

As Morgan was passing Tracy to get to her spot to judge, she laughed when Tracy whispered, "Twenty minutes tops. Let's make this quick, shall we? Fair but quick. I need to use the bathroom!"

"With you on that twenty! I'm famished," Morgan answered.

This was a class for strictly beginner riders. Most shows placed the Beginner classes at the beginning of the day, but Morgan liked to space it out a bit more. It seemed to her that spreading the classes throughout the day gave the younger riders (really meaning their parents) more time to prepare for the unexpected things bound to happen. It also gave them the opportunity to watch the more experienced riders and horses. Sometimes, it was best to just watch and learn from peers.

As the announcer instructed them all to a posting trot, Morgan carefully watched them, making notes on her clipboard as the horses and riders went around and around.

She looked for easy, smooth transitions going into the canter, and then looked for eyes up, heels down, easy hands and seats, straight backs, and steady legs in the correct positions. Seeing some open fingers on some riders, she made her notes. She also watched to see if the horse was fighting its rider.

She made sure she wouldn't get run over as the announcer gave the instruction to walk and then reverse direction. As she turned, she noticed Renae barely got out of the way of a nervous Shetland pony who didn't like the larger horse beside it. She couldn't help but smile. Looking into the bleachers, she saw some parents laughing who had seen it happen too.

Watching the little girl on the Shetland pony, Morgan thought she handled it all quite well. No white, scared face on this girl, Morgan noted with some satisfaction as the girl concentrated on getting her pony back to the rail.

The riders and horses just had to learn how to deal with it. Things like that happen. That's one reason she hosted these shows. Riding a horse in a crowded ring wasn't too much different than driving a car in traffic: Everyone had to pay attention, anticipate others, and be prepared for the unexpected.

At the end of the class, the riders lined up in the middle of the arena. As the judges walked by each horse, the rider asked their horse to back up a few paces. The judges looked for smoothness of the transition, how the horse responded, if they fought their rider, how straight they backed up, and how well they stopped.

Finally, the three judges met and compared notes. Tracy had them laughing when she said, "Man, I sure hope we all agree on this! That bathroom better *not* have a line! Give me your choices, ladies."

Morgan said, "If there's a line, Tracy, I have plenty of other stalls to choose from. We just need to find one that's not already occupied with something big and hairy..."

"*Don't* make me laugh! If you do, something embarrassing will happen, and I'll never be able to show my face here again!"

Smiling, Renae and Morgan handed over their sheets. After a quick discussion, they finally decided on the winners.

Tracy handed the final form to Kim to take to the announcer's stand. Morgan motioned for the ribbons to be brought out. In her Strictly Beginner classes, Morgan liked to have a ribbon for every contestant. She had the standard top three ribbons for the better riders, but then she'd also designed a special Participant ribbon for them all so they could have at least a memento of their first show.

It wasn't a consolation prize, as she explained in her Show Programs, but merely a keepsake of their first horse show, something to remember it with. She only did this for this Beginner class. In all of her other classes, either they won a ribbon, or they didn't. That's how life worked.

As Morgan assisted in handing out the ribbons with Tracy and Renae, she smiled back at the young riders whose faces were alive with excitement. There were a few disappointed ones too. You can't win them all, she thought as they rode by. But she'd give a word of encouragement to those as they walked by her.

She took a second to pet the Shetland pony because he was just so darn cute, she couldn't possibly resist him. The Shetland pony was so short, even sitting on its back, the little girl was barely eye-level with Morgan. She had to look up a bit at Morgan when she pulled her adorable pony to a stop.

Her face was glowing in excitement under her tiny helmet covered in black velvet as Morgan spoke to her, praising her for her cool head when her pony spooked earlier. From the grin on the little girl's face, Morgan was sure she'd been hooked by the love of horses already.

As Morgan watched the last ones walk toward the arena gate to leave, she thought her day just couldn't get any better than this. She hoped she was making happy memories for these young kids.

She and the other judges joked with each other as they made their way out of the arena as the announcer's voice came over the loudspeaker about the thirty-minute intermission.

Chapter 10

LAURA FOUND A DROPPED show program on the ground and, after shaking off what she hoped was dirt, read that after this current class there would be a thirty-minute intermission. It didn't take a college graduate, and surely not four of them, to know what that meant. They practically raced each other to get in line at the food truck they chose before the line got any longer.

Josh stepped up to the wide window and spoke to the young woman taking orders. "Hi, what's your name?"

Alexis, helping out a worker on a break, smiled. She leaned down on her elbows and answered, "I'm Alexis. What can I get you?"

"Well, Alexis, I was wondering if you could do me a small favor here. See these two lovely ladies? Well, I'd like to pay for both of them as well as for myself but *not* for this guy here. Can you ring it up that way?" He kept his eyes on the smiling Alexis even when he felt Damien poke him in his ribs.

When Laura heard what he said, she let loose with a hearty laugh. Still laughing, she wrapped her arms around Josh's waist from behind and squeezed him. Josh smiled and patted her hands but still didn't look at Damien.

Damien looked confused and poked his friend in his ribs again. "Hey! What about me? Why do I have to pay for my own?"

Josh didn't answer. Instead, he placed his order, and after Laura and Abby placed theirs, Alexis rang up the total for the three of them. Josh swiped his debit card instead of using his cash but threw in a few dollars in the tip jar.

Looking directly at Laura, he said, "Well, it's not exactly ten dollars, but it's pretty close. We even now?"

Laura nodded with a smile, also not saying a word to her husband.

After Damien ordered his food, he looked back and forth from his wife and his best friend. After a minute of thinking, he finally got what it was all about. He wrapped his arms around her waist, hauling her close to dramatically kiss her and made her laugh again. He pulled away, sending a *behave yourself* look to his wife.

Pointing his finger in the air toward his friend, Damien said, "Don't you try to steal my girl, Josh. Your charm won't work with her."

Leaning back in her husband's arms, resting against his chest, Laura smiled. "Don't be too sure about that, darlin'. He's awfully cute!" She heard him growl at her teasing and laughed again. "Okay, okay, okay. The man's no good for me!"

They'd been eating and joking with each other for about twenty minutes, enjoying the fact they beat the mad rush for food. They heard over the PA system about the intermission and watched hungry people line up.

After a couple of minutes, Josh noticed they could get some dessert at the other food truck without too much of a wait, so he volunteered to go get in line. Holding out his hand, palm up, in front of Damien, he wiggled his fingers.

Damien rolled his eyes but good-naturedly pulled out some money from his wallet and placed it in Josh's palm. Laura volunteered to tag along with him. She stayed for an extra moment to order her husband and Abby to gather up their trash and leave the table to let someone else sit there while they were gone. After all, they didn't need a table to eat dessert.

Already making his way toward the food truck, Josh was jostled by a large group of running, yelling children. Trying to regain his balance, he practically fell over a person walking by him, knocking into them hard.

Reacting quickly, he grabbed the person's arms to keep them from falling down. As he turned to apologize, he found himself staring directly into the startled, deep green eyes of a woman.

And in that split second, he felt a hit to his gut.

MORGAN WAS PITCHED FORWARD and would've taken a nose dive in the dirt if somebody hadn't grabbed her arms when they did. She felt herself being hauled upright and spun around. With the momentum carrying her around, she felt her right hand land solidly in somebody's torso. Looking up, she was suddenly looking directly into a set of gorgeous brown eyes.

She read the instant concern—and was that shock?— in them and felt her heart just plummet to the bottom of her stomach. She was locked in eye contact with this person.

Although feeling faintly embarrassed, she couldn't seem to look away. She felt his hands tighten on her upper arms but didn't feel fear. She wasn't sure what she felt, but whatever it was, it was powerful.

She thought about stepping back but wasn't sure she wanted to. Or even could.

Josh couldn't help staring. God knows he was trying to look away. It took him a moment to realize he was holding his breath. Or had she knocked it out of him? He had to consciously soften his grip on her after he realized he'd unknowingly tightened it. Slowly, he released the breath he'd been holding and tried to get his wits about him.

It occurred to him he should step back to give her some space. But try as he might, he couldn't seem to move his legs. He wasn't sure he wanted to.

"Josh! Are you guys all right? Did you *see* those awful kids? Of course you did since it was those kids who just practically shoved you two completely over! *Where* are their parents? They shouldn't be running like that!" Laura fumed, looking around like she was ready to give somebody a piece of her mind.

She paused and looked at Josh when he didn't answer her immediately. He wasn't paying her any attention at all. Her glance went from one to the other. Her angry eyes quickly turned into curious ones. Well, well, well... Wasn't *this* interesting? Laura thought. It looked like somebody here just lost a piece of their own minds. Or their hearts.

Clearing her throat, Laura gently laid her hand on Josh's shoulder. She wondered if she should retreat, but she couldn't now. It would've been too awkward. Like this wasn't. "Josh."

It was the voice that broke the spell. Josh suddenly came to his senses. He slowly dropped his hands from the woman's arms. He had to learn to breathe again. And fast. "I'm so sorry about knocking into you like I did." Seeing her dazed face, he asked, "Are you okay?"

Morgan blinked. She couldn't seem to do anything else. She slowly came to her senses. It occurred to her that he'd let go of her arms and was now looking at her intently. It suddenly dawned on her they weren't alone. She finally got her wits about her and glanced at the woman beside them.

Suddenly, the noise of the show and the people around them penetrated through the fog she felt she was in. Embarrassed beyond a doubt, Morgan took a quick step back. "I'm... I'm fine." She ran her tongue over her lips. "It's okay. And I'm not sure, but I think I also punched you. I didn't mean to. Sorry about that. Maybe I should be asking you if *you're* all right?"

Looking at the pretty blonde woman who was now looking at her with more than a little curiosity, she apologized to her also. Morgan prayed it wasn't a jealous wife or girlfriend. "I'm sorry. Those kids just came out of nowhere, didn't they? They'd better not be doing that around the horses! Well, I have to go..." She waved vaguely in the direction of the food trucks. "I need to get something to eat while I'm on break. I don't have much time left."

Turning back to look at the man who was still intently looking at her, Morgan took a deep breath. She gave a small smile, saying, "Thank you for breaking my imminent fall. I wouldn't have liked to have taken a nose dive without being prepared for it first. Thanks again." Morgan made herself stop babbling and turned to walk away.

Reaching up to straighten her hat, she went directly to the food truck she saw Alexis at and noticed she was looking her way. She had to act like nothing had just happened. But after she greeted Alexis and was handed her order which Alexis had known to have ready for the judges once she heard the intermission called out, she wondered, *What* just happened?

LAURA WATCHED THE BEAUTIFUL woman walk away. She released a breath she wasn't even aware she was holding. She shot her glance back to Josh.

Almost squinting, his eyes followed the retreating woman's every move. He was watching her walk away, watching as she righted her black cowgirl hat. His eyes took in almost instantly her slim, tight body. He noticed how the black slacks she wore fit her very well. Raining down her back, her wavy brown hair looked thick and soft. Why did he have the sudden urge to bury his hands in it, to feel it?

She was getting food now at the same food truck they'd gone to, talking to the same young woman they'd ordered from previously. He watched as she took her tray of food and walked away.

Laura just looked at her friend, whose gaze was still glued to the woman at the food truck. Trying to hide her smile was like spitting to put out a raging forest fire. It just wasn't worth the effort. She simply couldn't help it when her smile crept across her face.

Josh felt Laura's hand tighten on his shoulder. He'd forgotten she was even there. *What* just happened? *Who* was that woman? he wondered.

"Josh?"

He turned and looked at Laura. He couldn't have missed her smile even if his eyes were taped shut. "Did I just make a complete fool of myself? Be honest. I'll know if you're lying to me."

Laura didn't think so since he looked a bit thunderstruck still. "Are you kidding? I couldn't have made a better introduction myself. I *would* offer a small piece of advice for the next time. I mean, if it should ever happen again."

Feeling worse than a fool, Josh looked at her. "Okay. I'll bite. What's your advice?"

"I'd suggest giving her your name and phone number. Or maybe getting hers. You know, the essentials to make meeting her again possible. But this whole mystery thing is pretty romantic too."

Josh blew out a breath as he searched for the sharp-dressed woman, but she was gone. He had an almost insane urge to run after her.

That shimmering green blouse had brought out the color of her vivid green eyes. He'd noticed her black hat had the same green material in its wide band. Pretty sharp outfit, he thought. He wondered vaguely if her outfit added to her effect, or if it actually detracted from it. He felt sure she'd make an impact no matter what she was wearing.

Without realizing he was speaking out loud, he muttered, "I don't know if I could live through another meeting like that."

Hearing him, Laura laughed. She couldn't help it. Wrapping her arm around his waist, she looked up at him. When he looked down at her finally, she shook her head. "You're going to have to thank her, you know."

"Who?"

"Elise."

"Why in the world would I thank Elise?"

"Because if she hadn't set you up with Abby, you would've never come here. And if you hadn't come here, you'd never have met, more or less, your Mystery Woman."

Suddenly reality crashed in. "Oh, man. Abby."

Chapter 11

MORGAN TOOK OFF FROM work the day after the Shamrocks and Dreams show because taking off when you wanted to was a perk of being the owner. And she could do that because she knew her employees were trustworthy. Ty had checked in with her earlier, making sure she was fine.

Overall, it was a nice, easy day in which to recharge and relax at home. Even if the barns were busy, her house was far enough away to have complete privacy. She needed to think and sort out some unexpected feelings.

She was sitting in a wicker chair on her patio, Darrell B stretched out on the cool tiles near her feet. Darrell G was propped against the side of the chair, looking up at Morgan with her chocolate brown eyes. Brown eyes that reminded her of another pair of brown eyes. Only that other pair belonged to a man she'd spoken to for only a short, but oddly momentous, minute. Or was that just her take on it?

Morgan ran her hand over Darrell G's head again as she looked out at the mountains edging her property. Her eyes followed three turkey vultures that were lazily riding the wind currents, patiently waiting to smell where their next meal would be coming from. She watched as the large bodies bookended with long black and white wings glided effortlessly around and around the endless blue sky.

What was *with* yesterday? she wondered. First, there were the sudden, heart-wrenching memories in the morning. Then she about got knocked down. And what *was* it about that guy? Who was he? Was he a local guy, or was he from elsewhere and there just for the show? Was he some kid's dad? Her hand paused, resting on the dog's head. Darrell G nudged Morgan's hand with her nose to get her attention again. Absentmindedly, Morgan began petting her again.

Why had he affected her that way? All he did was save her from taking a nose dive in the dirt. As she replayed the scene in her mind, she saw again the dazed look in his eyes. No, it was more than just a quick save. Had he felt it too?

Closing her eyes, Morgan also remembered the pretty woman beside him. Was that his girlfriend? Wife? Sister? A relative? A friend? As Morgan replayed the scene in her mind yet again, she recalled the woman didn't seem upset or jealous of her. She'd just been curious. It took Morgan a while to remember that. The blonde woman had been simply curious.

But the thought that nagged her the most, and the deepest, was *why* she'd felt anything at all. She hadn't been affected by anyone since... Well, in years.

Darrell B suddenly sat up, whined and cocked his head to the side like he was studying her. His sister was looking at Morgan with the same wondering look.

"That's enough, you two." Reaching forward, she rubbed them both behind their ears and kissed their noses. They began thumping their tails on the ground. "You're beginning to look like Ty with those worried eyes of yours. Although I do appreciate the concern from you guys, too, I'm fine. Are you listening to me, Darrell?"

Morgan needed air. She needed space. She needed her horse, and a good ride in her mountains. "You wanna go for a ride? Huh? Do ya? Do ya?" The dogs jumped up and started wagging their tails wildly. Darrell B barked in anticipation of an adventure. "Me too. Let me get my phone and canteen, then we'll go for a ride in our mountains. You'd better go get a drink because it's liable to be a long one."

The dogs bounded around the porch in excitement as Morgan headed inside, both waiting impatiently for her to return to them.

IT WAS TWO IN the afternoon, and Josh was still sitting on his couch, thinking. He'd been sitting there for a while now. He hadn't thought this much about anything with such singular focus since he'd rescued a sick, lost kitten on the highway, took her to the vet, and promptly decided to keep her.

Freeway was curled up beside him. He reached over again to stroke her yellow fur. She sleepily raised her head, looked at him and slowly blinked her green eyes. She then rested her head back down on her white front paws, her eyes closing again in sleep. But he heard her soft purring.

He just couldn't get the Mystery Woman from yesterday out of his mind. Who was she? Josh wondered. Was she a local, or was she from somewhere else and just there for the show?

He never got the chance to ask around because as soon as he and Laura had turned around, Abby and Damien were standing there. Abby had quietly asked to go home a moment later.

Josh stroked Freeway as he talked to her, "What could I do? I tried to explain it to her as I drove her back to her place. How could I explain it to her when *I* didn't know? I'd bet my next paycheck I had more questions than she did... And still do. What do *you* think I should do, Freeway?"

Unconcerned with human affairs, Freeway just continued to purr with her eyes closed, a satisfied look on her face.

Hearing his doorbell chime, he walked to his front door and looked through the peephole. He smiled in spite of himself as he saw Damien standing at his door and waving as if he knew Josh was not only home, but was looking through the peephole at that exact moment. Josh briefly toyed with the idea of not answering the door just to make Damien feel like an idiot. What were best friends for?

"Josh, I know you're in there, and you're thinking about not opening the door. Admit it, man. I'm smarter than you think I am. Open up." Damien smiled as he raised one arm. "I got beer!" He then raised his other arm. "And pretzels!" After another moment, he added, "And I know where you keep your spare key!"

Josh smiled again but still didn't make a sound or attempt to open the door. He was curious to see what Damien would do. He felt Freeway wind her way around his legs and heard her loud meow. Quickly, he looked down. She was intently looking up at him. She meowed loudly again as her tail whipped against his leg.

Damien began laughing on the other side of the door. "Thanks, Freeway! Now open up, Josh. She wouldn't be there if you weren't. She gave you away."

Scooping up Freeway in his arms before opening the door, he muttered, "Traitor."

Chapter 12

"So, what're you going to do about your Mystery Woman?" Damien was leaning back in one of Josh's chaise lounge chairs on the patio. Looking over at his longtime best friend, he popped the top of a cold can of beer.

"What do you mean?" Josh asked him.

Freeway jumped into his lap. Josh ran his hand down her back and up her tail a few times. He could hear her purring in contentment. Her purrs always made him feel happy. Animals had a tendency to do that for him. They were the best companions. She enjoyed pestering him for as much attention as she could get when he was home, but Josh didn't mind at all.

In fact, if she were the type of cat who didn't ever *want* to be pet, he wouldn't want her. He might as well come home to a completely empty house if that was the case. Freeway at least let him know she appreciated him as well as the cat food, toys, and treats he bought her.

With a raised eyebrow, Damien smiled. "Well, I came in at the end of the little fireworks show, and I still saw some bright, pretty sparklers. No one can be a part of a show like that and not want to see the finale."

Damien took a couple gulps of beer as he waited for Josh's reply. He didn't want to pry too much into his friend's business. As a matter of fact, if it wasn't for Laura, he may not have been there at all. He tried to explain to his wife guys just don't interfere with other guys' lives the way women do. She wouldn't take no for an answer and had practically shoved her husband out the door. She'd threatened him that if he didn't go to Josh, she would. He wouldn't put it past her to actually do that, so he'd grabbed his keys and wallet and left.

Josh's eyes remained on the view before him. It was one of the reasons he loved it there. Having a mountain view whenever he wanted it was hard to beat. Catching movement out of the corner of his eye, he spotted a cottontail rabbit slowly hopping along before abruptly stopping in the shade of a tree. He watched as its ears twitched, listening. After a moment or two, the rabbit continued on, stopping every few feet to pause and listen again.

Freeway watched the rabbit too. But she was more content to sit on Josh's lap, her front paws rhythmically kneading his leg.

Josh finally answered, "I've been running different scenarios through my head all night and most of today. But I've also had other things on my mind beside the Mystery Woman. Well, related to her, I guess." At his friend's raised eyebrow, he clarified, "Abby."

"Yeah, better you than me on that one. But surely she couldn't seriously think you were throwing her over for some girl you literally just ran into. What? Did she think it was pre-arranged or something? And it's not like you two have been dating for a year or something. Geez, it was just a single date that was barely a few hours long.

"I bet that drive home was a bit awkward, huh? It's a shame the day ended like that too. It seemed to be going well."

"Yeah, it was a little awkward. But she still wasn't who, or what, I'm looking for. And you can't stop feeling the way you're feeling. If she felt she was being thrown over, as you put it, then that's the way she feels.

"I tried to explain it to her logically, but logic can't always convince someone's mind or heart to see it the way you do." Josh drank some more beer before he reached over for the bag of pretzels Damien had set on the little table between them. "I guess she was embarrassed or felt humiliated."

He gently scooted Freeway off his lap so he could open the bag. "I called and left a message earlier letting her know I won't be calling her again. And to once again apologize for something I couldn't control." He dug his hand into the bag and took out some pretzels, popped a couple in his mouth.

"Yeah, that was good for you to do, typical even. If Abby *is* that overly sensitive, you wouldn't have wanted to be with her anyway. Maybe it was a blessing in disguise this all happened. It *did* save you from wasting your time, or having to tell yet another bachelorette to move along."

He reached over and got a handful of pretzels for himself. He grinned when Freeway jumped into his lap, stretching up to sniff his face. "Hey, girl," he said to her, scratching her cheek the way he knew she liked.

Josh lifted his beer in a small toast of agreement. "I agree." He paused for a moment. "Okay, so here's the thing. And I feel like a complete idiot for even saying this... But I really need to know who this woman is, Damien. I *need* to know.

"I mean, even if it's to find out she's already taken and has a happy life with a household of kids and pets. She'd better not, but I can't move on unless I know for sure." He tried for a little humor, and his friend smiled.

Josh slowly broke apart the pretzel in his hand. "I know it sounds crazy. I also know I could be setting myself up for some major disappointment. But I can't live with the not-knowing, the what-ifs of it.

"There was *such* an unexplainable connection in that one moment of time. I have to believe there could be a possibility for something more, the potential for more, whatever it may be. But even if it's actually nothing at all, I just need to *know*."

Damien nodded. "According to my intelligent wife, she's in full agreement with you. She did mention to me on the way home that the woman looked faintly familiar to her."

He shrugged his shoulders when Josh quickly looked over at him. "Laura tried to remember where she may have seen her before, but she couldn't think of it. Maybe this woman just reminded her of someone she'd seen before somewhere else. Maybe even of an actress on one of her TV shows. Who knows?

"But knowing Laura as I do, and her knack for remembering faces, I'm betting this Mystery Woman is a local. She said it all just happened so quickly, and it just seemed so surreal, she couldn't be certain." Damien brushed the salt from his fingers.

"What should I do? Drive over to the stable someday and ask that guy we met, Ty, if he knows of a knockout that has brown hair and amazing green eyes?" Josh took another pretzel and studied it. Wishing they weren't so salty, he flicked off a few grains of the salt stuck on it before popping it in his mouth.

Damien shrugged his shoulders.

"Should I see when their next horse show is, and then just wander around like a mad stalker? What would she think of me if I did that? I'd probably come across as seriously deranged and scare her off."

Damien was chewing on a mouthful of pretzel, contemplating their options. He saw himself as part of an investigative team now. "It seems to me the most practical thing to do would be to do what you just suggested yourself. As terrifying and simple as a plan that it is, it really makes the most sense."

He looked at Josh again. "And if you meet her again, and she does think you're a stalker, Laura and I would vouch for you." He smiled when he heard his friend chuckle. "We'd give you really good references. Glowing ones. Seriously, man.

"You're a good, decent human being. You treat women with respect, even if you don't really want to. You're patient with people. Elise is a prime example of that. You and your family are close and on friendly terms. You can speak without lacing what you say with profanity. I know most people don't care anymore, but many still do.

"You have your own successful business, and you have pretty decent people skills. You handle your finances better than most. You aren't into kinky or serial killer types of things, at least any that I know about. You're slightly older than me and never been married. And no kids, crazy ex-girlfriends, no baggage to drag around to boot.

"All of that really shows you're a patient, selective person in this area. If I were a woman that alone would turn me on." He popped another pretzel in his mouth, grinning broadly at his friend. Freeway stretched out beside him, eyeing the pretzel in his hand but not begging for a bite.

Josh looked over at him, saying dryly, "Thanks for the pep talk and credit reference. You're suggesting I call up the stables and start making regular trail-riding reservations in the, most likely, vain hope of meeting this woman again? Banking that just one day we'd run into each other again either literally or figuratively speaking?"

"No, *you* suggested that. I just happen to agree." Damien considered again. "It really makes the most sense, at least right now it does. It can't hurt anyway.

"Besides, it was really nice to be on a horse again. I know you had to have loved it, too, even though we were just walking. You don't have to go by yourself unless you want to. Laura and I would go with you now and then if you wanted company.

"You'll get bored going on that little ride all the time, though, so you'd probably want to reserve a spot on the other rides instead. Laura said they offer all sorts of rides there, even ones where you can take a little lunch with you. She's been on that one once before and said it was nice and relaxing. Check out their website."

"I guess I could spend some of my future retirement money on horseback rides. Maybe I'll think of it as an investment in myself. And I'd be helping to keep a local business going, I suppose."

Crushing his empty beer can and setting it aside, Josh looked out at his wide, open view. He saw small little birds hopping from one branch to another in a tree close by. He listened to their chirping and watched as a few of them flew down to the ground, then began pecking at it with their little beaks. "I'll think about it some more, and let you know."

Damien had a sudden thought. "Hey, I almost forgot. Laura did mention something else that slipped my mind until just now. It may be with you locked in that staring contest and all, you may not have noticed it." He paused for effect.

"Spit it out, or I'll sic my ferocious cat on you."

Looking down at the purring cat stretched out beside him, Damien said, "Yeah, she's ferocious all right."

"I just haven't activated her silent killer cat mode. Yet."

Not bothering to hide his grin, Damien pointed out, "Did you notice how she was dressed? Sharp, really sharp. Now normally Laura would've thought this woman was a show rider, but she doesn't think so. Laura thinks it was one of the judges. She said she recalled the woman saying something like she was in a hurry because she was on break."

"Well, maybe she was just in-between classes or something. She could still be a rider from anywhere if that's the case. That hardly helps me."

"Laura's power of observation is legendary, my man. My wife also noticed she went to the food truck and got her food pretty quickly."

Confused, Josh looked at him. He couldn't see what that had to do with anything. "Yeah, I saw that. So what?"

"According to my observant Laura, your lady didn't pay for it. Did you see her pay? She just took it and walked off. That means she had to have been someone of importance to the show itself. She gets free meals. Who'd get free meals besides a judge?"

"In order to save my retirement money I could simply ask that guy if he knew who the judges were at the show? Or maybe he could ask the owner of that place. Surely the owner would be the one who hired the judges, right? Tell Laura thanks."

Looking over at Damien, he added, "And thanks for coming by too. I do appreciate you coming over, whether you'd wanted to or not. I'm guessing Laura was curious and booted you out the front door. Am I right?"

"No, you're *not* right." Looking slightly sheepish, Damien had the good grace to grin. "It was the garage door. And it was *my* idea to bring the beer and the pretzels."

Josh laughed. "Well, we men can't live on beer alone."

"Nope. That's why I grabbed the pretzels."

"All are appreciated."

Chapter 13

MORGAN HAD BEEN SWAMPED with business since the Shamrocks and Dreams Show. The past two weeks were amazingly busy, but she loved it. She, Kat, and Mel were getting calls for more riding lessons, questions about boarding new horses, horses needing more training, offers from other facilities looking for a new judge, and even inquiries about taking private trail rides in the mountains for a change of pace and for fun.

And she was tinkering with maybe doing a Father-Son Weekend in the next month or two. Father's Day Weekend, maybe? She jotted down a note to look at the summer schedule. She might have clinics to go to herself or shows to judge, but Kat and Mel could handle an event for a couple of days. The Mother-Daughter Weekend was the third weekend in June, so do two weekends in a row? The Fourth of July was always a big event, so she'd have to think on it some more.

She still wondered at times about the guy who accidentally ran her down, but she kept those thoughts strictly to herself. When he crossed her mind, she simply dismissed him, believing it was just a weird thing that happened. She was simply making more out of it than it was based on her frayed emotions that day.

It was now a bright, cheery Saturday afternoon. Tomorrow she'd be off. She was glad about that as tomorrow was April Fool's Day. She knew her workers would respect her time off, so they wouldn't play any jokes on her. Well, she assumed they wouldn't. *That* could be just what they were hoping! She grinned to herself thinking of some of the past jokes they'd all played on each other.

She knew Alexis and Maya would again tie little green ribbons and bows in the horses' manes and tails in the morning to make it festive. She'd have to remind them to take photos so she could put them on the website. Alexis had started decorating the horses for the holidays years earlier, and it just became a fun tradition.

Morgan was sitting at her desk in the Sunset Ridge office re-writing her notes from a phone call she'd taken earlier. She was just now getting the time to try to decipher her quick writing. She studied a hastily scribbled word, sighing as even the context of what she wrote didn't help her. It didn't make any sense. She looked up when Ty walked in with lunch from the food truck.

"Good. You're back. Can you read my handwriting? Please tell me you know what this word is!" She flipped the paper around so he could see it, pointing to the word with her finger.

Ty glanced down at it, concentrating. He put the drinks down, so she took one as he studied the word. "I don't think it's an actual word. I think it's a scribble."

Flipping the paper back around, she studied it. "Oh. You know what? I think you're right. Maybe I'm so hungry I'm losing my mind!" She laughed as she looked up at him to see him grinning at her. Morgan just shrugged her shoulders before she said, changing the subject, "I was wondering if you got lost or something. I'm starving." She was practically licking her lips at the mere thought of food. "Hurry up, Ty!"

Ty smiled as he handed her the sandwich he got for her. "I swear you're acting like The Darrells. You know, if you'd eat more breakfast, and maybe bring a snack, you wouldn't be so hungry. Which bag of chips do you want?" He held a bag of chips in each hand for her to choose from. She reached for the Doritos.

"Yes, Dad. Thanks for reminding me. And I did eat breakfast as well as a snack. I also shared that orange with you, remember? Who knew we'd both get so busy we'd have to wait until this late in the day to even eat? I was planning on going to the house to grab something, but all those last-minute walk-ins kinda shot down that idea." Morgan took a big bite of her chicken salad sandwich on whole wheat bread.

"A candy bar isn't really a snack, Morg." Ty opened his bag of chips and leaned against the counter, facing her. "I'm not sure you can even call it a snack."

"Then why do they sell them as snack bars?"

He chuckled as he watched her take another big bite. "Hits the spot, doesn't it?" Ty took a bite of his barbeque sandwich before sitting down on the stool.

Her mouth full, all she could do was nod her head. After she swallowed, she said, "It may not be enough though. I swear I could eat a horse."

Both of them winced at her choice of words.

One of her wranglers had just walked in and asked her, "Did I just hear you say you could eat a *horse?*" Maya Barton, having worked for Morgan for the past five years, stood there, her eyes wide in surprise.

"I know. It was a poor choice of words, but I'm just so hungry I feel like maybe I could!" Morgan took another big bite.

Ty smiled as he pulled out a second sandwich from the bag and handed it to her. "That's why I got you two. Gotta save our stock!"

Laughing, Morgan took it. "You know me too well. Did you get yourself two?"

"Of course."

"Well, where's your other one?"

"I ate it at the food truck." Ty grinned at her. "I was starving!"

She pointed her finger accusingly at him and shook it. "Ha! So, *that's* why it took so long for you to come back!" She grinned at him before sinking her teeth into her sandwich.

Smiling at her bosses, Maya turned around at the sound of footsteps behind her. Bo and Eric had just returned from a two-hour ride and were on schedule to do another one in an hour.

"Hey, you guys. Our animal-loving boss lady just said she was so hungry she could eat a horse. Has anyone in particular been misbehaving today? I'd hate to have her starve to death with so many around to choose from!"

Bo and Eric laughed as they removed their chaps and hung them on a large hook on the wall. It was cooler without them on, so when they had a chance to relax, off they came. Bo reached over and ate a couple of Ty's potato chips before Ty jokingly slapped his hand away. Smiling at him, Bo stole another one.

Ty said, "I can fire you, you know."

Bo shrugged his shoulders as he said with an unrepentant grin, "Yeah, but you won't."

Morgan watched them and warned Bo, "Don't even *think* about stealing my Doritos, Bo!"

"I wouldn't dream of it." He quickly ducked away when Ty reached out to jokingly punch his arm. Smelling their food, he said, "You're both making me hungry now! I'm gonna go get something before our next ride." He headed off to the food truck.

Morgan popped a couple of the orange triangular chips into her mouth as she grabbed her other sandwich.

Ty was pulling the last bag of chips from the carryout bag when the phone began ringing. Since he was closer to it, Ty reached over and picked it up after wiping his hand on his jeans. Listening to the one-sided conversation, Morgan gathered there was a last-minute addition to the two-hour ride going out.

After hanging up, Ty reached over Morgan's arm for the reservation book and added a name and an "A" for "Adult." Putting down the pen, he reached for his drink again. Morgan turned the book around so she could read who he'd added: *Josh Wright*. She read through the rest of the names and ages for the ride.

"That's a good-sized ride going out." Looking at Eric sitting in the corner chair, she asked, "Do you want Maya to go with you on this ride? Or are you and Bo okay with it?"

Eric seemed to be thinking. "How many now total?"

"With this last guy, you've got fifteen. I'd feel better, Maya, if you went with them. There are a few teenagers on it, so Eric and Bo may need the back-up. State Regs are covered with two wranglers, but..."

Morgan and Ty weren't surprised when they saw that both Maya and Eric were already nodding their heads. Having a bunch of teenagers on a ride, even with their parents along, usually caused extra work for the wranglers. Having another wrangler there seemed to be the best route for averting situations before they started.

Now that she had food in her stomach, Morgan felt better. With a smile, she reached over and took some of Ty's chips from his newly-opened second bag, popping them in her mouth. She leaned back in her chair and ran a pen through her fingers a few times. "You have it all under control here, right? I think we're caught up now."

Ty answered as he wiped his hands on his jeans. "Sure do. If you want to go ride, we've got it covered here. I don't think we'll have any problems if you leave now even with this big ride."

Morgan scooted her chair back. "Okay. Well, I'm going to head on down, and do some riding myself then. I'll most likely be in the outdoor arena, or maybe just riding around if you should need me. I won't have on my two-way if you do."

As she stood up, Ty said, "We should be fine. I see people showing up now, so we'll have plenty of time to get people up. Bo should be on his way back, so we're good. Maya and I can sign them in, and begin loading them up after a while. Toby's ride should be back soon too.

"Go on, Morgan. Bombay's waiting on you." He watched as she opened the tack cabinet and grabbed her personal riding helmet she kept in there. She'd already taken her tack down when she'd had to go to the other barn earlier.

"Okay. If you change your mind, come get me." Morgan said as she headed out the door.

Morgan walked around the corner of Sunset Ridge just as a silver pickup truck pulled into the Center's main entrance from the highway and began making its way slowly up the driveway. She greeted Bo as they neared each other and stopped to mention they had another customer on the ride going out. She also mentioned Maya was tagging along to help run herd on the teenagers, if needed.

Bo nodded. "That'll help for sure." Seeing the helmet dangling from her fingers, he smiled. "I swear Bombay knows you're coming. When I passed by Quail Run, I saw him in his pen looking over this way like he was just waiting for you to get down there and give him some attention."

"Oddly enough, Ty just said the same thing. I'd best get moving. I sure don't want to disappoint my boy! Have fun on your ride. You all should make good tips on it."

As Morgan made her way down to Quail Run to ride her personal horse, a tall bay Thoroughbred gelding named Bombay Attraction, Josh was walking toward the office. He smiled as he spotted Ty coming out the office door.

Chapter 14

Ty walked out of the office and headed toward Josh when he saw him walking over from the parking lot. They shook hands like old friends and stood in the shade while a few other people walked by them.

Looking over toward a neighboring barn, Josh noticed two large German Shepherds streaking toward a slim figure clad in blue jeans and a red shirt heading toward them. Josh watched as the woman got down on one knee, setting something down on the ground beside her before she began wrestling with the dogs.

Josh glanced at Ty, who was also watching the scene. "I assume those are your dogs, or maybe hers? I don't remember seeing dogs when I was here before."

"Technically those are her dogs, but she got them for the Center. If there's a show or something, she puts them in the kennel run to keep them from getting into trouble or even stolen.

"She claims they're for security, but I think she just fell in love with them when she saw them as puppies. They were going to be split up, and she couldn't bear the thought of breaking up a family. It was just the two pups in the litter, thankfully, otherwise she would've bought them all."

With a smile, he remembered the day Morgan had happily carried the two squirming puppies into the office, handing him one of them. Puppy breath. He still could remember its puppy breath as the squirming puppy licked his cheek. And the little black triangular ears that didn't quite stand up straight yet.

He continued, saying fondly, "She paid a little extra for them both in order to outbid the two other buyers who were going to split them up. That's the story she told to me anyway. Her heart has always been a good one. Getting them for security is just an angle she uses so nobody thinks she's got a mushy heart."

"Were they from a puppy mill or something? How'd she run across them?"

Ty shrugged his shoulders before answering. "I'm not sure. They look like pure-breds to me, but I'm no dog expert. We're both against puppy mills. She came across them at a horse show she was a judge at about three years ago now. They've got their shots, in case you're worried." Josh shook his head. "And both are fixed. Morgan's responsible when it comes to things like that. They even have a microchip in them in case they get lost or stolen."

"Morgan?"

"Morgan O'Connell. She owns the place. I've been her manager for all but a few years of her being here."

Thinking quickly, Josh thought this might offer an easy segue into asking Ty if he happened to know the judges from that show a couple of weekends ago. He ventured, "So you being here such a long time, you probably know all of the people who come and go, work here?"

"Yes. Well, the workers anyway. Customers I sometimes know if they're regulars. I mainly stay here at Sunset Ridge since Kat and Mel handle Quail Run. I'm kept in the loop on everything, but I don't know every single person down there personally. Why?"

"When my friends and I were at the show a couple of weekends ago, we ran into a woman there. We were wondering if she might've been a judge. We didn't really have time to talk for long, but we were curious as to who she was. Do you know who the judges were that day, by any chance?"

"Sure. There were three of them. Morgan was one, the others were Renae and Tracy. Those two have judged here before. Morgan likes them so she asked them to come back for this past show. What did this woman you're wondering about look like? She may have just been a visitor or a contestant. If so, I most likely wouldn't know her."

Josh looked around for a moment. He felt he was close to her, and yet so far out of reach. "Well, I remember she had long, dark brown hair and vivid green eyes. She had on a black hat with a green band, green blouse." Josh raised his right hand to his forehead. "About this tall. Possibly about our age, but I'm guessing on that. We're not sure she was a judge. We're just wondering and guessing that she was."

Ty looked at Josh curiously. It sounded like Morgan. He was instantly hesitant to tell Josh her name until he knew more. "Why do you guys want to know about her?"

"We just ran into each other, and she seemed like an interesting person. But like I said, it was a quick conversation. She was apparently in a hurry."

Ty stared straight ahead. This was interesting, he thought. It sounded like maybe Josh was the guy Alexis had mentioned to him later that evening of the show when they saw each other before leaving the Center. Alexis made it sound like a little bomb had gone off when Morgan had collided with some guy near the food trucks during the intermission.

If it *had* been Josh, it'd be no small coincidence that he was back now asking about a dark-haired woman with green eyes. *Vivid* green eyes, he corrected himself.

But wasn't Josh with another woman that day? Ty didn't like the fact it seemed like Josh could be a player. Granted, Ty didn't know him that well. And as a guy himself, he just wasn't seeing Josh as that player type. Although this was only the second time they'd spoken in person, Ty was a great judge of character. Still, he'd prefer to know more about Josh Wright as a person before he gave up Morgan's identity and whereabouts.

Josh wondered what was running through Ty's mind. He seemed to be pondering something, tapping his fingers against his thigh as he thought it all out. After a moment, Josh thought he hit upon a possible cause. Seeing as Ty appeared hesitant to answer, Josh jumped to the conclusion Ty knew exactly who he was asking about. No use beating about the bush, he thought to himself.

Waiting for a small group of laughing teenagers to pass by them, Josh's gaze followed them until they all neared the office. Their parents were still at their van. Looking around to be sure they were alone for the most part, Josh spoke up in his direct way. "You know who I'm asking about, don't you?"

Ty just glanced at him, but Josh could read his eyes. Yeah, Ty knew her all right.

Josh also had the sense Ty knew it was he himself asking about this woman. Treading carefully now, Josh asked, "From the look on your face and your silence, I'm guessing she's close to you, otherwise you wouldn't be feeling protective of her." A sudden thought came to Josh's mind. One he didn't care for. "Is she your wife or girlfriend?"

Ty smiled slightly at the question. He respected the directness of this guy. He also respected his tenacity. He was also sharp. "No, I have neither at the moment. If I *do* know who you're asking about, she's not married or seeing anybody herself. But I'm not quite sure I'd say she's completely available either."

At first, Josh breathed a sigh of relief at hearing his Mystery Woman wasn't married. But then he tried to guess at Ty's cryptic statement.

Ty decided to be direct himself in Morgan's interest. "It seems *you're* interested in this woman who you claim you only spoke to for an instant. Why the sudden interest in her? Weren't you with another woman at the time?"

Josh was impressed with Ty's memory. How could Ty remember so easily that he'd been with Abby that day? One part of him resented the implication that he was a player, but another part of him completely respected Ty for asking about it.

Feeling that Ty was testing him in some way, he didn't really have a choice but to tell the truth. "Abby and I were on a blind date set up by my friend Damien's cousin. It was the first time we'd met at all. As a matter of fact, just an hour or so earlier when I went to pick her up.

"Damien and Laura came along to make it more of a social function than a date to relieve some of the pressure. It was kind-of sprung on me to do, so I asked them to come along."

Josh blew out a breath, then continued, "Elise, that's Damien's cousin, has been setting me up on blind dates against my wishes for longer than I care to recall. If I try to back out, two things would most likely happen. One, I'd feel guilty or like a jerk, which amounts to about the same thing. And two, it would probably hurt the woman's feelings, and I try to spare anyone that. If my mother found out I'd hurt a woman's feelings, she'd skin me alive.

"At the advice of another friend, actually a client of mine, I decided to take Abby on a short horseback ride. Abby was the absolute last date. Elise will no longer be setting me up on any more blind dates unless she has the money to bail herself out of jail after I make a citizen's arrest."

Ty smiled at the last. He believed Josh was telling the truth. If nothing else, it was due to the slight disgust in his voice at the end. He turned his head to reply and saw the dogs chase a small rabbit near the driveway. It practically flew under the bottom fence rail toward some bushes for cover. The dogs were hardly distracted by the fence and continued after the rabbit.

They soon had the front halves of their bodies plunged into the brush trying to either get at the rabbit, or flush it out. He could see their tails waving wildly. He heard their high, excited barks despite the strong breeze that was blowing.

Ty hoped there wasn't a rattlesnake in there. If so, he hoped all that snake training Morgan paid for her dogs to have took effect. Would they smell a snake in there if they rushed in like that? Probably not. Of course, unfortunately for the little rabbit, if there *was* a snake in there, the rabbit would've most likely taken the snake's bite. That didn't mean the snake didn't have more venom to use though, he thought.

Josh was instantly concerned about the poor rabbit. Before he could stop himself, he asked, "They won't get the little guy, will they?"

Ty grinned at the grown man beside him showing concern for a rabbit. But if the truth was told, he felt the same way.

"Nah. For being what they are, and two of them, we've never once seen them actually hurt another animal. And never a kill. They just like the chase, I guess. Morgan was always on them when they were little. Same with deer. They just want to play with them. It's never anything more. They lose interest in relatively quick time. The dogs are gentle and friendly, not a mean bone in their bodies. Hopefully it will stay that way."

As they watched the dogs try to get to the rabbit, he saw Morgan come out of the barn and saw her apparently calling them. She was too far away for Ty to worry about Josh recognizing her. The dogs gave a last, imploring look at the brush but trotted over to her in obedience, their heads down to show her they knew they were in trouble. The men watched as she pet them a minute before turning to go back into the barn, the dogs meekly following.

After another moment, Josh said softly, "Ah! There's the little guy! Now he has something to brag about to his friends later!"

Ty looked back at the bushes and saw the rabbit cautiously poke his head out, wait a moment, and then take off away from the barn into the desert. "He left sooner than I would have."

Ty decided he'd feel out Morgan first before giving up her identity to a guy. He liked Josh though. He just had a certain quality about him. But he still needed to learn more about him because he wasn't going to be a part of allowing anything to happen to her if he could help it. He wouldn't knowingly hurt a woman's feelings either. He figured he and Josh had that in common.

Looking at Josh he said, "Tell you what, Josh. I'll speak plain with you. I *think* I know who you're asking about." As Josh opened his mouth to speak, Ty held up a hand. "But I'm still not going to tell you her name just yet, and I have my reasons. You'll just have to deal with that."

Ty turned when he heard Maya calling his name. Standing in the doorway, she held up the phone and wiggled it. He nodded, then gestured for Josh to follow him. "And if she's who you're looking for, I want it clear that if for whatever reason she doesn't want to go out with you or give you the time of day, you must respect that. Respect her, and don't pull any of the typical guy games or stunts with her."

Josh stopped him by laying a firm hand on Ty's arm. "I don't play those games because I was raised to respect women."

Ty smiled to himself and nodded in satisfaction at the annoyance he heard in Josh's voice. "But I'm also going to give you a tip because so far I like you. The way is clear for you. She and I are just friends. There's nothing romantic between us, but we *are* extremely close—and that's not likely to ever change. If you should ever run across her again, you may want to know that. If you can't handle or accept the fact her best friend is a man, then don't even start with her."

"I thought you were going to give me a tip, *if* it's the same person?"

"That was one. Another is to be patient with her, Josh. I almost guarantee she'll be resistant to you no matter what approach you use. Most likely, she won't be interested. If not, just leave her be. If she shows any interest or is even being open to seeing you, then don't give up on her if you find you really and truly are attracted to her. Don't ever push or rush her.

"After you've been around her, you may change your mind. It could happen. If it does, then no games. You just end it gently but quickly. You treat her with full-out respect, you understand me? You seem the type that would, but I want to be quite clear on that. Because if you don't, then you'll be dealing with me."

Smiling again as he put his hand out to open the office door, Ty added, "That is, if you even get that far."

Chapter 15

April

HAVING SOME TIME OFF together, Ty and Morgan were saddling up their personal horses for a ride just for their own enjoyment. Being with the horses had to be fun for them as well, otherwise they'd burn themselves out with the long hours they put in with them. When they rode on their off time, they always rode their own horses. They didn't allow the wranglers, and for sure not the customers, to ride their private horses.

Morgan was wrapping the strap to her canteen around her saddle horn as Ty mounted up. Looking down at her, he waited patiently. The Darrells were sitting beside his tall golden palomino, Monte, watching Morgan with an excited light beaming out of their deep brown eyes. Occasionally one would let out a bark as if the excitement of a ride in the mountains was simply too much to hold in.

She checked the cinch again to make sure Bombay hadn't filled his belly with air so the saddle would slip when she got on. Bombay turned his brown head to look back at her when she began to tighten the cinch. Morgan gave him a disapproving look before stroking her hand down his sleek nose. "You're a bad boy, Bombay." She tapped the large white star on his forehead and straightened his forelock. "But I still love you bunches and bunches."

She shortened her reins and slipped her left foot in the stirrup. With a slight hop, she easily swung her right leg up and over Bombay's rear. Her right foot slipped unerringly into the other stirrup as she gently landed in her saddle. Looking over at Ty, they clicked in unison to their horses, easing them into a walk. The dogs whipped past them in a black and brown blur.

"Which trail this time, Morgan? It's your turn today."

"Let's do the middle trail. I've got things to do later so I don't want to be out too long." She steered Bombay toward the middle trail, whistling for the dogs who were heading up the longer trail.

Ty said, "We need to go to the range sometime soon to make sure your shooting skills are still good, don't you think? It's been a while."

"Hmm. I notice you mention the shooting range and not your place to kickbox. Worried I might knock you down for the count again?"

"You didn't knock me down. I tripped." He grinned at her, knowing she was teasing him.

Fact was, she'd come a long way on her self-defense skills. He'd told her once she was the perfect pal for him. She was someone to dance with, ride horses with, shoot guns, kickbox, or to just chill with. She'd agreed.

They rode in companionable silence for about ten minutes. Ty was mentally working on a way to introduce the subject matter he wanted to discuss with her. He'd been working on this for the past week and *still* hadn't figured out a way to approach her. He wondered if he should just be direct like Josh.

If he didn't like Josh, he wouldn't even be having this argument with himself, he thought. But the fact was, he *did* like Josh. The guy seemed solid. Ty didn't think he was a player or a jerk. Just from their few conversations in person, and two lengthy talks on the phone over the past few days, Ty was getting a good feeling about Josh as a person. He liked him enough to go to bat for him with Morgan, hoping he wasn't making a mistake. He glanced over at Morgan as she gazed at the scenery to their right.

Just yesterday, Ty had purposely driven by Josh's office to get a look at it. It looked clean and orderly from the outside. The landscaped yard around the well-kept buildings was obviously cared for. His construction equipment in the locked, fenced area looked in good condition. His sign was clear, concise, and in good shape. He noticed the security cameras on his property.

Josh paid attention to details, which showed he had pride in what he did, and that he took care with what mattered to him. You can tell a lot about a person by simply observing their surroundings and how they care for things.

He'd also done a little digging into Josh and his business and liked what he knew so far. Knowing he was a horse person and seemed to love being with them was a big bonus. Ty saw his sincere enjoyment just petting a horse across the fence. A man who loved animals like that was telling. Josh Wright came across as an all-around decent man.

Morgan rode along, watching as her dogs zigzagged back and forth across the trail in front of them, their noses to the ground. She was enjoying the silence and wasn't really thinking about anything at all. She slid her cowgirl hat to her back, loosening the stampede string so it didn't pull on her throat.

Once they neared the more open ground, she nudged Bombay into his slow, rocking canter. His brown ears perked up as he stretched his long legs over the ground. Morgan smiled as she felt him wanting to run faster. She gave him a little more rein to let him know it was more than fine with her. As they flew along, she heard Monte gaining on them. She looked over her shoulder and saw Ty's big grin. In unison, they both leaned forward a bit in their saddles and let their horses just gallop as they wanted to.

Ty's palomino was competitive and didn't like the large bay in front of him. Monte seemed to be running with his belly on the ground as he put his heart into catching the bigger Bombay. Ty was laughing as he felt his horse switch gears and take off after Morgan and her horse. Soon they were side by side, each trying to pass the other.

Morgan and Ty at this point were merely passengers as the horses were competing against each other now. The humans on their backs were simply afterthoughts to them as they pounded down the sandy trail, leaving a dust trail blowing in the breeze behind them.

The racing horses were neck and neck as they rounded the bend in the trail. Morgan glanced over at Ty and saw he'd reached up with his hand to keep his hat on. Morgan laughed at him as they flew along.

Finally, they agreed to slow up the pace and gradually brought their horses down to a trot. After a while, they transitioned smoothly into a walk, with the horses moving into a slow trot on their own volition now and again. Morgan reached down and gave loud, praising pats to Bombay's sweaty neck as she smiled over at Ty. Her smirk said it all.

He reached down to praise his gallant Monte.

She turned around in her saddle to look for her dogs. They stopped to give the horses a quick breather as she looked around. Finally spotting The Darrells far behind them, she whistled to get their attention. She didn't mind them roaming, but she at least liked to know in general where they were. She watched as they romped toward them, their tongues hanging out the sides of their mouths. Most of the time, they had to be on leashes if on public land, but this area was all right for them to be free. Turning to face forward again, she adjusted her canteen.

Once the dogs caught up, they still waited to let them rest for a few moments. In silent unison, the horses and dogs began walking again.

Ty said a quick but fervent prayer and took the plunge. "Morgan, I was wondering how you're doing. I know on the day of the show, you were pretty beaten up. And you've seemed to have moved on. But how are you *really?* As in a day-to-day basis, just life in general. Do you ever get lonely?"

Morgan was taken by complete surprise by the questions. It'd been about three weeks since the show so she figured he'd forgotten about that morning, or at least let it go. She looked over at her friend and wondered where this had come from. Thinking about it, she took a few moments to answer him.

She ran the ends of her leather reins through her fingers to occupy her hands. "Well, I'm fine. I told you those old memories were just triggered that morning, and it was unexpected.

"But I'm good in day-to-day life. It's been quite a while since that's happened, but it *can* still happen. It just will. I can't bottle up my emotions. As I seem to recall, *you* were the one who ordered me not to bottle them up some time ago."

Ty was looking at her intently. "Yes, you seem fine right now, but do you feel like you're moving on any? Apart from work, I mean. Why not live life more? Your personal time is limited like mine, but why don't you go out sometime? I'm asking as your best friend. I'm not trying to pry."

Her look told him she felt he was. He had to step carefully or else she'd throw up her defenses. If she did, he'd probably never get through them short of using a sledgehammer or dynamite. She was as stubborn as they came sometimes.

"Sweetheart, what you went through all those years ago was more than just hard. It was more than many people could even take, let alone come out as well as you did. You were devastated. You were on an emotional roller coaster for a long time.

"I can't say I know exactly what you went through because I haven't gone through it like you did. I have lost loved ones, though, so I know some of what you went through. And most of what you went through you dealt with all on your own. And that was scary to do.

"What you had with Shane was real, and it was cut short way too soon. But life doesn't have to be over for you." He saw the tears pooling in her eyes. "I'm not asking to make you drudge up old memories. You know that."

Before he could continue, she interrupted, "Then why are you doing it for me? Where's all this coming from? I told you I was fine. It's been years now. I *have* moved on."

She bit down on her lower lip to keep it from quivering. One thing she hated to do was cry, and she fought against it as hard as she could. Ty had seen her cry before. He was one of the very few who ever had. And the only one here.

Watching her fight to keep her composure made him feel rotten to the core, but he felt he had to do this in order to help her move on. He reached over, took her hand in his and held it as they rode along.

Picking his words with care, he asked softly, "Do you think Shane would want you to remain alone for the rest of your life? You're too young to throw away your love life, darling. Shane would've wanted you to move on.

"You know that in your heart, but you rarely date anybody. I can take you out, but it's not really the same thing. I'm just a transition for you. I'm more like your security blanket."

She quickly turned her head, looking at him for a moment. She looked away again, her green eyes bright with the unshed tears she was fighting to hold back. She'd never thought of him in that way, but maybe he was right.

She'd told herself countless times the same thing Ty was saying to her right now. Shane *wouldn't* have wanted her to remain alone, just as she truly wouldn't have wanted him to mourn over her for the rest of his life if something had happened to her. That was the pact they'd solemnly made soon after getting married, wasn't it?

She *had* tried to go out on dates a few times long ago, but she just couldn't feel at ease with anybody. Her guilt at trying to have fun without Shane, knowing he was gone, had been unbearable. She just wasn't ready. And really, she had no desire to push the issue. Nobody seemed able to make her laugh, truly laugh, like Shane could. Did.

Feeling more depressed, guilty, and empty *after* the date than before it, she finally just quit trying the dating scene altogether. There was no one who even remotely caught her interest or could make her laugh. And who could she possibly trust enough?

Except for Ty. She felt extraordinarily comfortable with Ty. And he could make her laugh. Who knows where they could've ended up if they'd met under different circumstances? But now, well, he was just her best friend. How could she ever find another friend like Ty?

He'd been there for her like no one else she knew. When at some of her lowest and darkest points all those years ago, she'd often wondered if God had sent her Ty Stanton to help keep her going. Maybe God sent him to help pick her up, especially in those dark moments when she didn't know why it was worth the bother to even try.

Keeping quiet, Ty let her work through her thought process on her own. He let go of her hand after he squeezed it. He could see the wheels turning in her head as they rode along. He kept his mouth shut to let her think in peace and quiet. Although they rode along in silence for what seemed like long, never-ending minutes, it didn't feel uncomfortable to either of them.

She just needed to collect her thoughts. When she had, Morgan looked over at him. She raised her chin a notch. "You may be right, Ty." She turned her head, facing forward as she felt tears well up again as soon as she began to speak. She admitted in a shaky voice, "Maybe you *are* my security blanket. I've never thought of you in that sense, but underneath it all, perhaps I was. *Am*," she corrected.

Looking directly at him now, she said, "But in all fairness, I could never have found a better security blanket than you. Or a better friend, Ty. I need you to know that's the plain truth."

He reached over again to hold her hand in a firm, comforting grip for a moment. Giving her hand another hard squeeze, he released it. With his eyes on hers, he said, "You know I'm more than happy to be here for you, Morgan. And no matter what happens, I *will* be here for you. I will be here for you for as long as you want me to be, and maybe even longer than that. We're pals for life, so don't you ever forget that. Okay?"

Pausing a split second before he took another leap of faith, he joked, "I hope your future boyfriend or husband doesn't have a jealous or insecure side because you know I'm not giving you up. He won't be able to run me off, no matter what he tries. Best friends stick together, you know. He'll just have to deal with it. If he's man enough, it won't matter to him I'm your friend."

"Who says I'm ever going to get married? Didn't we just establish I don't even date? And now you're speaking of a future husband?" A pair of chocolate brown eyes that held a look of shock unwillingly popped into her mind at that moment.

"Well, one just never knows who may one day sweep you off your feet." Or knock you off them, he thought to himself. "Besides, didn't we just establish that maybe you *should* date, at least for fun? Even if it's to just get out on the town some, vary the routine?"

He figured he'd planted the seed of at least dating in her mind. He knew her well enough to know he'd have to back off or else Josh wouldn't have a chance at all with her.

"Ty, I need to think about this. When I've tried dating in the past, it never worked out in any way. I felt worse after the date than before it, so why even bother? I've completely lost interest in the whole scene. And I don't want to mislead some unsuspecting guy or hurt someone's feelings.

"Besides, it seems like anymore you go out one time, and they think you're an instant couple. I'm just not into that—at all. I'm actually pretty happy on my own.

"On top of that, it can be truly dangerous nowadays to date. There are too many crazies out there. Haven't you warned me about that? And taught me how to shoot even better, and drilled me relentlessly in self-defense? I don't trust people. You know that. And why. Besides, I watch TV. Those crime dramas are enough to make me want to never be around people period!"

He had to give her that. He *had* taught her quite a number of ways to protect and defend herself just like he had to his sisters and young nieces. Morgan had already known some skills, but he'd taught her even more.

Looking at her, he said, "You're a natural judge of character. Always listen to your gut, Morgan. If you're uncomfortable, then get out or away. But remember, there *are* still good people out there. Look at me!" He grinned at her.

Morgan replied seriously, "But *you're* one in a million. You're my lucky star. And I for sure don't want to get hurt. Can't you understand that? I just can't rush into this whole idea." Morgan felt her heart tighten up a bit just thinking about it. "I'm actually quite happy the way I am right now anyway."

A sudden thought popped into her head, and she blurted out, "Why don't *you* date? When was the last time *you* went out on the town?"

"We're not talking about me. And you know I've had a few girlfriends over the years we've known each other. I don't want to have all the fun. It's your turn to go out now."

Clicking to Monte and nudging him with his heels, Ty cantered off with a big smile on his face.

Morgan followed along behind him, her two dogs running with her, one on each side as if they were protecting her.

Chapter 16

JOSH WAS READY TO lose his ever-loving mind. The more he thought about his Mystery Woman, the more he wanted to meet her. He needed to know if their first meeting was a figment of his imagination. Or not.

The more he thought about her, the more he was building up this image of her in his mind. And he was afraid if he kept conjuring up this great woman he was hoping, or expecting, to meet that when he finally did, he'd be sorely disappointed.

Hammering in a small nail, he momentarily pictured it being Ty. With a small grin, he hit the nail again with the hammer. Josh *knew* Ty knew who this woman was. And Josh *knew* that Ty knew that he knew.

Holding the hammer in the air still for a second, Josh paused to think that through. Yes, he was sure of it. Besides, Ty had even admitted he knew who he was asking about. So *why* wasn't Ty willing to tell Josh her name, or at least where Josh could find her?

He pounded in the nail, some of his frustration coming through the force of the small hammer in his hand but not enough to damage his own wall. Bending down to grab the level, he raised it and adjusted the board slightly. Finishing some trim work in his own house in whatever spare time he could find was a great distraction.

It was a hot and sticky early Saturday afternoon with the forecasters predicting a heavy thunderstorm later in the afternoon or early evening. It wasn't monsoon season yet, being only the end of April, but this sounded like a potentially dangerous storm.

Josh figured he'd get some work done now in case he lost electricity later on. If he did, then he could just sit on his covered patio or in the living room watching the storm roll across the mountains outside his windows. He and Freeway had seen some amazing lightning storms and cloud formations over the years safely from his living room.

He'd already checked his flashlights and had a few gallons of water in his fridge. His parents had taught him when he was younger to be prepared so he had at least the basics.

Josh continued to work on the room for another couple of hours. Standing back to look at it, he approved of his work. He didn't consider himself much of an interior designer, but he liked what he saw so far. He'd recently gone to the local hardware store, bought some primer and mixed up some paint.

For some reason, he'd chosen green paint, in two contrasting shades. One shade was a light mint, and the other was a darker hunter green. He experimented by painting three of the four walls the mint shade. For contrast, he painted the main wall the hunter green.

As the second coat of paint dried, he refinished and stained the wood trim, letting it also dry. He tried to imagine the wood-framed bed that was normally in this room in front of the hunter green wall. He thought it would turn out nicely.

After returning his tools to his garage, he made a sandwich, eating it while standing over his kitchen sink so he didn't have to use any dishes. He'd always thought it was just a perk of being a bachelor to be able to eat like this whenever he felt like it. Any crumbs from his sandwich would fall directly into the sink so all he had to do to clean up was run the faucet for a moment.

He rinsed off his hands and washed the crumbs down the drain when he finished eating. He walked over to his upgraded refrigerator, debated his drink choices for a moment and took out an ice-cold Pepsi. Gulping some down, he then grabbed a couple of cookies, popping them in his mouth as he tried to get his mind to settle.

He finished off his drink and rinsed out the can before tossing it into his aluminum can recycling bin in the corner of the kitchen. He gave in and grabbed another cookie and leaned against the counter to eat it.

Meanwhile, Freeway sat at his feet, looking up at him expectantly. Although Josh never fed his cat human food, it didn't stop Freeway from being ready for the day he might change his mind. She gave up, though, when Josh walked out of the kitchen. She trotted after him, darting around his moving legs. He scooped her up in his arms and smiled at her satisfied look of being carried. She rubbed her head against his shoulder as he walked.

Deciding to take a fresh look at his newly-remodeled room, he made his way through the living room, up the stairs and down the hallway. Stepping inside, he critiqued it in his mind. Should he get light green mini-blinds or just stick with the white ones? Or maybe get some dark green ones instead? Wooden slats would look really classy, and would go with the trim. He tried to imagine which ones would look best, but he decided he needed to actually see the choices in here.

"What do you think, little girl?" He scratched her cheek as she purred. "Which are the easiest to clean?"

Looking at his watch, he figured if traffic wasn't too bad, he could drive to the home improvement store, buy the blinds in the different colors he was debating on and still get back before the storm came. He already knew the measurements of the window, so he walked downstairs, putting Freeway down so he could grab his wallet and keys. He checked for cat hair. Not seeing any, he was satisfied he was cleared to be seen in public.

Figuring he'd better be prepared, he flipped on his porch and hallway lights and grabbed his rain slicker from the hook by his door.

He bent over to pet Freeway. "I'll be back in just a little bit, okay, girl? Then we can watch the storm together. You hold down the fort until I get back, all right? No parties while I'm gone!"

He chuckled when Freeway whipped her tail across the floor like she was upset with his last order. He rubbed her head with his hand before standing back up.

Shutting the door behind him, he hurried to his truck. Sliding inside, he glanced through his windshield at the darkening sky. The wind was picking up already. He'd better hurry if he wanted to make it there and back. There was definitely a storm brewing.

MORGAN LOOKED UP AT the sky through her windshield as she drove toward home. The radio station's meteorologist had just reported they were expecting a heavy downpour with lots of strong wind and dangerous lightning.

Warning of flooding roads and dangerous rushing water in the washes, he advised if one didn't have to be out, they needed to stay home. He warned residents and any tourists alike about the Stupid Motorist Law, reminding them if they needed rescuing because they drove through flooded streets or washes, especially around barricades, they'd have to literally pay for it. He again reminded people to just stay home.

"I'm working on it, mister. But I also don't want a ticket," she muttered.

Where she currently was, it didn't look too bad to her, but she knew once she got into the mountains closer to home, it could be a different story. She was also actually driving toward the storm rather than away from it. But it wasn't a storm yet. It was still building. Looking at the clouds again, she also knew how quickly it could turn bad. She turned up the air conditioner and the country music station as she drove down the highway.

Spending the past couple of days at the horse and tack auction outside of Phoenix had been fun for her. She enjoyed looking at the tack, clothes, and knickknacks that people wanted to sell. Picking through a lot of the lightly-used tack carefully, Morgan bought what she needed for the Center.

One vendor had a great deal on halters and lead ropes, so she bought some of those too. When she saw another vendor selling nice saddle blankets, she'd sighed. She took what she'd already bought to her truck and came back for more. With what she bought there over the past couple of days, the Center should have enough spare supplies for quite a while. As always, buying tack and toys for her horses and The Darrells had been a blast.

She'd also spent the last few days seriously thinking about what Ty had asked her weeks ago. *Was* she moving on at all? *Had* she moved on at all?

All alone, she could be brutally honest with herself. She could honestly say she *had* moved on in many ways. But she also had to admit she had been, and probably still was, using Shane as a crutch, an excuse to not go out on a date but rather to immerse herself into her work. She *was* hiding. Behind Shane, the Center, and maybe even behind Ty.

It took Ty to make her realize it. It took time to allow herself to accept it. It took courage for her to make the decision to change.

She was scared stiff.

Driving down the wide two-lane highway now since she left the interstate, Morgan wiped her suddenly nervous hands on her jeans, one at a time. She was going to make herself go out on a date. She didn't know with *who* yet, but she'd find somebody.

If she got desperate enough, she'd even swallow her pride and ask Ty if he had anybody nice in mind. But she'd have to get desperate to do that, she decided. But she knew in her gut anybody Ty would suggest would have to be a decent guy. She could absolutely trust Ty with that. But who did he know that she didn't? They both spent so much of their time at Harmony Hills, neither got out much.

Just thinking about going on a date with a stranger made her stomach tighten. She'd better just concentrate on the road for now. Forget future dates with strange men, she told herself. She'd just wreck if she thought about it too much.

This topic would be just one more she could send up a prayer about too. God would listen to her. She often talked to Him like He was sitting right there beside her at any given time. Morgan thought of God as a friend, someone who never judged her—even though He was the Ultimate Judge.

And ever since she could remember, she took comfort thinking, *knowing*, He was there for her. She had faith that whatever happened, there had to be a reason for it. Sometimes she realized it months or even years later, but she never questioned Him. Trials were how one grew, she'd told herself since she was a teenager.

She figured if He was too busy, He'd send an angel down in His stead to listen to her one-sided conversations. Her angel would pass along the news if he, or she, thought it relevant enough for God to know about. Could angels be female? she wondered sometimes. She'd never heard or read about one. They were always referred to as males. What did her angel look like? Did she have more than one?

Morgan often wondered if she bored Him or her angel. Did they have to take breaks from her? Did things she say or do ever make them laugh? Or embarrass them? Did they cry when she did?

She also always thanked Him for the good things that happened to her. Every day, she told her Friend Upstairs thanks for watching over her, for helping her miss an accident, or for sending business her way. Just whatever good came along.

Even if it was when she didn't have those horrible monthly cramps or other sick feelings He cursed women with over the past couple thousand years. She always asked (more accurately, *begged*) Him to not make her suffer every month. The older she got, the better she was, and she *never* forgot to thank Him for that. She hoped she didn't embarrass God or her angel with those private pleas, but she figured they'd probably heard worse. And He could always make them stop, couldn't He?

With a deep sigh, Morgan looked out her side window. She always prayed for a safe trip, even if it was simply going into town. And she always said thank you when she arrived safely home. But a large part of arriving safely was in her hands so she also paid attention to what she was doing.

But as she drove, her mind wondered again with random thoughts. She often imagined what God looked like. Pictures always portrayed him as an older, grandfatherly type. She assumed that was because feeble human minds had to be able to 'see' Him in order to comprehend Him. Some artist or priest decided to make Him old. But *did* He age? If He'd been around forever, she doubted it. Was He middle-aged? Surely not a *child*? Heaven help her if her life was being run by an immortal teenager!

In her mind, she assumed when God made Adam and Eve, they were in their mid-twenties, maybe thirties. So if Adam was made after His image, then Eve from Adam, that meant that was how old *He* was too, right? And Adam and Eve would be the same age, she assumed.

He didn't make them old people, or did He? Morgan mused. Why didn't He age but humans did? How'd He decide on how to *make* a human age? Not to mention how to *look* and even *feel* old? If we are in perfect bodies, why do we have sickness and ailments? Morgan wondered yet again.

And the biggest question of all is *where* did God even come from? If He wasn't an actual child from another God, then where did the concept of children come from? It was all something a human mind simply couldn't fathom.

Keeping herself occupied with these thoughts, Morgan soon forgot all about going out with potentially dangerous, crazy, boring, strange men. She forgot all about the feelings she'd always ended up with after going on a date. Her dates with God were far more interesting and calming. And safer.

Picking up her fast food cup, she sipped some more iced tea. Setting it back into the cup holder, Morgan glanced up at the sky again. It was getting slightly darker. She did not want to get caught in any kind of storm if she could help it, but her gut was telling her she was headed straight into one.

Chapter 17

Josh turned on his windshield wipers as fast as they could go. Peering through his truck's windshield, he silently lectured himself for getting carried away in the home improvement store. If he'd just stuck to his plan of getting the window blinds for his newly-remodeled room, he most likely would've been home by now, putting up the first one to see how it looked. But he just *had* to stop and look at other things too.

And then he'd stopped at the store to get more Temptations and cat litter for Freeway. The beer, potato chips, and dip were just a bonus for being a good dad to his cat. But *now* he was stuck driving home in a severe thunderstorm amid a torrential downpour. But in his defense, he justified to himself, this storm *had* arrived a lot sooner than expected. With some of the roads already barricaded, he'd had to find an alternate route home.

The recurring lightning lit up the roadway far better than his headlights did. The downside to those sporadic spurts of light was they were blindingly bright, especially coming randomly in the pitch-black darkness. And driving blind was dangerous.

When there was no lightning trying to burn out his retinas, he concentrated on navigating through semi-flooded roads, throwing up big water sprays from his truck tires as he drove through fast-flowing rivers running down the sides of the road. Glancing in his rearview mirror, he felt sorry for the guy behind him as he knew he was being pelted not only by the fury of this storm but by Josh's truck spray.

Well, he shouldn't be trailing so closely in this kind of weather, he thought.

As he rounded the large bend in the road, he noticed a pickup truck pulled over on the shoulder of the opposite lane, its hazard lights blinking brightly in the dark and gloom. As his truck pulled even with it, he quickly glanced over. Although his window was splattered with rain, the reflection of an oncoming car lit up the business logo painted on the side of the driver side door. *Harmony Hills Equestrian Center*.

His first thought was that it was Ty, who could handle himself. As a matter of fact, Josh took a little bit of devilish delight in thinking it *was* Ty on the side of the road. It served him right for tormenting Josh by not giving up Mystery Woman's name to him. He'd been waiting for *weeks*. Weeks that felt like eternity.

Josh drove less than a mile before his mind took another route and got in touch with his feminine side, as Damien jokingly referred to it. What if it *wasn't* Ty but one of the female workers from the Center? If it was one of the girls, they could be scared and alone.

"Okay," he muttered to himself. "I'd better make sure."

Besides, even if it *was* Ty, he may still need some assistance. Everybody needed help at times, he reasoned. If he didn't turn around and check, the uncertainty and guilt would eat him alive.

Turning on his left turn signal, he gently pumped his brakes to slow down—and to warn the driver behind him to back off—and pulled into an empty lot he knew was there but could barely see. Driving through the running groundwater and the puddles getting deeper by the second, he pulled back onto the highway, driving back toward the Center's stranded truck.

He slowed down as he neared the blinking amber lights of the stranded truck, turning on his right turn signal in plenty of time so the car behind him wouldn't ram into him. Carefully he pulled up behind the truck, leaving some space between them for safety. Putting on his own hazard lights and turning off his headlights so he wouldn't blind the person inside, Josh reached over to his passenger seat and quickly slid his arms into his hi-vis rain slicker, zipping it and flipping up the hood.

Looking carefully for oncoming cars, Josh exited his truck and walked to the driver's side window. He normally would've preferred the passenger's side so he wouldn't get hit by a car, but it was too dark to see how deep the ditch was over there. All he knew was it had to be running fast with deep, churning water and most likely debris like wire, pieces of broken cactus, and trash.

Not to mention snakes. Josh did *not* like snakes. Just thinking of them running up against his legs made him shiver.

He stepped up to the driver's side window and glanced inside to see if there was even anyone inside of it. Seeing a dark figure in the driver's seat, he tapped on the window to get their attention.

"YOU'VE *GOT* TO BE kidding me!" Morgan said to herself as the truck began pulling to the side. "A flat tire this close to home in a downpour?"

At first she thought it was just the pull of the water on the road, but she soon knew better.

She quickly turned on her hazards, carefully pulling over as far as she could without ending up in the deep ditch she knew was there. Thankfully, there wasn't anybody behind her as she pulled over. She was doubly thankful most roads out here in Arizona had very wide shoulders.

She sat there for a moment, thinking. Should she get out and at least look at the tire? Or just call the Center for someone to come and get her? It'd be safer to do that last option, she thought.

Trying to change a tire in pitch-black darkness, beside a deep ditch, *and* on the side of a two-lane highway in a downpour was far from smart or safe. Not to mention, she knew she didn't have a raincoat in the truck. Not even her cowgirl hat was on the seat beside her. She just had what she was wearing. There wasn't anything suitable in her little suitcase in the back seat either.

Morgan pulled her cellphone from her phone case attached to her belt, wondering if she should call the Center or Ty. Looking down at the phone in her lap, she debated with herself. She needed to hurry, or she'd probably get hit from behind from some idiot who was driving and not paying attention. Or simply couldn't see very well in this storm. Sometimes accidents are simply accidents after all.

Looking at the clock, she doubted anyone was still at the barn. With a storm like this on the way, they would've cancelled rides long ago and closed down early. But she didn't want to call Ty as she knew he'd be home, happy with an early night off. And his house was at least twenty minutes away in good weather. He'd been working more since she was out of town too. No, she didn't want to call him yet. Let him enjoy being home, safe and dry.

She'd try the Center first as it was closer. Maybe someone was still there. Well, no, she thought again, because if so, it'd be Kat or Mel. She didn't want them to come and get her. Surely they cancelled their lessons and left early too. This was a pretty significant storm, and she always stressed safety with her employees and clients.

Shaking her head, Morgan made her decision: She'd just call Ty after all.

She'd just opened her cellphone when she heard a knock on her window.

EVEN IN THE DARKNESS, Josh saw the figure inside the truck jump a good foot when he tapped on the glass. And that was pretty amazing considering they were in a seated position, probably with a seatbelt on. He would've thought it funny except for the conditions. There was nothing funny about being stranded on this highway at night in a storm.

He lightly tapped again and spoke this time, hoping to ease the person's fears. He felt sure now it wasn't Ty.

"Hi there! Do you need help? I saw you pulled over so I came back to see if you were all right." He had to speak loudly to be heard over the thunder rumbling overhead. No answer. "I ride there at the Center sometimes and recognized your truck. My name is Josh. Josh Wright." He paused, waiting for the thunder to die down. "Ty knows me, if that makes you feel better."

He waited in the pouring rain for the person to respond in some way. He adjusted his hood from the blowing wind. He was thankful it was his hi-vis raincoat as the bright yellow should help him not get hit by a passing car.

Josh could feel the fast-running water streaming around and under his boots as he waited. If he didn't know better, he would've thought he was standing in the ocean. The water was running so quickly the pavement actually felt like it was moving, and his balance felt off kilter. The bright lightning that suddenly came out of the pitch-black sky made his eyes automatically close in an effort to avoid the blinding light.

Morgan's heart was racing, and she was fully occupied in trying to control it. She'd been so focused on the phone call she wanted to place, she hadn't even noticed the vehicle pulled up behind her.

"Stupid. *Stupid!*" she quietly berated herself.

Looking in her mirror, she could tell the other truck's parking lights were on, and could just make out the hazards flashing on the wet pavement. She could barely hear the male voice on the other side of the glass. Feeling jittery, she realized there was only a sliver of breakable glass between her and a perfect stranger.

Once the rumbling thunder quieted down, she was able to hear the guy more clearly. She heard him say he knew Ty. Still, Morgan made sure her doors were locked before she pushed the button to partly roll down the window so she could see this person better. A rush of cold wind and rain blew into her truck, making her shiver. She peeked out over the top of the window and asked the guy his name again.

As an oncoming car neared them, its headlights flashed some light onto her face. All Josh was able to see were her eyes. And they were a vivid green.

He swore his heart just stopped. *No, it couldn't be.* He was imagining things. He had to be losing his ever-loving mind. He'd been afraid of that happening for weeks now. It just finally happened. Like in a dream, he heard a voice asking something, but he had no clue what. All he could do was stare like a deer caught in the headlights.

He looked closely as another car went by to make sure he wasn't hallucinating. No, they were green. *That* green. Those green eyes that'd been haunting him for weeks, day in and day out, were right in front of him!

He'd dreamed and he'd fantasized about what he'd do if—or rather *when*—they met again. He'd never once pictured *this* scenario though. Maybe God was on his side after all. Who needed Ty? He smiled like a puppy just let loose in the dog food aisle.

Morgan just stared at the person getting soaked on the other side of the window. She couldn't see his face in the darkness and with that hood on. Why wasn't he saying anything? Maybe he hadn't heard her since a car had been passing. She raised her voice and asked again, "What did you say your name was again?"

Josh heard her this time. It was *her* voice. *He'd found her!* It was his heart and not the sky thundering now, but he could hear over it just fine. Trying to keep the excitement out of his voice so he didn't scare her, he replied, "Josh. Josh Wright. I'm assuming you know Ty at the Center? We're kinda friends now.

"And I've met Bo, Toby, and there's a girl, but I can't think of her name right now. Wait... Maya? Yeah, Maya. I just wanted to see if you needed any help. I'm just here to help if you need it."

"Hang on a second, okay? Don't go anywhere."

To his surprise, she rolled up the window. What was she doing? he wondered.

Morgan rolled up the window, took a breath and a chance, and hit her speed dial for Ty. "Please pick up. Please pick up," she chanted as she heard his phone ring.

On the third ring, right before it went to voicemail, she heard Ty's voice. "Hello?"

Thank you, God. Thank you so very much! she thought. "Oh, good. You're up."

"Of course I'm up. It's hardly late. Can you call back later? I'm watching a really good movie right now."

"Wait! Don't hang up on me! I'm on the side of the road. Are you still there?"

Instant concern was in his voice. "Are you all right? Were you in a wreck? Where are you? I can come and get you. Tell me where you are."

Reliable Ty, always ready to come to her aid. She heard the television volume in the background simply disappear. "No, I'm fine. Really, I am. But listen, there's a guy here. He says you know him. He stopped to help when he saw me pulled over. I'm about fifteen minutes from the Center on the highway. I'm on the shoulder by that really deep ditch past the curves. I just want to make sure you know him though."

There's my girl. She's using the head God gave her, he thought proudly. "What's his name?" Ty asked her as he put his bowl of popcorn on the table beside him.

"He said Josh. I think he said Josh Wright. It sounds familiar to me, but I don't know why. He said he's come out to ride, and he knows our names. Do you know him? Can I trust him?" Morgan mentally crossed her fingers, eyes, and toes that Ty would give big thumbs up on this guy.

"Did you say *Josh Wright?* Josh Wright is standing there beside you, right now?" Ty couldn't keep the shock and disbelief from his voice. What was *he* doing there?

"What? What's wrong? He's not beside me. Not really. I'm in the cab, and my doors are locked."

"So where's Josh?"

"He's outside my window. I rolled up my window before calling you, but I can see him standing there. He's waiting for me."

"In this rain? You're telling me Josh Wright is standing in a torrential downpour waiting for you? At night? Is he on the driver side or the passenger side of your truck?"

"Why in the world does that make a difference? Is he a crazy?" Morgan cast a quick glance out her window.

Ty was picturing this in his mind. He needed details. "Just answer me. Which side is he on?"

Morgan quickly glanced outside again to make sure the guy named Josh was still there. He was. "On the driver's side. Is he safe? Ty, I need to know now. He's standing on the road, and it can't be safe for him to stay there much longer! Plus, there's lightning. Hurry up and answer me. If he's not safe, I need to get rid of him so you can come get me."

Ty didn't answer her because he couldn't. Instead, he burst out laughing. He laughed so hard, he had tears in his eyes.

To her utter astonishment, Morgan heard Ty laughing. *What* was going on with him? Morgan had thoughts running through her mind as quickly as the rain was falling from the heavens.

Finally, he got control of himself, with a little laugh escaping now and then.

"What is *wrong* with you, Ty?" she demanded.

"Nothing, darling." He got himself together before he said, "Morgan, yes, you can trust Josh. I really do like him. He's a top-notch guy. He'll take care of you. I know he will." His voice changed as he added, "Just trust him, and me, okay? Let Josh help you, Morgan." Ty was suddenly being serious.

"Okay. I trust you, Ty. How about I give you a call when I get home so you know I'm okay? Is he safe to know where I live? Or should I have him take me to town, and you come get me?"

Morgan couldn't help but wonder at her friend's words and his serious tone. It seemed like he was saying one thing but meaning something completely different.

"He's safe to know. But if that makes *you* uncomfortable, just have him take you to the office and wait for him to leave. Or ask him to drop you wherever, and I'll come get you. But you *call*, not text, me when you get home. Do that for sure so I know. You can relax with Josh. Don't worry. Call me when you get home."

"I promise I'll call you."

"There's no hurry. I'll wait up." With that, he disconnected the call. He hoped he wasn't making a mistake with Josh. His gut said he wasn't though.

Morgan looked at her cellphone for a second before she put it in the holder attached to her belt. She slowly rolled down her window again. The rain and wind whipped inside as she called out, "Josh?"

TY GOT OUT OF his recliner, his mind running as fast as a jubilant runaway horse. He walked around his living room as thoughts flew around in his mind. How about that? he thought. He smiled as he again pictured Josh standing in the downpour, playing a Good Samaritan. And who in this whole blessed country did he happen upon but the very woman he'd been searching for?

Shaking his head in disbelief, he laughed again. What was Josh thinking right now? Did he know yet who it was he'd stopped to help? Man, oh man. Ty would give *anything* to be there right now watching this scene unfold.

Looking at his watch, he read 8:32pm. It's not that late, he thought. It doesn't give them much time to get acquainted with each other, yet more than enough if Josh was smart. And Ty was positive he was.

Smiling broadly, he also thought if this was a nudge from the Man Upstairs, time was irrelevant. They had no choice in the matter and were just going to go along for the ride. And what a ride it could be!

Settling back into his recliner, he rested his bare feet on the footrest, crossing his ankles. It did occur to him briefly that Josh was also smart enough to make the connection between Ty and Morgan. When he did, he was probably going to be just short of livid with Ty for not saying a word to him. When Josh realized she'd been right in front of him all this time, he probably wouldn't be too happy about it. Maybe later but not when he first found out. Ty shamelessly grinned.

He couldn't blame Josh if he got pissed at him, but in the end Ty was betting his silence would prove beneficial. He'd wanted to work on Morgan a little more first, just a little more time spent getting her comfortable with the idea of going out with someone. Well, that couldn't be helped now. He just hoped Morgan took to heart what he'd said that day on their ride as well as a few small talks since then. Was she able to open her mind and heart enough to give Josh a chance? Ty just didn't know.

Grabbing the remote, he turned the volume back on and rewound the movie. He couldn't keep his mind from wandering. Morgan had now spoiled his movie. He'd have to watch it again another time if he couldn't get back into it soon. But this distraction was worth it.

He wouldn't say anything to Morgan when she called to let him know she got home safely. He wouldn't say anything at all about it until he saw her first so he could read her body language.

He couldn't wait until morning.

JOSH STOOD IN THE pouring rain, leaning against her truck as the wind pelted him. What was she doing? Did she want help or not? He stayed plastered to the truck in the hopes a passing car wouldn't sideswipe him as he did Good Samaritan Duty. It also kept him from being knocked over by the wind or the water running underneath his boots.

After another strong gust of wind roared by, he reached up to adjust his hood again. He'd moved to the back door of the truck in case she wanted to open her door.

He turned toward the front of the truck. Maybe she'd been calling him, but he hadn't heard her. He walked a little closer to the driver's door so she'd know he was still there. Did she want him to go? Fat chance there was of that! he thought. He was getting ready to knock on her window again when he saw it slowly roll down. He heard her call his name.

Stepping up to the window, he tried to use his body as a shield against the wind and rain coming down. Looking into her eyes at close range, his heart stopped again. He was going to have to work on keeping that from happening every time he saw her.

"Do you want me to give you a ride home? Or to the Center, if that makes you more comfortable? Or to some other public spot? Or I'll wait with you until a ride comes, if that's what you want. I'm just here to help."

Morgan listened to his voice. It was calming in its confidence and not patronizing. Good, he didn't feel the need to soothe and pamper a woman stuck on the side of the road. "If you wouldn't mind giving me a lift, I'd appreciate it. Give me a second to grab a couple of things, okay?" She didn't wait for his answer but rolled the window back up.

She turned off everything she could think of. As a precaution, she removed her pepper spray from inside her purse, slipping it into a side pocket for faster access. She hung her purse across her body to keep her hands free, making sure her phone was secure at her waist. Taking a breath, she reached for the door handle. Holding her keys in her hand, she waited for some cars to pass by before opening her door. She briefly ducked her head to try to keep her hair dry.

She suddenly laughed at the ridiculous action. Her entire body is going to get pummeled by rain, and she was worried about her hair getting wet? Working with horses, she worked in all types of weather and didn't care what she looked like.

Josh heard her laugh and smiled. Wow, could she get any better? She had to be scared of getting a ride with a complete stranger at night, but she was laughing. Maybe she was getting hysterical. At this precise moment, Josh didn't care. She had a terrific laugh.

As Morgan slipped out of her truck, she quickly shut the door and clicked her key fob to lock the doors and set the alarm. As she turned, her mouth practically fell open. This Josh guy had taken off his slicker and was already wrapping it around her shoulders. He quickly covered her head with the hood. Now *he* was getting drenched, and she was the one who was covered up.

He waited for another car to pass before guiding her to his truck. Instead of taking her straight to it, though, he paused to quickly test her truck's tailgate and cover. She looked around in surprise as she instantly realized he was making sure her truck was secure before leaving it. When he turned back to her, he guided her to the driver's side of the truck.

"Why are you leading me over here? Do you think I'll be more comfortable driving your truck? You can drive." Morgan had to speak loudly to be heard over the storm around them. She felt the rain hit her like a hard, random massage and saw how soaked he was getting.

Shaking his head at her, he opened the door slightly at first and gestured for her to get ready to get in. "Climb over to the other side. I'm driving." When she hesitated, he answered her unspoken question. "You can't get in from the other side because of the ditch, and my back seat is full of supplies so there's no room for you." He smiled at her in the dark, but she could barely see his face.

Morgan nodded her head and opened the door wider before she stepped between him and the truck door. She practically jumped in, trying to hurry over the center console so he could get inside. The rain slicker hem got caught on his seatbelt lock, and she struggled to get it loose. The poor guy was stuck in the rain while she fought with it.

"I'm so sorry! I'm stuck on the seatbelt thing!"

She felt his hand untangle and move the material away so she'd be free to scramble across and get in the passenger's seat. She adjusted her purse and checked for her phone and pepper spray when she finally got seated. He climbed in after her, slamming his door shut.

Morgan watched as he ran his right hand through his hair a few times, trying to rid it of some of the rain water that had drenched it. When he turned his face toward her, the overhead light was just beginning its automatic dimming.

But there was just enough light to see his face fully for the first time for a split second or two before it went completely dark.

Brown eyes. Gorgeous brown eyes that held more than just a bit of emotion in them.

She gasped out loud before she could stop herself. In the dark, she reached up and put a hand over her suddenly racing heart.

Chapter 18

JOSH HEARD HER GASP of surprise when the overhead light went dark.

He smiled. He simply couldn't help it. She recognized him! He was elated to know she hadn't forgotten him. Her involuntary reaction to recognizing him was sweet music to his heart. And he wasn't above taking a minute to appreciate this moment. He wanted to simply savor it. Moments like these don't come along every day after all.

He turned the key in the ignition and started up his truck. Reaching over to adjust the fan vents, he shivered. He turned on the heat a little, just enough to take the chill off his wet skin.

He shivered again before he said, "I need to dry off a bit here. I think I have something in the back seat, so I'm just going to reach back there, okay? I don't want to spook you."

Carefully reaching into the back seat so as not to touch her even by accident, he grabbed a towel and dried off his face, hair, and arms as best he could. He quickly wiped down his door and the control buttons since they were drenched too.

Whether he was shivering because he was soaked through to his bones, or if it was because he was miraculously sitting in the dark—in his own truck of all places!—with his Mystery Woman, he couldn't honestly say. But either way, his skin was covered in goose bumps.

The flashing amber hazard lights lit up his profile as he thought for a moment. The only sounds in the truck were of the pounding rain and wind on the metal roof, covering up the sounds from the emergency lights clicking on and off as well as the windshield wipers frantically swinging back and forth.

One thing he did know, however, was good advice was good advice. Reaching up to turn the overhead light back on, he glanced over at her. She still had a fair amount of shock on her face. He could appreciate that as he was sure he'd had the same look himself as he'd stood in the rain waiting for her to roll her window back down. He also noticed she'd moved ever so slightly a bit closer to her door. He completely respected her feelings.

He handed her the towel and reached down into a little cubby hole and dug out a crisp, new business card. Wiping away a few drops of rain dripping from his forehead and hair first, he turned to her and, hoping to calm her, put on a cheerful smile.

With a slight flourish of his hand, he held out his business card. "Just in case you disappear on me again, I want to give this to you now, before anything else."

Morgan was frantically trying to get her mind in gear. It's him, she thought. It's really him. What happens now? Looking up into his eyes, it seemed as if she had a thousand thoughts fly through her mind, but she was unable to capture a single one. She automatically wiped her arms dry.

His hand waved a little to get her attention, and her eyes glanced to the card. Slowly, she took it from his fingers. She felt their fingers touch for just a split second and again felt that unexpected zing. She looked up in time to see that he'd reacted the same way as she had. Oh boy.

She forced her eyes down to read the card in the dim light. She moved her head so her shadow got out of the way. She then smiled as she realized she was unaccountably happy he'd taken the initiative to give her his numbers. She now even had his email and business addresses. He apparently wasn't leaving anything to chance. That could only mean one thing: He wanted to see her again. He was confident and that immediately impressed her.

Josh Wright already just seemed different. She couldn't help but be interested in him simply for his confidence as well as his compassion for stopping on a rainy night to help out a stranger. He'd given her his rain slicker, and he'd made sure her truck was locked.

Yes, this man was different. Looking up, she met his eyes. He didn't break eye contact at all. That made her think he was a man who was confident enough in himself that he didn't need to.

When she looked back up at him, Josh couldn't look away. They could've been rear-ended by a car, and he wouldn't have even noticed it. Her smile was contagious. He smiled in return and stuck out his hand for her to shake. He was intensely aware of her reaching over to take it.

The jolt they each felt as their hands made contact for the very first time was probably strong enough to at least jiggle the needle on the Richter Scale. Neither felt like letting go immediately.

Josh spoke first. "Hello, I'm Josh Wright. I'm thirty-five years old, have a clean criminal record, and run my own successful business. I have a great relationship with my family, no kids, no wife, fiancée, or girlfriend. My last physical showed I'm in excellent health. I don't smoke, do drugs, or get drunk. And I have friends who will vouch for me. I've been waiting a lifetime to meet you."

Touched by his gentle and sincere impromptu speech, Morgan thought about it for a moment. Her hand was still held firmly but gently in his as she wondered what to say back.

She decided to return the favor, choosing her words carefully. "Hi back. I'm the owner of a successful business myself, as you may or may not be aware of already. I haven't had a physical in who knows how many years, so I have no idea how healthy I am... Or even if at all. I don't smoke, do drugs, or get drunk either. I also don't have a criminal record.

"And I want to thank you for stopping tonight because not many people do that anymore. My name's Morgan O'Connell."

"Did you say Morgan O'Connell?" Josh couldn't stop himself in his surprise. "*You* own Harmony Hills?"

Sensing something was going on here, she pulled her hand away and laid it in her lap. "Yes, I'm the Morgan O'Connell who owns Harmony Hills Equestrian Center."

She paused as he looked out the windshield into the darkness, the hazard lights still blinking. Since the overhead light was still on, she could see his profile fairly well even though parts of his face were in shadow. "Is there something wrong? You don't like my place? Did one of my horses bite you or something?"

Josh was mentally pounding the crap out of Ty as he looked out into nothing. Ty had known exactly who Morgan was and where to find her this whole time all right. He worked with her on a daily basis.

Josh's mind went racing back to the day when he and Ty had seen a lone figure clad in jeans wrestling with the dogs after they'd chased a rabbit. Ty had said the dogs belonged to her, that her name was Morgan O'Connell, and that she owned the place.

Josh had been looking right at her the very first day he returned to the Center and didn't even know it. But Ty had. He also remembered Ty had mentioned one of the judges at the show was named Morgan. She'd been right in front of him this entire time, and Ty said *nothing?* His brows furrowed as he thought this through. He couldn't wait until he and Ty got together again. He really couldn't.

Turning back to Morgan, he finally answered her quietly-asked question. "No, there's no problem at all. Not with you, or your place. It's a fantastic place, what I've seen of it so far. It's just a coincidence, that's all. Just another small shock to the system to know I've been out at your place on different occasions, but for whatever reason, we never actually met while I was there." He decided it best to not mention Ty and their conversations about her.

Morgan nodded her head, replying thoughtfully, "You're right. That is odd. I'm almost always there, but I do roam the entire place. Plus, I do work at other places for clinics, shows, and things like that." Smiling at him, she quipped, "We were just two ships passing in the night. Is that what you're saying? This must be fate, huh?"

Josh smiled back when he said, "You have no idea. And two ships in the night is a great metaphor taking in the current situation!"

Glancing at the digital clock on his dashboard, he noticed it wasn't even nine yet. It wasn't really *that* late, was it? It was also a Saturday night, and places stayed open later on the weekend. He thought he'd take a chance since fate seemed to be on their side tonight. It wouldn't hurt to ask. It'd only hurt if she said no.

Looking back into those captivating eyes, he asked, "Since we're here, and it's a crappy evening, how about I buy you a drink? Or if you're hungry, we could grab dinner. You can pick the place. Would you be willing to go out with me right now?"

Before taking her normal route of thinking it through—and declining—Morgan went with her gut that was telling her differently this time. It was time she put her newly-formed decision about getting a little bit of a social life into play.

And Ty knew who she was with, so she had a sense of safety already. Just like one shouldn't go hiking alone, one shouldn't go out on a date with a stranger without letting someone else know. Safety first.

Hoping she didn't sound nervous, she answered, "I'd like that. And I know a great place that's fairly close to here that does both." Reaching for her seatbelt, she grinned at him, saying, "Tell you what, how about you drive?"

Josh smiled back as he reached for his own seatbelt. "I guess I could do that. Where to?"

Chapter 19

JOSH HELD OPEN THE door to The Neon Moon so Morgan could go in first. What guy wouldn't hold open a door, any door, for the woman he'd been waiting to meet for what seemed his whole lifetime?

He followed her inside, both stopping to allow their eyes to adjust to the dim light while they looked around for an empty table in a quiet area. A song by Mark Chestnutt was playing from the juke box and a few people were on the dance floor. It wasn't overly busy in here tonight, most likely because of the storm.

Josh lightly touched her elbow to get her attention and pointed to a table near a flashing neon blue moon.

Morgan excused herself first to go the restroom and try to collect her thoughts. This was all happening so quickly she needed to make sure her head was screwed on tight. She didn't want to say or do anything that she may regret later.

After using the restroom and washing her hands, she looked at herself in the mirror and whispered to herself, "I'm on a date. A real date." She kept saying it over and over under her breath, but it still didn't feel real to her.

Life was sure odd, she thought to herself as she swung her hair around and ran her fingers through it a few times. Digging into her purse, she found her little brush and took the time to brush out the tangles. She added a little ChapStick to her lips and decided it would have to do.

She studied herself in the mirror. Nothing looked different about her, but she *felt* different. She, Morgan O'Connell, was on a date. With a guy who'd picked her up on the side of the road in the middle of a thunderstorm of all things. She wondered why she'd been so worried about finding a guy to go out with. It took her less than two hours and one flat tire.

Smiling inside at her thoughts, she headed back to the table. While she did feel some nerves vibrating through her veins, she hoped they didn't show.

Josh had headed to the men's room while she went to the women's. When he saw himself in the mirror, he actually frowned. He looked like a hobo who'd been kicked out of his cardboard box from underneath a bridge.

He quickly tried to make himself look at least somewhat presentable. But then he figured since she'd come this far willingly, first impressions were already made. Of course, first impressions were made weeks ago, weren't they?

He now slightly regretted he hadn't shaved that morning. But it wasn't like he knew when he left earlier that he was going to get an impromptu date with his Mystery Woman!

Removing his soaking wet shirt, he wrung it out in the sink before reluctantly slipping it back on. He walked over to the hot air dryers, tilting up the nozzles and pushing them both on. Standing in front of the hot air, he kept pushing the metal knobs to keep them on to warm the chill on his skin from being soaked from the wind and rain. If he stayed there long enough, his shirt may even dry out some. He held out his shirt a little to let the air get through the thin material.

A man walked in, took in Josh's soaked appearance and shot a look of sympathy at him. Josh said, "Thanks. I was just telling myself I didn't look all that bad."

The man chuckled as he made his way to a urinal, saying, "Well, I just thought how much I hate wearing wet jeans. Uncomfortable is a mild way of putting it." He paused before adding, "I don't know if you've been here before, but they have a nice gift shop. They sell clothes in it. Well, they don't sell jeans, but you could at least get a dry shirt. Just a thought."

Josh nodded his thanks. As the hot air blew over him, he was still finding it hard to believe his stroke of luck at finding her like he did. What if he hadn't decided to turn around when he saw the truck on the shoulder? He adjusted the nozzles before turning to let the warmer air hit his back too. He pushed them both back on again, hoping to get his shirt to dry just a little bit. He wished he could do the same to his jeans, but knew these little hand dryers were no match for thick denim.

The man washed his hands, which Josh silently approved of him doing, used one of the hand dryers and left. Alone again, he took another moment to fix his hair with wet fingertips. He finally headed back to the table they'd settled on.

Morgan was in her chair talking to a waitress as he approached. He smiled back at her when he noticed she was smiling at him as he got closer to their table. He chose a chair across from Morgan and sat down in his wet jeans as she continued speaking with the waitress.

"Oh, sure, I'm all right. This is Josh Wright. He's apparently a friend of sorts of Ty's who came to my rescue. Josh, this is Jo."

Morgan watched as Jo took in their wet appearances, grinning when she noticed Jo's gaze was stuck on him. Well, he *was* really attractive even soaked to the skin as he was. Both women could see the muscle definition in his bare arms and his chest through the wet t-shirt that was clinging to him.

Morgan continued to speak as if Jo wasn't fixated on the man seated across from her. "We thought we'd stop in here for a bit before he dropped me off. I'll have my usual drink, I guess. What about you, Josh? And I'm buying since you rescued me."

She shook her head as he began to object. "No, I insist. I'm stubborn, so you won't win this one. I'll let you win the next one. Deal?" She tilted her head and waited expectantly for him to give his order to Jo.

Grinning, Josh looked up at the smiling waitress. How could he argue with her on their first date? Maybe on the second one, but not the first.

"Okay, Jo. I'll start with a Budweiser. Bottled." He paused. "You don't happen to have any spare clothes, do you?"

Jo laughed along with Morgan. "No, sorry. I wish I could help you. We have the gift shop though." With a wicked grin, she said, "I can loan you an apron from the kitchen, or a pair of chaps I can jerk off the wall over there, but that's about it!"

Picturing it, he laughed. "Uh, no. That's all right. I'll live."

Jo chuckled. "Well, *there* went this evening's entertainment." She looked at Morgan and winked. Morgan laughed heartily and told her to get moving. "Yes, ma'am. Coming right up." With a friendly smile, Jo turned away to go back to the bar.

Taking pity on him and knowing she'd like one herself since she also got drenched before he gave her his raincoat, she said, "Let's run to the gift shop, and get dry shirts, okay? We might as well be halfway comfortable."

They both got up and made their way to the gift shop. Morgan saw Jo and pointed to the gift shop. Jo nodded, smiling in understanding.

Josh insisted on buying their t-shirts so Morgan accepted his offer. They both headed back to the restrooms to change into them, returning to their table feeling somewhat better.

Looking at her, Josh was glad she seemed to be relaxed. He sure felt relaxed with her. Part of him was slightly wound up, sure, but he didn't feel overly anxious. He figured with all the experience he'd gained with Elise's numerous blind dates, he was a professional dater by now. He still wasn't going to thank her though.

"I heard you say you have a 'usual' drink here. I guess you come here pretty often. They give you a discount for being a repeat customer?"

Folding a paper napkin to keep her hands occupied, she replied, "As a matter of fact, they do. It's why I'm willing to buy!" She grinned when he laughed. "It's actually a business arrangement. It took me a little while to convince the owner of this place to do it, but I finally convinced Kyle it was a win-win for us both."

Morgan pushed the napkin aside and leaned forward. "See, he gives me and my crew a small discount. This encourages them to come here to wind down after a long day of work. Sometimes they'll bring their friends, but the friends have to pay normal prices. That's more business.

"And when I have tourist-type customers who ask for a good place to go that isn't a chain restaurant, I send them here. They're told to mention how they were referred. If they do, they get a small discount. We have these little cards we hand out for each other for the discounts and to keep track of it all. Here, I'll show you."

She reached into her purse and removed one, handing it to him. "Kyle and I keep track of it all as well as we can just so we know how it's working, and if it needs tweaked. We've tweaked it only once so far. It's been working great for us both since then."

"And that's it? You don't get free meals, drinks, or get to stay after hours?" Josh asked her with a smile, looking at the card again.

"Well, there is a bit more. See, it works both ways. If his workers are asked by a tourist, 'What's fun to do around here?' they recommend my place. See how simple it is?" She grinned. "But no free meals although a drink does get through sometimes!"

"So that's why you're buying, huh? Because you get a discount? Does this mean that you're frugal, or just cheap?" he teased her.

Morgan laughed, sensing he was teasing. "I can be both, but frugal and *resourceful* are my choice of terms. And no way will I cheat you. You can even keep that card in case you come back here. I'll pay full price tonight just to prove to you how grateful I am you decided to stop, and for the shirt."

She looked straight into his eyes. "Seriously, thank you for stopping. I was getting ready to call the Center to see if someone could come and get me, or maybe Ty. We'll fix the truck in the morning when it's safer and drier."

"You're very welcome on all accounts. Just so you know, but not to belittle your gesture, you aren't required to buy me a drink," Josh replied. "However, it's been a while since I've eaten which means I'm also hungry. You want some food too?"

He was going on instinct and waited to see if she'd accept an impromptu dinner with him even if she was the one buying.

Ty said to trust him, she reminded herself. "Fine with me. Do you want an appetizer, a meal, or both?" She glanced at her watch and then handed him one of the plastic-coated menus Jo had left behind. "We'll both eat since I'm also hungry. This morning feels like it belongs to another day!"

Putting a finger on the top edge of the menu he was now holding up to read in the dim light, she pushed it down slightly. Giving him a look that told him not to argue with her, she added, "And I'm still buying."

He chuckled. "Yes, ma'am. Thank you in advance."

Good, she had some guts, he thought. She didn't appear to be a flaky, coy type of a woman. She wasn't afraid to tell a guy what she wanted. She had self-confidence. He'd hoped for that.

He saw Jo coming over with their drinks and read quickly through the menu. He picked out a meal combo. He noticed Morgan hadn't even looked at a menu, so she must have a 'usual' in the food department too.

Jo placed their drinks on the table and, with a flashing smile, handed each of them a dry towel she'd tossed across her shoulders. "From Kyle. He said he doesn't want his chairs wet."

Laughing, Josh and Morgan thanked her as they took the towels.

Josh sat on his before adding, "Too bad you don't sell jeans. But I graciously accept his offer of a towel. Tell him thanks."

Jo grinned back. "Sure will. And that you bought some merchandise. Our shirts look good on you!"

Just as Morgan was getting ready to speak, a large group of people came hustling through the door. They sat near Josh and Morgan but not too close. So much for people staying home for safety, she thought. The live band had just gone on stage from their break so it got noisier.

Morgan spoke above the added noise so Jo could hear her, "We're also going to eat, okay?"

"You know we're more than happy to take all the money you want to give us. We're gonna make a *mint* off you two tonight." She grinned at them. "What'll it be?"

She took their orders, promising to get them out as soon as she could.

As the band played, a few couples began heading toward the large dance floor. Josh and Morgan watched for a few minutes, entertained.

Turning to her, he said, "Okay, I've just got to ask you this. I hope it's not personal or anything." He kept a straight face when she turned to face him directly. He leaned forward to be heard over the music. "*What* in the world were you doing in your truck while I was standing in the middle of a raging thunderstorm on the side of the road getting drenched?"

At the unexpected question, not at all what she thought he might ask, she flashed a smile. She could see the humor lurking in his eyes and tried to keep a straight face when she answered him. "I was running you."

Confused, he asked, "Running me?"

Morgan tried to make her voice serious and official sounding. "I mean I did a background check on you. I don't just get in cars with strange men at night. A quick, unofficial one since you were standing in said storm getting drenched. I have friends in high places, you see. I needed to make sure you were genuinely there to help me and not just after a free meal and a drink or two."

"Really? I guess I passed then. Who's your friend in high places that you called?" He took a drink of his chilled beer. It tasted great to him.

"Ty."

"You called Ty and asked him if I was safe?" He tried to sound nonchalant about it. Resting his beer on the table, he turned it around a couple of times. "Hmm. Exactly what did he have to say?"

"He said you were, and I could, so I did. And here we are."

"What?"

She expounded for him, humor in her eyes, "I asked Ty if you were safe. He said you were. I asked Ty if I could trust you, and he said I could, and should. So I did, and I am. And so, therefore..." She spread her hands out to encompass the restaurant, and then their small table. "Here we are."

She smiled again, her green eyes sparkling at him even in the dim light. The flashing blue moon light glowed for a moment, illuminating her face, and then went dark again.

Josh smiled. Okay, so Ty had actually backed him up tonight. Josh supposed it was a good thing he could score a point in Ty's positive tally column. But he was going to need a good deal more of them before Josh decided to not pound him into a huge pile of horse manure for keeping Morgan and himself apart all this time.

Raising his beer in a toast, he waited for her to raise her Fuzzy Navel. "To Ty, and his accurate and timely background check."

They smiled at each other and touched glasses.

A thought popped into Morgan's mind as she sat there. "Excuse me for just a second, Josh. Normally I don't do this and be rude, but I need to send off a text."

She took out her phone and texted Ty where they were since she was supposed to call him when she got home. An unplanned night out would delay that call, and she didn't want him to worry about her. She promised she'd call him when she got home and added their private *I'm fine* code so he knew this was her texting him now.

He immediately texted her back so she knew he got it. He told her to take her time. He'd be up late anyway.

As she texted someone, Josh reached for the salt shaker, shook out some salt on the coaster, then put his beer back down on it. Motioning for her to pick up her drink, he repeated his actions on her coaster.

At her questioning look, he explained, "Salt is basically a buffer between the glass of your choice and the coaster or even a napkin. The salt keeps the coaster or napkin from sticking to the bottom of the glass. See?" He demonstrated it to her.

"But yet the condensation on the glass can still be absorbed by the coaster or napkin. It doesn't take much salt, so you don't want to go crazy with it. You also don't want to leave a big mess for the server to clean up because that's just rude."

She studied him for a moment. "Drink at bars often? Or is this something you learned in science class? How'd you know to do that?"

"Nah. Not a drunk, remember?" He smiled. "I honestly don't remember how I learned this trick. One of two ways, probably. My friend Damien or Google."

Morgan grinned as Josh continued, "Damien doesn't drink a lot either, just so you know. It's simply something that was picked up somewhere sometime, I guess. Maybe like how you just picked it up from me."

Morgan was curious about something else and she just had to ask. "Okay, I need some clarification on something." At his nod, she considered how to broach this subject. "The first thing you did in the truck was give me all of your contact information like your phone numbers."

Finding it was harder to ask than she anticipated, she forced herself to ask what was nagging her. "Why exactly did you just assume I was single? How do you know I'm not married or dating someone? That was a bit on the presumptuous side, don't you think? Do I somehow just come across as single? Or do you just always hand out your personal contact information to anyone and everyone?"

Josh hesitated for a moment before answering. He didn't want to lie, but he felt she may not like the fact he and Ty had been talking about her for the past month or so without her apparently knowing. Would she get spooked if she knew he'd been searching for her since they ran into each other that day at her show?

"Well?" Morgan asked when he didn't immediately answer her.

"It was simply a chance I took. My hope was that you weren't with anyone. Since you took my card readily, and we're here now, I assume you're not."

It was the truth. It *was* a chance he took from the very beginning when he first approached Ty about possibly knowing who she was. It was all a leap of faith.

After a pause, he added, "And to be honest, yeah. I *do* hand out my contact information to just about anyone who's willing to take my business card."

"Fair enough." Inwardly, Morgan appreciated his reply. His apparent honesty made sense; therefore, it helped her relax a bit more.

Jo came over with their nachos, two little plates, silverware, and extra napkins. "Here ya go. I added the extra jalapenos like you usually get, Morg. The main course will be out soon. Your drinks good for now?"

Morgan nodded. "Yeah, thanks."

Her tray full of drinks, Jo took off again with a smile.

"Well, dig in here, Josh. Don't be shy!" Morgan smiled as she prepared to do the same herself.

With a smile, he reached for the nachos, playfully swatting her hand away from the one he wanted.

She chewed on chips topped with the best cheese and toppings around while she thought about something. Pointing her finger at him, she asked, "What about you? Am I just to assume *you're* single because you told me so in the truck? How do I know that's truth, and you don't have a wife and kids at home, wondering where you are right now?"

Josh picked up his beer to wash down the tasty nachos. "Well, I guess you caught me. I do have a little girl waiting for me at home as a matter of fact. But she knows I have off hours and is content overall to wait for me. No worries."

Morgan felt an unexpected stab of disappointment. How could the very first man she went out with be like that? Surely Ty would know, wouldn't he? She put down her nacho and didn't know how to proceed. She looked at the man across from her, thinking it through.

When he didn't say anything else, she prompted, "And...?"

Josh decided to see how far he could tease her. "I don't have her baby pictures with me, but I can assure you she's adorable. She's the current love of my life and has been for a couple of years now. She's also a terrific little snuggler."

"But you said you didn't have any kids and all that earlier."

"I don't."

"Then...?"

Josh leaned back in his chair, deciding to not push her too far too soon. With a smile, he said, "I'm just teasing you. She was barely more than a kitten when I rescued her from the side of the road one day coming home from work. She was just a scrawny little ball of fluff I just happened to notice. I looked all around for more kittens or her mom, but I didn't see anything at all.

"My best guess is some awful piece of pure filth dumped her. She was too tiny to have gotten way out there by herself. Unless she was born out there, and her mom maybe got killed somehow. She looked to be starving, so it's hard to say. I took her to the vet first thing the next morning and decided to keep her. I named her Freeway."

Surprised at the relief she felt, Morgan popped a gooey nacho into her mouth, keeping her eyes down for a moment. She immediately realized he hadn't actually answered her. She decided to call him out on that fact.

"That's incredibly sweet of you. You seem to have a habit of being there to rescue damsels in distress on the sides of roads." She said firmly, "But you didn't answer me."

Josh respected her intelligence and tenacity. "How do you know I'm single? Well, Ty believes me. I guess the only way for you to be sure is to go home with me. I guess it also depends on how well your friend is at judging the sincerity in people, and if you believe him."

Morgan leaned back in her chair, studied this stranger eating nachos with her. She watched as he took a drink of his beer, then casually took another nacho from the plate.

She finally replied, "I can tell you right off, I'm not going home with you."

He just smiled and took another nacho.

"And as for Ty, I trust him with my life."

"Then I guess you can trust that I am indeed single." For now, he added to himself.

Chapter 20

WHILE THEY ATE THEIR impromptu dinner, Josh and Morgan talked with an ease most people don't usually have until they've been together for weeks or even months.

Both of them were mildly surprised at how much they had in common. They noticed their senses of humor were also similar, as in warped. They sensed the other had strength and values by discussing their respective businesses. Both wanted them run with honesty and integrity being at the core. And both having a lifelong interest in horses specifically and animals in general, and how they should be treated, were just more traits they had in common.

They leaned forward so they could hear each other better over the increased noise. To others watching, they appeared to be a cohesive couple rather than just two people who'd met only a couple of hours before on a dark and stormy highway.

Morgan excused herself for a moment and made her way to the restroom. Josh leaned back in his chair and watched the dancing. He wondered if Morgan danced, and if she would if he asked. With his impression of her so far, he decided she'd have too much class and manners to say no if he asked even if she didn't. But seeing as this was a familiar place for her, he was willing to bet she did.

He watched as she made her way back toward their table. It was taking her some time to get back over to their corner as she was stopped every few feet by some guy, probably wanting her to dance with him. Josh really liked how she shook her head at each one.

Suddenly, a man unexpectedly wrapped his arm around her waist as she was walking by him, hauling her close to his body. Yanked into his side, Morgan instantly removed his unwanted hand from around her waist by bending a few of his fingers backwards. Hard. His face showed both surprise and extreme pain. The look on her face made it clear she was being firm while her automatic move was more than a little persuasive.

Robby, the bartender, happened to look over and noticed what was happening. He quickly dropped his towel and rushed over to assist her. When he reached them, he simply stopped, scowling at the man before looking at Morgan. She said something to him that made him grin. Robby then stepped back to let her have some space.

A few other patrons close to them had stopped drinking and were watching the scene unfold before them. More than a few women showed their support by yelling, "You tell him, honey!" and "Show him who's boss, girl!" There was a smattering of applause while Robby waited to grab the offending man, but Morgan didn't appear to want to let up on bending backwards those fingers anytime soon.

Impressed, Josh could only look at the pained look on the man's face. His first instinct had been to run over to help her and was halfway out of his seat when she took matters into her own hands. It looked like she knew how to take care of herself. He'd be wise to remember that. Not only had she not made a scene (everyone else was doing that), but she hadn't wasted a moment of time in getting the man to remove his arm from her body. Smooth. Quick. Decisive. More importantly, effective.

Although Josh was highly curious to see what else she'd do, he also decided not to waste such an opportunity.

Quickly making his way over to her, he lightly rested his hand on the small of her back for a moment before letting it glide to her waist. He gently pulled her toward him and away from the offending man. He sincerely hoped she didn't bend his fingers backwards too. He tried to ignore the jolt he felt as he held her close. She felt so completely right by his side.

She didn't resist at all when he rested his hand on her waist. When she looked up at him with her expressive green eyes, Josh saw a little anger. But he also saw a calmness that told him she was in complete control of herself.

Looking at her, he smiled in quiet understanding. "Sweetheart," the term came out as though it were natural, "I've been waiting for our dance." Looking at the man who'd placed his hand on her, Josh stared him down before he spoke to her again. "Let's go." He neatly swung Morgan onto the dance floor.

Robby grabbed the man and was escorting him to the door as Josh turned her into his arms. Jo stood at the bar to watch it until Robby came back. She'd worked in bars long enough to know some scenes were created to cause a distraction. While the bartender was offering assistance at the scene, friends of the person causing the scene would quickly lean or even jump over the bar to steal bottles of beer or whatever they could get their hands on in record time. Jo was no fool.

On the dance floor, Morgan was able to instantly match Josh's steps as they two-stepped around the floor. She wasn't sure what made her heart race like it was doing at that moment. Was it the guy who'd dared to try and stop her when she refused his invitation? Was it Josh's neat and very smooth save? Or was it being held so closely in his arms? She didn't know.

What she *did* know was she was having a surprisingly great time. And that she was in the arms of a guy she felt more comfortable with than any other man she could remember in years—besides Ty.

His voice full of humor, he leaned down to speak into her ear. "Thank you."

Morgan shivered at his lips and warm breath being so close to her ear. When she tilted her head up, he could see the slight confusion in her eyes. "For what?" she asked.

"For not breaking my fingers like you did his. That was very well done by the way. It impressed the heck out of me, that's for sure. I wouldn't have even noticed it if I hadn't been watching you."

She shook her head. "I didn't break his fingers. I just made them sore enough to slow down his drinking pace and make him keep his hands to himself. I could've, though, but I thought I'd go with a warning first. Lawyers don't normally get involved that way." She grinned at him. "Injure his dominant hand slightly, and his weaker one would be no match for the likes of me."

Josh could only shake his head. "I guess not, but you don't depend on that rational thinking entirely, do you? Men are still physically stronger than women."

"It's not all about strength though. Women simply need to be more clever, and act more quickly. It's more in the timing. But in a place where someone, if not everyone, else possibly knows me? Sure, I'll go with that thinking. If he tried anything else, most of this crowd would be all over him. That is, if there was anything left of him after I got done with him."

"I'll try my best to remember that about you."

"Behave yourself, and you won't need to be reminded," she replied lightly.

He smiled inside at her humor while fully respecting her warning and abilities.

Josh guided her around the dance floor, warning her it'd been a long time since he'd danced so he was rusty. She smiled and said not to worry. As they went around the floor, he realized how much he really enjoyed it. She responded to his invisible cues for a changed tempo, to twirl in his arms, or roll out and then back in.

Now and then, they did step on the other's toes, laughing as they got their feet sorted out. He joked it was because of his wet jeans and the weight was slowing him down, making her laugh.

When the music switched seamlessly into a slow Vince Gill ballad, they stepped right into it without either of them having a thought of not doing so. As the slow country song went on, she felt his hands slide down her sides and wrap loosely around her waist. He gently pulled her slightly closer to him, being mindful of not crowding her. Almost of their own accord, her own arms slid up over his hard biceps to his wide shoulders and then around his neck. She stepped minutely closer to him by her own choice.

Her own heart had gone from a nervous racing when he pulled her closer and wrapped his arms loosely around her waist to a slow thudding that was almost painful to her. When she realized he was intentionally giving her personal space, she began to relax. She soon felt simple contentment flow through her.

As the song wound down to the final, drawn-out notes, Josh and Morgan simply stopped, still holding on to each other. After a few seconds, Morgan tilted her head back and found herself looking into those brown eyes that had captivated her all those weeks before. She could see the emotion in them and wondered if he saw the same in her own.

Morgan took a breath and a small step away from him. Josh easily released his grip on her to let her go. He was amazed at how much he wanted to kiss her, right then and there. The desire she'd unwittingly stirred in him shook him to his core. But he wanted her to know she had his full respect. He didn't want a one-night stand, no matter how enticing it may sound. He'd never had one, and never wanted one. Morgan, he knew instinctively, wasn't the type of woman to simply walk out of a bar and go to bed with a guy she'd just met. And that was one of the reasons he wanted her.

Smiling at her, he said softly, "Thank you for the dances, Morgan. I really enjoyed them." Then Josh simply took her left hand in his right one and headed back to their table in the corner.

As they sat down across from each like before, Jo soon walked over. Asking if they wanted anything else, both Morgan and Josh shook their heads.

Josh said, "But thank you very much, Jo. The food and drinks were worth every penny Morgan here has to shell out. I think we should be going soon since I still need to drive her home. I think it's been a long day for her."

He would've loved to stay until closing, but he remembered Ty's talks. He thought it best he move slowly with her. This first date would just be like an appetizer, that's all. He excused himself to go to the restroom before they left.

Jo looked at Morgan a moment before saying, "It looks like your evening turned out quite well for you."

Morgan knew what her friend was alluding to but just said, "Unexpectedly so."

Jo wasn't blind to the attraction between this man and her friend. She'd watched them dance that last slow song, and it made her heart happy to see her friend taking a chance. While she'd never met this man before, Jo already had hopes he was a keeper. "He seems fun, polite, and respectful. That's a hard combo to find these days, isn't it?"

"Unexpectedly so," Morgan replied again, causing Jo to chuckle.

Morgan paid and tipped Jo as Josh returned. When they grabbed his raincoat and their damp shirts hanging over the spare chair, Jo reminded them to not steal the towels. They laughed as they made their way toward the door.

As Morgan walked out behind Josh, she wondered about him. What was she to do with a tanned, muscular man who was a good six feet tall? One blessed by the gods with thick, brown hair and eyes that seemed to read her like she was an interesting book he hated to put down?

She had absolutely no idea.

Chapter 21

THEY LISTENED TO HIS Gordon Lightfoot CD playing softly in the background as he drove. Driving down the rain-soaked roads, he automatically turned onto the highway that led toward Harmony Hills. Now and then, a flash of lightning and rumble of thunder reminded them of the storm that had come through earlier, but the rain thankfully had stopped.

He'd offered to help change her tire, but she said it'd be okay until the morning. It was still safer to do in the daylight. She was worried some drunk or sleepy person might hit them.

They made small talk as he drove, mainly discussing his music choice.

Morgan said, "I'd forgotten all about Gordon Lightfoot, but man! He was so great. His voice, the lyrics, the melody... Just all of it! The other day they played Marty Robbins on the radio, and he's another favorite of mine I hadn't heard in forever. They made real music back then, didn't they? These were *their* voices, not auto-tuned ones. The instruments were real. The talent was real."

Josh agreed. "Neil Diamond is another I really like. These guys are overlooked nowadays. Personally, I love the music I don't have to worry about hearing vulgar language in, especially with kids around.

"Of course, this could be irrelevant considering how foul-mouthed so much of the youth is today. It's considered normal by almost everyone now. But I myself don't want to hear profanity in music, or even in general.

"I still remember when the FCC banned swear words on TV and radio. Now it's the worst words being used as common vocabulary. How profanity is put into lyrics and is considered music is beyond me. But I doubt those songs will hold up as classics like these guys will."

"But if they aren't remembered at all, nothing can even *be* a classic. There are too many to remember them all."

"That's one way to look at it." He smiled after a moment. "Since we seem to agree on what's considered good music, everything else will be smooth sailing between us, y'know."

Morgan chuckled. "You could be right."

Looking at the clock radio on his dash, he saw that it was well past midnight. He'd had no idea so many hours had passed. They'd almost closed down the bar. Maybe they should've stayed a while longer just to say they did. But something told him to trust Ty's advice about going slowly with her and not being pushy. Not that he ever considered himself pushy with any woman, but he was taking more care with Morgan O'Connell.

In the dark, he glanced at her to see what she was doing. She was looking out her window, watching the clouds go by in the light of the moon. Josh bet there'd be a lot of flooded areas tonight and tomorrow. He tried not to think about his work sites and the mess they'd be in on Monday. Hopefully by then, they'll have dried up.

It suddenly occurred to him he really didn't know where Morgan lived, or know where he was supposed to be taking her. He'd just automatically begun driving toward the Center since that was where her truck was headed when he pulled over to help. She hadn't once said anything about their direction of travel.

Josh said, "It just occurred to me that I don't know where you live. I was assuming toward Harmony Hills since that looked like the direction you were heading when you got the flat. Is that where you want to go, or do you want me to drop you off somewhere else?"

Morgan replied, "I not only work at the Center, but I live there too."

She'd already debated with herself about telling him she actually *lived* at the Center but figured he may already know, so what would be the point in lying to him? Since she owned Harmony Hills, it only made sense that she lived there too. A horse facility that large had to have somebody living on property for safety and security.

Turning her head toward him, she joked, "Trying to get rid of me already, are you?"

Turning to look at her, he could see her face partially lit up by the lights from the dashboard. Smiling, he looked back at the road. That's all they needed, for him to not pay attention himself and to run off the road and get stuck in the ditch in the middle of the night. His four-wheel drive would probably get them out, but if not then she *would* have to call Ty and have him bail them both out. Ty would never let him live it down.

"Well, you're pretty tough to be around." Quickly looking at her again, he saw her smile. Looking back to the dark road even with his high beams on, he said, "As long as it took for me to meet you, one of the last things I want to do is let you out of my sight." He gave a long, drawn-out sigh. "But I guess I have to be a gentleman like my parents would expect of me."

"I appreciate that." Morgan smiled at his humor while also wondering about his comment about meeting her.

He waited a moment before sincerely saying, "I had a great time with you. Stopping to help you, and then spending time with you has made for an unexpectedly nice and special night. It'd be great if we could do it again sometime—minus the flat."

Morgan was paying attention to him as he drove, silently approving of his driving habits so far. Some people nearly scared her spitless when they drove, but she had once to grab onto the door handle or slam her feet into the floorboard.

She finally answered, "I admit I had a great time too. It's been a long time since I had a good time with someone who didn't work for me. Well, excluding Ty. I don't really see him as an employee but as my best friend." She paused. "And although I hardly know you from Adam, I think Ty is correct when he says you're a good guy."

She looked at his profile that was softly highlighted from the dashboard lights. With the music in the background, and the fresh memories of a surprisingly fun and enjoyable night in her mind, Morgan actually felt her strong mistrust about dating begin to shake. She had to keep her head on her shoulders, but she was willing to take a chance.

She said, "Tomorrow we both go back to our own worlds. Tonight may have just been a slice out of time for us both. That being said, I'd also like to see you again sometime. But I also need time to think. I'm not one to rush into things like this."

If he pushed her, he'd sorely disappoint her and crush her newfound fragile spark of hope. On the other hand, if he respected her wishes? Well.

He replied, "I completely understand. And you're not alone in those thoughts or feelings, Morgan. I want you to *know* that. I've never been one to rush into relationships of any nature myself. There's no pressure here, all right? But we connected somehow weeks ago, and I think it's safe to say we've *both* known it.

"Maybe I've conjured up this image of you in my head over the past few weeks, but so far the reality is even better. It's you, not an image of you, which has me interested in seeing you again. I'm more than willing to give you time to think."

Josh paused as he switched off his high beams and slowed down so the car in front of them could turn right onto another road. As he picked up speed again, his thoughts fanned out. "How about this? Let's plan on seeing each other again, but we'll set some basic ground rules to keep off any pressure. Does that sound all right to you?"

"I suppose if we have ground rules we both respect, that'd be good." Her heart was thudding, and she was already feeling anxious. She had to keep her head on straight here, so she made herself focus on their conversation.

He said, "First off, we're honest with each other. No matter what, we must be honest. Even if we're worried it might hurt the other's feelings, we do it. We can be honest *and* tactful.

"Secondly, no games. I hate mental or emotional games. They're hurtful, damaging, and disrespectful. I don't ever want to feel like I'm being used or manipulated. And I can only imagine you feel the same way. Agreed?"

Morgan nodded, realized he couldn't see her, so quickly spoke up. "Absolutely. Yes to honesty, and no to games from either of us. I also don't like people who play games. It's a form of control, and I won't put up with that."

"Exactly. Let's start off just like most people do, or should anyway. We want to be friends, so let's be friends first and foremost. We'll just hang out, go to the movies, maybe back to the bar there, maybe meet for lunch or dinner now and then.

"We don't even have to call them dates. We're just two friends meeting up and hanging out with no pressure to go any further until or unless we're both ready to. Is this comfortable for you?"

"Agreeing so far." She let out a small, quiet sigh of relief.

"See? We work well together."

Morgan smiled. Looking at him, she quipped, "I see we've graduated to 'we' already. That was pretty fast, Josh."

He laughed. "Okay, Morgan, if this is going to work with us, you're going to have to keep up."

He heard the smile in her voice when she replied, "Duly noted. Next?"

"You can join in anytime you think of anything, you know. Anything *you* feel uncomfortable with, or want us to pay attention to, just say it. Ground rules are really good to have. The rest is either going to happen or not. We may not ever go beyond friendship, and that could be all right too. I don't think a person can have too many friends, not if they're real ones."

He paused, thinking. "Most importantly, if either of us is feeling pressured in any way, if we're moving too fast to handle, or don't like something the other is doing or saying, we have to speak up right away so we can back off and talk it out. It's not good to let things simmer and fester. It'll just get blown out of proportion doing that."

A man who was willing to talk? Morgan thought that was a myth like humble religious leaders and honest politicians. Sure, there were some men she knew who did, but they sure seemed to be few and far between. Actually, now that she was thinking about it, Ty was the only one she knew.

She asked, "What if we're in a group, or in public, or just need to ease into a sensitive topic about the other? We need a code word or phrase, something we can say to the other without anybody else knowing what we're talking about. A code can prepare the other for any topic or issue we want to bring up. Our own secret language would be fun."

She was having fun, Morgan realized.

"See? Now you've caught on! Did you notice you just said 'we' and 'our'? And you didn't even flinch or choke. If we have our own secret language, we must have something between us. We're already together, but we just can't admit it yet because that'd prove we're moving at supersonic speed. And that is just completely unacceptable."

They smiled at each other in the dark.

She said, "Okay, so if we're feeling something is out of whack, whatever it is that makes either of us uncomfortable or upset, our code will be..." She thought for a moment. "How about 'polar bears like to slide on snow.' That work for you?"

Josh was puzzled at her choice of a code phrase. It was interesting, he had to give her that. "Yep, that works for me. I have no idea how you came up with that phrase, but sure. So all we have to do is say 'polar bears like to slide on snow,' and we'll know there's something we need to discuss and take care of to move forward. Have I got that right?"

Morgan was truly having fun now and thought about it some more. "Yes. And we can add, delete, or change something as we come to it like the rational and mature adults we're hoping the other is."

"Agreed. There *is* just one more thing. I want this to happen if we can possibly do it at all. Okay?"

"Well, I have to know what it is first before I can agree." Morgan picked up the seriousness of his tone.

"Okay, let's just say, for whatever reason, as impossible as it may seem right now... Well, if we move beyond friendship but decide later that *we* just won't work out, we still try to remain friends and not become hostile, bitter enemies. I really am serious about this. If we don't work out, then we just don't. I know it can sometimes be easier said than done because of hurt and disappointment.

"But I also don't see why people have to become mortal combatants for eternity just because their personal relationship didn't work out. I'm talking other than major issues like abuse in any form, things along those lines.

"But I think we have enough in common if we saw each other in public, we wouldn't talk trash to, or about, the other. Or key the other's truck or anything else stupid and immature. Let's not hate each other if it just doesn't go the way we want it to. Either it will, or it won't. Let's try and stay friends. Can we do that?" Josh glanced over at her.

"Well, I haven't made enemies with ex-boyfriends in the past, so I'm good with it. All right, I just need to see if I'm clear on this. So are we kind of going out now, just getting into the very beginning stages, I mean?" Morgan's voice had hitched a little, but Josh didn't seem to notice it. "We just met, and we're just testing the water? We *aren't* boyfriend/girlfriend, but *are* just becoming friends?"

Morgan had thoughts racing through her mind. This was only the first night they'd even met, so weren't they moving too quickly already? So they had a strong chemistry and a spark that could probably ignite a forest fire. That really didn't mean anything. It could be loneliness or just old-fashioned puppy love. It could wear off, and probably would.

Josh answering her questions broke into her thoughts. "I'd like to think so. We just met and think we could be good friends with the *potential* for more. But we'll always have our ground rules and boundaries we don't cross unless we agree on them."

Morgan said, "Okay. As I said, I still need to think about all of this, okay? However, if we can start off just as friends who hang out, that's a good start."

"You bet. And maybe one more thing?"

"What would that be?"

"What happens between us always stays between us. I don't go telling my friends any juicy secrets, gossip, or personal details. And you don't go telling Ty and all your friends. I say Ty specifically because I know you two are very close friends. I want *us* to work it out if something comes up.

"I don't mean we can't ever say *anything* about the other at all. I'm talking about decency, respect, and privacy. We keep private things between us. I don't like sharing my personal life with others. I don't air out my laundry or spread gossip to others, so it'd be great to know someone else like this.

"Is this okay with you? Neither of us kiss and tell?" Josh wondered if he was being controlling or pushy, but this was important to him.

Morgan thought about it. "Ty is by far the closest friend I have. If I went to anybody, it'd be him, but I understand what you're saying. Private details are ours and ours alone. Okay, I'll try to not divulge any details that would be deemed private or personal."

"That sounds good to me." Josh released a small sigh.

They were almost to the Center now. They'd passed her truck on the side of the road about ten minutes back. It seemed like days, even weeks, ago when he'd stopped to see if anybody needed help. Time is relative, he supposed. Look how his life had changed in a mere few hours. Or really, in just a few seconds. Wasn't it crazy to know one's life can completely go in another direction in literally the time it takes to blink your eyes?

As he was turning into the Center's main gate, he slowed down. "Where to, Miss O'Connell?"

"Oh, sorry. You just turn right on this lane coming up. See the red reflectors? Then veer off there by the *Private Drive* sign. Just follow it around until it stops at my house."

He turned onto the lane which was basically just a bladed path in the sand wide enough for vehicles to drive on and followed it around to the two-story house. They saw a huge jackrabbit freeze in the lights, and then quickly bound away in a zigzag pattern.

He thought he might have to turn on his four-wheel drive in the deeper, soaking wet sand, but his truck rolled on through with no problems. It was rough and bouncy since the hard rain had created trenches and holes.

As the truck bounced over a particularly big bump, she groaned. "I know what *I'll* be doing tomorrow—smoothing out my driveways with the tractor again!"

He said, "Hey, at least you have your own tractor and *can* do it. That also saves me from bringing mine over, and doing it for you!"

She laughed. "I appreciate the thought!"

"That's what friends are for." He glanced at her and saw her smile.

Her house looked like it was well-cared for and looked natural there. From the beams of his headlights, he could make out archways in her porch with landscaped foliage around them.

"Wow. I don't remember even seeing this here when I've been out before. It blends in very well, doesn't it? I'll stop here to avoid any of those puddles so we can see to walk around them." Coming to a stop, he put the gear shift into *park*. "Hang on a second."

Making a quick decision, Josh left the truck running before he got out and walked around to her side. He figured it might make her feel less nervous knowing he wasn't planning on staying if the engine was running. He noticed she came across just a tad nervous, or maybe it was shyness, now. He didn't want her to feel that way with him.

As he rounded the front of his truck, automatic lights flooded the area. Safety lights. Were they there for convenience, for strangers lurking in the dark, or for venomous snakes and other wildlife? he wondered. Either way, he approved.

When he got to her side of the truck, he opened the door for her and waited for her to grab her things to climb out. Walking her to her front door, he raised her hand, kissed it, held it gently in his hand for a second, and then let it go.

Morgan couldn't speak. What could she say? He'd melted her heart, and a good portion of her resolve, with his words and actions all night long. When had a guy last kissed the back of her hand? Ever? Morgan wondered, in a daze. It was unexpectedly, amazingly romantic—more than if he'd kissed her cheek or mouth. Either of those would've made her feel very uncomfortable, but that single action of his had her heart pounding in her chest.

She smiled, laid her hand on his arm. "Thank you for everything, Josh. From stopping to help, the shirt, the dances, the great time. And I'll talk to you soon?" At his smile and nod, she put her key in the door. "Have a safe drive to your home. Hopefully you can get through with no problems. I bet the flash flood warnings are still on, so be careful."

"I will. And thank you for the dinner and great time too. Let me know if you need anything, all right? I'll wait for your call." Josh stood there quietly as she unlocked her door but didn't open it.

She looked at him one more time. "Good night." With that, she walked in and closed her door.

He waited until he heard her lock engage and saw an inside light come on. With a light heart and a big smile, he returned to his truck and happily made his way home.

Morgan sat down on her couch in a hazy state of disbelief. She'd turned off her house alarm when she'd walked in and then reset it for nighttime protection. She put her purse, keys, damp shirt, and his business card on the table by her door before she made her way to her couch, plopping down on it. The silent house was a comfort to her.

Thoughts raced through her mind as she sat there, hugging a pillow to her chest. This was moving along way too quickly. They just met a few hours ago, and they were basically already thinking they were a couple? Didn't she even tell Ty she hated that instant jump?

We have to slow down. *Way* down! Morgan thought. He was reading way too much into it. Or was he? Wasn't she doing the same thing? Besides, she was in no way wanting or needing to be in a relationship. Why did she tell him she'd go out with him again?

The only answer she had that covered all of her questions was one: Either one or both of them had lost their ever-loving minds. With a small grin, she admitted to herself it felt great.

Besides, they had ground rules. They were just going to be friends first. No harm, no pressure in gaining a new friend with a man that Ty already knew and approved of, right?

She was heading upstairs for bed when she remembered she was supposed to call Ty when she got home. Looking at her clock, she realized it was after one in the morning. She looked again, not believing it. She didn't realize it'd been over five hours since she first spoke with Ty when she was in her truck. What could Ty be thinking?

She hit the speed-dial on her phone, wondering what she was supposed to say when he picked up, as she knew he would. He picked up on the first ring.

"Morgan, did you forget to call me?" He sounded awfully chipper for as late as it was. Ty didn't even say hello, or ask how she was. "Or are you just now getting home?"

Feeling like she was checking in with a guardian or a father, she felt more than a little foolish calling him at one in the morning to let him know she just got home. She couldn't lie because she knew the truth was bound to come out. Besides, she and Ty never lied to the other.

"Yeah, I just walked in the door a few minutes ago. Sorry it's so late!"

"Not a problem at all. I told you I'd wait up. I was watching movies." Or rather, the same one over and over again since his thoughts kept revolving around her and Josh. "So how'd your night go?"

Ty was trying to sound only mildly curious when he was fairly bursting at the seams.

He'd already come to the conclusion that since she didn't call back soon after she called from the truck, she was out on a date with Josh. He didn't think Josh would let her go that easily. Josh wasn't stupid after all. When he got her text letting him know they were at The Neon Moon for dinner, he'd smiled.

"Well, like I texted you, I treated Josh to a meal since he came to my rescue. He seems like a nice, funny, and decent guy. Honestly, he was a gentleman the entire time. I don't know if he's always like that, but he was very easy to get along with."

Remembering a comment Josh had made while they'd talked over dinner, she added, "He did say he couldn't wait to talk to you. I had a feeling it'd be soon, but I don't know what about."

She heard Ty start laughing on the other end of the phone. Apparently, *he* knew what it was about. Dismissing it, she moved on.

Deciding to sum it up quickly and get to bed, Morgan thought for a moment. No details, she told herself. Hoping to change the subject, she added, "We'll need to fix the truck in the morning. The bed has all the supplies and tack I bought. It's locked, but I want to get it as soon as we can.

"Do you want to come and get me in the morning so we can get it all taken care of? Or I can have one of the others drive me there, and I can change it myself. The water level in that ditch should be down by then."

Ty could tell she wasn't going to tell him what went on during the last five hours. He had to respect her privacy even though it was killing him.

With unmistakable humor in his voice, he replied, "Sure, darling. But since it's so late, how about I come to your place around noon? That should give you enough time to sleep in and get up. That work for you?"

Rolling her eyes because she knew he was teasing her, she held back her chuckle. Answering her best friend with a wry tone, she said, "I'll be up long before that, but around noon sounds just fine. The earlier, the better. I'm assuming Drew and Maya are covering tomorrow morning still?"

"Yeah."

"Good. Thank you for being there when I called you tonight. And sorry I called so late. I just didn't realize how much time had gone by until I got home."

Oops. If *that* wasn't a starry-eyed girl admission, she didn't know what was. She heard Ty start to break in and hurried to stop him. "Good night, Ty. See ya later." She quickly hung up but couldn't stop the smile that spread across her face.

At the sound of the call being disconnected, Ty grinned. Well now, *that* was a very good sign. He sat there for a moment, thinking.

Morgan was a little bit nervous. If she hadn't cared at all about going out to dinner with Josh, if she'd seen him as just another guy, she would've been her normal, controlled self. But she *wasn't* her normal, controlled self. Her nerves and calm demeanor seemed to be a bit shaken, and *that* had to mean they hit it off pretty well. And now she was feeling skittish about it.

Perfect. He smiled again.

His next step was to make sure she didn't bolt.

His heart was actually feeling lighter just at the thought of her maybe—finally—breaking free of her tormenting memories. Not that she actively carried them around everywhere she went, but he also knew they were always there. So, in essence, that was exactly what she was doing.

Ty turned off his lights and headed upstairs to bed. He set his alarm on his phone and fell back onto his big bed. His mind was still swirling with thoughts about his best friend and a possible romance blooming for her. He finally drifted into sleep with a smile on his face.

Chapter 22

May

MONDAYS WERE A BEAR to get through sometimes, making the week start out roughly. But it seemed even worse when a Tuesday was too. Josh had his hands full from downed computers as well as flooded and partially washed-out work sites because of the weekend storm. And now his receptionist told him some family member was on the phone.

"Is it really important, or can they call back later?" He hadn't wanted to be interrupted until he had this paperwork all caught up, but Kristi knew she could always interrupt if it concerned his family or Damien, who was pretty much family in Josh's eyes. He just had so much to do still and didn't want to break the zone he was in. He made fewer mistakes that way. "Let me know, please."

"Okay." Kristi Adams pushed the blinking button for the line holding on her phone, asking, "Ma'am? He's in the middle of something right now. Can you call back, or do you want to leave a message for him? If it's important, I can send you through."

She listened to the person speaking. "How long for him to call you back? Oh, well..." Kristi mentally listed all the things her employer was in the middle of doing, then looked at the stacks of paperwork on her own desk. "Let's see, it's the first of May now, right? I'm estimating sometime around June or July."

The caller laughed. They spoke on the phone for a while, Kristi writing out the message for Josh on the pink message pad. As they finished up, she said, "I'll make sure he gets this right away. After that, it's out of my hands." Kristi heard the woman laughing again before asking another question. "Yes, he is. He's just really busy, but it'll calm down soon." She listened again before replying, "Okay, you have a good day too."

Kristi smiled as she hung up. She ripped the message off the pad and placed it in Josh's inbox tray. She beeped him on the intercom. "They left a message. It's in your tray whenever you come out here."

"Thanks," Josh replied, deep in his zone. He more or less answered her automatically, not really paying attention to what she said as he was engrossed in running figures.

Still immersed in work a couple of hours later, Josh had completely forgotten about the phone call. If he wasn't concentrating on work, his mind was full of Morgan O'Connell. He hadn't called her back or seen her since he'd dropped her off at her place late Saturday night. He figured a couple of days apart would let her settle, and give her a chance to make sure her feet were firmly on the ground.

For some reason, he sensed she was a flight risk if they moved too fast too early. She apparently needed to feel in some control, and he was in no hurry to rush things. If his gut instincts were correct, she'd be worth it.

He also remembered Ty's subtle warnings and hints about her possibly feeling resistant to going out with not only him, but anyone. His mind raced over possibilities of why this would be the case, and why Ty would know the reasons for it. Ty had told him over and over to just be patient, give her space. So, he would. He figured it wouldn't hurt to settle himself either.

It wasn't until he realized how hungry he was getting that he finally decided to stop for a while, and go grab something to eat. He sat back in his big chair and tried to let his mind clear. Business was booming so that made him happy. He'd had Damien come over the afternoon before to fix the computers, and Josh was now caught up for the most part.

The flooded and washed-out worksites just had to be dealt with as they got to them. His crews were experienced and good workers, so after he'd driven to all the sites and talked with the guys, he knew all would be fine. His foreman, Ryan March, was an ace, and Josh was letting Ryan handle most of the outside work for now so he could catch up on the paperwork and logistics.

He relaxed for a couple of minutes and looked out the window, seeing the sun shining brightly and not a cloud in the sky. He'd better go get something to eat, and then get back to work, he told himself.

Josh was walking by Kristi's desk when he saw a pink message slip in his inbox. He picked it up to see if it was important.

Kristi's message was spelled out neatly for him: *WHEN YOU DECIDE YOUR MOTHER IS MORE IMPORTANT THAN YOUR WORK, SHE'LL BE WAITING FOR YOUR CALL. PS: TURN YOUR CELL BACK ON.*

He read it twice, and then he laughed.

Kristi was walking toward her desk from the hallway that led to the breakroom as he stuffed the note in his pocket. "You're alive! Ready to join civilization again?" she teased.

"For a little while. I'm going to grab a bite to eat. Do you want me to pick you up anything?"

She shook her head. "Thanks, but I already ate."

He held up the pink note. "Thanks for the message. Your words, or hers?"

"A mixture of us both. Her sentiment. My words. She did say it wasn't an emergency, so there's no rush. Just call her whenever you find a free moment." Kristi set her mug of hot tea on her desk, slid it out of the way. As he was opening the door, she added cheerfully, "I told her to expect your call around June or July."

She heard his laughter as the door closed behind him.

Josh drove to a local subway shop for lunch. As he was sitting in the booth getting ready to eat, who should walk in but Ty? Since Josh was sitting in a corner booth, he wasn't sure if Ty had seen him yet or not. He took a bite of his sub as he listened to Ty ordering his food. He opened his bag of chips and kept on eating, watching as Ty's meal was being placed on a tray.

As Ty turned away from the counter after filling his cup with iced tea, he caught sight of Josh sitting in a corner booth, watching him. He smiled broadly and made his way around the empty booths and chairs toward him. There were only a handful of customers in there eating so they had the place almost to themselves.

"Have a seat. Good to see you again." Josh smiled at Ty as he slid into the booth seat across from him. "Why aren't you at work?"

Ty grinned. "Don't rat on me, okay? I didn't think anybody would miss me for a while. Figures I'd run into someone I knew." Ty arranged his food before he picked up his sub. Keeping a straight face, he inquired blandly, "How was your weekend?" He took a bite to hide his smile.

Josh drummed his fingers for a moment, deciding on which route to take. "It went well. Faster than I wanted it to go, but that tends to happen on weekends for most people. I think I finished up a bedroom I've been remodeling for a while in my spare time." Picking up the last of his own sub, he asked, "How was yours?"

Ty held his smile. Josh was quick on his feet. It didn't look like Josh was going to be any more forthcoming about Saturday night than Morgan had been. It was actually throwing him for a loop. Were they playing a game with him? Did they figure out he'd deliberately kept them apart and were in league now to get even with him? He wouldn't put it past Morgan. Her sense of humor could be wicked at times.

Ty could see the humor in Josh's eyes now and knew he was laughing at him. "Mine? Busy, what with my boss being out of town and all. And that storm. That was a pretty bad one according to all the news reports. Then waiting up late one night and then having to go out to change a flat tire that same day."

Ty took another bite of his turkey sub. "But my weekend was not nearly as interesting as yours was, I bet."

Enjoying Ty's company, Josh could see they were playing a little game now. Holding up his bag of chips, he tapped it and poured the little crumbs into his mouth. Scrunching up the empty bag, he reviewed the situation. He was getting the idea that Morgan was sticking to their deal and hadn't said a word to her best friend. He would do no less.

"Well, I suppose it was a nice weekend overall. I got a lot done, met some interesting people, had a good meal. Good company does a lot for one's soul, don't you think?" Josh replied calmly. He reached for one of the three chocolate chip cookies that came with his meal and took a bite.

Ty nodded. His respect for Josh went up another notch. It wasn't often to run into a guy who'd keep the privacy of someone he was interested in without his wanting to spill details or secrets. Or even make up some to impress another guy.

But Josh was calm as a cucumber. He was in no way eager to tell exaggerated tales of a wild weekend with a certain dark-haired, green-eyed beauty.

"I agree. Friends and family make the world worth living for. Without true friends, it can seem to be a very empty and lonely existence." Looking directly at Josh, Ty spoke honestly, "I know you and Morgan met and spent some time together. And considering how late it was when she called to tell me she was home safe and sound, and how she seemed, I'd say you both are off to a good start."

Seeing how Josh was about to interrupt him, Ty held up his hand. "No, she didn't give me details nor will you. And that right there tells me a lot. And I will absolutely respect that, and be grateful for her finding someone like you—how I *believe* you are anyway. There's a lot I could say, but I won't. Just remember all that I told you earlier, and go slow with her. Respect her."

He grinned before adding, "And I'm also guessing you were pretty stoked about me not letting you know she was right there in front of you all this time."

At Josh's intense look, Ty had the audacity to laugh. "I thought so! That's why I'm bringing this up in a public place because you won't beat me up where there are witnesses." They smiled at each other before Ty got serious again. "But like I told you that first day, I had my reasons, and I still stand by them. I'll always look out for her because I *am* protective of her.

"But no matter what happens, I think you'll be very good for her. I believe you'll treat her better than most any guy I know of around here, and you'd better. I'm backing your play, in a manner of speaking, so you treat her with respect."

Pausing, Ty added, "Don't make a liar or a fool out of me, Josh. If you do, *I* won't care if there are witnesses or not." His tone was serious as he made his last remark.

"If I didn't, you'd have every right to. But on the other hand, I don't think either Morgan or I need to be accountable to anyone but each other. You're hardly her father, Ty. I don't mind her having a man as her best friend. Not at all. It's different for sure, but in some ways, there are more plusses than minuses with that being the case. Only time will tell."

Josh paused, weighing what he wanted to say, feeling like he needed to say it. "Just so we understand each other, I'm going to be blunt. I'm not going to walk on eggshells wondering if you approve of anything we do. If you mind, that's your problem. She's not a teenager out on her first date, and you're not going to be her overly protective father sitting on the porch with a shotgun full of buckshot waiting for her to come home before curfew.

"We just met, and no one knows if we'll work out. We may not even see each other again. If we do, that's between us. We're starting off as friends. We're also both old enough now that we don't need a chaperone."

Ty was silent for a moment. He got the message loud and clear: Josh was telling him to mind his own business. And he didn't mind at all. It was actually what he was looking for.

Josh was man enough to stand his ground even to her male best friend. As long as the rest of him was decent, Josh was along the lines of who Ty would want for his best friend. Ty didn't want her to hook up with some weak guy who couldn't speak his mind. Josh had the confidence and steadfastness that Morgan would rely on if they did become serious later on.

But to Ty's mind, it was also best to make certain Josh knew he *was* going to be watched because he was certainly going to be watching out for his best friend.

Josh wasn't prepared for Ty's wide smile. He was expecting some sort of male pissing match over a yellow and white checkered tabletop and chocolate chip cookies. He really didn't want one, but he wasn't going to back down either.

He should've known it was another test he had to pass before Ty would accept him. It irritated him a bit to know he'd walked right into it again, but he felt better about saying what he did. It seemed they had stated their positions, and each accepted the other's.

When Ty reached over the table to slap him on the shoulder, he couldn't help but smile back. He grabbed another cookie and took a big bite as Ty held up the last bite of his sub. Before popping it in his mouth, he asked, "So when are you planning on coming out for another ride?"

Chapter 23

IT WAS AFTER SEVEN o'clock that night before Josh was able to call back his mom. When she answered the phone, he could hear the smile in her voice. "Hello? Now I wonder who this could be? Could it be my son? Are you sure you dialed the correct number?"

"Hi, Mom. Come on now. Don't give me a hard time. It's been a long day, and it's not over yet. How have you and Pops been?"

"Well, right now I'm really confused," she answered. "Kristi swore it'd be at least June or July before you called me back. What happened?"

"Nothing happened. I just figured you were more important than my work."

He heard her soft laugh and could picture her getting more comfortable in her favorite chair. He asked, "What's happening at home? You and dad get more animals to chase around the farm? The last time I spoke with Angie, she said Dad went to a cattle auction a little while ago."

"Heavens, no, dear. We've enough as it is. We're supposed to be retired, but that only lasted those few months, as I'm sure your sister informed you. This semi-retirement thing is going all right though. It gives us something to do, keeps your dad occupied, and keeps some money coming in."

She paused, taking a drink of her tea. "And I've been out riding almost daily. It's been great weather to ride in. I really wish you'd come home, and spend some time here. It gets lonely with all you kids gone."

"Angie doesn't live that far away. Don't you get to see her and her family fairly often?"

"Yes, but it's just not the same as you. You were the one who really loved to ride with me, and who could keep up. Angie comes with the kids, so she can't always ride. None of her kids are into horses like you were. I love them, don't get me wrong, but you know how it is. Your dad rides with me sometimes, so I don't always have to ride alone."

Josh felt a little stab of guilt and sadness at hearing his mom's words. The two of them were closer than she and his sisters simply for their shared love of horses. With his being the only child of hers with not only the deep love of horses, he was also the only one with no children to slow them down when they got together.

Although she truly loved her grandchildren, of course, Annabelle Wright missed riding for hours on end, running, walking, or jumping her horse on the trail as the whim hit her. She couldn't do those rides with her grandchildren.

But she and her son reveled in those rides, and she missed both them and him. They had a strong bond, and the horses kept it going. She knew there could come a day when she could no longer ride, no longer work with her horses, that her life could either be altered, or even end. And it *would* one day. She wanted her son to have as many great memories as she could give him. She missed her son.

"I'll come back to visit when I can, Mom. We'll ride those trails again, I promise. I miss them as much as you do." He paused, hoping he wasn't getting her excited as he couldn't imagine anytime soon that he could leave Arizona for Kentucky for a long visit.

His dad got on the line, and they spoke for a while before he handed the phone back to his wife. "I gotta go watch my weekly show so I can keep track of what day it is, son."

Josh laughed. "Don't let me stop you, Pops!"

"I won't. I love you, but I got to go. Bye, Josh!"

"Love you, too, Pops. Bye." Josh heard his mom laughing before she got back on the line. "So, Mom, did you call just to talk, check up on me, or was there something in particular you wanted to talk about?"

"Well, there is, actually. Your father and I were thinking of taking a vacation to enjoy this semi-retirement thing we're trying out. It's been a while since we've seen you, and since you can't seem to come here, we thought we'd pop out there.

"The neighbors have already volunteered to keep an eye on the place while we're gone. They said to just let them know when, and they'll be here. Is there any time that doesn't work for you, preferably before winter time?"

"Well, isn't winter time the *best* time to leave Kentucky and head to Arizona? Thousands of people do it every year!"

Annabelle chuckled. "I know, but that's just too long to wait. And I'd hate for the neighbors to have to come down here in the cold. And maybe snow and ice, in case we get some this year. The Millers were kind enough to offer, so I'd rather not make it a hassle for them."

"True. You can come anytime you want to. I've got a spare room freshly remodeled just waiting for someone to use it. When are you thinking of flying over here? I'll juggle my schedule to make sure nothing more important than my mom and dad comes up."

They made tentative plans, both excited at the prospect of seeing each other again. His family was very close, so getting together again was special.

Looking at his clock, he groaned inside. "Well, Mom, it was great talking to you and Pops, but I need to get some things done before I turn in. That all right with you?"

"Sure, honey. It's pretty late here too. Remember we're on a later time zone. But a perk of being retired is we can stay up as long as we want to, and it doesn't matter. You take care, Josh. Love you!"

"Love you too. Tell Pops I said good night. See you soon, Mom. It'll be so great to see you both!"

Hanging up his phone, Josh leaned back and closed his eyes. He always felt good after talking with his parents. He really missed them, but he loved living here too. It made him really happy to know they'd be coming out to visit fairly soon. It was easier for them to come to him because if Ryan or Kristi needed him, he'd still be around. But he really needed to make the time to go to them, especially so he and his mom could take those rides again.

Getting up to grab something to eat, he vaguely wondered if he should call Morgan. It was hard to not call her, especially since he'd looked for her for so long. Now that he had her number but he wasn't calling, it seemed counterintuitive. But he'd deliberately not called her as he wanted her to take the next step when she was ready.

Well, that and the only number he knew to call her on was a business line. He'd not asked for her cell to let her feel more comfortable. Maybe it'd be more fun to just drop in at her place, and go for a ride. Just make it a casual thing. Or would that be awkward?

As he closed the refrigerator door, he wondered if she was thinking about him.

MORGAN WAS EATING ZUCCHINI lasagna and drinking a Pepsi at her desk as she worked on some ideas for the Fourth of July. She thought of ideas, then discarded them. She'd been so busy since the weekend, she needed a breather. But she noticed anytime she wasn't engaging her brain at full capacity for her business, thoughts of Josh Wright would invariably crowd in.

Was she ready to take a chance on him? She couldn't fool herself and say he was interested in only friendship. They both knew it too. She wasn't born yesterday. The question was: What was *she* interested in, if anything?

Why hadn't he called? she wondered again. Had he changed his mind? Or was he simply waiting for her to call him? Giving her his phone numbers was putting the ball in her court. Maybe he was just going out of his way to not pressure her, to let her come to him. Whenever she felt ready to call, she would?

If she was right, she had to respect that about him. After all, being pressured was one major reason she didn't want to date in the first place. But it also made her a little insecure, wondering if she'd done or said something wrong that caused him to not be excited enough to call her back first.

Was dating always such a psychological game? she wondered. Or was she just analyzing it way too much? The answer was yes to both.

Rolling her chair back from her desk, she stretched her legs. She'd already showered and changed into her pjs, so she was relaxed and at ease. Well, as long as Josh stayed out of her mind. She reached over and read his business card yet again. She held the card in her hand, letting her fingers flip it over and over as she wondered if she should call him.

Morgan was nervous. Well, it was more like terrified, if she was really being honest with herself. Not to mention feeling quite vulnerable. She also wondered what would happen if she fell in love with this guy? What if they ended up going their separate ways, and it broke her heart? Was she strong enough to move on? How would it affect her?

Shaking her head, she berated herself for jumping to conclusions. And for moving a thousand steps into the future when she had yet to really take even the first one.

Why did she do this to herself? Because she was a woman, she thought wryly. It's what we do. But she was a woman with a past she had to seriously consider.

She recalled something Ty had told her as they'd driven together down the highway to fix her truck on Sunday. He wasn't prying into what had happened between her and Josh the night before (she imagined it was killing him not to), but he certainly was gently encouraging her to give Josh a chance. To not shut him out and end any type of relationship before they really even got started on one.

It was almost annoying, yet sweetly endearing, how well Ty knew her, and how her brain worked.

He knew she was ready to bolt.

They'd been driving down the road, not in any rush to get to the truck. The sun was out, and the sky was back to being the calming blue it normally was there. After a light conversation about the weather, Ty had briefly mentioned her being with Josh. She'd answered his neutral questions with neutral answers.

After a moment he said, "Morgan, I think it's great that you took a chance last night. If you ever need or want to talk to me about anything, you know I'm always here, right?"

She nodded her head, looking at the huge puddles of water atop the sandy ground as they drove. Broken branches from some mesquite trees littered the side of the road.

He glanced at her while he waited for the car in front of them to turn. "Morgan, I feel that you are in *that* moment right now. That sliver of space of deciding what you're going to do next. This is an opportunity that may not come along again anytime soon, if ever. It may not work out with him, but I think it's worth you giving Josh an honest chance. You don't know where it could lead."

The car in front of them finally was able to turn, and he began to drive again. "This could be that opportunity that allows you to grow. And maybe to really get your freedom back. Or maybe to simply gain a new friend. Don't just ignore it. That's all I'm saying."

Morgan nodded and said softly, "It's just a lot to think about, Ty. I enjoyed being with him. I mean, I really did. If this is an opportunity for me, I want to grab onto it, and see where it takes me.

"But on the other hand, I need to keep myself grounded. You know all the reasons why. What would happen if we broke up? Or maybe worse, if we stayed together? It's safer to stay grounded. I just need to make sure I *am* grounded in order to think clearly."

Ty nodded before saying gently, "But if you keep yourself grounded for too long, you may never be able to fly again. The view can be awfully pretty when you're flying."

"I know. But sometimes, it's safer to just stay on the ground where you can't fall so hard. The view from down here can be pretty great too."

Understanding her reticence, Ty sighed quietly.

Meeting him halfway, she said, "But you're right. Flying can be great all on its own too. I know that." She added softly, "I flew once before, and sometimes I do miss it."

Ty heard her softly spoken comment and drove on, not saying a word in response. He just reached over, gently squeezing her hand in comfort.

Now here she was, sitting alone and pondering what to do. Did she want to stay grounded forever, or learn to fly again? Was she brave enough to chance this? If anything, maybe she'd gain a new friend. But what if she could gain *more?*

Just the thought of calling Josh made her palms sweaty. How did she *ever* get through Saturday night without losing her composure? It must've been a miracle, she thought. Then she realized it was the fact it all happened so quickly, she didn't have time to sit and let herself analyze it all to death.

They'd made ground rules together, so she should be willing to give them a chance to work. It's the least she could do, wasn't it? If they didn't work out in the end, then at least she tried. But she had to be willing to give the man a true chance. Could she even do that? she asked herself. They were starting out as friends, she reminded herself yet again.

She took a deep breath and picked up the phone. Laughing nervously to herself, she set it back down. She got up and walked around her living room a couple of times to work off her nervous energy. She even gave herself a pep talk. She picked up the phone again.

Setting it back down yet again, she procrastinated by going to the kitchen to get some iced tea. Lecturing herself sternly, she picked up her phone and made herself dial his cell number before she lost her courage.

Flipping through some paperwork he really didn't feel like doing right then, Josh automatically reached for his cellphone when it rang, barely glancing at the Caller ID. Showing a local number, he figured it wasn't spam. "Hello."

"Hi. It's me, Morgan. It's been a few days, and I haven't heard from you. I decided to see what you've been up to. Am I calling too late?"

Quickly turning off the TV he had playing in the background, he smiled when he heard her voice. His plan had worked.

"Hey there! It's really good to hear from you. It's not too late at all. I was just..." What had he been doing? He'd forgotten the second he recognized her voice on the other end of the line. "It doesn't matter. It's great to hear your voice again. I've been thinking about you, and wondering how you've been."

"Really?" Morgan didn't know what to say to that bit of honesty. "That's good to know. I have to admit you've been in my thoughts too. A lot, actually."

"Yeah?" Josh smiled. "How much is a lot?"

She heard the smile in his voice. Although her heart was pounding in nervousness, she began to relax because of it. "Well, apparently more than you thought about me."

"Doubt that," he said before he could stop himself. He heard her soft chuckle and smiled again. "No need to compare, is there?"

"I guess not," Morgan replied before changing the subject. "Being in the construction business, I was also thinking about your work sites because of the storms. How did those turn out?"

And so they spoke with each other on the phone like old friends do. Morgan relaxed even more as Josh seemed completely at ease. Just hearing his voice on the other end of the line had her nervousness disappearing a little at a time. It reminded her how easy it had been to be in his company on Saturday night.

Neither worrying about the time, and the fact both of them had jobs that required them to be up practically at the break of day, Josh and Morgan talked until almost midnight.

Chapter 24

THE FRIENDSHIP BETWEEN MORGAN and Josh grew stronger as time passed. They met for rides in her mountains, had an occasional lunch or dinner together, and hung out at each other's house a couple of times. Taking it one more step forward, Morgan invited him and his two friends to her house for game night with her staff.

She felt like they were working on a recipe together. They had all the ingredients, so now they were slowing mixing them together. It helped that Ty already knew not only Josh but also Damien and Laura from their ride that day. Gaining approval from friends could be trickier than family. In her case, her staff were basically both.

Damien and Laura had been astounded when they heard Josh had finally met his Mystery Woman, and how it had come about. When they recently met Morgan in person over a casual dinner, they couldn't believe it was her.

Josh was relieved his two friends accepted Morgan—and she them—as he didn't want any tense relationship drama in his life. He wouldn't be able to choose between them. He was thankful it didn't appear he'd need to.

Seeing Morgan in nice blue jeans and a t-shirt had triggered Laura's memory that evening. She finally remembered she'd seen Morgan at the Center on her previous rides. Apparently, the dressier clothing Morgan had worn and their first dreamy meeting threw off Laura's normally natural gift of remembering names and faces. And where she'd seen them.

When she'd exuberantly told Josh she remembered now, he'd just groaned, putting his hands over his face. Between his groans and laughter, he'd replied, "*Now* you remember? A lot of good that does me *now*, Laura!"

Morgan had smiled and told him, "All good things come to those who wait. It all worked out in the end though. Timing *is* everything, Josh. We just had to wait for our time to come. Maybe we wouldn't have been ready for each other before."

But she knew she was really referring to herself.

W<small>HEN SHE HEARD HER</small> doorbell chime, she walked to her door and looked through the window beside it. Seeing Josh with his arms full of food, she smiled. Opening her door, she welcomed him into her home. "Hi! I'm glad you made it! It looks like you've come prepared. Let's head to the kitchen."

"Hi back!" He smiled at her as he walked into her home. Loving its Spanish architecture and its coziness, he followed her to the large kitchen. After setting his bags on the counter, he asked, "Is it just us here?"

"Yeah. The others should be coming up here in about fifteen minutes or so. Why?"

"Well, I suddenly realized I had poor manners and barely greeted my hostess. My mom wouldn't approve at all. My rudeness is nearly unforgiveable."

"Oh." Morgan found herself suddenly caught up in Josh's strong arms. Putting on a stern face as she rested her hands on his shoulders, she lectured him, "That *is* pretty rude of you. Your mother would certainly be ashamed. I'm ready for your apology."

Laughing, he slowly lowered his head. She smiled and the giggle that bubbled from her was cut off when his warm mouth met hers. Their shared kiss began as a teasing one, with Josh intending it to just be a quick one. But that was hard to do with her. Ever since he took the chance and kissed her one night after he'd taken her out to dinner, there was always this current between them. And it only seemed to grow stronger and more intense the longer they were together.

It didn't take but a few seconds for their passion to ignite, and Morgan's hands brought him just a little closer. Hungrily they kissed each other, neither one caring about the time, the food waiting on the counter, or the guests that were coming.

Slowly backing her against the counter, he pressed against her as he devoured her mouth. Morgan moaned softly in her throat, reveling in the sensations he had coursing through her. Every kiss they shared just seemed to get better and better.

She ran her fingers through his thick hair, pulling him even closer. She felt his hands run up and down her sides, then slide around and rest at the small of her back. His mouth finally left hers to press a soft kiss against her cheek before resting his own cheek against hers.

She said in a breathless whisper, "You're forgiven."

Barely hearing her, Josh slowly pulled away after pressing another soft kiss to her cheek. Breathless himself, he ran his hands over the top of her head and then gently down the sides of the face that captivated him.

"What did you say?" he asked, trying to regain his senses and calm his racing heart. His hands finally rested, linked around her slim waist.

Their foreheads now resting together, her heart still pounding, she repeated, "I said you're forgiven."

It took him a moment for her words to register. The spell she wove around him was a powerful one. When he realized what she'd said, he hugged her tightly and laughed. "I'm glad to hear that. Of course, if I'm not completely forgiven, I could work on it a little more." He raised his eyebrows and wiggled them at her.

Smiling, she slid away from him to break free. "It's a minor offense this first time, so bail isn't too steep." She tried to get her heart rate and blood pressure under control before any guests arrived.

He was about to answer her when they heard a quick knock at the front door, then Ty calling out, "Hello! Okay to come in? Morg, you here somewhere?"

"He's early, I see." Smiling as he ran his hands through his hair quickly, Josh walked around the corner. Calling out to his newest friend, he said, "She's in the kitchen."

Ty smiled when he saw Josh, noting the slightly disheveled hair. Stopping beside Josh as he made his way toward the kitchen, he reached over to wipe off an imaginary lipstick smear from Josh's face, humor easily seen in his eyes.

Slightly embarrassed, Josh shook his head but grinned.

With a grin directed at Josh, Ty called out, "What have you two been doing that took precedence over putting out the game tables?"

Morgan quickly righted herself as Josh was talking with her best friend. Feeling back in control of herself, she called out, "Hey, Ty!" She looked around the wall, a bag of tortilla chips in her hands. "Why don't you two set up the tables while I finish up in here?"

She took the bag of snacks he held out and returned to the kitchen.

It didn't escape Ty's attention she'd avoided his last question. With another smile, he motioned for Josh to follow him to get the tables and games from where she stored them.

Morgan had made her game night potluck-style so no one person got stuck with a big bill. She also figured everyone contributing something made them all feel more welcome and relaxed. Morgan had started her game nights years ago when she was looking to fill up lonely hours, and to become more familiar with those she employed.

It hadn't taken her long to realize some of her workers didn't really have anywhere inexpensive to go to have fun. And since the younger ones couldn't go to bars, her house became a safe place all felt comfortable going to. All the food, drinks, games, joking, laughter, and company made Morgan feel like her house was more of an actual home—something she'd always wanted. Over time, she and her employees had bonded into more of a family.

Damien and Laura arrived, bringing some drinks and a dessert as their contribution. As her staff trickled in carrying various food items, Morgan made the introductions. When Bo and Drew walked in, they all recognized each other from their ride. Pleased, Morgan felt like these three new people had already been sifted before being added to the mix. By the time this party was over, she felt they'd all be blended together.

Alexis recognized Josh as soon as she saw him. With a big smile, she said, "Hey, I know you! *You're* the guy who ran over Morgan, aren't you?"

Josh also remembered meeting Alexis that day and laughed. "I didn't run her over. I ran *into* her!"

"Same difference!" Alexis replied, laughing. "Either way, welcome to our little unofficial social club!"

Chapter 25

THE FOURTH OF JULY weekend was one of Morgan's best money-earning events of the year... As long as the monsoons didn't hit. This year they were in the clear as the weather was spectacular because it was cooler than normal.

It'd actually rained a couple of days earlier, and the unique, distinctive smells of the desert were lingering in the air. Parts of the desert turned a little bit greener, and some varieties of cactus got just a tad thicker after soaking up the rainwater. Some even bloomed with colorful blossoms.

Morgan had every ride booked to capacity, even adding the lesson horses from Quail Run to accommodate extra rides. She had all of her Sunset Ridge wranglers on the grounds as well as all of her stable hands from Quail Run. Morgan had even asked a few boarders and students' parents if they wanted to help for some extra cash, or a discount, due to the response she'd had from her ads and flyers placed around town.

Thankfully, Ty didn't have any problems returning from Illinois the day before from his annual family reunion. Not having Ty there would've made a huge dent in the smooth running of the Center. Morgan was relieved to hear his voice on the phone the evening before telling her he was back home, and he was good to go in the morning. His family reunion was held a little later this year, so it'd been a worry the planes returning him home would be late, or even cancelled.

Damien and Laura followed Josh as he made his way to Sunset Ridge. Morgan had told them to meet there at precisely nine o'clock—which actually meant fifteen minutes earlier. She had this personal rule about fifteen minutes early was actually on time, and on time was actually late. Josh walked his two friends around so they could see everything.

Damien looked around, whistling. "Man! You weren't kidding, Josh. She *does* throw one hell of a party. This took a lot of planning!"

Josh and Laura could only nod in agreement.

They could see small carnival-style booths in the outdoor arenas. Josh told them Morgan's stable hands from Quail Run and a few volunteers were running those events. He told them there were even small, inexpensive prizes for the winners. They were more of a memento and for bragging rights than anything else, but they were still prizes.

Morgan was creative at getting her business name out there, and each prize had the Center's logo and contact information on it. "I try to never miss an opportunity to promote my place," she'd explained to Josh when he saw all of the boxes of prizes in her living room one evening.

He'd felt like a kid at a birthday party looking through the variety of coolies, hats, pens, lanyards, sunglass holders, mugs, reusable bags and water bottles. She even had small bottles of sunblock with clips on them that were printed with her business logo. She also had special T-shirts made up for the staff to wear so the visitors knew who was a staff member in case of an accident.

Her arm looped through her husband's, Laura laughed in excitement at the transformation in the Center. Red, white, and blue streamers seemed to be everywhere near the booths, but Morgan wouldn't allow any near the barn and horses being used for the trail rides for safety purposes. She banned all balloons for safety reasons. If any got away, she was also worried some wild animal would eat it, causing them a slow, horrible death.

Morgan had a couple more food trucks come for the expected large crowd. Looking around, Laura noticed the numerous tables and trash cans by the three food trucks were decorated in patriotic colors.

Damien tugged at her arm. When she looked, she smiled as she saw blue porta-potties being lined up by two men in overalls. They saw the new signs warning of *No glass, no alcohol, no balloons, no firecrackers, no dogs (except legitimate service dogs, of course)*, and *No unaccompanied minors allowed on the premises.*

Morgan's other, permanent signs also warned that this was a horse business; therefore, there were risks involved. All visitors were accepting those risks by being there. She had jokingly labeled some as *Exhibit A* and *Exhibit B* as a nod to anyone who thought about suing her for anything. Damien laughed when he noticed them.

There was even a DJ, who was currently cranking out modern pop tunes from his booth.

Some of the privately-owned horses in the nearby pastures and pens were standing by their fences, their eyes alert, and their ears pricked up in interest at all of the action, colors, and music. A few nervous or excited ones tossed their heads and trotted around, their tails raised high, before stopping and blowing a short, quick breath through their flared nostrils before tossing their heads again. The veteran horses just ignored it all by napping in the warm sunshine.

As they neared Sunset Ridge, Josh, Damien, and Laura could see Morgan speaking with some of the parents who were running the pony rides for the children who were six and under. Insurance regulations wouldn't allow for children under seven to ride on the trails, so she offered pony rides at the barn and around the grounds today for those younger ones who wanted to ride.

With the ponies being led around by an adult, helmets on the children, and buddy stirrups attached to the saddles, she figured it'd be safe. She didn't want anyone to be disappointed. With their compatibility with kids, she'd decided that was where Damien and Laura would be spending their time.

Ty saw them coming and walked over, a big smile on his face as he greeted them. "Welcome to our humble little shindig! I sure hope you're ready. We're already feeling busy, and we're not even officially open yet."

He gestured to the dozens of trail horses that were lined up at the hitching rails, wearing their saddles and bridles already. They saw Toby, Maya, Bo, Eric, and Drew leading others to and from the water troughs.

"Josh, you're now an honorary wrangler as well as an office aide. By the end of tonight, your feet are probably going to be really sore. Maybe our girl will give you a foot massage as payment for you working here on your day off."

Ty grinned at Josh's laugh. Ty liked to refer to Morgan as 'their' girl, and Josh didn't miss the tease.

"I'll be sure to mention that to her," Josh deadpanned.

"I'm sure you will." Looking at Damien and Laura, who were still trying to take it all in, Ty said, "And you two. I won't envy you your feet after about two or three hours of walking all over this place. It won't be as bad as it was going to be though. Morgan sweet-talked some of her students' parents into taking a couple of shifts. We're going to do our best to rotate through the five ponies so they don't get bored and cantankerous. The last thing we want or need is a pony popping a three-year old through the air."

They laughed as Ty motioned for them to follow him. "As honorary staff today, you also get some free swag. Hats, water bottles, whatever. You can choose. That's on top of the shirts you're wearing which are yours to keep, in case you forgot. There's a box of that stuff over there." Ty pointed to a table as he spoke. "That box is for staff only. If there's anything left over at the end of the day elsewhere, you're allowed to take it to give away to your friends or family. Whoever you know."

Josh asked, "As free advertising, I assume?"

Ty grinned. "Of course."

Josh headed over toward Morgan while Ty introduced Damien and Laura to the parents. She was so engrossed in her clipboard, she didn't even notice him there. He moved so his shadow covered up part of the clipboard. He didn't have to wait long until she looked up.

"Josh! I didn't even hear you come over. I'm *so* glad you're here! This has grown a bit larger than we originally planned on, which for business is great, but we're going to be worked to death today. I was just thinking I should've charged a bit more so we could all retire early." She tossed a grin his way and shrugged. "Maybe next year."

He kissed her on the cheek and smiled. "Well, show me the way, and I'll do my best to ease your burden, madam. What do you want me to do?"

"Well, the plan right now is for Ty and I to do the signing in, getting payments, and completing waivers. But I'm going to show you what to do with signing in people in case we need a break or something.

"But your main job is to fit helmets on those who want them, and to keep the helmets in order to make the next ride go out smoothly. I put them outside of the office for more space, so they're over there on that folding table. They're in tubs labeled by size. Only you are allowed back there to keep track of them.

"Once their helmets are chosen and fitted, you send them to the picnic tables. There's some sunblock available over there too. My new *specially-labeled* bottles, of course, because I'm sure someone is bound to steal them," she joked.

"We roped off areas to keep people organized and safe. See there?" She pointed to where they'd used ropes and signs to designate where people should wait. "When Ty or I signal that's all of them, the wranglers will begin loading them up. Then, I'll need either you or Ty, maybe both of you, to help with that. Teach them the KISS method, adjust reins and stirrups, keep them in line until the ride leaves. Watch for idiots. That kind of thing."

"Wait. The KISS method? What's that?" Josh looked confused.

"Keep It Simple, Stupid. Just give them the basics. You know... How to stop, turn, go. Stay in line, one horse length in-between. Walk only. Don't try to get on or off the horse unless we're there to help them. The same speech you heard us give when you took a ride here when you used to pay for them."

"Oh, well... I should admit now that I never paid any attention to you guys when you did that. It's like listening to the flight attendants telling people how to save themselves in an emergency. It just didn't apply to *me*." He grinned broadly at the look of consternation on her face. "I'm just teasing you, sweetheart!"

"You'd better be." Morgan shook her finger at him. "But it's annoying, and even dangerous, when others don't listen."

Scratching his head underneath his cowboy hat, he thought over what he had to do. "Ok, I can handle that. Do I stand out there to gather all the helmets when the ride is back?"

"Yeah. Probably. Some riders may try to return them to the office, some will leave them on the tables, some will hand them to any adult who looks like they work here. I'm sure some will just drop them on the ground, and leave them there. Basically, just make sure no one steals my helmets."

With a straight face, he offered a suggestion. "Maybe you should put your logo on them."

Instead of laughing him off as he expected, she got a thoughtful look on her face. "You know, that's actually not a bad idea. I've never thought of that before. We'll need to revisit that idea of yours later." She made a note on her clipboard, making him grin.

Seeing the rest of her wranglers, staff, and volunteers show up at the barn, she called everyone together for a quick huddle. "C'mon, honey." Morgan looped her arm through Josh's as she led the way over to the barn. "Let's get this party started."

After a few minutes, she got everyone quieted down to explain how everything was going to work. With a straight face, she began, "I need you all to listen to me, okay? If you're one of those people who ignore flight attendants when they're telling you how to save yourself in an emergency, you'd better *not* be ignoring *me* right now." She looked pointedly at Josh, making him smile.

She pointed to the stations around the Center so everyone knew where everything was located. She then described how the ride getting ready to go out would be in this spot, and those getting back from a ride needed to be unloaded over there, pointing to an area away from them.

"Keep them in the roped areas if at all possible, please. Safety is priority one here for my horses, staff, and, of course, the guests."

Many laughed at her humor at listing her guests last. Only her staff knew she was actually listing them in order as she saw it should be.

"The roped sections will keep the horses and people separated, and theoretically, lessen the chances of injuries and avoidable accidents. No running, umbrellas, balloons, firecracker poppers, loose dogs, or anything you think could spook the horses are allowed over here. Use your best judgment if you're unsure. Call for me, Ty, or Josh here if you need help. Err on the side of safety, please.

"First-aid stations are at all major events. Sun block and water should be used regularly. I'd highly suggest wearing a hat if you have one. Staff has access to the swag table over there, including hats."

She made sure the team leader at each station had a two-way radio and that they were on the same channel. "No chatter, please. Keep it open so if it's needed, it's available. Remember the wranglers need these in case of emergencies on the trail, so no playing on them. If your batteries run low, we'll get them replaced before they die, if we can. They all have freshly charged batteries in them now so they should be fine."

Josh watched as she seemed to have everyone in attendance in the palm of her hand. He hadn't realized she was so organized and such an event coordinator. He enjoyed seeing yet another side to her.

She answered questions, and then sent everybody to their stations. Standing between Josh and Ty, she confessed with a tight smile, "I think I'm gonna be sick."

They laughed at her as they ushered her into the office.

With a straight face, Josh said, "Flight attendants have barf bags. Are those included in your box of swag, or did I miss hearing you mention them? I may have zoned out."

"Seriously, Josh?" she asked, exasperated. At both men's wide smiles, she laughed. "Get to your station. People are heading over. The Lysol cans are out there to clean them with too. Don't let anyone steal them."

Josh laughed as he walked out the back door and headed to his station.

Behind her, the door opened for the first customers of the day. Turning around, she greeted them and proceeded to the counter so she and Ty could sign them in.

As the afternoon wore on, Josh thought running a construction business was a breeze compared to a horse business on a busy holiday. He lost count of how many helmets he'd fitted, cleaned, replaced—just to send them right back out again.

He'd loaded and unloaded every type of human being born on the planet onto the most patient of horses. He'd tied and untied ropes, adjusted reins and stirrups so many times, he wondered if they really needed to have stirrups in the first place. Couldn't they just ride without them?

He also assisted the wranglers in watering the trail horses and filling the hay nets that were tied above the covered hitching rails to keep the horses happy, occupied, and energized when they were given a break from a ride.

Sometimes he'd see Damien and Laura walking endlessly around and around, leading the ponies while smiling and excited children sat in the saddle acting as if they were the ones steering their mighty and hairy steeds around. Happy parents took pictures to make fond memories.

On his way back to his station from replacing a radio battery, Josh heard his name called out and turned around. "Hey, Leslie! I haven't seen you in a while."

Leslie introduced her family to Josh, introducing him as her "all-around guru for her gym." With a curious look, she inquired, "So the last time I saw you, you were going on that blind date. Whatever happened with that?"

Josh smiled broadly. "You wouldn't believe it if I told you."

"It worked *out* with her?" she asked, obviously thrilled.

"Well, no. Thankfully! I'd never live it down if it had." She laughed gaily as he continued with the rest of the story, "But I sorta ran into someone *else* while here, and now *we're* seeing each other. It was just one of those things, I guess."

Leslie grinned. "You came here for the ride?"

"We did. It was an excellent suggestion, so thanks again."

"So where's the person you ran into that you're seeing now? Is she here with you today?"

Josh grinned as he pointed to Sunset Ridge. "She's up at that barn signing in people for the trail rides as we speak."

With humor radiating from her eyes, Leslie asked, "You're telling me that you brought a date here for a ride and ended up with a staff member? I bet that was a *very* interesting day, Josh."

The teasing in her voice and the sparkle in her eyes had Josh, her husband, and teenaged sons laughing.

Josh couldn't hold back his smile. "You have *no* idea. As it happens, she's a bit more than a staff member. She owns this place."

Dumbfounded, his client just stared at him for a moment.

Her husband joked, "Well, *that* has never happened before. You made her speechless. I've been doing it all wrong for almost twenty years."

Josh laughed when Leslie playfully slapped her husband's arm.

Leslie finally wrapped her head around what he'd just said. "Well, *wow*. I have so many questions right now. I'm happy for you, Josh. And I can see how happy *you* are just by lookin' at ya. Love has a nice look on you."

Studying him for a moment, Leslie teased, "Just remember it was *my* idea for you to come here. If it all works out, I think there's a future discount for your services in there somewhere."

Josh chuckled. "Yes, ma'am. I won't forget. And if it *doesn't* work out, I'll charge you extra for the heartbreak and crushing disappointment. I won't forget that either."

Her husband laughed. "Then let's hope it works out for you both. We have a scheduled ride in about an hour, so we'll get to meet this lady ourselves, right?"

Josh nodded.

Wrapping her arm around her husband's waist, Leslie said, "Wonderful. I'll give you a glowing review so I can get my discount."

"You do that. Morgan would probably like to hear how great I am from somebody else other than me by now." They laughed at him as he excused himself. "I'd better get back up there as it's a madhouse today. She's got me working. Can you believe that?"

Leslie laughed. "It *must* be love."

"Must be," Josh replied, smiling.

When the local TV station sent out reporter Brenda Michaels and a cameraman for a story, Morgan didn't want to be on camera at all.

She did, however, answer every question Brenda asked her and gave them permission to film whatever caught their fancy. She could interview anybody else she wanted to—as long as they stayed away from the horses themselves. Morgan didn't want a spooked horse dumping its rider on TV because a cameraman didn't have enough sense to use his zoom feature instead of walking right up to a horse who'd never seen a camera that large before.

Throughout the rest of the day, the local TV station began airing snippets of *The Harmony Hills Equestrian Center's Fourth of July Bash* on the news and during breaks. They had film on everything Morgan had on her property: The carnival booths, trail rides, pony rides, food trucks, and people having picnic lunches. Even the DJ got some interview time in. Brenda Michaels interviewed anyone who wanted to be on TV, so in the end, she was almost as busy as the actual workers were.

By eight o'clock that night, when the last ride was done and the customers were unloaded from the tired horses and heading off to their vehicles, everyone was drained of energy. As they all cleaned up, turned out the horses and fed them, Morgan began cooking dinner for everyone on her own grill. They hoped they could eat before watching the fireworks that were to be set off outside of town.

Before she walked away to let The Darrells out of the kennel run, Morgan stopped beside Josh. She asked, "So who's Leslie Travis again?"

Shaking his head, he laughed.

Chapter 26

September

MORGAN HAD JUST FINISHED giving a riding lesson to a new young rider and had walked outside with her and her mom to their car. She waved again as they drove away. Standing there with the sun warming her while the cool breeze blew gently around her, Morgan took a moment to relax and appreciate the gorgeous weather.

She was turning to go back into Quail Run when she spotted Josh's truck turning into the gate from the highway. Happy at seeing it, she was also puzzled as she knew his parents were coming into town. She thought he'd driven to Sky Harbor Airport in Phoenix to get them.

Maybe he just wanted to stop by for something after dropping his parents off at his house. Maybe their flight was cancelled or delayed. She hoped not because she knew how excited he was to see them.

Morgan turned to make her way up to Sunset Ridge because that's where Josh would assume she'd be. She stopped in surprise when he suddenly turned away from the lane that led to Sunset Ridge, and instead headed toward Quail Run. He pulled up in the Quail Run parking lot, rolling down his windows just a little. He must've spotted her standing in the sunshine or recognized her walk, she figured.

Curious, Morgan saw what looked like a slim figure in the seat beside him, or maybe it was just a shadow. It was hard to tell with his tinted side windows even with her eyes shielded from the sun's bright glare. She immediately began to walk toward his truck.

As Josh got out and walked around the hood of his truck, she yelled out, "Hey, honey! What's that in your front seat? Another blind date?" She was laughing as she walked toward him, wishing she'd brought her sunglasses out. She'd left them on the desk in the barn, but at least she had her ball cap on to help shield some of the brightness.

Josh's answering laughter carried over to her, and his smile was wide as he opened the passenger front door. He'd once casually mentioned being on a few blind dates over the years, so she teased him now and then about it.

As a slim, tall, and attractive woman stepped down from his truck, Morgan came to an abrupt halt. His mom. He brought her over *today?* Morgan had wanted to meet his parents, well, more formally than this. At least cleaner. She felt her face turn slightly red, hoping it would be back to normal by the time she reached them.

Suddenly nervous, she wondered if they'd like her. Would she like them? Josh had repeatedly told her they'd love her, but she assumed he was just biased until even Damien and Laura agreed. And all three told her she'd love his parents back. Damien had said they were the coolest people ever.

Morgan saw Josh open the back door just as it was opening on its own. She stopped again when she saw a handsome, tall, and older man step down, reaching over to hold the hand of the woman who was looking directly at her. *No, he didn't.* Josh brought both of his parents *now?* She was such a mess! She smelled of horses, dirt, and sweat—probably both from herself and the horses. What kind of first impression was *this* going to make?

Her heart beating rapidly, Morgan gamely smiled as she continued toward the three people watching her every move.

Josh watched Morgan as she slowly made her way over to them. Although she was still a little way off, he could tell she was either embarrassed or shy. He grinned because that didn't happen very often with her. He might feel bad about that later on, but right now he was savoring the moment. His parents were meeting his Morgan for the very first time.

Looking quickly over at his mom, Josh continued to grin as he watched her try to take in not only the attractive woman walking slowly toward them but also the entire grounds. His father was riveted on the woman, naturally. Josh watched as Morgan made her way around the fence, running her hand down Ivy's nose as the pony shoved her head through the top and middle rails for some loving when she got closer.

When Morgan finally reached them, she gave a quick glare to Josh that clearly meant *Wait until I get you alone!*

He just smiled as he reached for her hand, gave it a reassuring squeeze. Bending down, he gave her a quick kiss on her mouth, which only embarrassed her more. Whispering in her ear, he said, "It's okay, sweetheart. Relax."

Moving to stand beside her, Josh made the introductions. "Morgan, I'd like you to meet my parents, Patrick and Annabelle Wright. Mom, Pops, this is Morgan O'Connell." Josh's smile couldn't possibly get any larger. He was so happy, he thought he'd bust.

Morgan smiled and turned to Patrick first. She did a quick study of him. He looked to be as tall as his son and looked similar to him in some of his features. A handsome man, he epitomized a Western cattle rancher even though they lived in Kentucky.

She offered her hand to shake his. Morgan then got a small heart flutter when, instead of shaking it, he smoothly raised her hand in his before kissing the back of it and smiling. He didn't release her hand right away but held it gently in his own as he looked at her.

He couldn't remove his gaze from this woman who'd caught his son's eye. She was stunning. Even an old man like himself could say that, noticing her captivating green eyes even in the shadow of her ball cap. The green shirt she wore seemed to enhance their color. He could see the faint embarrassment in them, but there was confidence and determination in them as well.

"Call me Patrick, Dad, Pops. Whatever. I'll answer to anything you want me to."

Morgan laughed. Although looking at Patrick, she was clearly talking to his son. "Hmm. Now I know where you get your charm and your gift of poetic words from. Quick, sweet, cute, and funny."

Turning her full attention on Josh's dad now, she gave him a careful, assessing look. "Hmm. Yes," she murmured as she looked him over. "And *you*. I'm going to keep my eyes on you too. It's not like I don't have enough to do as it is, but it's a real pleasure to meet you. Even under these circumstances."

That dig was for Josh. Knowing it, he chuckled.

Still speaking to Patrick, she said, "Call me Morgan. I'll answer you if I'm in the mood to." Humor lit up her green eyes.

Father and son had something else in common now: Patrick didn't have a chance either. Once her vivid green eyes and bright smile took full aim on him, he was half in love himself.

Annabelle grinned at the spell this young lady was casting on her husband. She noticed Josh was still beside her, looking as pleased as any young man in love could look. Smiling, she held out her hand to Morgan, saying, "Patrick, let the poor woman loose. It's so wonderful to meet you, Morgan. You just call me Annabelle or Mom.

"As impossible as it sounds, we've heard nothing about you until we were halfway here. And that was very little. Josh does enjoy his little surprises, doesn't he? Either you or I will be talking to him about that, I'm sure. Probably both of us. My husband and I are overflowing with curiosity about you, and we're so very pleased to meet you!"

Morgan smiled back as Annabelle was nothing like she was expecting. Morgan didn't really have a concrete idea of what Josh's mother would look like, but it wasn't this. Laura had told her just the other day that Josh's mom was still beautiful, and Morgan now understood what she meant.

Annabelle was tall, slim, looking quite healthy, energetic, and young even though she was in her mid-sixties according to Josh. Her lush brown hair barely had any gray in it. She had some fantastic genes, Morgan thought. Annabelle looked as interested in her as she was in her place of business.

"Welcome to Arizona, and to Harmony Hills. It's so nice to meet you, Annabelle. I have to say you both look really, really good from coming off a plane ride across the country. I usually look worn-out and sloppy by the time I get off any plane, especially a long trip with connections. It's why I don't fly much anymore."

Still smiling in genuine pleasure, Morgan released Annabelle's hand and took a step back. She felt Josh's arm come around her waist, his fingers slipping through one of her belt loops.

Annabelle noticed how her son pulled his girl closer. Her heart sang with happiness. What a striking pair they made. She didn't care how the woman her son finally chose would physically look. As long as she had strong character and values, then Annabelle would be happy. But it was a nice bonus they looked so good, so natural together. She saw Morgan's arm go around Josh's waist, her hand anchored into the top of his belt.

Patrick and Annabelle looked around for a moment. Annabelle asked, "You work with horses? That's a wonderful coincidence. They're a lifelong passion of mine. It's always nice to meet a fellow horse-worshipper."

Annabelle smiled in amusement when she heard the pony whinny softly in their direction. Her little ears were pricked up, and her eyes were still locked on Morgan. It hadn't escaped Annabelle's attention that the cute pony had followed Morgan as far as the fence allowed when Morgan had been walking toward them a minute ago.

She looked back at Morgan, commenting, "And it's a beautiful place here. I love the Harmony Hills theme too. Josh explained it a little, but you'll have to fill me in on the rest of it. You must love working here."

"Yes, I do. It's a lot of work, and I don't have much free time. But since I love what I'm doing, it doesn't always feel like work. I spend more time here at the barns than at my house. I'm sure Josh mentioned that to you. Then again, I guess he probably didn't since he never mentioned me to you earlier. At all. As in *ever.*" She felt Josh give a quick tug on her belt loop, and she grinned up at him.

Patrick spoke up, pleased with this situation. He saw his son was very much at ease with the young woman beside him. "Well, he did mention you're a workaholic who puts his work ethic to shame. And that's saying something because he's been a hard worker as long as I've known him." Patrick smiled at his little joke.

Morgan nodded. "Yes, I am. And I do. But he still is."

It took Patrick and his wife a moment to mentally sort through her reply, but once they did, they laughed along with their son. Josh piped up, "I told you she was quick. She'll keep you on your toes."

Josh's mother looked around. She was itching to ask Morgan to give her a tour of where she worked. It was a really nice set-up and obviously well-taken care of, but she wouldn't push for a tour so soon. They'd be here a while, so she was sure she'd get a tour sooner or later. Watching some riders coming in from an outdoor arena, she inquired, "Do you live around here, or do you have a long commute to work?"

Morgan looked confused. Looking up at Josh when she felt him squeeze her waist, she immediately noticed his bland look as well as the humor lurking in his eyes. Catching on, Morgan smiled. Yes, Josh did love his little surprises. She nodded slightly to let him know she understood they had no clue about her position at Harmony Hills.

Turning back to his parents, she was getting ready to answer when she felt Josh's arm release from around her waist. From the corner of her eye, she saw him pull something out of his back pocket. She looked back at him to see what he was doing, wondering about the camera in his hand. He began backing up a couple of steps. She frowned at him.

Josh noticed her perplexed look. "I just want a quick picture. Keep talking, sweetheart, and tell them where you live."

Morgan gave him another look but dutifully turned back to his parents. Casually looking around, she finally answered the question his mom had posed. "Well, I live pretty close by, so I generally just walk to work. It saves mileage and gas on my truck. And you know what they say about walking being really good exercise."

Josh was trying not to laugh at how Morgan was stringing his parents along. He had the camera prepped. He simply waited for her to drop her bombshell on them.

"Oh, so you're a close neighbor then? Where's your house, Morgan?" Annabelle asked politely.

Morgan pointed to her house on the rise above the barns. "I live right up there. It's usually pretty handy living where you work, especially when you own both places."

She heard Josh's camera click when their faces showed their shock.

Patrick looked around them. He took in all the barns, horses, people, landscaping, and fencing. She seemed fairly young to own a place of this magnitude, but maybe it was passed down from her parents. "You mean, *you* own this place? The whole damned thing?" His eyes were wide and suddenly overflowing with humor. The laugh lines around his eyes showed as he smiled broadly.

"Yes, sir. The whole damned thing." Morgan grinned as she threw his phrase back at him.

He chuckled in appreciation of her humor.

She expounded for their benefit, "I am the proud, and sometimes exhausted, owner of Harmony Hills. I built it from the ground up with a lot of help from some great people, and lots of faith and prayers along the way. One of those people still works for me as a matter of fact. I couldn't have done it without their experience, labor, and loyalty.

"Oh, and my clientele, of course. *Somebody* has to pay for all of this to keep it running." She paused, a grin tilting up the corners of her mouth. "I assume Josh didn't tell you this either?"

Annabelle shook her head. "No. My son left out all sorts of information. It's very impressive, Morgan." She looked at her son with humor in her eyes. "You, young man, are in need of a whipping."

"If it's all the same to you, Mom, Morgan has dibs on doing that now!"

Morgan blushed but grinned at him while his mom shook her head in exasperation with her son. But her grin couldn't be held back either.

His dad was laughing too. Father and son were sharing the same thoughts. Patrick was savoring this moment as he thought it all through. Not only did this Morgan seem to be great all on her own, but she was just like his Annabelle. And both women obviously loved their horses. Leave it to his son to find a woman who owned a horse business!

And both father and son knew Annabelle would never want to leave a horse center like this for long. She'd be camped out in an empty stall within the next day or two if she could. But maybe best of all, Patrick thought, his son had chosen a woman just like his mother. Smiling to himself, he reached for his wife's hand and pulled her close to his side. He watched as his son looped his arm around his girl's shoulders.

Yes, indeed. The Wright men had excellent taste in women.

Chapter 27

WITH A STRAIGHT FACE, Morgan asked her unexpected visitors, "Now that the highlight of your day is over since you've met me, what are your plans for what's left of the day?" With a grin, she added, "Or is this something else your son has neglected to tell you?"

His parents laughed as Josh looked over Morgan's head when he saw Mel walking out of Quail Run. He returned her wave and smile. Looking back at Morgan, he said, "We were planning on going to dinner at a nice but casual restaurant later on. Wanna come along?"

He was inadvertently putting her on the spot.

Morgan looked up at him for a moment. Hedging, she commented, "I figured you'd want them all to yourself, and they you, at least for the first night." Looking at his parents, she added, "And you must be tired from your trip. You'll probably want to go to bed early since you've had such a long day. Jet lag does wear one out, especially when you cross more than one time zone like you have today. How about I take a rain check?"

Josh smiled down at her as his fingers toyed with a stray wisp of her hair that the wind had blown loose from her braid. "You're asking for a rain check in Arizona? What's wrong with you, sweetheart? And you saying they may need to go to bed early implies they're getting old. Are you calling my parents old? You don't think they can stay up long enough to eat dinner?"

His parents knew what he was doing and tried not to smile.

Morgan realized what she'd said may not have come out as intended. "Oh! No, of course not! I'm just simply saying they've had a long day, been up a long time, flew almost two thousand miles, drove some more, and would want to settle in to spend some time alone with their son. Although at this precise moment, I don't know why they would."

Josh grinned at her needling him. Turning to his parents, he shook his head. "She's got sass, doesn't she? Are you sure you want her to come along? I mean, you *are* the ones who insisted we come over here now, and that she come to dinner with us." Glancing at

Morgan, he added, almost as an afterthought, "She's cranky too. Maybe *she* needs to go to bed early."

Morgan knew he was playing games with her now. She could give as good as she got. Stepping away from him, she looked at him for a moment. Trying her best to ignore that charming grin, she frowned. Crossing her arms and narrowing her eyes slightly, she asked, "Is that so?"

His parents watched, fascinated by their fun bantering. They were learning about Morgan as they bantered with each other, which is why Josh was teasing her like he was. She wouldn't back down easily, and showed some spunk. Annabelle could feel the sparks flying between them.

Turning her head, Morgan saw Mel waiting by the end of the barn for her. Morgan waved to her, holding up a finger signaling she'd be up in a minute. Mel waved back and returned inside the barn.

Morgan looked at Josh out of the corner of her eye then transferred her gaze back to his parents. Adjusting her ball cap first, she explained the situation to them. "Okay, here's the thing. I've still got work to do."

"See, Pops? I told you she was a workaholic."

She ignored their smiles and continued, "The blacksmith is here. Kat and Mel have lessons to give, otherwise they could hang out with Rick. If Ty's not back from running errands when the rides are done, I'll need to go up and do all the paperwork too. Bo, Drew, Maya, and Toby are there now, but Bo and Drew will be leaving fairly soon as it's their early night tonight."

"We'll wait," Josh said.

"Plus, I'm a mess. I stink, Josh. Can you smell me? I'd need a shower, and time to get ready. I'm sure you guys want to eat dinner tonight before it's time for breakfast tomorrow morning."

Josh said, "We don't mean right now, but later on today. And IHOP's open twenty-four hours a day. So's Waffle House. As it's a beautiful day, we can walk around, play with The Darrells, or sit at your picnic tables in the shade there. That'd be a nice spot to spend some of that alone time together that you think we need."

He apparently wasn't going to take no for an answer. Morgan sighed and turned to his parents, who were silently watching with humor in their eyes. "Okay, I want to know right now. Whose fault is it?"

Patrick frowned. "Pardon me? Whose fault is what?"

"Well, *one* of you gave him a good dose of stubbornness. Which one of you did it?"

Laughing, both Patrick and Annabelle spoke at the same time and pointed at the other.

"Him."

"Her."

Morgan gave up. "Okay, you guys do whatever you want to do while I'm busy. You can walk around, play with The Darrells, or sit on the picnic tables in the shade. If you want to just chill out and rest, you can go up to my house and wait. Make yourselves at home, raid the fridge if there's anything you want to snag, watch TV.

"You can even use the spare bedroom downstairs if you'd like to get in a little nap. Sometimes we young people need one of those, so I can only assume anyone older than us may want one now and then themselves."

Patrick and Annabelle laughed at her little dig, but with a straight face Morgan rolled right along. "If you even feel like taking a shower, be my guest. The downstairs bathroom is always ready for guests. Josh can show you. Is this all right with you?"

Annabelle said, "That'd be fine, Morgan. We'd really love for you to come with us. We insisted. Josh knew you were busy, but we wouldn't take no for an answer. It's that stubbornness you just mentioned. Since we showed up without any warning, it's no problem for us to wait for you.

"We're not in any hurry. We grabbed a little bite to eat on the way back from the airport, so we're good to go for a while yet. The horses come first. Do you mind if I tag along in a bit?" She smiled warmly and waited for the young woman to reply.

Morgan just shook her head at Annabelle, and then looked down at her scuffed cowboy boots. She dug her toe in the dirt for a moment. "I don't know how you guys do it. I simply can't fathom it."

Looking up, she gave her attention to his parents. "He's just like you, you know. He seems very easy-going and happy-go-lucky most of the time. Affable, even. But when he wants something, he just hangs in there, patiently chipping away until you cave in. I haven't decided if this is to be a pro or a con yet," she added when she saw them both smile and nod at her in agreement.

Morgan sighed and relented. "Fine. If one of us falls asleep as we're eating, and their head drops down into their plate, I go on record right now as it not being my fault. I wonder if I'm the only one with sense right now." She paused, thinking. "All right, I'm game. One condition though."

Josh looked at his parents with a sparkle in his eyes. "Ah, we've now reached her negotiating phase. We got to it faster than I expected."

"That's because I'm busy."

They laughed at her quick retort. Morgan threw Josh a look that warned him to behave. He just grinned and waited for her to speak.

She offered her compromise saying, "I'll go out to dinner with you, but I drive my own truck. And you drive yours so you don't have to drive all the way back out here afterward just to drop me off. If you did that, you'd then have to drive all the way back to your place. That's just impractical. I'm perfectly capable of dropping myself off at my own door. I've been doing it flawlessly for years. Deal?"

Josh tried to look like he was thinking about it. "Deal. Do we draw up formal papers, shake hands, or give blood now?"

She playfully shoved him. "I accept your verbal agreements as you all seem to be the trustworthy type. If you want to go to the house, let me know first because my alarm is on. Give me about two or three hours. Maybe more, depending on Ty."

Annabelle and Patrick watched as Morgan made her way back to the barn. Annabelle noticed she naturally veered over to pet the nose of the pony that was still waiting for her. As she walked toward the barn, the pony followed her, making Annabelle grin. She saw a woman coming out of the barn to meet Morgan, followed by two large German Shepherds. The dogs immediately saw Josh and were running toward him when Morgan called them back.

Josh and his parents watched as the two dogs instantly slowed down and made a wide circle back to her. Their tails were wagging as they ran straight to her. When they reached her, they began licking her hands and nudging her with their heads like they were apologizing to her. She bent down and praised them for coming to her.

Josh's parents smiled as she played with the dogs before heading inside the barn with the other woman who was talking with her. Looking at his parents, Josh commented softly, "Ty told me she paid well over what two other people were bidding for those dogs. He said it would've broken her heart to have them separated from the only family they had, each other. So she became their family. And they hers."

Patrick asked, "Who's Ty?"

"Like The Darrells, Ty is her family. He's been her best friend for a lot of years. He's also her unofficial partner, or manager. I'm actually not sure what his exact title is here, but he runs it if she's gone.

"He and I have become good friends ourselves which makes it all even better. It was a little hard to win his trust, but he was just making sure I wasn't going to mess with her, and then simply walk away. You'll like him a lot too. Her friends stick tight with her. You'll see that in no time."

Josh motioned for them to walk with him toward Sunset Ridge. "We'll leave the truck here for now to stretch our legs. Let me show you around."

His dad nodded as they began to walk. "And who's Darrell?"

"The Darrells."

"What?"

"*The* Darrells. She named both of her dogs Darrell. It was a joke of hers to name them the same thing, claiming it doesn't take as long to call them when she wants them."

His mom was intrigued. "She earns loyalty from those around her by thinking long-term. She still has her original employees, or at least one, she said. And now these dogs she wouldn't break up. I can tell she treats her horses quite well as that little pony is clear evidence of that. And she has her best friend near her who protects her from unsavory men.

"It seems to me her desire is to make a family, whether animal or human, blood relative or not. In my experience, this would promote the idea that she seems to have a desire to create a unit. And to provide a safe place so everyone has somewhere to go to, a place where they really belong. And someone to belong to. And that would also apply to her in a mirror image so she'd have them. Is that accurate?"

Josh thought about it as they walked. His mom had a knack for summing things up, and reading people like some would read and absorb a book. "That's her in a nutshell. You summed it up better than I could.

"Her employees are very loyal to her. One of the trail-riding guides, Toby, told me once he was fairly sure there was an unwritten waiting list for people who want to work for her. But she's got who she needs and wants. She's very selective and won't hire just anybody. She has her barn rules and policies, and she isn't shy about enforcing them. She uses her head along with her heart."

Patrick reached over to take his wife's hand. "The best of both worlds, the heart and mind, when used properly."

Josh nodded. "Even when she's in a difficult position, she keeps her head on straight and thinks." He remembered when they met how she called Ty to run an unofficial background check on him before she'd roll down her window and accept his help. He thought it was a good example of how her thought process worked, so Josh told them briefly about that first meeting.

Both of his parents nodded in approval when he finished. Patrick lay his other hand on Josh's shoulder as he commented, "Son, I'd say you found yourself a keeper."

"I knew it the first time I laid eyes on her. Mom, you were right all along. She came out of nowhere. Right now, we're just taking our time to learn about the other. Neither one of us know if we'll work out, but it's my hope we do. We're just taking our time, keeping a slow and steady pace. But I think she's the one for me."

Annabelle smiled. "I told you I knew what I was talking about. You're just like all the Wright men. You're all full of good looks, charm, humor, and intelligence. And you're selective, and so very patient when it comes to the important matters in life. And that's the way you should be. Rushing can cause mistakes, or make you miss seeing them. And that can make them even bigger."

Patrick agreed. "Taking your time, and making sure is never a bad thing."

She looked at the barn they were nearing and saw the horses tied to the hitching rails. "My goodness! This place looks incredible. Give us a tour, Josh, so we can learn even more about your lady."

"Sure. Let's start with her staff."

Chapter 28

THE TWO WEEKS JOSH'S parents visited him were eye-opening for everyone. Morgan got a deeper and wider sense of this man she was falling for more every single day because his family connection was strong, solid, and comforting. Their love and humor were contagious as she spent time with them touring the area, riding horses, or relaxing at one of their homes.

They, in turn, learned about the woman their son had fallen for by meeting her staff, and watching how she ran her business. It took a strong and smart person to be able to successfully run an operation this large. They were impressed that she didn't skim the details, but rather knew every one of them.

Both took note of how well her horses were cared for, and the attention she put into making her place safe and inviting for everyone. They admired the respect and loyalty from her staff, understanding quickly she'd earned both by pitching in as much as they did. They also took note of the close friendship between Morgan and Ty.

Ty understood Josh even more now that he'd met his parents. The humor, loyalty, respect, values, and their personal friendship even though they were family were right there for anyone to see.

As Ty spent more time with Josh, and now his parents, he couldn't help but wish that Josh and Morgan did stick together. He wanted to see Morgan happily married again, and he wanted Josh to be the one. Of course, it wasn't up to him. It would either work out between them, or it wouldn't. He knew he couldn't have chosen a better family for her to join though.

THE NIGHT BEFORE HIS parents were to leave, Josh and Morgan threw them a little farewell party at The Neon Moon. Damien and Laura joined them as well as Ty. Although

Ty was the only one without a partner, he didn't seem to mind, or act like the odd man out. He was a part of this group, and Morgan didn't think it would feel the same without him in it.

She'd asked Josh if he minded if she invited Ty. Josh had appreciated her asking, and had no qualms at all about Ty coming along. It was a little going-away party for his parents, so the more, the merrier, he'd told her.

During their dinner, Laura and Damien spilled the beans about Josh's blind dates over the years. Josh had glared at them as they happily dished all. Even Ty added some since he knew about Abby.

Morgan was as dumbfounded as his parents. Josh was more worried about Morgan's reaction than his parents'. He was immensely relieved Morgan took it in stride once it was all explained to her.

He also had a feeling she'd never let him live it down. Neither would Ty.

Almost appalled, Annabelle had asked, "Are you telling me my son is a... a *womanizer?*"

Damien had laughed. "No, not at all, Annabelle. He's far from one. It's all because of Elise. You remember meeting my cousin when we were kids, right?"

At their nods, he and Laura went on to explain in detail about Elise's meddling.

Morgan was more shocked to hear Josh had brought another woman to her property. They had all laughed at her reaction to hearing that news.

At the end, Annabelle had proposed a toast. Looking at Morgan, she'd said, "You can't fight fate, honey. Welcome to the family!"

After they ate their dinner, they made their way over to the saloon and dance floor area of The Neon Moon. They pushed a few tables together that would seat them all, and sat down to let their food settle a little before getting energetic. They talked as they watched couples dancing to the live band. Annabelle and Patrick were having a fine time. They soon rushed onto the dance floor.

Josh smiled fondly as they danced. Looking over at Damien, he said, "We're going to have yet another firm talk with those two kids when we get home."

Damien laughed. As long as he'd known Josh's parents—and it'd been a long time—they always seemed to be kids at heart. It was probably one of the reasons they'd stayed together so long—and so happily. Taking their cue, he stood up, holding out his hand to Laura. She quickly got up and followed her husband onto the dance floor.

Ty had a feeling Morgan wouldn't really be happy dancing with Josh if she knew he was sitting there by himself. He casually looked around and spotted a table of women.

"Hey, Josh."

"Yeah?"

Ty jerked his head in the direction of the table nearby that had all women at it. Keeping a straight face, he asked, "See anybody you recognize at that table?"

Morgan laughed as Josh glared at Ty. But he dutifully looked over at the women. "No. Why?"

Ty stood up as he said, "I just needed to know if I had some other guy's sparkling reputation to work against. I like to know my odds before I go into battle." With that, Ty made his way over to the table of women and asked one of them to dance.

Morgan watched them dancing for a minute, smiling. She said to Josh, "When we came here before you, we tended to stick together to help keep the crazies away. He'd sometimes dance with other women, but I tended to stick with just him."

Josh nodded before he asked, "What will Ty do now that you're with me?"

"I think he's man enough to figure out something." Morgan then shrugged her shoulder and said blandly, "But I guess he'll now just have to choose from any possible woman you've maybe missed, or passed by on—"

She laughed as Josh quickly stood up and dragged her onto the dance floor.

Pops and Annabelle saw their son grab a laughing Morgan and haul her to the dance floor. Laughing themselves, they figured she'd once again shown their son some sass. And they couldn't be any happier about it.

Chapter 29

November

MORGAN WAS COOKING FETTUCCINE alfredo from scratch while Josh sat at her kitchen bar and watched with interest. He mused, "You just keep getting better and better. I love that you know how to cook. It wouldn't be a deal breaker if you didn't, but it's a definite check in the She's Got Long-Term Potential column."

Stirring the sauce, she grinned at him. "Even though I still often drink Pepsi for breakfast?"

He grinned back at her. "Yep, even with that. You also balance it out with healthy stuff, so it's not that huge a concern to me. It also adds to your charm."

"I have charm now?"

"You always did. That particular quirk of yours just adds to it."

She smiled as she turned off the heat. "It's all ready. You want to eat on the patio? It's pretty nice out."

"Sure. I got the wine." He scooped up the silverware, napkins, and glasses in one hand, took hold of the bottle in the other and still managed to open the door to her shaded patio. She walked through the doorway and over to the table, partially in the warm November sun. After setting down their plates and the warm rolls, she pulled out the chairs while Josh opened the wine bottle.

"Man, you've got great views out here. And it's so peaceful." He poured the wine as she went back in for the salads and dressing.

She answered him as she came back out. "It's one of the reasons I fought so hard to get this place. It's hard not to get good views in these parts, but I really liked this one here. Besides, I needed the space it provided. And the highway was handy for giving out directions, and there's a good volume of traffic for free advertising."

They sat at the little table casually talking as they ate the homemade meal and sipped wine while the Arizona breeze gently blew and the sun kept them comfortably warm. The Darrells made an appearance soon after they sat down to eat, making them laugh. Josh wondered if they'd smelled the food all the way from Quail Run, where they seemed to spend most of their daylight hours.

Morgan wouldn't give them human food so they didn't beg. They just stretched out on the warm tiles in the sun to watch them eat. Their pointed and alert ears up, their deep brown eyes switched back and forth from one human to the other as if they were not only listening to their conversation, but understanding it completely.

Morgan was feeling relaxed. It occurred to her as they sat there that she'd been feeling tense and stressed a bit about work until Josh arrived. She now realized he had a calming effect on her. He was very patient with her too. It must've been interesting watching him being raised in a house with a loving family around him, most of which were female. Morgan wondered if that was why he was able to be so patient with her.

Josh barely noticed their slide into their peaceful quietness. He felt relaxed sitting there with her. He drank some more wine and grabbed another roll and used it to wipe up some leftover sauce on his plate. He wasn't sure what she put in her sauce exactly that made it so different, but it was delicious. He thought about a second helping as he ate the rest of the roll.

He looked at the mountains around them, dotted with a mixture of natural fauna. It was so peaceful out here, but it wasn't just the area. It was her. Whenever he was around her, he just felt more complete. He felt whole. When he was home alone now, he often found himself wondering about her, and what she was doing. Now and then, he even felt a little lonely, which he had never felt before.

"What's on your mind?" he asked her as he sipped his wine.

She looked over at him, wondering how honest she should be. She decided to just say what she was feeling. "I was thinking it's really nice having you here. Anytime I've felt anxious about something, and you've shown up, I've calmed right down. You're good for me," she admitted seriously.

She looked at him for another moment before saying, "Before you came along, I was fine, good, and even great. But try as I might, it's hard now to remember what I was doing, and how I was, before you came into my life. It just feels like you've always been there. The changes are so subtle over the months they practically go unnoticed. Isn't that odd?"

Josh's heart glowed. Reaching over to run his fingers over her hand, he admitted to her, "I was thinking somewhat along the same lines. About how peaceful it is here, especially with you. And how when I'm home now, sometimes I feel lonely because you're not there. I've never really felt lonely at my house before.

"Most of the time, I couldn't wait to get home to the solitude so I could *be* alone. But that's changed since I met you. I mean, I still enjoy being alone. But it's different now."

He gazed at her mountains while he thought about it all for a minute. "So I make you calm, and you make me anxious and lonely." He smiled when he heard her chuckle.

"I do what I can." She smiled at him as she picked up her wine glass. She sipped some before twirling the wine and watching it spin inside the delicate glass.

He continued after a moment of watching her, "I also have the same thoughts as you. That life as I knew it was going along just great. Then one day, our two lives collided, and now here we are. Isn't it weird to think this time last year we were strangers? We wouldn't have known each other if we passed the other on the street in town. Maybe we even have, but see? We didn't know it. Just look at what we'd be missing out on."

"Maybe it was just not our time *to* meet until recently." Morgan tore open a warm roll. "Going from strangers to being a couple is interesting, isn't it?" She studied him as she chewed. "You're learning so much about this new person in your life, but yet you're also learning about yourself. Even seeing how you're changing, and most times hardly even noticing you *have* until it just hits you one day. Because on a day-to-day basis, nothing really seems to be different. But now when we look back, a whole *lot* has changed.

"It makes you wonder why you didn't change for the better before. And you also begin making compromises, many times hardly realizing that you are. And if it's for the right person, making those compromises really isn't even a big deal. You just do it. Everything changes—how you look at things, do things, think about things. It's not just about you anymore."

"Love changes everything?" he asked quietly.

Morgan quickly looked up, and their eyes locked. Her breath got stuck somewhere in her throat. She felt his hand tighten on hers just a bit. She answered quietly, "Yes, it does."

He leaned closer to her over the patio table, the two German Shepherds watching with acute interest with their alert and all-knowing eyes. With a soft conviction in his voice, he said, "I love you, Morgan. I've loved you from pretty much the very beginning. But even more so now that I've grown to know you. The real you."

Her eyes glistened with sudden tears.

The real you. She was real to him. Who she was now was real to him.

Should she risk it? *Could* she?

Speaking softly but with confidence, she finally said what she'd held inside, wanting to be sure of it herself. Once she said it, it could change everything. "You do? That's good to know because I love you, too, Josh. More and more every single day."

They smiled at each other, both of their faces glowing. Pulling on her hand to get her up, he stood up with her. Pulling each other close, they sealed their love with a tender kiss as her guard dogs looked on, wagging their tails.

Chapter 30

Late November

"I THINK WE SHOULD call her to let her know. She needs the closure of this case. The last I heard she was doing well for herself, but it's been a major ordeal for her."

Agent Jerrod Landon advised, "She deserves to know the truth. To get some closure, and to be able to move on. Of course, we still have time to call her. Maybe we should just wait until we get a little closer?"

Agent Nick Malone was seated in his chair, elbows resting on his paper-covered desk as he leaned forward. "I agree something could still go wrong, some technicality we missed. We've been very careful and have solid evidence. But what if we get her hopes up, just to have something unforeseen happen and have her crashing again?

"Besides, I don't know if I'd want to do this one over the phone. She deserves to have this done in a more personal way. The bigger issue to keep in mind is she doesn't even know we found her. No, we *must* do this one in person. And we need someone she knows informing her. How's our contact doing out there? When was the last time we checked in with Miles?"

"He called in a few months ago. He said she's dealing with it, has made big improvements and headway. But he also doesn't believe she can really move forward until she has the closure. It's hard on family and relatives when they don't have it."

Tapping his ankle with the file folder he was holding, he thought for a moment. "We could just pass along all the information to Miles, and he could tell her. She could make a decision from there. If she wanted to come back for the trial, she could. If not, we could at least let her know how it ends.

"One way or another, she needs to be allowed to make her own decision on how she wants to handle it. We still have until at least spring to make a decision. That's still a long way off."

Nick agreed. "Yeah, it is. The trial is set for the beginning of April. It's almost December now, so that gives us about five months. But news like this is going to take some time to adjust to. It's bound to rip open old memories and emotions.

"I think we should call Miles now. Bring him up to speed on the case, and see how he'd suggest handling it. He knows her better than anybody else. Why don't you call him, and run it by him? Let me know what he thinks."

"I'll go call him now. I'll get back to you once I talk with him." Jerrod stood up, picking up the thick file folders on the desk, adding them to his own.

Walking out the door and down the pristine tiled floor toward his own office, he both dreaded and looked forward to making this phone call. He looked forward to it because he and a few selected others had worked very hard to bring this felon down. They did every possible move by the book to avoid any type of mistrial, or losing on a technicality.

But the agent also dreaded making this call, knowing it'd re-open the deep, gashing wounds on a woman. A woman who'd been trying valiantly to pick up the pieces of her shattered life, and make a new one all alone.

IT WAS HIS DAY off, and he was comfortable in his recliner, reading a suspense thriller while nursing a cold beer. He'd just flipped the page in a gripping scene when he heard his phone ring softly.

Initially, he decided to just ignore it—there was a reason his ringer was turned down after all—but then thought better of it. Marking his page, he set down the book to pick up his phone. He glanced at the Caller ID. It showed a missed call with an unlisted, restricted number message.

He quickly dialed a number from memory. "Hello, this is Miles. I just received a call and missed answering it."

He gave them the secure information requested to verify his identity. He waited a brief moment until a familiar voice came on the line. "This is Trapper."

"Hey, Trapper. It's Miles here. Has something happened?"

As Miles listened to the person speaking on the other end, he couldn't believe what he was hearing. After all these years, they had him. He sat there in stunned disbelief as Jerrod

Landon, code name Trapper, explained the particulars, laying everything out for him. He never interrupted as he listened to his fellow agent.

Agent Landon ended with more than one question. They were questions Miles could hardly answer at that precise moment. "How do you want to handle this? Do you think she'll want to come to the trial? Or will she just want to know what happens?"

"She'll want to know. She *needs* to know. There's no doubt about that in my mind. The questions are *how* and *when* though. I'll sit her down, and tell her myself when it's just the two of us, and we're secure."

Jerrod understood. "I know this is a difficult decision. You've been closer to her than anyone we could ever have found for her. I'm personally worried she won't trust you again when she learns you've been working with us. Or rather, *are* one of us. Or does she know already?"

He answered quietly, "No, she doesn't know, or even suspects anything at all. I'm sure I would've picked up on it if she did. She'll feel betrayed, I'm afraid. This will be a huge blow for her to absorb. When she finds out about me, well, our dynamic will undergo a radical shift. I can't see how it wouldn't."

Jerrod sympathized with his fellow agent. He said, "We never expected you two to become so close, Miles. It's good that you did, of course, as she needed a true friend and that extra safety measure. But it does present new obstacles we never foresaw. I'm sorry about that. I really am."

He paused before offering another option, "How about this? To keep your cover, we could send someone else to her. She need never know about you. She'll need you when she hears all of this. And if you're a part of her issue, who will she be able to go to for support? It'd be easier, wouldn't it? After she's told, you're still there for her in the same role."

For what may be the first time in his life, he was completely unsure about the best course to take. Normally everything seemed so naturally easy for him to do. But this was very different. He didn't want to lose her. What would happen if she couldn't accept it all? He knew she depended on him. And as Trapper asked, who could she go to? No one knew her situation except him.

"Trapper, let me think about this for a bit, okay? We could have another agent tell her to keep my cover, but I feel that's wrong. My gut doesn't like that option at all. Besides, if she ever found out the truth about me, *that* would make it all a thousand times worse.

She'd wonder why I didn't tell her face to face about the most important thing in her life. She's going to go through a whirlwind of emotions hearing all of this.

"I need to run this through my head first to analyze all options and possible endings. It's different since I'm here on the ground with her, not in an office thousands of miles away. Once I figure it out, I'll let you know. I'm assuming Malone knows you've called me? Who else?"

"Yes, he knows. We discussed it in his office just a while ago. No one else knows I'm calling you though. He wants me to tell him what you decide to do. He'll pass it up the ladder once you decide what route to take. No one knows her identity still but for a few of us. And you know who we are. We just can't take any chances with her, so obviously none of us want to expose her. We don't have intel on everyone involved, but we do on this one. Maybe we don't even need to worry about that anymore. But it still pays to be careful."

"I can't believe this is actually happening. I need to deal with it myself. Just give me the time I need to work it out. I'll get in touch with you when I'm ready, okay? Just don't have anyone else leak the news." A sudden thought came to him. "What about the media? Have they gotten wind of all this yet?"

"No. We've been really careful about it so it won't compromise the trial. We're feeding information and evidence to the LEOs since they'll be the ones actually handling the trial to keep the Agency out of the limelight. Being a covert agency doesn't work if everyone knows there is one."

"True enough. There are still crime news reporters out there, Trap. It wouldn't surprise me at all to hear one or more check the court dockets for stories. Most of them aren't any good and will just sensationalize something for ratings. And with everything online nowadays, once it's out there, it can't be roped back in. This could become a nightmare for her to deal with just in that aspect."

Both were silent for a moment, both thinking. A sudden thought popped into Mile's head, and it made a ball of dread form in his belly. "What about the family? They could stir this up like a hornet's nest."

"We haven't contacted them yet. None of us even want to, so we're dragging our feet on it. The LEOs would be the ones to actually do it, but hopefully they'll wait until the last minute."

"Thankfully her cover has never been blown. It should be strong enough for this." But *was* her cover strong enough to avoid an onslaught of media attention?

"Yeah, her cover is rock solid. It'd be nearly impossible, if not impossible, for the media to track her down." Jerrod paused, hoping he was right. "He did a great job with that." Both men understood who he was referring to without naming him.

"Well, you take the time you need to do this, Miles. Just fill us in so we know what's happening. If anything happens on our end, I'll inform you." The agent leaned forward in his chair before adding, "And Miles? Good luck, to both of you. I mean that sincerely."

"Thanks, Trapper. We'll be needing more than luck to get through this, I'm afraid. But we will. I just don't know how to start it. Thanks for the update." He hung up his phone, placing it on the end table beside him. He got up and walked to his window, looking out as a myriad of thoughts raced through his mind.

How was he to tell his best friend that not only was her husband's murderer caught and set for trial, but that he'd been working undercover with the Agency all these years? And that he knew of her cover even before she broke down and told him that long ago night? He was suddenly feeling a great pressing weight upon his wide shoulders.

As he looked out the window, he pictured every awful scenario in his head of what could happen when he told Morgan the news. Would she fire him on the spot? Would she ever trust him again? Would she trust *anyone* again? How *could* she? Was their friendship strong enough to withstand this brutal storm of truth and consequence? She was just now making strides forward, taking chances.

She had Josh now, but only to an extent. Josh knew nothing of her past, so could she even go to him? Of course not. What if she told him? How would Josh react learning that the woman he was getting to know now wasn't who she *really* was? Was he strong enough to handle it all? Could he be trusted to know?

His heart pounded in his chest as he tried to imagine living away from Harmony Hills, his best friend Morgan, the friends he'd made, and the life he loved here. Where would he go? What would he do? He'd been trying to do more than undercover work with his life, and he'd found a new life out here in the wild desert of Arizona. He'd known this day *might* come, but he'd just never planned on what he'd do if it actually did.

He'd never planned on becoming such a close and personal friend of the one he was keeping an eye on. He'd do anything for Morgan to keep her safe and happy. He'd promised himself to never let her down. But how could the news he needed to tell her do anything but that?

As Ty's future turned bleak and utterly unpredictable in every way, he returned to his recliner and sat down. He was running options through his mind when his phone rang again.

Chapter 31

Mid-December

MORGAN COULDN'T WAIT UNTIL tomorrow. Ty had said he needed to speak to her after work the next day when she wasn't so busy. With his recent distracted nature—which was highly unusual for him—she decided to get it over with.

After she'd showered and grabbed a bite to eat, she drove over to Ty's to see what he wanted to talk about. If it was just that he wanted to talk, she would've simply waited. If he'd just been distracted, she would've waited on that too. Actually, she *had* been doing just that for weeks now. But Ty was now both distracted *and* wanted to talk to her.

She couldn't shake the feeling something was wrong. Her first thought was he'd found a new job and was giving her notice. Just thinking about that made her heart twist, her stomach tighten, and tears spring to her eyes. She couldn't lose Ty. He'd been her longest, closest, best friend, and was practically her business partner. He wouldn't leave here, or her, would he? she wondered. She felt anxiety building inside of her.

Was it about Josh? Had Ty learned something about him and didn't want to tell her? That thought scared her. She'd already put her heart on the chopping block.

Maybe he just wanted Christmas or New Year's off. He hadn't gone to visit his family since the summer, so maybe he wanted the whole week off. He knew how swamped they were at this time of year, so maybe he wasn't sure about asking her. She'd let him off if he wanted to go. It'd be harder without him, but they could do it. A few other members of her staff were already taking off, but she could handle it all for a week or so. Morgan knew his family was close, and he'd be willing to pay for a last-minute plane ticket to see them over the holidays.

She sat there running endless scenarios through her head. Finally, she couldn't stand it anymore. She'd just drive herself crazy and analyze it to death.

She grabbed her phone, truck keys, and purse. She'd just go over there and ask him herself. Her gut feeling told her it wasn't a conversation to be done over the phone. Leaving on her hallway light, she set the alarm and pulled the locked door firmly closed behind her.

TY HAD TAKEN A hot shower, eaten dinner, and was relaxed in what he referred to as his civilian clothes—which was basically anything that wasn't a pair of dirty blue jeans and dusty boots. Tonight, he was just in a pair of sweats and a t-shirt, looking like a guy who was more than ready to chill out in his warm home on a cold night. Hearing his doorbell chime, he wondered who it was.

He went to his door and looked out the window beside it. He automatically opened his door to let her in. His heart was suddenly beating faster, even as his skin felt suddenly chilled. And it wasn't from the chilly night air as he opened the door for her.

"Hey Morgan. Why are you here?"

"Well, I have a feeling there's something important you'd like to talk to me about. It was driving me insane wondering what it could be. So I thought I'd just come over now and see what's what. You haven't been acting like yourself, and that makes me wonder what's going on because something obviously is."

As her eyes roamed the room, they finally came back to rest on his face. No doubt about it, she thought. He wasn't acting like himself. She could also feel it in the air.

He asked, "You want some iced tea? It's all I got that's non-alcoholic. Or water. This is all you can have since you're driving." And with what he had to tell her, they'd both better be sober and alert, he thought to himself.

"Sure, tea's fine."

She walked into his living room, again looking around for a possible clue. She turned around when Ty came in with two glasses of tea. He handed her one, and then set his own down on his coffee table. Ty motioned for her to sit down as he did. Morgan's stomach began twisting in knots as she sat on the couch beside him. She put her tea down beside his. And waited.

Ty just sat there, wondering how to start. He'd rehearsed every opening he could think of, but none were any easier than the one before. Just as he was about to speak, Morgan jumped in.

"You're not leaving me, are you? Have you found another job? Are you moving away?"

The look on her face broke Ty's heart. She looked scared, heartbroken, and crushed all at once. He grabbed her hands, held them tightly. "No. *No,* Morgan. I'm not leaving you. Not for another job. Not for moving away. I'm here to stay." Almost as an afterthought, he added, "I haven't been looking for another job. I wouldn't know what else I'd want to do."

She believed him. See? she reprimanded herself. She was working herself into an awful frenzy for no reason.

Ty held onto her hands still, looking down at them. He had to tell her. He simply had no other choice. He refused to let go of her hands. Partly because he didn't want her storming out the door before she could think straight, and equally importantly, he needed the contact.

He cleared his throat, took a deep breath and slowly released it. Looking directly into her trusting green eyes, Ty took the plunge.

"The truth is, Morgan, after you hear what I have to tell you, you may *want* me to leave. I'm sincerely praying that you won't, but if you decide it'd be better for you, we'll go from there. But I want you to know, first and foremost, I *am* your best friend, and I love you. And I've only done what I was hoping was the best for you. And I'm always, *always,* going to be here for you. You can still trust me even though I'm very much afraid you won't be able to. But it's a risk I must take."

"You're not in love, like in *love* with me, are you?" Morgan asked. It was the only thing she could think of. "It's not Josh, is it? You're not jealous of him, are you? I thought you guys liked each other and were friends." Her voice was full of worry. "Or did you find out something about him I need to know?"

Ty shook his head. "No, I'm not in love with you. I love you to pieces, but not in that way. Besides, you have Josh now. And I think you two are great together. I couldn't have picked a better guy for you. Since I'm a guy, I can give you the guy's view on him. He won't mess with, or around, on you. Remember, he's the good-guy type. The one who rides in on a gallant white stallion saving the day."

He tried to smile at her. He knew she wasn't really the fairy-tale ending kind of woman. After what she'd been through, how could she be?

"Ty, then *what* is wrong? You're scaring me. Can't you just say it?" Morgan implored him with those green eyes of hers. "Are you... sick?"

"No, nothing like that." Still holding onto her hands, he said softly, "As long as we've known each other, we've always been honest to a fault with the other. But there's one thing that I never told you, and it's a whopper that will test your trust in me. I hope our trust, love, and friendship in each other is strong enough to withstand this.

"I've never lied to you, but there *is* something about me you don't know. I just never told you because it wasn't supposed to *be* known. But now I *have* to tell you, and it's honest to God the hardest and scariest thing I've ever had to do in my entire life. And that's really saying something if you only knew. I need you to hear me out, all right?"

Morgan sat there, her back ramrod straight, her hands still held firmly in his. She waited, having no choice in the matter. She felt his strong grip on her hands getting tighter.

"Remember when we first met, and then later on when you told me about Shane? And then about what all you'd gone through after he was killed? That he *had* been killed?" Ty looked at her, trying to read her expression.

Morgan slowly nodded yes. If it had to do with Shane, this couldn't be good news at all. But *why* would this have *anything* to do with Shane? she wondered.

"Well, the truth is I already knew about Shane."

"*What?*" Morgan's perplexed voice was barely above a whisper. "What are you saying? *How* could've you already known? That'd be impossible. I did what Shane told me to do when I left. *No one* knows... So you couldn't... How could you..." Her voice sputtered in her confusion.

Taking the final step off that cliff he was on was one of the hardest steps he'd ever taken. An old friend had once told him, "The first step is always the hardest." This was more than just a step though. It was a leap of faith.

"The truth is, Morgan, I knew horses when I applied to work for you—but not like I do now. And I *am* your friend, and I truly care about and love you." Ty felt he couldn't stress that enough.

"But my other line of work before I walked through your door was quite different. I came here for *you*. I came here to watch over you, ready to protect you. I'm also an undercover agent like your husband Shane was.

"In short, I know who you really are. You're really Natasha. Natasha Borden. And Shane and I? Well, we're from the same Agency."

Chapter 32

MORGAN SAT THERE IN absolute, stunned silence. She couldn't move, or even think. She just sat there, still as a stone statue, scared to death to even move a muscle.

Ty's heart was twisted so much at that moment, it actually ached. He waited for her to react. The shock was written across her face. But it was more than just shock, which would've been huge on its own. There was also disbelief, denial, anger, betrayal, and hurt running across her face and shooting from those expressive green eyes of hers. Enormous emotions each on their own. And she was feeling them all.

It took a minute for her brain to engage, for her to be able to think, to comprehend. *I know who you really are. You're really Natasha. Natasha Borden.* He knew who she was. He knew her *real* name! She'd never told anybody her real name since she disappeared years ago. Not Ty. Not *anyone*.

Her hands began shaking. She looked down at them, still being held firmly in his. Hers were shaking so badly, they made his shake too. She felt dizzy, and she swayed backwards for a second. She barely felt Ty's hand move to steady her. He left his hand on her shoulder.

It took her a couple of tries to get the words out. Her throat was so dry, she couldn't even swallow. "What? *What* did you just say? You're an *agent?* You've been pretending to be my best friend, but you're really an *agent?*"

Ty could barely hear her, but he could hear the anger building in her voice. He instinctively knew what she was asking. She was asking for everything.

He again took hold of her hands, knowing she could strike out at him. But he also wanted the contact between them again, to keep a connection with her. When she tried to pull her hands away from his, he held on. She fought him, hard.

"Morgan, *wait!* Morgan, *listen* to me! I need you to listen to me. It's very important." He held on while she continued to struggle to get free of him. He was struggling to hold on to her, hoping to not bruise her.

Knowing he'd taught her a number of self-defense techniques, he also watched for any of those moves coming his way at the same time. She was quite strong and could inflict some major damage, especially if she wasn't thinking straight. And right now, she was far from being able to think straight. When he saw one coming, he blocked her.

"NO! No. You *lied* to me! You're a *liar*. You're a liar! The worst kind of liar! *How* could you do this to me? How *could* you? I trusted you. I *trusted* you! I'm leaving. Now. Right now." Her voice went from a low hoarse tone, to a yell, to a scream, back down to the hoarse. It was getting choppier. "Get away from me! Stay away from me. You aren't my friend! You're a liar! How could..." A look of pure panic crossed her face.

Ty was immediately worried she was hyperventilating as she was now gasping for air. Ty felt like his soul had just been ripped from his body. He called upon everything he had to stay calm and focused for her.

"Breathe, baby. Look at me. *Breathe.* Slowly. Watch me..." Ty pursed his lips, inhaling through his nose before slowly exhaling through his lips. "Follow me, Morgan. Slowly... Slowly... There you go. In through your nose... Out through your mouth. Good... Good." Ty coached her, relief shooting through him as he saw the panic leave her face. "There you go, baby. Just breathe..."

It took a few minutes for her to calm herself and begin to breathe normally although it was still coming in slight hitches of breaths. Her body shook like she was having chills.

Ty heard her tormented sobs begin as he laid his hand on her shoulder. He moved his hand to her upper back, rubbing it in a soothing motion. She needed to release some of her emotions now, and he was going to give her all the time she needed. He fought the tears in his own eyes as she continued to cry, shake, and take great gulps of air. He held her tightly against him as he kept rubbing her back, arms, and shoulders in the only source of comfort he could offer her. He waited a long time before her sobs lessened, and she began to quiet.

He grabbed some napkins from his coffee table so she could wipe her eyes and blow her nose. He kept his arms around her, holding her close. She was stiff as a surfboard against him, but he felt her ever so slowly begin to relax.

Finally, he said softly, "Morgan, sweetheart, I never lied to you. I know that's a moot point right now, but you were never to know. Our becoming friends like we did... That *wasn't* planned. But now I wouldn't give up your friendship for the world. I need you to believe in that, and in me.

"I know this is hard. I really do. It's been breaking my heart trying to figure out how to tell you. The longer I put it off, the worse it got. Then I hoped I just never *would* have to tell you. There wasn't any reason to tell you before, but now I have to."

He slowly got down on the floor in front of her. He raised her chin, then gently cupped her face with his warm hands before he spoke to her. Her tears silently streamed down her cheeks now. Her eyes looked devastated and deeply wounded. He reached over to grab more napkins from his coffee table, handing them to her. She blew her nose again and looked anywhere but at him. He leaned forward, placed a tender kiss on her forehead.

"You need to hear me out although I know you don't want to. I've been trying for weeks to figure out how to do this, but there's no easy way." Ty wiped her streaming tears away with his fingers. His own eyes were misty. He knew the hurt he'd just caused.

Morgan was far from wanting to have anything to do with Ty at that moment. She would've just stood up and left if her legs were strong enough to support her weight. Right now, they were weak and shaky. She absentmindedly wondered if she was going into shock because she couldn't get her legs or hands to stop shaking.

"How do I *know* I can trust you? How do I *know* you're one of the good guys?" Morgan finally whispered in anguish.

Resting his hands on her legs, Ty drew upon details from a long-ago conversation. "You and Shane... You two had a password. A code phrase. He told me what it was one time. Do you remember it? I'm sure you do."

She nodded, unable to speak. Her heart pounded painfully as she waited.

"It was Tomorrow," Ty said softly. "His Tomorrow. It was what he called you."

She let out a small gasp at his words. Her instinct for self-preservation, for her very survival, was telling her to get as far away from him as she could, as fast as she could. But he knew her code name. Only Shane knew that. This could only mean Shane and Ty *had* known each other. And not only that, but that her husband had trusted Ty Stanton so deeply, with no reservations, he actually shared her code name with him. But *why* would Shane have done that?

While her instinct was to run, her broken and smashed heart was urging her to stay and listen. But her mind was also racing in another direction. She *couldn't* run now. She was the owner of Harmony Hills, and she had a home here. What about her horses? Her dogs? How could she get another new identity?

And now there was Josh. She *knew* she shouldn't have gotten involved with him for this very reason. She *knew* it. Was she going to have to run again? What would Josh think?

What would he do? He'd be so hurt! Tears ran down her face as panic and hurt rushed through her.

Her breath got choppy again, and her eyes showed her fear. Again, Ty ordered her to take deep breaths and release them slowly. The shock of his statements was slow to wear off. All she could do now was stare at him out of pain-filled eyes.

He tenderly brushed her hair away from her face. He shouldn't have allowed himself to get so attached to her, but it'd been impossible to stop it. Didn't Shane say that's exactly what had happened to him? He just couldn't stop himself? Now Ty understood.

For him, it was her inner strength, drive, determination, courage, ethics, love for animals, compassion, and humor that had sucked him in all those years ago. His respect for her had only grown over the years. She'd given him her trust, friendship, and full access to her life. And he now repaid her with betrayal although his intentions had been pure. He had a great love for her. There was just something about her that pulled him in.

He couldn't stand to see those expressive eyes of hers boring into his anymore. He gently yet firmly enveloped her into a hug even when she fought to get away. But her fight was weak and short-lived. Soon her arms came around him, holding on for dear life. Ty held onto her tightly, scared of letting her go. He was scared she'd never let him near her again if he broke contact with her. He heard her soft sobs start again and felt her tears on his shoulder through his thin shirt as he held her closely against him.

When her sobs died away, he got up to get her some tissues. He sat down again on the couch beside her. She was still shaking. She blew her nose again, wiped her eyes and cheeks before she drank some of her tea. Finally, she leaned back and waited for him to explain.

He drank some of his own tea while he decided how best to tell her. He finally said, "I'll give you the summary version first. Afterwards, I'll answer any and all questions you have, all right?" At her nod, he wrapped his arms back around her, feeling they both needed the contact. When she leaned against him, he softly kissed her hair.

As he held her, he said, "While I'm an active agent now, I also resigned years ago in order to look for you. It was months after Shane had been killed before I even heard about it because I was in deep on another assignment.

"Once I did, and then found out you'd disappeared, I recalled all the conversations he and I had shared. There weren't many, but they all seemed to be for a purpose. I felt like Shane told me what he did just in case something ever happened to him. I don't know if he actually expected me to step up and find you or not, but I that's exactly what I did.

"When you disappeared, no one could find you. I used the resources the Agency had on the down-low to get a jumpstart on my personal quest, and then I left. I had to use our past conversations, what I'd previously learned and eliminated, and my own talents in order to locate you.

"It was like this all-consuming need to find you, to make sure you were all right. I was basically obsessed in finding you, sweetheart. It's the only way I can say it. It still took me time to find you, and part of it was probably dumb luck. But I did it for Shane, for you, maybe even myself.

"When I miraculously found you, I couldn't believe it. I didn't know if you even needed protection, but I wasn't about to leave you. I needed to process the situation, get my bearings. I watched you for a while to get the lay of the land. That's about the time I came up with the wild idea to apply for a job with you, which you gave me practically on the spot.

"The Agency contacted me about the second year I was working for you for another assignment, but I turned it down. Then they learned I was working for you, as in Natasha. I still don't know how. I never ever reveal any information on those I protect to this day. And I never once even mentioned where I worked to them. They found out somehow on their own. Maybe I should ask them about that someday.

"They then offered me the opportunity to protect you as an active agent. Originally, I turned them down, but they insisted. I finally decided it might be beneficial in case something came up so we'd have their protection and full resources. So I came back on. But I'd told them I will only do it for you, not to be sent on any other assignments. They easily agreed, which made me suspicious. However, they've kept their word."

Rubbing his thumb over her knuckles, he eased into his next bombshell. "A few weeks ago I got a call. They had an update for me to do with as I saw fit. I knew immediately what I wanted to do, *needed* to do, but doing it was another thing. And here we are tonight, getting it done."

Ty gently moved away from her so he could look her in her eyes. "According to them, they caught Shane's murderer. They want to know if you want to go to his trial."

Chapter 33

MORGAN STILL DIDN'T KNOW what to do. It'd been over a week since Ty had confided in her about who he really was, and about the upcoming trial. She could hardly deny she was distracted, but she simply couldn't show it. Now that she understood what Ty had been pondering on his own during those weeks, she was currently in the same predicament. It was just worse for her since it was *all* staggering news.

Alone that next day in the safety and comfort of her own home, Morgan had curled up on her couch and replayed her life in her mind. Some things seemed completely different to her now. Her viewpoint was now shaken. She didn't know who to trust, or what to believe. By the end of that night, after a couple of naps during the day to relieve her aching head, she'd come to a few conclusions about her life.

But only one she could do anything about.

The most important conclusion to her was that Ty had been, and still was, her best friend. And she *could* still trust him. It didn't mean she wasn't deeply hurt, and believed all would go back as it was before instantly, if ever. But she could easily see it from his viewpoint. They'd discussed his situation, and why he hadn't told her sooner in-depth, and it all made sense. She couldn't fault him and his reasoning.

Ty was worth the effort to do her part to rebuild their relationship. His code of honor ran deep. And he'd never intentionally hurt or betray her for his own gain. She knew him well enough to know that was factual.

When she recalled the tough times they'd gone through together over the years, knowing he could've easily bailed on her at any time but never once did, she knew he was there for *her*. He *wasn't* there because he was being paid to stay, whether by her or the Agency. It was always his own decision. Ty stuck to her like human superglue, and she loved him for it. It was just going to take them both some time to start their relationship on new ground, that's all.

Morgan had yet to tell Josh anything, mainly because she wasn't sure what to tell him. Honestly, she *couldn't* tell him anything. There were suddenly so many emotional entanglements to work through, and major decisions to be made very soon. She just needed to take her time in order to protect herself and her life. Both of them. She just needed time, but she was scared because she knew she didn't have nearly enough of it.

She was cleaning and re-organizing the back area adjacent to the tack room while Ty was in the office managing the trail rides. They had to work together and act like nothing at all was between them. The tension Morgan felt at times was gradually lessening. They were finding their common ground again, a little at a time.

When she vaguely heard the screen door on the other side of the wall open again and gently bang close, she assumed it was Ty coming out. She simply continued to sort items on the shelves on autopilot, lost in thought. She nearly jumped out of her skin when she felt two strong hands on her shoulders. Startled, she turned and saw Josh's smiling face. She smiled weakly when he leaned down and kissed the top of her head.

"Hey, sweetheart. I didn't mean to startle you. I'm sorry." Trying to control his smile, Josh massaged her shoulders for a moment.

"I can see how sorry you are just by looking at you. You're lucky I didn't karate chop you in half!" She tried to speak calmly while her heart still raced in her chest. "How'd you know where to find me?"

"Ty told me. He also said it was the perfect spot for making out."

"He did not!" She laughed and shook her head.

"It was implied."

"So why are you still standing there?" she teased, her eyes sparkling with humor.

He grinned as he took the brushes from her hands, tossed them on the shelf and grabbed her. Her laugh was cut off as he crushed his hot mouth to hers, walking her back against the wall to press against her. Her pulse skyrocketed as his hands cruised from her waist up her sides, then around to cup her breasts. She arched into his hands, a little moan escaping. His mouth slanted over hers again and again as his tongue dueled with hers. Her arms wrapped around his neck, pulling him even closer as she returned his fervor. Her breath rushed out of her lungs when his hot mouth moved to her neck.

His hands took hers, raised them over her head as his mouth returned to hers. She ran her tongue inside his mouth as she squeezed his fingers with hers. His soft groan as he pressed against her again made her blood boil. His hands released hers and ran down her arms, then over her shoulders before framing her face as their kiss went on and on. She wrapped her arms around him again and just held on tight.

With effort, Josh pulled back just enough to see the passion firing from her smoldering green eyes into his. He couldn't resist when she pulled him back for another scorching kiss. He felt her hands run firmly across his back.

He finally pulled back again, trying to regain his sensibilities. His hands were now against the wall on either side of her head as he tried to control his breathing. Morgan was grateful she had a wall to lean against to keep herself upright. She slid her fingers into his back pockets because she swore she didn't have the strength to hold them up on her own.

She smiled at the thought when she rested her head against the wall. They made eye contact, neither able to speak yet. Both worked on controlling their own breathing which was still far above normal. He leaned down again and nuzzled her neck before placing a soft kiss at the curve of her shoulder.

Softly, she asked, "You know what just happened?"

He replied just as softly, "What?"

"We just proved Ty right."

JOSH LEANED AGAINST THE wall as she finished up her project. He could tell she'd been at it for a little while. He said, "Doing something like this is just what I'd do if I was thinking about something. With me, it's normally working with wood or something. What about you? Are you cleaning because it needs it, or because you're thinking?"

"Both really, but more so the thinking part. I'll clean house, or do yard work too. You should see the house right now. It's spotless. I get a lot of free-thinking in when I work on stuff like this. Same as when I drive."

He nodded as he wondered what she was thinking about. It had to be pretty significant for her to clean the house like that, then do this project as she still worked. And there'd been an extra kick in that kiss... Why? What made her look the way she did?

She looked tired. He knew better than to say that, though, as his mom had taught him as a young man it was the last thing a woman needed to be told. Why tell her something she already knew? It was also disrespectful and insensitive because she probably looked that way for good reason. Possibly because he wasn't doing his fair share of the workload.

If so, telling her that would only lead to resentment and arguments. It could also hurt her feelings.

So while he wouldn't mention it, he *could* wonder about it.

She broke his thoughts when she said, "I'm almost done here. After this, I was going back to the house as I have the rest of the day off. Ty and I split the day. I took the morning shift, so he actually just got here. Did you want to come up with me, go for a ride, or hang out down here with him? You haven't gone on a ride for a while."

"I don't have any plans other than to spend some time with my girl." He watched as she closed the cabinet doors. "You cooking lunch? Or it could be my treat, unless we want to order something."

"Either. If you're hungry now, I could probably find some leftovers for you. I'm sure there's something up there that needs to be eaten before it goes bad."

He grinned and teased primly, "My goodness! That's very thoughtful of you. Am I the last stop before The Darrells would get it if they were allowed people food?"

"Sorry. I guess that came out all wrong, didn't it?" She laughed before she leaned up and placed a soft kiss on his mouth. Then another. "Why don't you go chat with Ty for a while so I can get cleaned up some? Then we'll go to the house. That good with you?"

"Sure."

They walked toward the office together, with her veering off to the restroom.

Josh found Ty sitting at Morgan's desk, just looking out the window. He was drumming his fingers on the desk, apparently absorbed in deep thoughts of his own. Josh wasn't sure if Ty even knew he was in the room. Just as he was getting ready to speak, Ty turned around.

"What're you guys up to today?" Ty was leaning back comfortably in Morgan's padded desk chair, looking as at home there as Morgan did.

"She's cleaning up, then we're getting some lunch. One of us may cook something at the house. Do you want us to bring you down something?" Josh sat down on the stool in front of the desk so he could face Ty. He wondered why Ty looked tired and distracted himself.

"No, she already brought down some leftovers for me. Thanks though. She told me she was just going to throw it out if somebody didn't eat it, so she thought of me." Ty smiled. "I'm just wondering how long it was sitting in her fridge before she remembered it was there. It crossed my mind she may want to poison me for something I did, so I smelled it after she left the room. It seems okay. Don't tell her I said that though. I'll deny it."

Laughing, Josh shook his head. "I won't say a word."

They were getting pretty animated about their sports players and teams when Morgan finally walked in. She leaned against the counter as she waited for them to wind down.

Ty got a look of mischief in his eyes as he glanced at Morgan then back over to Josh. Rubbing his hands together casually, he said, "I heard an interesting story lately, Josh. It came to my attention that our Morgan here—"

Josh interrupted him. "She's not *our* Morgan. She's *mine* now. Got it?"

Ty suddenly sported a broad smile. Teasing the man glowering at him, he said simply, "She's still mine too. Just differently. Besides, I knew her first."

Josh looked intently at him. "Doesn't matter."

"With all the girls you went out with before her, I think I should still have a claim on her."

"Shut up," Josh said although there was more humor than heat in his voice. "And that's not how it works anyway."

Both Ty and Morgan laughed at his discomfort. They both knew he didn't want to be thought of as a player, which they appreciated, of course. But it also didn't mean they couldn't tease him about it from time to time. Josh looked from one to the other, finally giving up and conceding defeat.

Addressing Ty, he said, "You wouldn't think it was so funny if it happened to you. Keep it up, and I'll unblock Elise and send word you're an eligible man. She won't stop, no matter what you say or do."

Ty smiled. "You blocked her?"

"Yeah, I did. I'm not taking any more chances with her." Smiling smugly, he added, "You'll be running away, looking for cover faster than you think."

Both Ty and Morgan laughed again.

Morgan said, "Honey, as a matter of fact, Ty would—"

Ty jumped in to shut her up. "Now then, Morgan, what're you going to feed our Josh? You want your leftovers back?"

She caught the 'our Josh' reference, knowing he was giving a gentle dig at him. Josh shook his head.

She grinned at Ty before answering. "Nah. I'll make something even better for him." She thought of Ty's favorite dessert. "Maybe some of my homemade peach cobbler, fresh from—"

Ty shot a rubber band at her. She squealed as Josh made a dash for the door, grabbing her arm as he passed by her. Laughing, he shoved her out the door. "See ya later, Ty! If she makes some, I'll let ya know." He tossed her coat to her as he shut the door to keep the heat inside.

Ty chuckled when he heard Josh through the closed window. "My kung fu warrior squeals like a girl! I can't believe it."

From the window, Ty watched and smiled when she threatened to karate kick him. Laughing, Josh quickly scooped her up in his arms, tossing her over his shoulder like a bag of feed and smacked her rear-end. He finally let her down so she could walk beside him. She reached over and took his hand.

As they made their way up the hill toward the house, Ty was still smiling. He truly believed that God was looking out for Morgan. She'd told him more than once she felt he'd been a gift from God to help her cope and to live life again. Now watching her with Josh, Ty felt the same applied to this new man who'd recently come into her life.

Morgan didn't believe in organized religions, but she was spiritual. She felt there was a Higher Power that watched over everyone. Blessings would come, and trials would come. But she never complained, or blamed God, when things went wrong. "Without the bad, how could we appreciate and be thankful for the good?" she'd once asked him.

Timing was everything, Ty thought as he sat back down in the chair. She was on the brink of getting closure over Shane at the same time Josh Wright entered her life. And now when she was unexpectedly on shaky ground with him, she had Josh to keep herself steady. How could God *not* be in on this? Ty wondered.

Thinking of what he knew about Josh, he idly wondered what Shane would've thought of him. He had an odd feeling Shane would approve.

Chapter 34

MORGAN HAD MADE UP her mind. The day after Christmas, she took actions that would probably change her life. Having closed the Center for two days to give both staff and horses a well-deserved rest, early that morning she first fed all of the horses before driving the tractor and manure wagon around to clean all of the stalls and pens by herself.

Josh was with Damien working on a project for Laura at their house. Morgan could've gone over there after cleaning the barns, but she decided to take advantage of the time off and being alone.

After she was done at the barns, she headed back to her house and took a long, hot shower. Having made her decision, she called Ty to be sure he was home before she drove over to his house. The closer she got to his house, the more her insides tied in a knot.

Ty opened his door for her before she even rang the doorbell. "How are you feeling about everything?"

"Overwhelmed. Sad. Scared. Unsure. Terrified." She shrugged her shoulders. "That about sums it up."

"Betrayed?" he asked quietly.

She looked into those eyes that she knew so well. She shook her head. "No, not anymore. You were doing it for me, for Shane. What could you gain from it?"

"Looking back, remembering how I couldn't believe I was alone and forgotten so soon after it all happened. Now knowing I wasn't... Because of you?"

Her eyes misted with unshed tears as she said earnestly, "You were there when I needed you. Someone. Anyone. You were there, here, for me. You were, and are, my best friend, Ty. How could I not forgive you when all you ever did was think of me?"

He nodded, looking down to hide his relief at her forgiving him. He took a minute to process that as it was so important for him to hear. When he looked up, he saw the understanding in her eyes. She got up, walked over to him, and made him stand up. She hugged him tightly, just hanging on to him. He did the same, resting his head against her hair.

Still in his arms, she murmured, "Don't get me wrong... I'm still hurting. But I can't separate the hurts inside. Some is from you. Some is from missing Shane. Some is from tearing open my past when I've tried for eight years to let it go. Some knowing I'm going to hurt Josh because of all this, and the uncertainty of how he'll react. All the hurt inside of me is just one big piece of pain." Morgan rubbed his back a few times before she stepped away.

He nodded in understanding, sorrow in his eyes. "I'm sorry for what I caused to hurt you. But I also wouldn't have done it any differently, you know? And that makes me sorry for that too."

"Don't be. I understand, so there's no need for you to feel that way. When I took that day off to analyze it all, I realized that you did the only sensible thing. If I put myself in your shoes, look at it all from your perspective, I can't say I wouldn't have done the same thing myself. And I'm not just saying that to make you feel better. It's the simple truth of the matter.

"I'm sorry I exploded at you and called you a liar. Since I'm not entirely sure what all I said, I just have to offer a blanket apology. Just apply it to whatever you want to..."

"You could've done far worse. And there's no need to apologize to me."

"There is if I value our friendship," she countered.

He gave her a small smile. "Well, let's sit down right here, and you can tell me how much I mean to you then."

She knew he was helping her get back on level ground and smiled back. Yes, this is just one of the many reasons he's my true friend, she thought to herself. He always had a way of smoothing things over, allowing open lines of communication between them. He didn't hold grudges either.

Sitting beside each other on the couch, she said after a while, "This is hard for me to say for a couple of reasons, but I love Josh. I know it seems fast, and I was never expecting it. He's just a phenomenal person. And I know he loves me."

Ty nodded, smiled. "I figured. And I don't judge things like that. You two seem to be a great match. You fit together very well in just about everything from what I can tell. I'm so happy about that, Morg. I really am."

She took a breath before saying, "That being the case, I've come to the conclusion that the only way he and I can move forward is if I tell him." She looked at her confidant, knowing what she was risking. "Everything."

Ty leaned back in thought. "Sweetheart, that's not a good thing to do. And I can't let everyone know I'm an agent. It's far too dangerous—for me, for you, for others I protect." He sighed. "I hate to say it, but I have to. What happens if you two break up? You've known him less than a year. That's not very long. So much could just change, things not even related to what only we know. It's a very big risk."

"I know, but I've thought this through a thousand times. He knows I'm holding back something. Originally I thought maybe we could just build from what we have now, that he'd never know about my former life. Why would he need to know? But then it occurred to me, isn't that secrecy the major issue that you and I just had to resolve? I hate all this secrecy!

"But more importantly, my past is always with me. It *has* come back to affect me over the years. It's back now, and it could again in the future. How could I explain it to him years down the road, when I should've told him already? What if you aren't around then for whatever reason to help me with it?

"Let's say he doesn't take it well at all. Although I'm sure I love him, wouldn't it be better to know this now rather than years later? If things go wrong with him, I'd rather be hurt and break things off now before we go any further in our relationship. What if we ever got married? What if we decided to have kids? And then this all comes up?

"The questions I keep coming back to are always the same two: Does he need to know? and Can we build a life together if he doesn't? He loves me right now for who he met months ago. And you know what? Maybe we *could've* built a life with him not knowing, except for what I said a second ago. But *now*..."

He understood what she was getting at. "But certainly not now because of what I just told you." At her nod, he sighed. He sat there thinking for a minute. "This must mean you want to go to the trial?"

"I think so. I think I need to, but I'm still debating. However, there's no way I'm going to tell the man I love that I'm going out of town for maybe a couple of months, but he can't even know why. At some point, he might find out why.

"Josh isn't stupid, and he doesn't deserve this. Especially not after all the patience he's put into me, and our relationship. He's far too great a person to lie to. And we promised each other, like you and I, to always be honest. No matter what. The trust we have in each other would be destroyed if I don't tell him. We'd be done.

"On top of everything else going on, I don't want to lose Josh because of some old secret that affects me to this day." She looked imploringly at him. "My past has made me who I am right now. It'll always be a part of me. Josh could very possibly be my future. How can we build one together if he's kept in the dark, with only me and you knowing it all?

"What if I told him only my side? To leave your involvement out altogether to keep your cover? There are too many variables to that. He's *still* being left out. And at some point, it's all going to come to a situation where it all clashes.

"At some point, I'm scared we're going to meet like this, he finds out, and wonders if we're having an affair or something. Or someone else sees us and wonders, tells him we're together. Imagine Josh asking me why we were together, and what we talked about. But I can't tell him, and I can't lie to him. That's a horrible situation to be in, Ty."

She sighed, patted his leg before saying, "He trusts us, by the way. He knows I'm over here right now, but obviously not why."

Ty got up to pace the room. It wasn't an easy decision. He looked at her, debating, weighing all the ramifications. He knew she fully understood the situation as she'd been married to Shane and had gone through all of this before. "He means that much to you?"

She nodded, her heart pounding. "Not only do I love him, but I *trust* him. I just don't see him taking our secret and spreading it for all to hear. He seems rock solid to me. After meeting his parents, he seems even more so. And look who he chooses as his friends, like Damien and Laura. They're solid people. Us.

"I've met his two key employees, and they seem like decent people too. Ryan is awesome. He's his right hand like you are to me. Kristi is pretty loyal to him, and she seems to truly enjoy working for him. Ryan and Kristi aren't just people off the street he hired. He took the time to know who he needed. I realized he hires people like I do. He's selective in everything that's important to him.

"And think of all those blind dates he was put on. He respected them all but never went beyond one or two dates. As far as I know, he never even slept with any of them. It takes a really decent man to not do that nowadays, don't you think?

"Josh is not just a guy from the streets who flies by the seat of his pants, or does things on a whim. Again, he's selective. He's solid, a different quality from any man I've known—besides Shane and you.

"No, I don't know what'd happen if we broke up. Maybe have him sign a confiden-tiality form now, just in case? I've tried to see it from every angle. I've even thought about breaking up with him now, and just never telling him the truth! But I can't. I just *can't* hurt him like that. I couldn't live with the guilt, Ty."

She summed it up the best way she could. "I'm taking a big risk either way. The only difference is one of the risks involves you."

"Let me think for a moment. Do you want anything to drink?"

"Bourbon? Rum?"

"You're not on an empty stomach, are you?"

"Tea's fine."

He chuckled. He poured them each a glass of tea. Like her, he'd prefer the stronger stuff but knew they had to keep a clear mind right now. Knowing she hadn't been eating much lately, a single beer would probably make her tipsy enough to not be able to drive any time soon. She was a lightweight when it came to alcohol. And she'd never get drunk. He respected that about her too. Drunks are dangerous. Especially those with loose lips.

After handing her a glass of tea, he sat down beside her, thinking it all through. He could completely see her point. And the fact was, if anyone *needed* to know, it was certainly Josh. And if anyone *could* know, it was also Josh.

But he also thought about the other side. *What if* they broke up? *What if* Josh told someone even by accident?

In the end, life was just a gamble. No matter which decision they agreed upon, there were repercussions. At least by telling Josh, she afforded herself the chance to move forward, to begin anew. And wasn't *that* his whole point of getting her together with Josh in the first place? And wasn't there a part of him, deep inside, that knew if they did get together, this subject would need to be dealt with?

At long last, he turned to her. His heart beat faster just thinking about what could happen. He controlled it before he asked, "Do you want to tell him by yourself, or together?"

Chapter 35

JOSH WAS SANDING DOWN the wood for a cabinet he was making with Laura, patiently showing her how to do it properly. When his cellphone rang, he recognized the ringtone he'd chosen for Morgan's calls. He stopped to answer it, motioning for Laura to continue.

"Hey there, sweetheart! Whatcha need?"

Morgan took a breath, glancing at Ty first. "Hey back. Are you still at Damien's?"

"Yeah. Laura's getting the hang of sanding right now. Damien hit his thumb with the hammer earlier so he's out of commission. Last I saw of him, he was watching cartoons."

He and Laura laughed which made Morgan smile. She'd been warned Damien was the worst with handyman projects.

Josh asked, "Did you need me for something?"

"I needed to talk to you. What time do you think you'll be done?"

He looked at his watch, thinking. "Oh, I'd say about another two or three hours. Is everything all right?" He left the room, hearing something different in her voice. "I can leave right now if you need me to, Morgan."

Morgan's heart was beating so furiously, it almost hurt to breathe. Ty rubbed his hand up and down her back, trying to get her to focus. "Well, the sooner the better. When you're done, can you come to my house? Would you mind?"

"Sweetheart, are you in trouble?"

"No. I just have something really important I need to discuss with you, and I hate waiting."

"I can be there in about half an hour, all right? Maybe forty-five minutes with traffic," Josh replied. "I'll just tell Laura I need to go."

Morgan's heart flipped over. Just like that. He was ready to drop what he was doing for her. "It's a polar bears love sliding on snow thing."

He was quiet for a moment. "I'm on my way."

"Thank you, Josh. I mean that."

"You bet." He hung up his phone, walked back to Laura. "Laura, something came up, and I need to go. Just keep sanding the wood like you are. Go with the grain. When you're done, clean it off like we did these over here, and then just stain them with the brush. Just do one coat for now.

"If you're unsure about the staining, we can get to it another day. But I think you can handle it just fine. Don't worry if you mess up something. We can always replace it if we can't fix it. If we keep a mistake, it'll just add character!"

Concerned, Laura looked up. "Is Morgan all right?"

"I think so. She just needs someone to talk to about something," Josh hedged. But it *was* the truth as he knew it.

"I hope she's okay. If you guys need anything, you just call."

"Thanks. Tell Damien to stop being such a wuss, and suck it up," he added with a smile as he removed his tool belt and dusted off his jeans. "He can do the staining. Surely *that* can't hurt him!"

She laughed, nodding. "Don't be too sure. If anything else, he can supervise me."

"Oh, no! Honey, don't do *that!* Not unless I get you in the divorce!"

She laughed hysterically, shoving her hair out of her way. "Josh, you're too funny! Go to Morgan now before Damien hears you!"

He smiled as he gathered his things, wondering what his lady needed to talk about.

Ty looked at Morgan after she hung up the phone. "What's with the polar bears?"

She actually found it in herself to smile. She explained, "It's our code we need to discuss something important. It just prepares the other. Sets the mood, I guess you could say. We only use it for important matters."

She drank down her tea as she made her way to his kitchen, leaving the glass in the sink and running some water in it. She went back to the living room to get her coat. "Let's go, Ty. For better or for worse, let's do this before I chicken out."

He drank his own tea before he got up, took his empty glass to his kitchen before running a little water in his glass as well. Hoping this wasn't a mistake, he went to get his own coat. "I'll be right behind you."

But then he quickly grabbed her, pulled her close, and tightly hugged her again before kissing her cheek. "It'll be okay, sweetheart. This will all work out. You'll see."

She hugged him back, nodding her head. "I sure hope so." Letting out a shaky sigh, she kissed his cheek before she stepped back and reached for his door.

As he closed the door behind them, they both wondered who he was trying to convince.

Chapter 36

JOSH HAD A BAD feeling all the way to Morgan's. He stopped to get a drink and use the bathroom when he filled his truck up with gas. His feeling of foreboding only got worse when he pulled up to Morgan's home and saw Ty's truck beside hers. Didn't she go to *his* house earlier?

Ty waited in the living room for them, knowing Morgan wanted a moment in private with Josh outside first. When they came inside, he glanced at Morgan and she nodded. Ty said, "Good to see you, Josh. Sorry we pulled you away from Damien and Laura."

"If it's important to Morgan, it's not a problem at all." Josh sat down on the couch at Morgan's urging. Sitting beside him, both were now facing Ty who sat in the chair she'd moved over while waiting for Josh to arrive. Josh looked at them before saying, "Okay, let's just hear it. Don't hold back whatever it is you have to say."

Morgan took a deep breath and said, "Josh, in the past when we've talked, I know you've felt me holding something back. I wasn't ready to share with you what it was until now. Ty knows, and is a part of it to a great degree, so I asked him to please come and be here for me.

"But I first must stress a few things. First off, no one else around here knows *any* of what we're going to tell you. And we need to keep it this way. Can we trust you to keep important information to yourself? To not tell anybody—not even your parents, Damien, Laura, your minister if you have one? No one... *Ever?*"

Josh nodded, wondering what could possibly be that important. "You both have my promise. If you don't want me to tell, and it's not something illegal or immoral, then I won't. I'm not exactly known for my spreading local gossip."

Despite the seriousness of the situation, Josh having the ethics to immediately point out he wasn't willing to do anything "illegal or immoral" impressed both Ty and Morgan.

"It's not either," she replied, reassuring him.

"We know, and that's just one reason we decided to tell you. And *only* you," Ty stressed.

"What's the other reason?"

Morgan answered, "Because I'm relying on my good judgment, and my love for you to not be steering me wrong. And for us to move forward with nothing between us, in my heart," she tapped it with her flat palm, "I made the decision to trust myself in order to trust you."

She waited, composed her thoughts before taking that plunge. "It's so hard to know where to start." Her glance flicked over to Ty, and then back to Josh. "Before I moved here to Arizona, I came from back East. The reason I left was..." She took a breath and said as calmly as she could, "The reason I left was because my husband had been brutally murdered, and my personal safety was in question."

Josh looked stunned. He just stared at her while her statement sunk in. She'd never even once mentioned having been married! She'd never let on at all. His glance went to Ty, who just quietly waited for Josh to process that first bombshell.

Ty could feel his heart kicking in his chest, imagining Morgan's was doing the same.

When he could speak, Josh said, "Honestly, I don't know what I should say right now. I never once even wondered if you'd been married before. It just never really entered my mind for some reason." He saw the sorrow and fear in her eyes. He asked quietly, "What happened? Do you want to tell me?"

"I can only tell you the major parts, at least for right now." At his nod of acceptance, she continued, "His name was Shane, and he worked for a... place... that was deeply involved in law enforcement." She hesitated to just say he was an undercover agent. "On one of his assignments, he was killed."

Her voice cracked, and her eyes filled with tears. She had to take a moment to pull herself together. When she felt ready, she explained, "I was told he was killed, and even how in grisly detail, by apparently the one who did it. He called me... at our *home*. The gist is, terrified and alone, I began a new life, and I chose Arizona to do it in."

Both Morgan and Ty searched Josh's face, his body language. She'd deliberately started with the most basic of the conversation, leaving Ty out on purpose, so they could judge how he was taking the news. What they both saw was sorrow for her, and some shock.

"Sweetheart, I'm so sorry. I can't imagine..." Quiet for a moment, he took hold of her hand, squeezed it. He finally asked, "How's Ty involved?"

At Ty's nod, Morgan again spoke. "Without my initially knowing, Ty came out here to protect me, to watch over me. In essence, he's my bodyguard and has been for the past six or so years."

Josh was flabbergasted. His glance went back and forth between the two silent people watching him intently. He could see they were dead serious. This wasn't some joke. Well, *that* explained quite a bit, he thought once he could think again. "If you didn't know then, how do you know it now?"

Ty said, "It's good to see you're taking this all so well. We were hoping you would. I'm sure as this all sinks in, and the shock wears down, you'll have questions.

"Just know that Morgan and I are still best friends, and we're tight simply because of the years we've known each other. I still work for her. None of that has changed in the scheme of things. But now there's you, and we decided to let you in on what's going on for reasons we'll get to shortly."

Ty leaned forward to tell their story. "Morgan didn't know until recently that I am in fact an agent. Or that I was here to see to her protection. We don't know if she's in the clear, but hopefully she is.

"However, the case of her husband's murder is not closed, so it still pays to be watchful and vigilant. There are still many things in my mind that aren't closed at all. Therefore, I'm still quietly protecting her. But something important came up recently so I was forced to tell her what she didn't know about me.

"But I want to say first that I also came out here because I wanted a new life, different from what I was doing. As the two of us worked together, we eventually became the friends we are today. The bond we have is tight, Josh, and it needs to be."

Josh leaned back, taking it all in. He ran a hand through his hair, before resting it on the arm of the couch. Minutes passed in silence. The clock on the wall softly clicked in the quiet as he processed what he'd been told so far. Reaching over, he took her hand again, squeezed it. "He told you this around the time you cleaned your house top to bottom and re-organized your tack room?"

Morgan was slightly surprised and glanced at Ty. She replied, "A bit before that, yes. How—"

Josh interrupted. "You both were acting out of character. And I thought I sensed a slight tension between you two in the office." And that'd also explain that boiling, underlying current he'd felt from her when he'd kissed her in the back room. Not that he'd minded, of course.

Ty was impressed. "As far as we know, you're the only one who picked up on that. I think the two of us have resolved that issue now. But we'll still need a little time for us to settle into this new dynamic." He looked at Morgan, who nodded.

She said, "Yes. It was a lot for me to take in. Just like this is a lot for you to take in, Josh."

Josh squeezed her hand again, rubbing his thumb over her knuckles. "Why are you scared of telling people?"

Morgan answered, "I can't have people know, Josh, because if my... former life... was exposed, I could be in danger. I may not be now, but neither of us know for sure. My Shane went to extraordinary lengths to protect me in case something happened to him. When it did, I disappeared like he'd ordered me to. He'd set up an escape plan for me in case something ever happened. He set me up so I could start a new life. Harmony Hills is what I built from the insurance policies he left me without me knowing he even had them.

"I started fresh for him because of his love for me, his desire for me to continue my life. It hasn't been easy, not in any way." She looked intently at Josh and said seriously, "I do not take what Shane did for me lightly. And one doesn't disappear just to tell everyone they had."

Ty nodded, helping her out. "Josh, you have to understand that Shane gave his life to protect the woman he loved. For Morgan here, he gave her everything she needed to live her own life again. We can't let anyone know because we still do not know exactly who it was who killed her husband, who *ordered* it. Or why. There's more than just one person involved here. As far as we know, this is part of a large, dangerous criminal organization.

"We in the Agency go to great lengths to protect those closest to us, so for her to be called at *home* is inconceivable. We had no way of knowing whether or not they thought she might know something and want to get to her to see for themselves. Her best bet was to just disappear."

Josh still held Morgan's hand, feeling her shaking a bit. Minutes later, after letting all of this sink in, he asked, "So why tell me now?"

"Because after almost nine years, I was recently notified through Ty that the man who killed Shane has been caught, and he's set to go on trial. They want to know if I want to go to it, and I'm still debating. It's in April, so I need to make up my mind fairly soon so they know and can be prepared.

"To say I'm feeling overwhelmed right now is an understatement, Josh. I never thought this day would come. I think I'd given up on it, deep inside.

"And why I needed to tell you all of this comes from several reasons. The first of which is if I decide to go, I could be gone for a couple of weeks... or a couple of months. I don't know. And I refuse to lie to you. I couldn't stand here and tell you I'd be going off somewhere, but not tell you where, why, or for how long. We promised to always be honest with each other. Lying to you or not even trusting you with something so vitally important would destroy us, wouldn't it? Especially if you somehow found out about it later on?"

Josh nodded, saying without hesitation, "Yes, it would. I'd feel hurt, disappointed, rejected, betrayed, and even maybe unworthy of your trust. And I couldn't trust you. It would be very hard to build a future upon that, if not impossible."

She looked at Ty, who nodded at her in silent communication. She then said, "Another reason is because of the kind of relationship Ty and I have. It's wrong for only us to know what we're talking about and doing while leaving the man I love completely on the outside. With you knowing, this means the three of us can be open with each other about this and not have those secrets.

"We go on as we always have. Ty and I are best friends and have been for years. I stick tight with my true friends, Josh. And I believe in my heart you're the same in this regard, which is yet another reason why we decided to risk an awful lot to let you in. Ty and I being tight like we are... I love you both, just differently.

"And as I've told you before, Ty and I have never once been together romantically even though many think we have or even are. We'll kiss on the cheek, maybe on the mouth on New Year's, and we're both comfortable with hugs and such. But nothing has ever gone beyond those plutonic touches."

Josh nodded and looked at Ty. "So, you're not just a bodyguard but an undercover agent?"

Ty nodded. "Yes. And only on a part-time basis with who I work for, and that's for Morgan. Other than that, I *am* her manager here at the Center. I have no plans on leaving her. Who I work for accepts this arrangement.

"When I leave here in a while, she can tell you all she feels comfortable with. She may tell you everything or nothing. Morgan is to only share with you what *she* feels she needs to, or wants to. Everything, *all* of this that we're doing right now, is *her* decision."

Ty gave Josh a firm look when he said, "We both need to know, Josh, that you fully understand this isn't a topic that any of us just brings up on a whim. Not that she's been married, not that she's a widow, not why she moved here, not how she started the Center, not that I'm an agent.

"*Nothing* we're discussing right now can be discussed with anyone. The only time we can bring it up with each other is when we know we're alone, like now, in our own homes, but being careful even then. It's best we come up with a code to alert the others beforehand, but we'll get to that later.

"You will need to be careful now because sometimes knowing something can just slip right out. It only takes one person to overhear, to spread the word. You might be amazed at how quickly information like this gets around to the wrong people. I've worked the underground for a very long time. Most of the intel I got was because someone opened their mouth when they shouldn't have, and it eventually got around.

"It only takes one person to kill me, her, or both of us, if this information got out. I'm positive there are people out there looking for me. My silence and my unknown location help protect many others, not just Morgan here. There are very few people even in my own family who know what I did, Josh. They all just know me now as working in Arizona with horses.

"If her cover is leaked, she's up a creek, to put it mildly. Having the Center, she's unable to just pack a suitcase and simply disappear again now. She gambled and put it all on the line to buy the Center, to build a business she couldn't just shut down and run from, if it ever became necessary.

"Her cover is solid, and she has a real life here. She met you and has chosen to share her life with you. I really like, approve of, and trust you, so I have few qualms about this. And those misgivings are only because having someone else know is unnerving and dangerous. However, in the big picture, I couldn't be happier for you two."

Josh said, "Thank you, really. I appreciate knowing that. And I appreciate your trust in me. I can only imagine this was a very difficult decision to have made. I admit I'm stunned, and I may have questions later. I probably will. It's *a lot* to take in!

"But I love Morgan here." He smiled at her. "And every relationship has its challenges. I believe I'm man enough to handle it, especially because there are actually three of us handling it." Josh paused. "Three of us, like three sides of a triangle. As you may know, the triangle is the strongest shape. This is a good omen."

Ty had to give a small grin, saying, "Immediate knowledge of geometry. I guess that comes from being a contractor."

Morgan pointed out, "But we're just not a love triangle! Not in the kinky sense anyway."

Josh returned their quick grins with a nod before getting serious again. "As for exposing either of you, I promise to carry your secrets to my grave. I mean that. I love Morgan here, and I don't take that lightly. I'd protect her with my life, if needed.

"You being a friend, one who I value quite a lot, it's not out of my thinking to say I'd try to do the same for you. What I know already about the two of you, I'm sure either of you would do a much better job of it than an amateur like me, but I sure would do what I could. At least, I hope I would. It's one of those things that you just don't know until it happens, if it ever does."

Morgan and Ty nodded, both appreciating his honesty.

She said, "You not telling anyone ever is a crucial part of protecting us though. Keeping what we're telling you to yourself means you're *already* doing your part."

Ty nodded. "She just made an excellent point, and it's one hundred percent spot on. It can be very stressful, Josh. If you ever feel the need to discuss this with us, don't hesitate. We just have to be secure first."

They sat there for a while in the quiet again, Ty and Morgan giving Josh plenty of time to think. Suddenly, Josh said, "Wait a minute. When you say her cover... She had a former life, and she disappeared. Are you *really* Morgan O'Connell?" He looked at her, his facial expression showing his surprise at this thought.

She said softly, "I am now."

He looked a little shell-shocked again, that was for sure. He just looked at her and then back at Ty.

Morgan said, still softly, "I am who I was before I called you this afternoon. Me—who you've known over these months—hasn't changed one iota in the past hour or two. Are you okay with this knowledge, Josh?"

He nodded. "It's just so much to take in! Surely you can understand that?"

Both Ty and Morgan nodded before watching, waiting.

For the next couple of hours, they patiently and honestly answered Josh's questions and answered some he hadn't even thought to ask.

When Ty finally got up to leave, Morgan hugged him tightly. He kissed her cheek, whispering, "I think this was the right decision for you, Morg. We'll see, I guess. I'll see you tomorrow morning. You call me if you need me, all right?"

"Absolutely. Thank you for being here once again for me. And for trusting me and him," she whispered back, kissing his cheek before letting him go.

He nodded before offering, "I guess you two will be talking about this for a while yet. How about I feed the horses and The Darrells so you don't have to worry about it? It's almost time to feed them anyway. And if you need me for something in the meantime, I'll still be here. When I'm done feeding and closing the place down, I'll just head on home."

"I honestly hadn't even considered asking you about doing that. It'd be really appreciated if you did. Thank you."

"Consider them fed then. I'll just earn a little of my holiday pay."

"You do that," she replied, smiling.

She headed to the kitchen when Josh said he wanted a word with Ty alone. They walked to the front door and stopped. Josh studied him for a moment before asking softly, "So *this* is why you kept us apart until you knew more about me? To protect her because of her past?"

Ty nodded. "I'd die to protect her whether or not I was being paid. I needed to know you were worthy of her. That you weren't going to mess with her, cheat on her, take advantage of her, use her, get to her to try and steal her business or her money. Or be someone who could jeopardize her life or business. I needed to know what kind of person you were at your core. I could be wrong about you, but I don't think so.

"But I also needed the time to work on her to even be open to you, and dating in general. As you can now probably understand, she would *not* have been."

Ty paused again, thinking. "Josh, her life for the past eight or nine years has been hard, getting easier in most respects simply due to time. But this will always be a part of who she is. But she honestly is who you met, chased after, and now are dating. Trust me when I say, if you didn't catch *her* attention, *her* heart, you wouldn't be here in any way right now. I could only do so much to get you two together. Staying together, well, that's between you two. It'll either happen, or it won't.

"You're not just someone, but *something*, special to her. I don't believe she sees you as just a man to date. I think she sees you as someone who is able to show her she still has a future worth living for. And you're possibly the one person who can help her move forward in this area.

"While I've gotten her started on this journey, it may well be your purpose to travel it now with her. Maybe not, but this is my opinion and feeling on it. And there's no pressure. Either you guys are committed to working it out and will, or you just don't. Time will tell. But you must *always* keep all of this to yourself, even if you two break up."

He said ruefully, "However the stars get aligned, they were that day you two met. I guess you could say both times you first met."

They both smiled at each other.

"And she saved my life, too, you know. She gave me a new life out here, on the spot, no questions. She helped me by giving me a new career, finding my house, and our friendship has enriched my entire life.

"My family is tight, where trust, honor, and loyalty are foremost with us. Therefore, I also expect and greatly value those qualities among friends. Morgan is all three to her bones. She'll stand strong and true to those she loves, like she did Shane. She's tough, Josh. She's tough, but sometimes she cries."

Josh nodded, and then with an impulse to do so, hugged Ty. "Thank you for being there for her, Ty. Really."

A bit surprised at the unexpected hug, Ty smiled. "You're both welcome. Now, go to her and just let her go at her own pace. I'm sure you two need to talk this out some more. It's completely up to her what she will do or say. Just be there for her, Josh. She doesn't want, or need, for either of us to fix anything for her even if we could. She just needs to know we're here for her if she needs us."

Josh thought that over. After a moment, he replied, "I can do that."

"Good." As Ty was walking out the door, he turned around again. After a second of hesitation, he said, "And I'm also warning you to not let our girl down."

"Don't plan on it. Later, Ty." He softly shut and locked the door after Ty walked out and headed toward his truck.

Taking a deep breath, Josh turned around to go look for their girl.

Chapter 37

HE FOUND MORGAN IN the kitchen, looking out her windows, staring at her mountains. Not saying a word, Josh walked up behind her, wrapped his arms around her and just held her. They both needed that. They didn't need words at that moment, but just the simple companionship, the acceptance. They were still standing there long after they saw Ty's truck disappear from their sight as he drove to the barns to feed the horses and dogs.

She finally turned around, and he saw the tear streaks down her cheeks. Silent tears she hadn't even known she was crying. He tenderly wiped her face with a damp paper towel, kissing her cheeks with a gentleness that just made her cry more of those silent, salty tears.

He held her against him, cradling her head against his chest as she tried to pull herself together. He figured it was the aftermath, or simply the *relief*, of telling him of her past. This was a serious step for her take, a leap of faith to entrust him with her secrets.

She finally pulled away so she could look up at him. With a tremor in her voice, she asked, "Are you okay?"

"I was just about to ask *you* that, sweetheart."

"I was so scared to tell you…" She took a breath, let it out slowly. "What do you think? How does this make you feel?"

"I think you are even more amazing than you were before I walked through your door a few hours ago." He kissed her forehead. "Do you want to tell me more of it? All of it? Any of it?"

At her nod, he tucked her hair behind her ears. "Then let's go back to the living room, all right?"

"I'll meet you there in a minute. Let me get something for you first."

JOSH WAS SITTING ON one end of her couch, not knowing exactly what was going to happen now. He'd used the restroom then sat back down on her couch as he waited for her to come back downstairs. He tried to comprehend everything this woman he loved had been living with.

This answered his personal questions about her reticence around men—except for Ty. Josh had wondered if maybe she'd been attacked or even raped. He'd prayed not as he wouldn't wish that on any woman. But it was the only answer that'd made sense to him. She was close only with Ty, very hesitant to date, knew how to protect herself with physical skills and guns, and had a security system as well as two guard dogs.

How does she manage to keep it all together? Josh wondered. How does she cope with it all so well? How was all of this going to affect him personally, once it sinks in? And most of all, how would it affect their growing relationship?

He heard her come down the stairs and watched her walk into the room carrying a safe box in her hands. She stood there for a moment before she placed it on the coffee table in front of him. "You want something to drink? I have Pepsi, iced tea, water. I'm going to grab a Pepsi. Would you like one?"

He could tell she was working her way up to this, so he'd help her out and have a drink too. "A Pepsi sounds good."

She walked back in, handing him a cold Pepsi and sat down in the chair closest to him. She sipped her drink, then placing her drink on the end table, she just looked at him.

Seeing her nervousness, he took her hands, kissed the backs of both. Pulling her over to sit beside him, he said, "Morgan, anything you tell me will stay with me. I'm a solid wall, not one made of rubber. Think of me as your attorney with that attorney/client privilege, but even more secure."

Morgan nodded. "I'm not sure I should tell you since we've not known each other all that long. I don't know how to say it except I *feel* I can trust you. And for the sake of *us*, I feel I need to tell you some more things about me. Just to get it all out in the open. We're in the zone right now, so I'd rather just get it all out now, you know? If you have questions, you can ask..." Her voice trailed off.

Looking into her green eyes, he said softly, "Sweetheart, whatever is in your past, it won't change how I feel about you. And you *can* trust me." Seeing the tears in her eyes, he reached up and wiped a few stray teardrops that spilled over and ran down her cheeks.

Softly he added, "Morgan, if you don't want to tell me anymore yet, don't. This is *your* decision. I won't push you into telling me more."

"I know you won't, but I need to tell you. I want us to not have secrets between us, but this is just so much for you to take in. I know when we began dating, this was hardly the kind of thing you wanted to deal with, or ever thought you'd need to." She looked down at their joined hands. She could hardly tell where hers ended and his began. "There's no easy way to tell you more, though, so I guess I just have to say it. But, I'm afraid to tell you more at the same time."

"What are you afraid of?"

"Maybe that you won't see me in the same way, or that it'll be too much for you to take in. Especially after it all begins to sink in." Looking into his brown eyes, so full of compassion, she added, "And telling you brings up pain and sadness that I've worked really hard at keeping under control so it doesn't overwhelm me."

Josh squeezed her hands tightly. "Morgan, look at me, really look at me." When her tear-misted eyes looked into his, he said, "I'm not going to leave you. I'm here to stay, all right? If it's a lot to handle, we'll work it out. It may take me time to really process all of this, or it may not.

"But I think you and Ty have told me the most important facts already. You've told me what happened to Shane, what you went through, how you came out here, how you started Harmony Hills. But I think there's more *you* need to say, to purge your emotions, to begin to truly heal. Let me help you. Just let me help you."

She slowly nodded her head. Saying a silent prayer for guidance and for strength, she sat there for a moment longer. She reached into her pocket, removed the key and unlocked the safe box. She lifted the heavy hinged lid. Moving aside some small, loose items that lay on the top, she pulled out a small photo album.

Handing the photo album to Josh, she hesitated. Quietly, she said, "These are some photos from my former life. Some are from my wedding album."

Chapter 38

HAVING PUT HER PAST behind them, they ate dinner at her table while talking about their future. They switched and talked about mundane, everyday topics as they washed the dishes together before heading to the couch. It was getting late and both needed to get up early, but neither felt like moving.

Josh didn't want to leave her alone. That was the one theme he got throughout the afternoon and evening as he'd listened: She was always alone. He wanted to change that. He wanted to spend the night with her so she wasn't alone. Not for sex, but for comfort, companionship, and support.

But how could he ask her to stay over without her getting anxious? They both agreed they didn't want their relationship based on sex, so they were waiting. It wasn't easy, but he felt she'd come to him when she was ready. She wasn't now. She had to come to terms with her past first. He only hoped it wouldn't be too much longer. But if he had to wait, he knew she was worth it. Wouldn't it mean that much more if they both knew her mind was clear... Focused solely on him, and them?

Quietly, Morgan asked, "I was wondering if you wouldn't mind staying over tonight? I don't want to be alone. Not tonight at least. I figured I would, but I don't. And I want you beside me, just holding me. I don't want you to get the wrong idea because I'm not looking for sex. I'm just not ready to take that step yet. I hope you can understand that."

"In that case, I guess I'll just go," he teased her. She gently elbowed him, smiling. She'd just neatly solved his own questioning mind. "Yes, I will stay with you. We'll just make sure the alarm is set so we both get to work on time. I head back tomorrow, and I think you do too?" She nodded. "Well, it wouldn't be wise to both be late and have our people out looking for us just to find us in such a compromising position." He smiled when he heard her chuckle.

Getting up, Morgan turned to look down at him. He looked decidedly relaxed and comfortable there on her couch. She put out her hand to him, tugging him into standing up. Motioning with her hand, she led him toward one of her spare bedrooms downstairs. She went to the middle drawers of a small dresser and slid them open. Removing some items, she tossed a pair of sweatpants and a shirt at him.

She answered before he could ask, "These are Ty's, so they should fit you." She smiled at the look he shot her. It's astounding what all a single raised eyebrow could convey. "Easy there, slugger. Don't get the wrong impression. Trust, remember?"

"Sometimes Ty, and even the others, will stay here at the last minute if we have a sick horse. Or in really bad weather or something. Plus, when I go on the road for clinics and shows, Ty stays here on property in case of an emergency. So I bought the bed, dresser, and bedside table for him to use. He used to sleep on the couch, but since I wanted spare rooms always available, I set up both bedrooms downstairs. This is basically his room."

"Makes sense to me. Mind if I take a quick shower? I probably have sawdust on me. I wouldn't want to get that in your bed."

"I don't mind at all. Towels, washcloths, whatever you probably need, are in the spare bathroom here. I keep it stocked with just about everything in case of emergencies. Have at 'em. I'm turning on my alarm in a minute. Do you need to go to your truck first for anything?"

"No, it's fine. I locked it already."

"Okay. Well, take your shower. I'll probably be upstairs when you're done."

Once in the bathroom, he opened one of the drawers, surprised by all of the items inside. She *was* prepared for about anything, he thought, smiling. Individually-sealed toothbrushes, full and travel-size tubes of toothpaste, travel-size containers of lotions, facial wash, deodorants, and even dental picks were in plastic organizers in the drawer. Curious now, he checked the other drawers. More plastic organizers holding travel-size shaving cream, hair-styling products, sealed lip balms, hair ties, a bag of disposable razors. Another drawer held a variety of organized feminine hygiene products.

He figured it made sense with all of the social gatherings she held up here, and as she said, in case of emergencies and last-minute overnight stays. He noticed from the first time he came over that Morgan tried to make her guests feel at home when they were there. A stocked bathroom would be a hit.

He easily found the towels and washcloths. When he pulled back the shower curtain, he noticed she bought regular-sized bottles of neutral shampoo, conditioner, and body wash. Appreciating her thoughtfulness, he turned on the water and took a quick shower. After he got out and dried off, he slipped on the sweatpants. Opening up one of the sealed toothbrushes and a mini tube of toothpaste, he brushed his teeth. After a moment, he took one of the little deodorants to use. He laid the items he'd used on top of his clothes, thinking he should replace them as a simple courtesy.

When he was done using the bathroom, he wiped down the counter and flipped off the light and fan. Carrying the t-shirt she'd given him back to the spare room, he returned it to the drawer. He left his own clothes in the bathroom to change back into in the morning. Or, he'd just wear these home in the morning, and bring them back later.

As he made his way upstairs to her room, he flipped off the last light she'd left on for him. Knowing the house was locked up tight made him wonder a little. Now that he knew her history, and knowing Ty knew it, too, Josh wondered if she would've had the security system if none of what she went through had ever happened. Many people had the paid protection, but now he wondered why *she* had it.

Was she afraid the men who killed her husband would show up here? Or was she just protecting herself from modern-day burglars, fire, and the like? Being a lone woman in the desert had to be unnerving at times. Then he remembered her guns. He smiled, doubting his little warrior worried about living alone.

When he entered her room, he heard her shower being turned off on the other side of the closed bathroom door. After a few minutes, he heard her blow dryer running. He walked around the upstairs a bit as he'd never been up here before and returned to her room. He was pulling back the blankets and sheets on the bed when the bathroom door opened and she walked out, dressed in shorts and a t-shirt.

Gesturing toward the fan in the corner, she inquired, "Will that bother you if it's on? I like the white noise and the moving air when I sleep. It helps keep it a bit cooler in here as well, but I can turn it off if it bothers you."

He stood there for a moment and just looked at her. He could tell she was slightly nervous. Looking at the fan, he replied, "No bother at all. I usually have my ceiling fan on at my place for the same reasons. I can't sleep if the room's too hot or stifling."

Nodding, she turned on the bedside light, motioning for him to shut off the overhead one. Just before she turned away, Morgan noticed he was getting a five-o'clock shadow and thought it looked quite sexy on him. And she couldn't miss the fact that his naked chest was very nicely formed. The sweatpants fit him pretty well too. She figured they would. She turned her attention back to the clock so she wouldn't end up staring at him any longer than she already had. Her pulse had quickened just looking at him in her bedroom. Seeing him half-naked with a five-o'clock shadow had her pulse revved up to warp speed.

Josh wasn't blind to her perusal of his body, how her eyes strayed and stayed. Fact was, he did the same to her. He did notice her chest moving in and out a little quicker than normal, and the knowledge made his ego swell up like a balloon. Every person wants to know they're desired, so to him this was simply a bonus knowing she noticed him as much as he noticed her. He slid his hand down the wall, darkening the room, but for the small light beside her.

Rubbing her hands on her pajama shorts, she informed him, "I plugged your phone in downstairs, in case you didn't notice. It's on the kitchen counter. Mine's charging in here. Do you need it?"

"No. I'll just have to remember to get it in the morning. And thanks for charging it."

"You're welcome. What time do you want me to set the alarm for? I usually get up around seven, but you'll need to go back to your place first. Do you want it earlier? Later?"

Josh thought about it, doing a quick time table in his mind including drive time back to his place, shaving, breakfast, and getting to his own office. "Let's do five-thirty. That'll give me a little extra time. Normally I'd sleep in a little later, but that should keep me on schedule."

She sat down on the bed to adjust the alarm. "Okay, you get the side closest to the clock and the alarm. This button here? That's the snooze button." They grinned at each other before she climbed in, scooted over, switched out her pillows so she had her favorites and stretched out.

When he sat on the side of the bed, she felt the mattress give under the added weight. "You know I won't take advantage of this, right? Pressure you to do anything you don't want to or are ready for?"

"Yes. If I didn't, you wouldn't even be offered the chance."

He lay down beside her before he turned off the lamp, throwing the room into darkness, with the exception of the little glow from her nightlights. He turned to his side, raised up on his elbow and looked down at her upturned face. The tiny reflections from the nightlights showed bits and pieces of her face to him. He ran his fingers over her face, reveling in how she automatically and trustingly leaned into his touch. He brushed her hair back from her face as he simply soaked in the moment. He liked the feel of her hair as he ran his fingers through it. He felt the cool air move over his bare chest from the fan. Outside, they could hear the yipping of coyotes.

A thought went through his mind, and he debated asking it. Finally, he decided he needed to know how she felt about it. "Can I ask you a question?"

"Sure."

"Do you ever want to be called by your old name? Do you miss being called by your real name?"

It hadn't escaped his notice she never once said what her name used to be. Not even her last name, before or after she'd been married. She'd only said Shane. Even her sparse photo album didn't list names. He knew because he'd checked when she went to use the restroom earlier before she put away her safe box.

Morgan was quiet for so long, Josh wondered if he'd somehow offended her or brought up bad memories. Before he could apologize, she answered quietly, "I don't know. It's been so long now, Morgan is who I am, and what I answer to. If someone called out my old name, even if they were calling out to someone else, I'm not sure I'd even acknowledge it. Do I miss it?"

She lapsed into silence again, thinking hard. "I guess deep down I may. But it seems like who I was before is simply another person. Like someone I *knew*, not someone I *was*. It was a family name so I'll never forget it, but it's not *me* anymore. Since I haven't seen my family since I left, it's honestly not a subject that comes up with me. They do know I go by Morgan now though. Besides, it's best to stay with only Morgan here. I'd not want to risk the chance of having my real name come out as it'd cause too much speculation."

Josh ran his hand over her hair. "I understand."

"Thank you for asking how I felt. It was something I've never really dwelt over. Maybe someday I'll tell you."

"I can give you a goodnight kiss in here, right?" he soon asked lightly, teasingly.

"By all means, please do," she replied, in the same light tone.

He leaned over, gave her a chaste kiss on her forehead. "Goodnight, darlin'." He stretched out beside her.

"Wait... What? That's... it? You seriously can't—"

He smiled, vastly amused at her sputtering. He leaned over her again, just looking at her. He then kissed her on the tip of her nose, then her temple, trailing his mouth alongside her face. He heard her soft sigh as he slowly made his way to kiss her chin, then each of her cheekbones. Finally, he moved his lips to hers in a kiss that was achingly gentle. Just a soft brush of his lips across hers, then again, and yet again.

When he pulled back just a bit, she followed him, seeking his mouth with her own. Her hands slowly pulled his head down until he was on top of her. Not being in any rush, they simply absorbed the other with sweet and gentle kisses. He heard her soft sighs and little gasps as he ran his hands gently across her neck and sides as his mouth coaxed her responses. His body, reacting as any healthy male would, naturally adjusted to hers.

Feeling him against her, Morgan tried not to tense up. Her faith in him was absolute, but she also wasn't a tease. But she was willing to take another step forward, albeit a small one.

Her hands explored his naked shoulders, feeling the ripples of his muscled torso with her fingertips. She felt his skin shiver at her soft, butterfly touch and smiled inside. All that construction work had made his muscles toned. She ran her hands slowly and firmly down his sides to his hips, slipping them just under the top edge of the sweatpants as his warm mouth made its way down her neck. Somewhere in the back of her mind, she reveled in feeling no excess body fat, but just nice toned muscle anywhere she touched him. She heard his low moan as her hands touched him, just as his mouth and hands touched her.

Her hands made their way around to his rear, and she marveled at the feel of his buttocks. The man felt like he was made of stone. Physical labor definitely had its benefits, she thought to herself. Her head moved on its own accord as his mouth nuzzled her by her ear. She shivered and gasped he used his mouth and tongue to taste her.

His mouth went back to hers to give her a long, hot kiss, his tongue dueling with hers, and then made its way slowly down her neck, making stops at the hollow of her throat and her collarbone, stopping where her shirt began. With no resistance on her part, she felt Josh's hands slowly push up her shirt, and both shivered in pleasure and anticipation.

She felt his tongue then his lips against her bare skin as they moved from one side of her chest to the other. She felt his body shudder as he adjusted his position over hers. Her body shivered in response, and she let out a moan. Josh felt her shiver, heard her low moan. He tried to keep attuned to any signs from her to stop.

Her breath hitched again as feelings she hadn't felt in almost a decade began to build and slowly wash over and through her. She'd forgotten how it felt to feel the loving touch of a man. Her hands held on to his trim waist before slowly cruising over his strong back and moving up to his neck, almost as if to help keep herself grounded. She arched against him as he continued to touch her as she hadn't been touched in years.

Her emotions and feelings of pleasure were flooding her with desire. She felt a throb deep within, her body naturally seeking more and more. She arched against him again as Josh made gentle love to her with his mouth and hands. She felt the heat radiating from both of their bodies and knew he was holding back... for her.

"Josh." She wasn't sure if she cried it out or whispered it. "Josh..."

Josh somehow heard her quiet voice through the roaring in his head. His body literally trembled as he pulled away from her. His heart was hammering inside of his chest, trying to pound its way out. He looked into her eyes, passion setting those eyes of hers aglow. He trembled again, pulling himself back to awareness. He hadn't meant to go this far, to allow so much passion to run free, but he couldn't help it. She made him weak yet incredibly strong. Her responses were instant, sweet, and hot.

Nodding slowly that he understood her, he took deep breaths of air. It didn't escape his notice she was doing the same thing. After a moment, he pulled her top back down, but pleased himself at the last second by pressing a wet kiss to her bare navel, feeling her skin flex in response. She gasped, and her fingers clenched in his hair. Moving up, his mouth gently kissed hers again, calming them both back down a little at a time. It was like allowing an all-out galloping race horse to slowly transition down to a canter, then to a trot, and then finally, to a walk.

In the glow of the nightlights, her eyes looked dazed. He figured his own weren't too far off. Morgan smiled at him, cupping his cheek in her hand that still wasn't too steady. Softly she said, "I'd forgotten what it felt like..."

He saw a glistening of tears in her eyes from the glow of the nightlight. Josh whispered, "Sweetheart, are you okay? Did I... I didn't mean to..."

Morgan's heart flipped over when she realized even now he was concerned about her. He was afraid he'd pushed her too far, maybe pressured her. She knew the guilt he'd feel if he thought he had. "I'm fine. It's just been... It's just been a really long time. You didn't do anything I didn't allow or want. I'd just forgotten how it can be... But I can't go any further, not yet..."

Her voice trailed off, partly in embarrassment and partly because she was feeling overwhelmed by her feelings for Josh. She was afraid of what she felt for him. She was afraid she couldn't hold herself back if they did this again. But would that be so wrong of her?

Almost instantly, rolling in on the heels of those feelings was guilt. Guilt that she could feel those intense physical emotions and have her body respond so willingly and so quickly to a man who wasn't Shane.

Josh tried to read the expressions as they crossed her face, but there just wasn't enough light to be sure. He swore he'd apologize a thousand times if he saw anything that told him she felt regret or guilt. "Baby, I didn't mean to push you. You're just so responsive. It's been a long time for me, too, to be honest. Not as long as I'm guessing it has been for you, but these feelings I have for you... Don't feel guilty, Morgan. Please don't. It's all right. There's no hurry with us, remember?"

Morgan's heart ached, and her eyes glistened with tears. Wordlessly, she nodded. It was her fault. She could've stopped him from the first passionate kiss. So why didn't she? Because she needed to feel... wanted? Loved? Cherished? Alive?

She raised her hands, sinking her fingers into his soft hair, loving its feel. Giving him a smile, she pulled his head down to hers and gently kissed him. Then again. She wanted to let him know it was all right. That she was fine. That *they* were fine.

Josh breathed in her scent as he slowly pulled back. Right now, she was vulnerable, and he was in no way wanting to take advantage of her in this state. He wanted her strong, confident, and sure of herself again. But he also wanted her to remember, maybe to even realize, that she was alive and more than capable of feeling emotion. Shane may be dead, but *she* wasn't.

Leaning over her, he decided one more kiss wouldn't hurt, and placed a sweet, gentle kiss on her lips that made her heart squeeze almost painfully. Then he rolled to his side and pulled her up against him. With his arm securely around her waist, he gently tugged her closer, so her back was firmly against his warm chest, his legs entwined with hers. He slid his other arm underneath her head and pillows, where she rested it.

Adjusting her head and her long hair on his arm, she lay there for a moment, trying to calm her racing heart. Morgan linked her fingers with his. She knew she wanted him, which worried her. She had to work through these feelings coursing through not only her body, but her mind, heart, and soul. There'd been no one except Shane for her. Morgan was sure Josh wanted her. And not just because he was a healthy, grown man, but because they had a very strong emotional connection.

They loved each other, but she just wasn't ready yet to go any further. She knew she needed something more to go any further. Closure? Healing? What? Until she knew what it was, she knew it was wiser to wait.

The man was amazingly understanding and patient. It brought tears of appreciation, of gratefulness, to her eyes that she'd found such a man. She didn't know there were men like this anymore. She'd hoped there were, and was sure there were, but she wasn't sure she'd ever find one. She was incredibly thankful she had. More importantly, she never thought she'd even want one again. But she did.

"Josh?" Morgan whispered. "I'm very glad I told you about Shane tonight. It's making me feel a lot better in ways I didn't know it would. I was really worried it'd change the way you'd feel about me, or make you nervous to be around me. Thank you for listening. And for staying."

"Thank you for trusting me with your secrets. And you're welcome, anytime."

"Josh? This feels pretty wonderful, doesn't it?"

"More than." Josh nuzzled her hair, breathed in her scent. He often would recall her scent as he was in his office working, or at his own house. He couldn't seem to get her out of his mind. He loved feeling her in his embrace like this. He'd dreamed about it more than once. Closing his eyes, he just soaked up the feelings that were coursing through him. After a moment, he softly chuckled.

Morgan was curious. "What?"

Josh smiled into the darkness as he said, "I'm suddenly thankful my truck is up here at your house instead of at the stables. And that I have a cat that has a litter box, automatic food and water dishes, and not a dog that needs to be walked. Freeway will be fine until the morning."

Morgan blushed in the darkened room. She never gave a thought to his truck. Well, that would've been a dead give-away having his truck down at the stables. And then having him make his way to it bright and early in the morning when the wranglers came in to feed. Not to mention Ty.

Her blush deepened so much she felt like her face was on fire as she wondered what Ty would say if he saw Josh's truck parked at her house all night. Not that they weren't adults, but, well... It was Ty. Although he was her best friend, he was still a *man*. She felt the heat burning from her face in silent embarrassment at her friend knowing she was sleeping with another man. It was just something else she'd have to get over, she figured.

A few minutes later, she tightened her grip on Josh's hand, sighing in contentment. "Goodnight, Josh. I love you."

"I love you, too, Morgan." He placed another kiss to her head.

Being held in each other's arms, they drifted off to sleep.

Chapter 39

Mid-January

At Josh's for dinner, he cooked while she watched from the comfort of a chair. Taking turns cooking their meals made for an equal workload as well as providing simple enjoyment. One could learn a lot by watching someone else cook.

After they ate and washed the dishes, Morgan began walking around his living room, looking at pictures on the walls as he watched her from the couch with a lazy interest. He wondered what she was thinking about as he knew it wasn't the pictures. You could only stare at the same one for so long before you went cross-eyed after all.

She finally turned around, setting down her glass of iced tea on the top of his entertainment center. She just looked at him, like she was going to say something, but yet didn't.

Morgan noticed his eyes kept glancing at her glass, and with an inward smile, she picked it up and moved it to the coffee table, placing it on a coaster. She fought to hide her smile when she saw him visibly relax. When she went back to standing near the entertainment center, she turned around and looked at him. Again, she still didn't speak, but it was obvious she wanted to.

"Yes?" Josh prompted her, a small smile lifting his lips. Even Freeway had been watching her with interest, curled up beside Josh's leg, her purrs vibrating against his hand as he stroked her fur.

"Okay. Here's the thing, Josh. I've been thinking a lot about it, and I need another opinion."

"About what?"

"The trial. I really think I should go to it. It'd be closure for me, and I think this'll be the opportunity for me to get it. Maybe the last opportunity. Ty needs to know, so I need to give him an answer really soon. Do *you* think I should go?"

Josh didn't need more than a few seconds to answer her. "No."

Morgan surely hadn't heard him correctly, had she? For some reason, she'd been certain he would've agreed with her and Ty. "*No?* You don't think I should go to the trial? Why not?"

Josh looked at her, crooking his index finger at her to come to him. She did but didn't sit down. When she just stood there, looking down at him with a confused—and slightly defiant—look on her face, he leaned forward and gently pulled her down beside him. Morgan didn't exactly come willingly. She tried to pull her hand out of his grasp. He raised his eyebrow, slightly amused, and put more muscle into it until she finally plopped down beside him. Freeway gave what could only be considered a glare in her direction for jostling her.

Holding her hand, he linked their fingers as he rubbed his thumb over hers. He was thinking, laying out his thoughts before he spoke them. "You said you love me. And you meant it, right?"

"Of course. I would never say it if I didn't!"

"Good, because you can't take it back. I happen to love you right back. And I wouldn't say it either unless I meant it. That makes us a couple, a pair, a team. Right?"

Morgan thought for a moment. "Yes, I suppose it does."

"Then I stand by what I just said. I don't think *you* should go to the trial, but *we* should."

She looked slightly dumbfounded. "You want to go *with* me? But why?" she blurted out before she could stop herself. At Josh's calm look, she reasoned it out for herself. "Because we're a pair. A team. But this is different. We're not making a decision on what movie to see, where to eat, whose basketball team we're going to play on, or what trail to ride. This is serious."

"All the more reason for you *not* to go through it alone." He leaned closer to her, kissed her temple. "Sweetheart, if there's one thing I remember you telling me when all of this began all those years ago, it's that you went through it alone. Well, you're not alone. Not anymore.

"I'm not going to stay behind here, writing up work bids, hammering in nails, and sipping coffee while you're a few thousand miles away dealing with a killer's trial on your own. You're crazy if you think I'd let you do that! Certifiably crazy."

She smiled broadly, her green eyes glowing. The feeling that overcame her, just knowing he supported her was great. But knowing he refused to let her deal with this alone, that he'd drop everything to be there with her, and for her, was overwhelming. The immense feeling of gratitude that bloomed inside her brought instant tears to her eyes. Someone not in her exact position wouldn't understand the depth of those emotions.

When she felt she could talk, she said as firmly as she could, "Well, one thing's for sure. I'm not crazy, certifiably or otherwise. So, I guess that means you're right. *I'm* not going to the trial." Smiling, she placed her free hand on his cheek. "But *we* are. But only if you're sure. Seriously, I wasn't expecting you to go.

"If something comes up and you can't go, I won't hold it against you. You're a business owner, and I know you have a lot on your own plate. It wouldn't become a hot topic I'd bring up down the road. I promise you that, and you know how I feel about making promises I can't keep."

He placed his hand over hers on his cheek, brought it down to his lap. "Good to know you're a smart woman too. And don't worry about me. I can take off from work. Like you mentioned, I *am* the owner. Ryan is a great employee, and the best foreman I could ever find. And Kristi handles everything in the office with me. Anything they can't deal with can either wait, or they can call, email, or fax me. Sometimes technology is a nice thing to have around. So don't worry about me and my business, all right?"

He took her other hand and laced his fingers through that one too. "What about Ty? Will he be going, or will he be staying here to run the Center in your absence?"

Morgan hadn't even thought about that. Her look of surprise let Josh know that right away. "Oh. I don't know. I didn't even ask him, and he didn't say one way or the other. If he wants to go, Toby and Maya can handle things here, I'm sure. Kat is already running Quail Run almost on her own. But Ty may not want to go. I'll need to ask him."

She looked over at the clock. "He should be done in another hour or so. I'll ask him to come over here, if that's okay with you?" Josh nodded. "He needs to know I've made the decision to go."

Seeing Josh's raised eyebrow, she hurriedly corrected herself. "I mean, that *we've* made the decision to go." At his nod of approval, she smiled. "And Josh, I truly didn't expect you to go. It never even occurred to me that you'd want to. I'm used to dealing with everything on my own. And I can already tell you, it's a huge relief and an amazing feeling to know there's someone I can lean on. Besides Ty, I mean. He's probably glad you came along to relieve some of the burden I place on him periodically."

Josh replied, "No, I don't think he is. I think he's happy you're moving forward, that you now have someone in your life. But not to just share any burden with them. True friends aren't burdens to carry. And I'd say Ty is a true friend to you. I bet if he heard you say that, he'd be insulted, maybe even hurt, you'd think of it like that. But I could be wrong."

"No, you're right. I'm sorry I said that. Ty would never think of me like that, just like I'd never think of him like that."

She looked up at him. "And I'm going to promise right now that I won't cry or fall apart anymore. Or at least *try* not to. It embarrasses me to no end to think of how many times I've cried around you and Ty recently, but especially you. I don't usually cry or fall apart at all. Just in case you were worried you were with a crybaby or something, I'm not one. I'm not normally a high-maintenance type of girl.

"In fact, it's rare for me to ever lose my composure. Except for goodbyes. I *always* cry at goodbyes. And I hate it, really hate it, when I do."

Josh smiled at her tenderly. "Morgan, I've never thought you were a crybaby. You went through some intense emotions when you told me about your husband being killed, and then what you went through afterwards. That just means you're human. Nothing more, nothing less. And except for when you were telling me about him, I don't think I've ever seen you cry, or get upset about much at all. It's not a crime or a shame to cry, sweetheart."

"I know. But I just needed to let *you* know, just in case you ever wondered."

"I didn't, so don't worry anymore about it." He looked at the clock. "Let's call Ty now, shall we?"

Ty SHUT OFF THE lights, set the alarm, and locked the door before pulling it closed behind him. He waved goodbye to Toby, Bo, and Maya as they headed toward their own vehicles.

He drove over to Josh's, which thankfully wasn't in the opposite direction of his own house. Since it wasn't too far out of his way, he said he'd swing over there to talk to them when they phoned earlier.

He pulled into the wide driveway beside Morgan's truck and shut off the engine. As he removed his keys from the ignition, he wondered if Josh and Morgan got married someday, would he sell his house or keep it? Then he wondered if Morgan would move in here, or if Josh would move into hers? He figured he'd move in with her as it made the most sense. As Ty walked up the sidewalk, he began wondering what they had for dinner, and if they'd kept any warm for him.

After he hopefully brushed off all the dirt from his jeans and boots, he rang the doorbell, hearing it chime through the heavy wooden door. Morgan opened it with a smile, waving him inside. Stepping inside a few feet, he saw Josh sprawled out on his couch as he watched a ballgame. Morgan took his coat, hanging it up on a peg beside the door.

Ty grinned at him. "Well, don't you look comfortable? You know you can come down to the office and keep me company anytime she gets on your nerves, right?"

"Hush, Ty!" she admonished him.

Josh laughed as she motioned for Ty to follow her as she headed toward the kitchen.

Seeing their boots by the door, Ty quickly popped off his own before making his way to the kitchen. The warmer air inside the house was welcomed. It was a bit colder outside than the weatherman had predicted, but he didn't mind.

Ty stopped at the sink to wash his hands when Morgan pointed to it and quickly took a second look at what she was doing. "Oh, you're not doing what I *think* you're doing, or are you?"

At her smile and nod, he hugged her. When she began laughing, Josh heard from the other room. Taking a gamble, he called out, "Ty Stanton! I *know* you've got your hands on my girl again. You'd better be taking them off her before I get in there!"

He heard them both laugh this time. He smiled, knowing he was right but also in satisfaction as he watched the rival team miss their shot of tying the game.

"Here, I saved you some dinner." Morgan removed a plate from the oven and set it on the stove. "Grab what you want to drink from the fridge."

As he did, she slid silverware onto the plate of lasagna and green beans. She added some buttered rolls to the plate. "It's okay to eat in there. Go keep him company and out of my hair for a bit, okay?"

Ty chuckled, knowing she was teasing. "Thanks for saving me some dinner." He took the napkins she held out to him before heading to the living room.

Good friends, a sports game on TV, a home-cooked meal, and fresh peach cobbler would really make his day complete.

Morgan could hear them really getting into the game while she finished making the peach cobbler. She'd grin at their cheers of triumph and howls of disappointment. Being a sports-minded girl herself, she thoughtfully waited until she heard it was half-time. Sliding the dish into the oven, she figured now was a good time to talk with Ty while the cobbler finished baking.

When she walked into the living room, Josh didn't need to be asked to turn off the TV. She sat down beside him on the couch since Ty was in the chair. His empty plate was on the end table beside him while Freeway lay comfortably in his lap. She grinned at the cat, who'd obviously taken to Ty like The Darrells had taken to Josh.

Plunging in, she said, "Ty, we've come to the decision that going to the trial is the best thing to do. And by that, I mean both Josh and myself. He refuses to let me go through this alone, which I seriously appreciate and was not expecting. And we were wondering about you. Are you going too?"

Ty sat there in silence for a couple of minutes, contemplating the situation. They could hear the icemaker drop newly-made ice cubes in the tray. In the absolute and sudden quiet, it sounded a lot louder than usual. Quickly running everything through his mind that she'd just blurted out, Ty was already running scenarios and options through his mind piece by piece.

Now that Josh knew Ty was an undercover agent, he admitted to himself he was fascinated by wondering what was running through Ty's mind. He saw his new friend in a whole different light now. He really wanted to ask Ty questions, but he figured they'd have to wait. Probably for eternity.

Morgan leaned back on the couch into Josh's side, hugging a big throw pillow in her arms. Josh sat there, his arm now draped over her shoulders. Whether for support and for simply a comfortable position, Morgan wasn't sure, but she liked having it there either way.

Ty said, "As to me going to the trial, although I'd be very interested in the evidence and hearing it all firsthand, I can always get transcripts. Well, unless they classify and seal them. Then I could also get information from... other places.

"But me showing up could also compromise my cover unless I went in disguise. If I did go, we couldn't meet or talk since that'd arouse interest or suspicion. There are too many variables."

He thought for another minute before saying, "I'll stay here and watch the place for you. The trial could last quite a while. I don't know about you, but to me it'd be too long to leave the Center in the hands of someone other than you or me. You agree?"

Morgan opened her mouth to speak, but Ty cut her off. "No, Morgan. I'm not doing it just for you, but for me and my safety. I don't know who else could show up there. What about reporters? No, I'll stay and run the place while you're gone."

"If you're sure?" At his nod, she continued, "I'll be sure to let everyone know you're in complete charge while I'm away, which they really already do. I know I can trust you here. Thank you, Ty, for everything I know about and for a lot I'm sure I don't." She smiled at him.

Ty said, "Well then, you're going to need a cover story for here. We have to give a partially-true story. Stick to the facts as much as we can to avoid mistakes and getting tripped up. Although it's not really any of their business, it will become theirs if I'm any judge.

"But honestly, someone, if not everyone, will ask sooner or later especially if it drags on for a long time. If we just tell everyone upfront, that'll stop the majority of any talk, and we definitely must be on the same page."

Josh said cheerfully, "I know. We'll just say Morgan and I went on a little trip together. A lover's retreat or something." He and Ty smiled when she snorted. Glancing at her, he asked, "No? Why not?"

"I don't want them thinking we're out having non-stop hot monkey sex. I don't want to be the topic of barn gossip. I'd have to fire everyone!"

"Sweetheart, you probably already are. *We* are, I mean. But okay. We'll just say I left you, and you couldn't stand it so you chased after me." He paused. "Then we'd have hot monkey sex after we made up."

Ty began laughing when Morgan's face turned red in embarrassment.

Josh said, "No matter what we say, they're going to think whatever they want."

Ty backed him up. "He's right, Morgan. Look, everyone around here knows you two are a couple. And as far as I've heard, they really like the concept. Besides, it got Kat and Mel off their hopes of me and you so that's a nice side benefit." Looking at Josh with a grin, he added, "Thanks, by the way."

"I could've helped out with that sooner, if you'd told me," he joked.

Ty chuckled. "Yeah, yeah."

Morgan had to agree with them even though she didn't want to. Thinking for a moment, she said, "All right. We'll just tell them I need to go and finish up some old family business, maybe have a bit of a vacation, and Josh went along. We won't have a definite time of return but until then, Ty is in charge. That covers all the bases. Will this work for all of us?"

The picture of pure innocence, Josh asked, "So we can't tell them we're having hot monkey sex?"

"No! Geez. Show some of that class I thought you had!" Morgan got up and stood there for a couple of seconds, looking down at her laughing boyfriend.

With a twinkle in his eyes still, Ty said, "We'll work out a story before you leave. But her story idea should be enough. Don't worry about it right now. I just wouldn't mention the trip to anyone until we work it out, cover any other bases. We'll wait until we get closer to the trial in case it gets moved or something."

"No problem there." She walked over to get Ty's empty plate, saying, "Boys, you're missing the game. I think our team was up by only two. Half-time is probably over. Why don't you see what the score is?"

She walked back into the kitchen, Freeway trotting along behind her.

Josh glanced at Ty as he reached for the remote. "Is she a dream come true or what?"

Ty chuckled and nodded. "You're a lucky man, Josh. A very lucky man."

Chapter 40

April

TY RANG MORGAN'S DOORBELL and patiently waited in the bright porch light for it to open. He'd stood there for just a short time before it was opened by Josh, who stepped out of the way to let him enter. They walked past the suitcases lined up neatly by the door and made their way to the living room. Each took a seat in the quiet room.

Looking around briefly, Ty asked, "Where's our little warrior?"

"Upstairs. She wanted a few minutes alone before we leave."

"How does she seem to you?"

Hearing the concern in his voice, Josh said, "Well, all things considered, I'd say she's holding up pretty well. Eating is the biggest thing I've noticed she's let go of, but she at least nibbles now and then. Maybe it will pick up once we're there."

"Yeah, I noticed she wasn't eating as much the other day. But her spirits have been up as usual, and no one has mentioned anything at all to me about her. They *are* surprised she's leaving the Center for weeks though. This was to be expected as she's never left it that long before.

"They all accept the story we gave them, so I don't see any issues coming up while you two are gone. They also all know I'll be staying here at her house while she's gone. Toby and Maya will run the rides while I drive you guys to and from the airport. What about your business?"

"I'm going on a vacation with my girlfriend who's also taking care of some family business. They know Ryan and Kristi are in charge. If anything comes up, they can contact me. I've got a good crew with only a couple of guys Ryan needs to keep an eye on, which he knows about already.

"I'm not too worried about my place. I'll add some extra pay to Ryan and Kristi to help with the extra workload too. Since he just got back from his vacation, Ryan's rested and good to go."

Ty deadpanned, "Well, let's hope neither business fails while you two are away."

"You'd better hope not, otherwise *you'll* be out of a job too!"

"Then I'll be sure *she* at least has something to come back to," Ty teased.

"Do you think she'll let me and my cat stay here if mine goes under?"

Ty laughed. "That's between you two. But if she says no, I'll let you and Freeway stay with me."

"I'd appreciate that." Josh grinned.

Glancing at their luggage, Ty asked, "Well? Should we begin loading the truck?"

Josh looked at the line of suitcases and bags before saying, "Yeah. She'll be down anytime."

Grabbing a couple of suitcases each, they made their way down her wide porch steps and loaded up the suitcases in the bed of the truck. Ty took the one he brought for himself inside to his room since it was going to be an extended stay there at the Center for him.

Although it wasn't even six in the morning yet and still more dark than light, they elected to sit on the porch steps in the cool, fresh air to wait for the woman who meant so much to them both, in such different ways.

Ty brushed off invisible dirt from his jeans before he asked seriously, "How are *you* doing?"

Josh looked out over the desert before him, his eyes resting on the dark mountains. "All right. It may be rougher once I'm there, but you know what? I guess maybe because it didn't happen to me directly, I can keep myself removed a little. And hearing what Morgan went through already has prepared me for what could come. It still won't be easy, and I'm aware of that.

"I know she'll need someone steady, and I plan on being that for her. My biggest wish is that by her going to this, she'll get the closure she needs so badly. Maybe this will help her let it all go, to be free. If not, then we'll just go on as we are. We can still move on, move forward. It'll just take longer probably.

"But I really think my knowing about her past has allowed her defenses to come down quite a bit. And the relief she feels because she isn't hiding that huge secret from me anymore has made a big difference already."

Ty said, "I'm with you on that. She *wants* to move forward with you. She's taking chances with you I never thought she would with anybody, so whatever you're doing seems to be working. You're a really decent human being, and I think just what she needs. If you ever need me for anything, you just let me know. I'll do whatever I can."

"You know I will. And I count you as a good friend too."

"Thanks. I appreciate knowing that."

Josh decided to take advantage of it just being the two of them for privacy. "And I'd also like to say that if I can ever help *you* with anything, I would. I've given you a lot of thought over the past few months. And I came to the conclusion that you walk a lonely road yourself."

"I'd be honored to know I could be a true friend to you, Ty. Maybe you have a bunch of trusted friends somewhere else, but I'm here if you ever need one. And since I also know about you... Well, you have someone else now besides Morgan you can talk to."

Ty was inexplicably touched by Josh's sincere words. It took him a moment to respond. "Thank you. You're right in saying I'm on my own in a lot of ways. It's safer that way. But yeah, it *can* be lonely at times. The always wondering of who's trustworthy?

"I've enjoyed your company since we all met and began to hang out together. A cousin of mine who's more like my brother is my closest friend besides Morgan. Obviously, he doesn't live anywhere around here. I'd be honored to have you as a friend."

"Good, because you have me as one whether you wanted to or not."

Ty smiled, appreciating even more this man his best friend was dating.

Josh grinned back, knowing it was a hard thing for men to let other men know they need help sometimes, or just to know they have a real friend they can go to. Men aren't that different from women in many respects. And everyone needs a trusted friend.

Just a couple of weeks ago while hanging out with Damien, it suddenly occurred to Josh that Ty had no male friends here. No one close to his age, someone he didn't work with. The only men Ty was around were the young wranglers, at least as far as he knew. Josh decided that needed to change, and he was ready to be a true friend to him.

The two men sat there in silence now as they each were absorbed in their own thoughts. The Darrells trotted over and sat down in front of them. Josh pet one on the head while the other walked over to Ty.

Ty absentmindedly pet the dog for a moment. "As far as I know, there haven't been any changes to your itinerary. Flights are for sure the same. Captain Sinclair will be waiting for you at the airport near the security checkpoint by the luggage carousel and will take you to where you guys will be staying. If you need anything, he's your contact person. You're to have free access to a car so anytime you need or want to get away, you can.

"As far as I know, the media still hasn't gotten wind of her coming in for this. My contacts have told me this trial is generating a bit of hype though. With any luck, they won't realize she's even there, but it's a foregone conclusion to know they will at some point. She's changed quite a bit, but she's hardly forgettable." They grinned at each other before he added, "I know my people are going to do what they can to minimize it."

"She'll be in disguise anytime we're not in our room so that should help. You did good with that."

"Let's hope it works."

Hearing faint sounds behind them, they turned in unison. Morgan opened the front door and walked out, knowing they were studying her like she was under a microscope. She knew they were worried about her, but oddly enough, she felt strong and sure of herself.

"If you guys are ready to go, let's hit the road. I don't want to be rushed in case we run into bad traffic. You guys ready?" she asked.

Josh stood up. "I'll just head to the bathroom first." He walked inside, deliberately leaving them alone.

Ty walked to her, cupped her face in his warm hands. "I know you're going to be just fine, Morgan, especially so since you've got Josh with you. But I want you to know you can still call me if anything feels off to you, okay? Use your instincts. If they alert you, *listen* to them.

"And I'd really appreciate it if you'd call me once you're there so I know you're all right. We'll go radio silent after that."

Morgan nodded as she reached up and held onto his wrists. "I promise. Please don't worry about me, Ty. I'm not alone anymore, remember?" She gave him a small smile.

She crouched down to say goodbye to her beautiful dogs, kissing them on their heads as she scratched them behind their ears. The Darrells seemed to know she was leaving them. They were now whining and begging her with those intelligent brown eyes of theirs to not go.

She had to look away from them before her own eyes teared up. She already missed them, and she was still right in front of them. Last night after she said goodbye to Bombay, she later cried in the shower. She couldn't even stand goodbyes when it came to her animals!

Josh came out the door with a small bag, figuring they were ready. "Ty, do you need the restroom? I grabbed some drinks."

Ty shook his head as Josh walked toward them.

"I'll get the alarm." Morgan slipped inside, set the alarm, locked, and closed the door.

They all clicked on their seatbelts, Morgan seated between them. Ty started the engine and asked, "You kids got everything? Correct IDs? Tickets? Money? Phones? Chargers? Computers and chargers? Is the iron off?" he asked with a grin.

"Yes, Dad," Morgan replied, grinning.

Smiling, he put the truck into *drive*, heading down her lane toward the open road. As he glanced at the clock on the radio display, all he could think was that it was about time for this to end, once and for all.

WHEN THEY GOT THE truck unloaded at the Departure doors, Ty looked at her. His worried look was gone. Now he just looked unhappy they were going, and he wasn't. She gave him a long hug, resting her head on his shoulder for a moment.

"I'll miss you too." Ty leaned back down, whispered in her ear, "I love you, Morg. I'll be here if you ever need me to be."

She nodded before she stepped back and just smiled at him, knowing she couldn't talk because she'd start bawling. How she *hated* goodbyes, even temporary ones!

Knowing this, Ty looked over at Josh. He shook his hand, warning him with a look. "You'd better watch yourself. She's sneaky."

Josh grinned at his warning. "I've got her all figured out." Hearing Morgan snort at him, he ignored her and said in a conspirator's tone, "I just let her think she's in control."

Ty grinned. "Well, I can see this will be an interesting plane ride," he said as he stepped back, shutting the tailgate. "Now I really *am* upset that I'm not going with you." Turning, he just looked at them. "Well, you're all set. Call me when you land and get settled. If anything doesn't seem right to you guys, you *call* me."

"Yes, Daddy." Morgan tapped his face lightly with her hand, trying to talk calmly without falling into tears.

Ty grinned. "If I *was* your daddy, you would *not* be going on a vacation with just your boyfriend!"

They laughed as she began picking up their carry-on bags, signaling to Josh to push the cart. Turning to him, she joked, "Babe, we'd better go before Dad decides to cancel our lover's retreat. Let's move it before he changes his mind."

She blew a kiss to Ty and spun around, heading toward the doors. The tears she fought gallantly to hold back began streaming down her cheeks.

Josh smiled and turned to follow her into the check-in area.

Ty said softly, "I'm very relieved you're going with her. Take care with our girl, all right?"

"I've got her. See you when we get back."

They exchanged a firm handshake before Josh solemnly nodded again. Pushing the cart, Josh went through the glass doors and wheeled it over to where she was waiting for him.

Ty watched them as they made their way to the check-in counter. He saw her wiping her cheeks with her hands. Sighing, he stood there for another moment. He watched Josh give her a hug and kiss the top of her hair in comfort.

His heart aching for his friend, he got back in his truck and began the lonely drive home.

Chapter 41

CAPTAIN TUCKER SINCLAIR MET them at the airport almost two thousand miles away. Both he and Josh used the pre-arranged code phrase to ensure their identities, with Josh and Morgan using their new fake names to add an additional layer of protection. Both were relieved their new IDs and Morgan's disguise passed airport security. Once they both got through without a single issue, their confidence was boosted.

As the friendly Captain Sinclair drove them to their hotel, he gave them a large envelope that contained their ID badges, maps, and a page of general information they needed. Pulling up to a swanky hotel, he smiled at their looks of surprise. "They decided to splurge a bit for you!"

Morgan said, "Please tell whoever 'they' is thank you! Wow. We weren't expecting this at all. We may never leave!"

After answering their questions, Captain Sinclair gave them the keys to the car he drove them in. He waited a distance away to be sure they got checked in with no problems. When he saw the desk clerk hand them room keys with a smile and point to the elevators where the bellman was waiting with their luggage cart, he knew they were set. Slipping into the car waiting for him, he drove away into the bustling city traffic.

WHEN THEY WALKED INTO what would be their home for the length of the trial, Morgan's eyes tried to take in everything at once. She toed off her shoes first thing so she didn't track in anything to mar the beautiful floors and carpeting. As Josh helped unload the suitcases and tipped the bellman, she walked around the spacious suite.

She was thankful their suite had a fully-equipped kitchenette in it. That'd save them quite a bit of money on food, not to mention being healthier than eating out. Plus, it'd give them privacy and security.

She looked through the cabinets and drawers. Pleased, she found there were actual dishes, glasses, pots, pans, cooking utensils, heating pads, and silverware. There was even dish soap, SOS pads, and a drying mat.

A hand towel and wash cloth were folded neatly beside the sink with a tented welcome note placed on top. Curious, Morgan opened it and saw it was a personalized, hand-written note and not just a form-written printed one. *LIAM AND JADE, WE HOPE YOUR STAY WITH US IS ENJOYABLE AND RELAXING. PLEASE LET US KNOW IF YOU NEED ANYTHING AS WE AIM FOR YOUR COMPLETE SATISFACTION!*

After they were alone, Morgan walked over to the couch. Sitting down, she simply sank into it. She smiled as Josh made his way over, sitting beside her. He smiled as he, too, seemed to sink into the cushions.

Sitting there for a moment in silence, he said, "Nice digs, huh?"

She casually looked around. "Not too shabby. It'll do in a pinch, I suppose." They smiled at each other. "This couch is something else, isn't it? Wow. If the couch is this comfy, it makes me wonder what the bed is like. If it's too soft, we'll need to request a firmer mattress. We could suffocate on one this soft!"

Her gaze took in the suite again. "Doesn't it seem odd they'd go all out for us? A car, and this suite? I mean, this suite is not inexpensive by any means. Where in their probably tight budget could they justify paying for a place like this for an extended period of time? For someone like us, on top of that?"

"Not us. You."

"What?"

"They didn't set *us* up, but *you*. They're doing this for you, sweetheart. I'm here just by accident, really."

Morgan understood. With a grin, she squeezed his knee and quipped, "Lucky you!"

They relaxed for a few minutes, each collecting their thoughts. She removed her fake glasses, wig, and hair net, placing them on the end table beside her. She sighed as her long hair fell loose. As usual, Morgan's mind soon turned to the practical.

Leaning back on the couch, she turned just her head as she looked over at him. "Well, let's make it a home, shall we?"

"Sure thing. I'll take a shower first. Want a quiet night in? We could call room service."

"Yeah. I'm sure it's expensive though. We could order in a pizza. That'd be way cheaper. But we *could* splurge on ourselves for at least one night! If it gets charged to the room, I wonder who will actually pay for it since we're responsible for our food? It's worth the risk, I think."

She faced forward again, looking at the tasteful artwork over the table that could maybe sit four people if they didn't care about having elbow room. "How come you get to take a shower before me?"

"Because girls take longer, and I don't want you to use up all the hot water." He saw her smile. "Besides that, you can start a dent in what you brought."

She grinned as she replied in a teasing tone herself, "You brought a lot too. I mean, your little printer, the laptop, some office supplies, files. And we haven't even mentioned all your clothes..."

"And I bet you'll be using all of my equipment before this trip is over too. And that's fine with me because Mom taught me to share my toys. You can just thank me later when you do." He held back his playful smile, but the humor was lurking there in his eyes as he said in a slow, deliberate tone, "Every. Single. Time."

Morgan reached over for one of the small throw pillows at the end of the couch, then swung around and hit him with it. He quickly grabbed his own pillow, hitting her back. She squealed as their impromptu pillow fight soon got competitive. Josh laughed at her as she threw herself to the floor to avoid a head shot.

As he leaned down to whack her again, she grabbed him and yanked him down, rolled him onto his stomach, and sat on his back. She was suddenly holding his arms behind his back so he couldn't move. She blew her hair out of her face as she tried to catch her breath.

It took Josh a moment to realize what had just happened. How had she done that so quickly? He'd ask her as soon as he got his breath back. When he finally did, he tried to lift his head up to look over his shoulder but couldn't.

With the side of his face on the plush carpet, he asked, "Where'd you learn moves like that? Or should I just guess?"

Still catching her breath, she answered, "Ty. His training is paying off. I always wondered if it'd ever come in handy besides at the bar."

Smiling, she leaned down, kissed his cheek, then his temple before nuzzling his ear. "Let's call him and tell him I already got to take someone down. It'll be sure to impress him," she whispered in his ear before she gently pulled on his earlobe with her teeth.

Josh couldn't laugh with her sitting on his back. He knew he couldn't really roll her off either. Strategically, he acted like he gave up, waiting for her to let his arms go. Once he was sure he could move them, he quickly moved, knocking her off his back. He then rolled over and now had her pinned to the carpet. He held her arms out to the sides and sat on her thighs so she couldn't move.

He grinned down at her as she just looked up at him, surprise on her face. With a smirk, he asked her, "Are you *sure* you want to call him?"

He leaned down to kiss her. He felt her laughter bubbling up as he nibbled on her lips. He ran his tongue over her lips before he kissed them gently and with care. He heard her long sigh as he moved down her throat to where her pulse beat rapidly. He felt her fingers lace together with his own and squeeze them.

Making his way back up to nibble on her earlobe, he felt her move her head so he'd have more access. Taking advantage of the exposed skin, he tasted her as he moved back down her neck again. Her soft moan made his heart race faster.

Patiently, he worked his way slowly and thoroughly around to the other side of her neck, then up to that earlobe. He could hear her breathing more quickly and felt her shiver. She let out a small gasp, and he felt her fingers tighten in his own again. His lips journeyed across her face, finally coming back to her tempting lips.

With a tenderness that made her heart ache, Josh made love to her using only his mouth on hers. She lifted her head up to follow him when he began pulling back. She held him prisoner with her mouth alone.

When they ended the kiss, he just looked into her eyes for a moment. Hers were dazed and filled with passion. He felt sure his were the same.

Taking a deep breath, he contented himself with just looking at her. She was so beautiful, he thought. Her brown hair was spread across the soft carpet, framing her exquisite face. Those captivating eyes were locked on his, her soft mouth slightly open as she caught her breath.

A moment later, he noticed the little sparkle that came into her eyes. He waited for the zinger he was sure was coming. She surprised him though.

"I'm sure now, Josh," she whispered.

"What'd you just say?"

"I said I'm sure."

Josh had to swallow the lump in his throat. Was she talking about what he thought she was talking about? He looked into her eyes again. He'd kept true to his promise of letting her choose when to take their relationship further. She was more than worth the wait to his way of thinking.

"You're sure?"

"Yes, without a doubt."

He released his breath. His only thought now was how odd her timing was. As he looked down at her, he realized her eyes still sparkled. He knew that look. She was up to something.

"And what exactly are you sure about, sweetheart?"

"You know." Smiling shyly, she gently loosened one of her hands from his and ran her fingertips down one of his muscular and tanned arms.

"No, I don't. Why don't you tell me?"

Morgan sighed. Pausing for a moment as she trailed her fingertip back up his arm, she finally spoke. "I'm sure I need to call Ty right now." She looked up at him, humor radiating from her eyes.

She squealed with laughter as he grabbed the nearest pillow and whacked her with it.

Chapter 42

THE COURTHOUSE WAS MADE of old stone, probably quarried from the nearby land over a century ago. Morgan and Josh walked up the wide steps and entered the bleak and colorless building. The elaborate stone reliefs were its only saving grace.

They passed through the metal detectors and courthouse security with no problem. After using the restrooms and noting all of the exits, they walked down the tiled hallway to their assigned courtroom.

Taking a seat on an old wooden pew near the back—and on an outside aisle in case she needed a quick getaway— they sat down and waited. There were quite a few other people in the room already. She hoped no one recognized her. With the disguise Ty had created for her, they all felt reasonably confident she could go unnoticed. It'd have to be someone who really knew her, or maybe remembered her voice, to recognize her. Morgan casually looked around her to see if she recognized anybody, but she didn't. Except for one man.

She did know Prosecuting Attorney Wilson Andrews. He'd been building a solid reputation when she'd been in the area all those years before. When Ty had mentioned his name weeks ago, it seemed like a really good omen to her. She wondered if he'd been assigned this case, or if he'd asked for it. Would he recognize her? They'd frequented some mutual parties back then—her for family obligations, him for probably networking opportunities.

Morgan and Josh sat there, quietly talking to each other while waiting for the judge and jury.

And for the man who'd killed her husband.

———◦⟨⟨⟩⟩◦———

THEY SAT THROUGH THE opening statements and the beginning of the trial for the next five hours. Morgan mentally told herself to bring something to sit on for the future days if she ever had hope of feeling her backside again. Even with the two fifteen-minute recesses the judge had called, her backside was still numb by the time they came back in from walking around and visiting the restrooms.

Morgan listened to every word, every detail as it was being presented. They had yet to get to the details of the murder but were still setting up the case. When she began to get agitated and held her hands together, Josh simply placed his hand on hers in support.

Morgan made herself look at the man who killed her husband and shattered her life, forcing her to begin an entirely new one. As the proceeding continued, as far as she could tell, he never showed any emotion.

Every now and then, he'd turn his head to look around, to look at his attorney, or the jury. His hair was short and dark, and his build was anything but slight. His bulk was from muscle—not fat—under the suit he was wearing. She still couldn't see his whole face, just a side profile. She decided it was better to see him in stages. She'd maybe see him better when they walked him out later on when they were finished for the day.

If she heard him speak, would she recognize his voice as the one who had called her that long ago night? For some reason, the voice she remembered didn't seem like it'd fit this man. He was too bulky for the voice to fit him. Of course, it *had* been almost a decade ago, and people *do* tend to change over time. But would his voice?

When Judge Emerson finally decided to end the proceedings for the day, Morgan was thankful. She figured she'd had enough. And this was the easy part. Everyone in the courtroom rose as the judge left through his private door.

She got her chance to look more fully at the man who'd killed her Shane after the judge left the room. She'd never seen him before, at least not that she recalled. But would he know *her* if she wasn't in a disguise? The officers escorted their bound prisoner from the courtroom as she studied him.

As the spectators filed through the doors, Josh and Morgan remained where they were, waiting for the crowd to leave. Josh made eye contact with Captain Sinclair, their known daily dose of protection detail. Josh gave him a small nod as the man made his way through the small crowd and out the double doors.

Once everyone had exited the room, Josh looked at her. "How are you feeling?" he asked quietly.

"Fine, for now. I'm more than ready to go though. You?"

"A little anxious for you. But other than that, and the fact I can't feel my butt, I'm fine." Josh gave her a small smile.

She smiled back at him, silently thanking him for his way of calming her as they quietly left the room.

Throughout the day, she'd debated with herself about the wisdom of speaking with Wilson Andrews. Once again, she'd decided against it. Maybe at the end of the trial but not on day one. The main goal was to avoid anyone who knew her, anyone who could expose her to the media. Or anyone else who could still be looking for her. While Wilson could probably be trusted, she just wasn't willing to risk it so soon.

At this point, staying incognito was going to hinge on Shane's family... If they even bothered to come. *Why* weren't they there on the first day of the trial for their own murdered son and brother?

LATER THAT EVENING, THEY stopped at a couple of stores for seat cushions and groceries. Paying with their new debit card in their new names, Josh felt like a fugitive. It didn't matter that he wasn't.

It was just the fear hanging over his head of being caught that made him feel like one. It was scary and more than uncomfortable to be living under a new name, even temporarily. It felt like he was living a lie. Because he was. The constant stress was always there, wondering if they'd get caught using their fake IDs, or these new cards, or if she'd be recognized.

They returned to their room with their purchases with no issues. Shutting the door behind them was a relief to them both.

The first thing she did was take a shower, just letting the hot water run down her back to relax. Slipping into her pjs—the shirt he'd bought her on their very first date at The Neon Moon and a pair of shorts—she sighed. Combing through her wet hair, she almost felt like herself again.

It wasn't until he was relaxed while cooking their dinner that Josh realized how he'd felt at the store was precisely how Morgan had lived on a daily basis for the past decade, especially in the very beginning. She still was even now. And she'd done it completely alone.

Feeling the depth of his own emotions just for that night at a store, he was stunned at the sheer magnitude of what she must've gone through. He was now in her shoes. He just stood there and watched her as she stirred the iced tea she was making.

How in the world had she done it? he wondered. Even without a recently-murdered husband, and a possible killer searching for her, creating a new life from scratch was a massive and terrifying undertaking.

Glancing at him, Morgan wondered at the look on his face. "Are you okay?"

"How'd you do it? How did you begin a new life with a new name? And then start a business? After everything you'd just gone through... You had to..." Josh's voice trailed off.

She put down the long wooden spoon and turned to face him. She was expecting this to hit him at some point.

She tried to explain it to him the best way she could. "It was a leap of faith. Faith, and a deep, unconditional trust in my Shane." Tears suddenly sprung to her eyes as those old feelings of sheer terror and panic were resurfacing. She was back and facing it all over again in order to answer him. "I had to be strong and fearless because he needed me to be. I couldn't shame my husband by being less than what he was, and what he expected... No, *needed*... me to be.

"I had absolute blind faith in Shane having seen to every detail. How could I question him? If I did, I'd be questioning his love, his experience, his intelligence, and his faith in me to follow his directions. Questioning him was the last thing I'd ever do because it would've dishonored him, and his memory."

Josh got misty tears in his eyes as he saw them run down her own cheeks. Her mental and inner strength were no less than astounding to him. He pulled her close to him and just held her against him, rubbing her back. She held on to him, fully realizing how the first time she went through this she'd been so alone. This time she wasn't. The feeling of relief for having support now was indescribable.

She finally pulled back, quickly taking over the cooking duties so their dinner didn't burn or set off the smoke alarm. She wiped her cheeks as she stirred the food in the pan before turning back to him. Seeing his tears for her was nearly her undoing. "Sweetheart, I made it. I made it because I had no other choice."

She wiped the few tears from his cheeks as he stood there, unable to comprehend what she went through.

Josh nodded. He stirred their food this time and turned back to her. "I'm sorry. It just hit me, and..."

"Don't be sorry or embarrassed, sweetheart. I was expecting it to hit you sooner or later. This is real life. It was bound to happen." She cupped his cheek to get his full attention.

"And I don't think less of you because you cried for me. Real men can cry too. Your tears show me your love. Why would I think less of you for them?"

"I wasn't expecting it to hit me. Not that part anyway. It just hit me in the store, and again now... How *so much* could go wrong, and we'd be caught.

"And I thought about what you went through alone. How you'd just lost Shane... *And* had a possible killer after you! Still, you then give up your life and all that you had and knew. How even now, you're living a lie that has become your truth." He cupped her cheek. "I want to be strong for you, and instead you're doing it for me."

She looked deeply into his eyes as she said, "You *have* been, and without question still are, my rock. We both can't be the strongest at the same time. *This* time? It's my turn." She smiled fully then. "That's because we're a couple, a pair, a team. Am I right, or am I right?"

He smiled at her throwing his words back at him. Turning off the burner, he removed the pan before turning back to her. Taking her hands in his, he sincerely replied, "You're wholly right. And I couldn't have found a better partner. I'm so proud of you, Morgan. So very proud."

Her heart thudded before she whispered, "Natasha. Natasha Borden."

Josh's heart stopped. She'd given him her real name. But it was more than just her name. She'd given him her full trust. It was a powerful gift.

He framed her face in his warm hands before he leaned down and kissed her gently, then just another brush of his lips against hers. Pulling back to look into her green eyes, he whispered, "I'm even more proud of you, Natasha. So very proud and honored to know you."

AFTER THEY ATE THEIR dinner and did the dishes, Morgan joined him on the couch. Josh had the remote, flipping through channels on the TV. When he landed on a program about endangered orangutans, he put it down. Watching it with genuine interest, she rested against him, his arm around her to hold her close.

Somewhere along the line, she simply fell asleep. Once he noticed, Josh eased her down and let her head rest in his lap, tucking a small pillow under her head to make her more comfortable. He slowly threaded his fingers through her hair as she slept, sometimes running his warm hand up and down her bare arm. About an hour later, his own eyes getting droopy, he turned off the TV. Easing away from her, he looked down at her, hating to wake her up since she needed the rest.

She'd exhausted herself mentally and emotionally over the past few weeks. She'd kept up with anything and everything related to Harmony Hills as she was dealing quietly with her past. He was proud of the way she handled herself.

She thought of herself as a crybaby. No, she was far from it.

Sighing, he knew today was just the beginning. But this would also hopefully be an ending for her. Then she could start again. Or more accurately, move forward even more.

He walked into the bedroom, drew back the bed covers. He turned on the little fan they got from the friendly front desk clerk for the background noise and air movement before returning to her. He gently picked her up and carried her to bed. She hardly stirred at all when her head hit the pillow, already fast asleep before he'd pulled the covers over her. He leaned down and kissed her cheek.

He went back into the other room, checking the door locks and the *Do Not Disturb* sign again before turning off the last light. He took his shower, made sure their phones were charging, and double-checked the alarm before he slipped in beside her and turned off the bedside lamp. Morgan instinctively rolled over to get closer to him. As his arms closed around her, he kissed her forehead. Closing his eyes, he joined her in sleep.

Chapter 43

THE COURTROOM HAD MORE people in it today. Morgan and Josh wondered why. Were they law students? Or possibly reporters?

Carrying their seat cushions, they found a place to sit. They'd worried at the last minute the courthouse security guards wouldn't allow their cushions, but once the cushions went through the X-ray machine and were hand-checked, the guards approved them. One of them even smiled in understanding.

Josh watched as more people filed in and took their seats. It was now almost time for the second day of the trial to start. They had a judge who demanded promptness, and if you weren't in your seat on time, no one could come in until a recess was called. Anyone with a cellphone had better turn it completely off because if it sounded in his courtroom, not only would the phone be thrown out, but so would its owner.

Just as the doors were closing to signal the start of the day's proceedings, Josh watched as an older woman and two middle-aged men walked in. They headed directly toward the bench at the front of the courtroom. He just realized it was still empty while most of the other benches were full.

He studied the three adults with curiosity. They didn't bother to hurry to get settled in even though the bailiff watched and waited with a look of frank disapproval and annoyance on his face.

They certainly hadn't been there the day before. Their clothing spoke of money while their straight backs and patrician features spoke of family pride and polished manners. He turned to Morgan to ask her if she knew who they were, as he had his suspicion. The look on her face answered his unspoken question. He had a sinking feeling that Shane's relatives had just arrived.

He reached over to hold her hand to remind her she wasn't here alone and faced forward again. He was curious to see them better. As the bailiff ordered everyone to rise so the judge could come in, he saw the woman turn to speak to one of the men beside her.

Josh watched as the man casually looked around the courtroom. As his gaze neared them, Josh felt Morgan squeeze his hand almost painfully.

Out of the corner of his eye, he saw Morgan look down. His guess was correct. Surely if they saw her, they'd single her out. The man's gaze rested on her downturned head for a moment before looking directly at Josh. Josh glanced at him with a casual indifference then switched his gaze to the judge who was walking into the room.

Morgan finally looked up, wondering again to herself if they'd recognize her in her disguise. She made eye contact for just a second with the man looking at her, seeing the faint questioning in his features before recognition lit in his eyes. She casually looked away, acting like nothing was wrong.

As everyone began seating themselves, she watched as the man leaned over to whisper in the ear of the woman beside him. The woman nodded her head. She slowly turned around to look back at them.

No! Morgan silently screamed.

She saw a few others in the room turn their heads to look at them, wondering who those in the front row were interested in. To add doubt to her identity, Morgan herself turned around as well as if to see who they were looking at, or for.

She knew it probably wouldn't work, but it was worth the try. Her cover was almost surely blown now, and it was only the second day!

When Judge Emerson ordered the first fifteen-minute recess, Josh and Morgan quickly slipped out the door. They made their way down the hallway, looking for an empty room. Morgan was fine with a janitor's closet just to avoid a confrontation so soon.

"*Liam!*"

They saw Captain Sinclair discreetly waving them over to an opened door. As soon as all three of them were in the room, Sinclair shut the door. "As soon as I saw them walk in earlier, I was thinking of a way to get you somewhere quiet and private. I figured you'd want a place to go to. You guys are *quick!*"

Standing by the window, Morgan sighed. "I feel like a coward, but I just don't want to see them right now. Or ever, actually."

Josh leaned against the long table. "Well, it was bound to happen. We figured it would, sooner or later. They may not even be sure it *is* you. They could be doubting themselves."

Sinclair asked, "How would you prefer to handle this? Do you want to go back in there, or set it up where you can hear it in a private room like this?"

"I'm going back in there. I'm not hiding from them. Shane would be ashamed of me if I did that. He deserves better from me.

"You know what? I'm going to go find them, and talk to them. If they walk off, that'd be nothing new. If they talk, well, at least it's over and done with. With these people, no matter what I do or say, it'll be downhill right after anyway. I might as well get it done now to save myself the ulcer later. After that, we'll decide if I want a private room. Does that work, Captain?"

He nodded. "They may not expose you, Jade. If they threaten to, we'll handle it. You've got protection here."

Josh smiled as he hugged her, rubbed her back. "That's my girl! Make me proud. No backing down, you hear me? If they make you mad, just don't karate chop them, all right?"

Morgan grinned at him, slipping the glasses back on. "You just took all the fun out of it. Why even bother to go out now?"

"If you go all kung fu warrior on them, you'll make the news for sure. Just keep that in mind!"

She smiled. Looking at them, she tilted her head. "Well? What are you two waiting for? Let's go."

She confidently walked out into the hallway and headed toward the courtroom. Josh and Sinclair smiled at each other before they followed her.

As long as Josh lived, he'd never forget what happened next. He was dying to call Ty and tell him how proud he was of her. He knew Ty would be kicking himself for not being here to see this in person.

Morgan practically marched down the glossy hallway. Josh and Captain Sinclair had to increase their pace to keep up with her. Even in her high heels that went nicely with her short but tasteful skirt and satin top, she could move.

Near the courtroom, Morgan spotted the relatives who'd left her on her own all those years ago. They saw her practically charging at them and could do no more than stand rooted to the spot.

She walked confidently right up to them, not offering to shake hands. Giving them a brittle smile, she said, "Clare. What a surprise to see you here, particularly since you weren't yesterday. As well as you, Charles, Allen." She nodded to them in turn, briefly. "And how have you all been the past decade?"

Clare Borden had never really known what to say to her late son's wife. How her precious son could've chosen someone who worked with animals she never understood. Her son had been destined for great accomplishments in his life. He'd had every advantage, and money was at his disposal.

Her Shane marrying such a lowly woman was just beyond her comprehension. She'd thought their dating was merely an act of boyhood indiscretion, like sowing his oats with the locals. She'd never seriously believed they'd marry. But they did.

Now here she was, a dignified lady of status, wealth, and breeding in her top-designer suit, her hair perfectly set even in the early spring humidity they were experiencing, in a type of stand-off with the younger woman.

Looking at her former daughter-in-law, she was refusing to be the one to break first. Clare Borden didn't see it as being stubborn or weak, but simply as the way it should be. *She* was an asset to the Borden family. Natasha hadn't been, and still wasn't one now. And one did not bow to those who were lower in status than you were.

Neither of her other two sons had said a word either. Her sons were probably just as spellbound with this woman as her Shane had been, if she went by the looks on their faces when they'd first spotted her. They should know better than to go by a person's looks. But they were men after all. It's what they did.

But at least she'd made sure her other two sons married well. She'd refused any other option by threatening to remove them from the Family Trust and thrown out of her will if they married beneath their stature.

Morgan sighed. "That's what I thought. I see nothing has changed at all with you. That's a shame. At some point, I hoped you'd grow up and see that no one gives a care about you with your uppity, self-righteous airs. I even used to pray for it. Did you know that, Clare? I prayed for you and your sons. And I thank God that He helped guide me through the hurt you caused me."

Seeing people begin filing back into the courtroom, she turned as if to follow everyone inside. "It's so nice to know some things never change. Actually, *nice* is the incorrect term to be used here. *Pathetic* is a much better choice."

As she was turning to go back inside, Morgan heard Clare say her name. She stopped, turned back to face Shane's mother. "My name is Jade now. The person you knew ceased to exist a long, long time ago. If you must address me, you call me Jade and *only* Jade. Am I making myself clear?"

Clare and her sons could only stare at this stranger in front of them. Clare lifted her chin and spoke, "Jade, then. I wanted to apologize for all that happened all those years ago. It was wrong of us to shut you out like we did."

Her sons nodded their heads in unison.

"And we wanted to be here not only for the trial of Shane's murderer, but for you as well. We wanted to come to support you as this must be difficult for you. We're here if you need us."

Josh was incredulous. He stood off a few feet, close enough to hear and to clearly see the disdain on Clare Borden's face. He could hardly believe she could look at her former daughter-in-law with such distaste and contempt while simultaneously apologizing to her and offering their support at the same time. Mesmerized, Josh was waiting to see if the older woman choked to death on her pride.

His gaze turned to Morgan. Her face was carefully guarded. She wasn't allowing any of her emotions through. She refused to give the bitter woman any satisfaction of seeing her beg, plead, or to appear weak. She had no reason to do either of those things anyway. Josh silently waited, knowing she could handle this on her own.

Captain Sinclair had stopped and moved away from them a bit, looking like a casual bystander. He'd almost forgotten he wasn't supposed to know them. But he stood where he could watch and listen himself—and to be available in case it turned physical. He hoped not, for Jade's sake.

Morgan looked directly in their eyes, one person at a time. Letting none of the hurt, betrayal, and disappointment through in her voice, she told it to them straight. Her voice was iron-strong when she finally spoke. "Your timing *sucks*."

She watched as their faces showed shock at her hard words. She felt great. She really did. And she was just warming up.

"When I needed you the most, you threw me to the street like I was just some penniless little beggar looking for scraps from your golden trash cans instead of your daughter-in-law who'd just lost her husband. I was his *wife*, who was now scared and alone. That meant *nothing* to you.

"Guess what? *I've* grown up. I've made a new life for myself. I have true friends who care for me, and I care for them. And I know in my heart they would never, ever leave me hanging the way all of you did.

"Not a single one of you offered me support in my darkest hours. Sure, you were hurting yourselves. But you had each other to go to for safety, and for consolation. I understood you were hurting. But you weren't hurting like I was. You weren't alone and scared like I was. I had *no one*.

"Shane was everything to me. I lost everything that mattered, everything that was good in my life in one snap of Fate's fingers."

Morgan looked at them in turn again. With her own disdain now, she practically spat at them. "As for your support? I don't need it. I have all the support I will ever need from people who accept and love me for who and what I am. And that's something none of you will ever get from anybody.

"Nobody loves you for *anything* except your money. And it's not even yours. You never earned a penny of it. As I recall, Clare, that money was never in your maiden name, was it?

"Those who love me are far better humans than you could comprehend, Clare. They love me for simply being *me*. For all that is in me that you and your pretentious, self-righteous and pathetic family could never see, but what Shane could see so clearly. *I* made him happy. It was never you, but me.

"And if you want to offer *me*, of all people, support then there *must* be something in it for you. Publicity? Sympathy from the press? A distasteful show of false support to a widow you ignored and disdain even to this very moment? If this trial hadn't come up, I bet you wouldn't even be giving me a second thought right now."

Her voice had turned harder as she spoke. Almost a decade of pent-up emotions from being a widow, and all those years of being united by marriage before then to this family were breaking free. She didn't have to try and please them anymore. She didn't need to keep peace in the family anymore. They weren't her family now, nor had they ever been.

At their closed-off looks, she felt she was right. Nodding her head, Morgan took a step closer to them. Speaking softly, but strongly, she said what she needed to make sure they knew. "This trial isn't about *us*. It's about *Shane*, and what was done to *him*. He *died*. Do any of you get that? Nothing you can do is going to bring him back so you can show him off.

"It's about justice for *my* husband, who I loved in more ways than you could ever understand. You never accepted me and never will, and I don't give a fat rat's ass about it either. And Shane was *never* one of you. He didn't want anything to do with you!

"Don't play to the crowd now. It's bad form. Shame on *all* of you for even trying to take away attention from Shane, and what he went through, to gain sympathy from those who don't really know you. None of you could even bother to be here on the first day of this trial! You're all *disgraceful*."

Morgan looked at them one more time. "I never knew what true family and friends were until I began a new life on my own. And now *that's* who I surround myself with. People who would drop literally everything in their lives to show unconditional love and support for those close to them.

"You can keep your false, conditional offers of support. I don't need them or you. Just stay *away* from me. That's been easy enough for you all to have done in the past, hasn't it? Now you can just continue. You come around me, or even tell anyone I'm here, and I'll be more than happy to let the press know *exactly* how you treated your dead son's wife. I've got it all documented, and I'm not afraid to air it.

"But I'm not here to rock your little pathetic boat. I'm here for my murdered husband. All of you just stay away from me. This time you have my absolute, complete permission."

With that, she turned around and walked confidently to Josh, who was at the door beside the guard. She saw Captain Sinclair off to the side. He winked at her and walked to the double doors to follow them in.

Josh and Morgan took their seats where they'd been barely fifteen minutes earlier. She put down the cushion he handed her, not even glancing at Shane's relatives as they made their way up the aisle to their front row seats. She was still so furious and filled with adrenaline, her hands were shaking, and her blood was still rushing through her veins.

After Judge Emerson came back in, and everyone got seated again, Josh reached over for her right hand. He spread it out flat, palm up, on his thigh. With his left index finger, he drew a straight line down her palm. Then he drew a heart, finishing it with the letter *U*.

I love you. Morgan's heart swelled, and her eyes got misty at his message. She reached over and did the same to his left palm. She then placed her right hand in his left one and firmly squeezed their hands together.

Chapter 44

IT'D BEEN OVER TWO weeks of testimonies and physical evidence about her husband's last days. His mission was considered classified, so she still didn't know the exact particulars of the situation he'd been in.

Listening to some of the testimonies, she wondered if they were agents like Shane and Ty, or maybe from somewhere else. She couldn't imagine they'd be in court if they worked for the Agency, or would they? Were they in disguise, and she couldn't tell? Who were these witnesses? How they presented this case wasn't at all how she'd expected, so she didn't know what to believe. She just had to trust that Wilson Andrews knew what he was doing.

She *did* notice that the Agency itself was never once mentioned. She was pondering that for a long while when a sudden thought came to her. Did Shane's own family know what he *really* did? He'd never trusted them, so Morgan didn't think he'd ever told them. But even now, did they know? She doubted it.

For some reason, this made her happy. Just to know something else about Shane that they didn't. It was like more proof she knew him better than they did, and that he thought more of her than them. They'd been a team. She took solace in that.

But Morgan was also nearing exhaustion from the mental and emotional roller coaster rides she'd been going through—from the trial itself, and from being in close proximity to her former in-laws. More of Shane's relatives had shown up as the days dragged on. She refused to speak with any of them. They didn't even look her way, so she assumed they didn't recognize her in her disguise. Or if they did, they didn't care.

Her exhaustion was also caused by her nightmares. Those began after the testimonies of the coroner and others who'd found Shane's remains after being tortured and burned. The photographs put on the board made her sick, and her heart tore in two. She saw Clare wipe her face with a handkerchief trimmed with lace, sometimes dabbing at her eyes.

To Morgan, it looked more like a publicity stunt, something for attention rather than a distraught mother weeping for her murdered son. Seeing Clare's actions made Morgan feel even sicker. Josh seemed to agree with her as he just stared at her former mother-in-law, sometimes even shaking his head.

When those people testified, and their evidence was shown, it was all Morgan could do to not fall apart. While Clare was petitely, carefully dabbing at her eyes, Morgan was barely able to hold herself together. She wanted to scream, cry, yell, rage at it all, throw furniture, and punch holes in the walls. She wanted to strangle the man who killed her Shane, witnesses or not. She had to force herself to stay seated while the madness was boiling inside of her like molten lava.

Josh would swear on that bible in the courtroom he could *feel* her anger, and the depths of her sadness, pouring off her in waves. He'd put his arm around her and pulled her tight to his side, holding her hand in his, mentally prepared to bodily carry her out if she so much as tried to stand up or open her mouth. But she held herself together... until they were alone. Once they reached their car, her emotions would just let loose. He'd just hold her, and let her cry.

On those nights when those dreams and images haunted her, Josh had been there to wake her up, hold and comfort her as she tried to get her bearings back. He'd kiss her tenderly and tell her to just hold on to him. He'd hold her close to his warmth and soothe her back to sleep in his arms, feeling her tears, shudders, and her racing heartbeat. He'd had bad dreams himself, but he dealt with his by helping her deal with hers.

As the trial continued, Josh's thoughts ran wild in every possible direction. The more he heard, the more he couldn't believe Morgan had endured it alone. How would *he* have coped if this had happened to him? If it was his *wife* who was brutally killed? And not knowing why or where? And he'd have to change his own identity, leave his family, friends, job, where he lived. Forever? He wouldn't even be able to put down where he went to college or use old job or personal references.

He'd have to start from square one when he was already on square one thousand. Could he do it? He honestly didn't know.

But Morgan had.

Josh had another startling realization one day during court. He felt so dense for the thoughts that just now popped into his head. Something a witness said triggered the realization of why Morgan avoided cameras and publicity.

She'd refused to be interviewed by the local TV news crew that came to Harmony Hills during her hugely popular Fourth of July event. She'd answered the questions—but not on camera. She'd instead directed the reporter, Brenda Michaels, to interview her guests and take video of everything she had going on there.

Morgan had refused not because she was so busy—which she was—but because she was scared someone somewhere would see the aired footage, or what was put online, recognize her, and know where she was.

There were no pictures of her family in her house. Certainly none of her and Shane. Even on her website, there wasn't a single photo of herself—or Ty—on it. Only photos of what she had and did there: The buildings, the scenery, wildlife seen on rides, her clients having lessons, events she put on there, certainly the horses. But there was *nothing* that could begin a conversation related to her past.

She still feared for her safety, or she was on auto-pilot after having to live that way for years. She still had the need to remain invisible to the world. Natasha Borden could not be discovered, so she kept her previous life completely away from her new one.

It all made sense to Josh now.

Having these thoughts slam into his head, he now understood more about her. She rarely shared stories of her past because she couldn't risk it. When she met new people, she had an incredible knack of always turning the conversation away from herself to whoever she was talking to.

"People love to talk about themselves. It was their favorite subject."

How many times had she said that to him, usually in a joking manner? It was her way of deflecting too many questions about herself onto others so she could learn about them. And for them to learn nothing about her.

She'd been living and traveling a long, lonely road. And she always would be to some extent, just like Ty. No wonder the two of them bonded like they did. Truly, they'd had only each other, Josh thought. Just like Shane seemed to have had only her.

And as it became clearer to him what she'd told him about Shane's family, he simply couldn't fathom how she'd survived them either. Now seeing them firsthand, he could understand the wonder Morgan had displayed at meeting *his* parents. His family was vastly different from Shane's family and apparently even her own.

She'd only recently told him she was closest with her grandparents growing up. They were the ones who'd had horses and recognized her talent and love of them. Both had encouraged their granddaughter to follow her passion. But both had passed away soon after she'd married Shane. Her immediate family wasn't close at all. She'd never spoken of her family except for that one long conversation during their recent ride in her mountains.

Josh had always thought he had the best parents and family. Now he was sure of it. Learning so much about her own, he really wanted to share his with her. He felt almost obligated to show her there were still great families out there. She needed one.

Whenever they returned to their hotel room, they didn't mention the trial at all. They'd talk about it in the car, whether in the parking lot or during the drive. But once they hit their room, it was their neutral space. Their safe space.

Every few days, she checked her personal emails just for normalcy. Of course, she thanked Josh each and every time for use of his laptop with a hug and a kiss, which always made him smile. She could've done it on her phone, but giving the affection they both loved to get from the other was simply more enjoyable.

As necessary, in the evenings and nights due to the time difference and court, Josh was taking care of his business via phone, fax, and email. Kristi was a godsend, and Josh swore he'd let her know how much he appreciated her when they got back.

Morgan agreed wholeheartedly. But she also asked, "Why wait?" So she happily ordered flowers and chocolate-covered strawberries to be delivered to Kristi to show their appreciation.

Ryan was also handling everything as Josh wished. He'd had to fire one guy they'd been trying to give another chance to, but Josh wasn't upset at the news. His business and reputation were more important. Josh fully supported Ryan and let him know it. Both men were prepared for it, so Ryan simply called in another guy he personally knew so they wouldn't get behind schedule. Josh made sure he let Ryan know how much he appreciated him while Morgan sent another box of the strawberries just to Ryan.

Some of the media personnel were rumored to know the victim's wife was in attendance, or at least that she was in town. Captain Sinclair had recently warned them about this. But so far, the people who knew her had kept mum about who and where she was. To their immense relief, Shane's relatives weren't giving her up. They'd been interviewed a couple of times by the local television news crew and said nothing about her—even when asked.

Morgan's opinion was they weren't *helping* her by not telling the media who or where she was. Rather, it was simply they—mainly Clare, she'd bet—wanted all the attention on themselves. Of course, Morgan's threat of exposing the family's treatment of her could've also played a role in their keeping silent about her. That'd be bad press for them and would likely permanently stain their perfect façade.

Either way, Josh was never so thankful for such a selfish, conceited family until now.

IT WAS A LATE, muggy Thursday afternoon when Judge Emerson ordered that the trial wouldn't start up again until next Wednesday. Josh and Morgan knew they couldn't stand staying holed up in their hotel for five days and wondered what to do with themselves. While they loved their lavish accommodations, they were still outdoors people. They needed to get away for a while, somewhere with no media.

As they cooked dinner in their suite that night, Josh hit up the perfect solution.

"Sweetheart, let's take a road trip. We've got the time, and it'll give us a break from here. We need to get away to recharge. We need to do something completely unrelated to why we're here. What do you think?"

"I agree. Do you have a place in mind?"

"Kentucky."

"Why there?"

"Pops and Mom are there, and I bet they'd love to see you again. We'd have a free place to stay, someone else to cook our meals, and be out in the country again. We'd even have animals to play with. We could also take our laundry. Best of all, you could be disguise-free."

"You don't think they'd want to see their son? You really think they'd just want to see me?"

"I'm sure of it. Besides, they've known me for years. They like new people now and then to talk to." He grinned at her. "Whatcha think?"

She smiled as she got the plates ready, and poured tea in tall glasses. "When do we leave?"

Chapter 45

EARLY THE NEXT MORNING, they drove down to a rental car facility to get a different car. They had the feeling some people were figuring out what they drove and didn't want to risk anybody following them to his parent's house.

If anyone traced their car to the hotel and looked for them, obviously they wouldn't be there to be found. With luck, anyone looking for them, thinking they'd found the widow, would assume they were wrong and leave.

After they got a compact car that had great gas mileage, they each drove a car back to the hotel parking lot.

They rushed upstairs to get their laundry, a pillow, and the suitcases they'd already packed and went right back down a different elevator to get to the new rental car. Josh made sure he took his laptop and business materials with him.

Morgan laughed as she confided she felt like a teenager running away. Josh's laughter joined hers as he pulled out of the hotel's parking lot and headed toward the interstate that would take them south to Kentucky.

Once they got far away from the hotel, Morgan removed her disguise and was able to just be herself again. She put it all in a plastic bag and tucked it underneath her seat.

It didn't take long until an exhausted Morgan fell asleep. She'd reclined her seat back and propped her pillow against the door, mindful of the airbags. She was sound asleep within two minutes. She never moved a muscle.

Josh was a little surprised when she awoke on her own about two hours later. He thought for sure she'd sleep until he woke her up. She stretched as much as she could in the small space and looked out her window. Running her hands through her hair, she waited for the grogginess to dissipate. After a few minutes, she felt almost human again and adjusted her seat to sit back up.

Josh waited until he felt she was awake before he spoke to her. "Hey, babe. Feeling better?"

"Yeah, a little. I konked out, huh?"

"Like a switch was flipped."

She watched the scenery zip by them. "Wow, I'd forgotten how beautiful this state is."

"That it is. I think it's one of the prettiest states in the country. Every state has its own pros and cons, but Kentucky has more in the plus column. At least most of it."

As they kept driving, Morgan exclaimed, *"Man!* There are *a lot* of trees in this state. They're everywhere, and they're so dense."

Josh laughed and had to agree. Hours later, he finally turned into a manicured gravel driveway that wound up a small rise. Morgan could see a small herd of black cattle grazing in a large pasture and a few horses in another. As they slowly drove up the lane, the barns and house came into full view.

"Oh... Josh... It's beautiful here! How could you have left it?" The awe in her voice was unmistakable and made him smile in genuine pleasure.

Annabelle obviously loved the outdoors. She'd landscaped the yard in her spare time over the years with large boulders, wooden split-rail fencing, and white gravel. Morgan could see flowers of every color strategically planted around the house, barns, and some of the fencing.

There was a screened-in gazebo near an old, very large oak tree with two rows of solar lights lining the walkway to the only door. Josh wasn't surprised to see the hanging porch swing inside of it facing the horse pasture. He smiled as he pictured his mom swinging in the mosquito-free gazebo, gazing at her horses as they grazed on the green grass.

After putting the car in *park* and cracking the windows, he turned it off. "You want a gazebo like that at your place? I could build you one."

"No, that's all right. Thanks though."

Surprised, he looked over at her to see if she was serious or not, but her faced was turned away. He then heard her laugh.

"Are you *serious?* Would I *like* one of those? Duh! What do *you* think?"

He laughed at her incredulous tone of voice. "When we get back, I'll probably need to catch up on work stuff, but I'll see what I can do for you. Your wish is my command, milady."

Morgan leaned over and kissed his cheek. "I don't deserve you, but that's too bad. I think you're a keeper, Josh."

Slowly, he smiled at her. "I really love the sound of that. I might just keep you around too. And Morgan," he placed his hand companionably on her left knee, "you *do* deserve me."

"Well, I'm sure not going to argue with you about it!"

They both smiled as they got out and stretched. Swinging his arms around to loosen them up, he waited for her to stop gawking and reach his side. He stood there, loving the feeling of coming back to his boyhood home. With the exception of the new gazebo, nothing had really changed all that much. He was excited to see his parents and could hardly wait to go inside.

As they made their way up the wide concrete sidewalk to the front porch, he held her hand. They hadn't made it to the bottom step of the porch before Annabelle came barreling out the front door, pure happiness and joy lighting up her face. His mom squealed in pure delight at her unexpected visitors and rushed to meet them.

Annabelle hugged Josh first then quickly enveloped Morgan. Annabelle wouldn't let go and just rocked back and forth with Morgan held tightly to her.

Josh grinned at Morgan. "I told you she wouldn't mind us coming!"

Morgan hugged Annabelle back. It was so comforting to be held in her arms.

Finally pulling back, Annabelle beamed at them. "What are you *doing* here? Oh, your dad is going to be so thrilled you're here! He's in town right now but should be back within the next couple of hours or so." She cupped Morgan's face and said with a twinkle in her eyes, "He talked of nothing but you for weeks. You impressed the socks off my Patrick!"

Josh laughed at his mom and pulled her away to hug her again. With an arm around each of his ladies, Josh walked up the porch steps and stopped at the open door so they could enter the house first.

Annabelle led the way to the living room and turned to face them. She was dying to ask if there was a certain kind of announcement they'd like to share that would explain why they suddenly showed up on her doorstep thousands of miles away from their own, but she didn't ask. She noticed Morgan's tired face but didn't mention that either.

Josh looked around. "The place never changes, Mom. You've added some more blue to the room, but that's about it." Turning to Morgan, he explained, "Mom has a penchant for cobalt blue and will buy about anything that was made from it." He looked at the fireplace, commenting, "The mantle looks nice, Mom. The bright flowers are a nice contrast to the blue, aren't they?"

"Thank you. Angie and I put that together a while back."

Morgan smiled, knowing Annabelle didn't want to talk about her living room. Morgan looked at her. "It's so good to see you again, Annabelle. We were in the neighborhood and thought we'd stop by for a while, if that's okay with you and Pops? Josh said it'd be fine with you two to come over with no warning."

Both mother and son heard the slight hesitation in Morgan's voice.

Annabelle answered quickly and with certainty, "Honey, in this family you never need permission to come over. Family members visiting the others shouldn't require making reservations! That's what family's for—to always be there for each other. My kids didn't need reservations when they lived here, so why would they now?

"Unexpected guests are what we live for around here anyway. And running a farm means we're rarely not here, so it'd be hard to miss us. You can come over anytime you'd like. Will you be staying here overnight, at least?"

Happily, Josh said, "You get us for a few nights!"

Her reassuring words calmed Morgan. Her family wasn't as open as Josh's, and she didn't always know how to come to terms with it. Her family practically demanded a minimum of one month's notice if you wanted to visit—even if it was just for the afternoon.

"That's wonderful!" Annabelle looked at them, wondering aloud, "Now, how could you just be 'in the neighborhood'?"

Morgan replied, "Why don't we tell both you and Pops at the same time, Annabelle? If that's okay with you, I mean? We could stretch our legs a bit and get settled in while we wait for him." To distract her a bit more and from the need to, she asked, "Can I use your bathroom?"

"Just this once!" she joked, making them laugh. "Go down this hall here, on the left. Then come upstairs, and I'll show you where you can stay. There's a guest bath up there that'll be all yours to use once I get it set up for you."

With that, Annabelle headed up the stairs to see about getting it done. Josh turned to go back outside to get their suitcases.

It felt great to be home.

Chapter 46

MORGAN HEARD MOVEMENT UPSTAIRS so she followed the sounds into a large bedroom. There was a calico cat sleeping in the middle of the bed. Closing the closet door with her foot, her arms full of clean linens, Annabelle nodded her head toward the cat. "That's Mercedes. She's a people cat so be prepared. You're not allergic to cats, are you?"

Morgan smiled. "No, I'm not. I'm not allergic to anything, knock on wood."

She watched as Mercedes opened her eyes, looking at Morgan with interest. She slowly got up and stretched, her front legs placed way out in front as her back arched, her tail and butt pointed up into the air. Then she confidently walked to the edge of the bed, waiting for someone to pet her. Morgan walked over and obligingly began to stroke her head. She heard the purring start almost immediately and smiled.

"She's friendly like Freeway, isn't she?"

Annabelle nodded with a smile. "That's right! I forgot you'd been around Freeway. I should've known you weren't allergic to cats. I'm sorry I forgot about that."

"I'll let it go this time. Just don't let it happen again," she teased.

Annabelle laughed. Placing the linens on a chair, she motioned for Morgan to help her with the bed sheets. "Let's get fresh sheets on here."

Obligingly, Morgan pulled back the comforter, making Mercedes jump down. Together, they stripped the linens from the bed and put on the fresh ones. Mercedes promptly jumped right back up as Morgan put on the pillowcases.

Watching Morgan, Annabelle explained, "We turned a couple of the kids' rooms into guest rooms. This used to be Josh's old room. We upgraded the beds a few years ago for visiting family."

She walked over to a shelf above a tall, beautiful cherry wood dresser. "These are his from when he was a teenager." She showed Morgan a model airplane, tank, and ship. Annabelle blew off some dust before handing them over to her to inspect. "He was big into constructing things even back then. He could sit up here for hours and work on these models. He'd be so quiet, we'd forget he was even home until he came downstairs for something to eat!" She smiled at the fond memories.

Annabelle heard the front door as Josh opened it to come in. Looking at Morgan as she gathered up the linens from the floor, she decided to just be blunt with the younger woman. "You and Josh can share this room, Morgan. Patrick and I aren't overly protective parents with our adult kids. Unless you prefer to have separate rooms, that is. I don't mean to assume anything and offend you."

Morgan's face showed a little surprise at her bluntness. "Well, um... We aren't sleeping together like you might be thinking, but we do sometimes sleep together. One room is fine with me, and I'm sure is fine with him." She didn't know what else to say, so she just shut her mouth.

Annabelle put the linens on the chair, walked over and shut the door. Looking at Morgan for a moment, she finally spoke. "What you're saying is that you will sometimes sleep with my son, but you aren't having sex with him?"

Morgan's face turned red. It took all she had to look his mother in the eyes. "Yes."

"Why not?"

Shocked, Morgan just stared. "Excuse me?"

"Why not? I can't imagine why a striking, successful woman like you wouldn't want to be with my good-looking, intelligent son."

After a moment, they heard Josh making his way up the stairs. Soon Annabelle felt the door she was leaning against begin to open as Josh turned the knob. She firmly leaned back on it, shutting the door again and quickly locking it.

Calling through the door, she told her son to go away for a bit. She smiled when he asked why. She answered like a true mother, "Because I'm your mother, and I said so. Do it." She added, "Morgan and I want to have a little chat."

Morgan knew she had to answer as Annabelle continued to look at her. Pausing to think about it, she chose her words with care. "Because of a few reasons. There's absolutely nothing wrong with Josh that I know of. As a matter of fact, it's been a real test to not, you know, have sex with him. But I'm not an easy woman, Annabelle. I need to be sure I have my head on my shoulders before I, or rather we, go any further.

"Besides the fact that once a couple has sex, it seems like that's all their relationship gets based on after that. And I don't want that. There's more to a real relationship than just sex. You have it once, and then it's just easier to continue on with it. This normally causes you to lose focus on the more important things. At least, that's how I see it. And although we'd be safe and careful, I myself don't want to deal with a pregnancy scare." Morgan left it at that.

Annabelle thought about her answer. As a mother, she loved her for it. As a woman, she accepted and fully respected her for it. She was very glad her son hadn't hooked up with an easy, loose woman.

Finally nodding her head, she said, "I know you're probably shocked at why I'd be asking, almost wanting, you to have an intimate relationship with my son. If I thought you were a loose, immoral woman, you'd bet your business I wouldn't want you to. But you're not that type at all. And if we raised him right, he wouldn't want to be with you if you were," she added simply.

"And I don't mean to sound like I'm actually encouraging you to do it—because I'm not—but merely asking why you haven't? And if you think it's none of my business—which it isn't—you just tell me that too."

Annabelle walked over to the window, drawing back the curtains to let in a little more light before opening the window to allow in some fresh air. She continued when her guest still hadn't said a word, "We'll just let this stay open for a little bit, okay? The AC is on, but since this room is normally closed up, we'll just air it out some more. Mercedes got lucky when I opened it up just yesterday to get linens from this closet. I didn't have the heart to kick her off the bed!"

She contemplated Morgan for a moment before she continued, "And although I'm an older person, I don't always agree with the saying one must have a marriage certificate in order to do it. That's something mankind came up with. I personally believe it's what's in a person's heart and soul that makes it right or wrong.

"What if there were no ministers around to perform a wedding ceremony? What then? Are people in other countries who are married there less married when they come here to the USA? And vice versa? Native tribes have their own customs too. What about the Quakers, Amish?

"How was it Adam and Eve were allowed to have sex and not be sinning? Or their kids later on? Heck, they had sex with each other, didn't they? Who else was there, if you believe everything you read? Some say there were gods and giants walking the earth, too, so maybe they all got together. But what happened to the gods and giants? Were all those first humans living in sin and slated to burn in hell for it? They couldn't have been forgiven for their sins through Christ because He hadn't been born, crucified, or resurrected yet.

"Have you ever wondered who was the very first couple married by man? And how did they decide what the vows would be? Most modern marriages take a good chunk of the ceremony from the New Testament, so what were marriage ceremonies like all those hundreds or thousands of years before those verses were even written? Did it mean they were living in sin?

"History has proven many marriages were arranged by parents or politicians wanting a political hold, an alliance, money, status. It was rarely from what was in their kids' hearts. For those marriages that were not from what their kids wanted, did them having sex make it wrong? It probably didn't come from their hearts. I'm quite confident and disgusted to say many times it was probably more like raping the young woman, likely for the rest of her life. What rights did women have? Even in these modern times, there are countries who still see women as less than oxen.

"What exactly are ministers, preachers, rabbis, and priests anyway? They're simply people who went to a school to be taught about a certain point-of-view about God. Then they get a certificate that tells the world they're godly? I don't agree with that. And I've heard one can actually get a minister's license just by paying twenty-five dollars online, and that's it! You can't buy your way into something like that.

"Some of the most God-fearing people I know live in shacks and sell vegetables for a living. They don't go to a church but believe in their hearts about God. Ministers and priests? They get charged with killing their spouses, stealing from the coffer, and molesting kids all the time. Child porn is not adult porn—it's child sex abuse. No ifs, ands, or buts. Think of how many so-called godly men, and even women, are child sex offenders. That's not to say they're *all* bad. I'm just saying they're no godlier than anyone else is."

She sighed, offered a smile. "And I've gone off on one of my tangents, haven't I? My kids hate it when I do that!"

Morgan had taken a seat on the side of the bed as the older woman spoke, captivated by her viewpoints. They were making her think. Mercedes crawled into her lap, nudging her hand for attention. As she stroked the cat, she confessed, "I've often wondered that myself. I mean, about the ministers and viewpoints on God. I believe He's been with me every step of the way in my life, but it's just my point-of-view of Him.

"I talk to Him daily like He's a friend of mine who's willing to just listen to me. Most of the time, it's in my head, but I talk out loud as well. And when something good happens, I always make sure I thank Him for it. I don't want to be one of those people who only cry out for help when things go wrong, you know? I'm far from perfect, but I try to live a good life, and keep God in it. I just don't go overboard, or to the extreme.

"And with what I've been given, as in my interests as well as natural talents, I try to use my talents to make it better. Like the Parable of the Talents, I think I need to find a way to make it more, or make it better. I don't want to waste anything I've been given or worked for, but how do I know for sure? It's just material stuff in this life, so does it really matter?"

Morgan paused, looking at the woman patiently listening to her. "As for religions, I'm not a church-goer anymore. Every religion out there can prove, more or less, their religion and viewpoint is the correct one. But they also don't agree on an awful lot of issues, and they can twist the scriptures around to fit their ideals. How's one to know which one is the *real* one? I've had friends over the years from every denomination out there, and I don't think there's just one, true religion.

"That's why I don't go to a specific church, or even like organized religion. I don't agree with religious leaders being seen as a prophet of God, or being worshipped as basically a god. I also don't agree with religious leaders who live in multi-million dollar mansions instead of a normal house. They live in excessive luxury while most of their congregation lives in cramped, rented apartments. Where's the humility? Why does a single man, or a couple, even *need* a mansion? They sure aren't taking in the homeless, widows, or orphans!

"On the other hand, the bible also talks about kings, queens, and riches. Men who owned thousands of sheep, goats, camels, slaves, or servants. I don't think of *being* rich as a sin, but the excessive and wasteful use of money? It sure *seems* like one! Those millions spent on a temporary house for one or two people's ego could be better used to help thousands of others. It's not for me to say or judge—but I *can* have an opinion.

"There was also far too much hypocrisy and passing judgment to suit me. I realize that no church is perfect because they all consist of imperfect people. A church is just a building, a location. But I find I feel closer to God when I'm not around people who spout religious views at me."

Looking up, she had to add, "But I do find it confusing, and maybe just a little shocking, to meet a mother who is basically encouraging her son's girlfriend to sleep with him. That's more than just a little modern thinking, don't you think?"

Annabelle smiled. "I've an open, realistic mind. The way I look at it is this, my dear. When two people love each other, progressing to that next step is natural. A piece of paper just means it's okay to have sex. In other peoples' eyes and minds you're allowed to now.

"Since when do people who are truly in love need to have others' permission on such a personal subject? That's just hogwash! It's none of their business at all. As long as there is mutual respect, maturity, and responsibility, it's a natural step. Unfortunately, most young people today don't wait to find that."

She cupped the younger woman's cheek for a moment and studied her face. "When I see you and my son together, I see a love that is real, deep, and natural. It's not a passing infatuation like a high school crush. Maybe you two are still learning about each other to be sure of it yourselves, but I feel it because it can't be faked. You'll need a lifetime together to learn about the other, but even that won't be long enough.

"Couples must realize they both will change over time, and be prepared to accept the differences as they grow and mature. Life itself, and all we experience in it, will inevitably cause us to change.

"Patrick and I are soul mates, but we also still change even after all these years together. It's what people *do*. We get along very well most of the time, but we still argue now and then. I've even made him sleep on the couch a couple of times, but that's just because I was feeling ornery."

Annabelle chuckled and walked to the other window, sliding back the curtains. "And that was quite a long time ago. The older we get, I've come to realize someday one of us won't be here for the other. I want to consciously cherish every moment I can with my love."

Seeing her son's girlfriend sitting on the bed dutifully petting Mercedes made Annabelle happy. It was a calming picture in her mind. "Neither one of you, as far as I know, are the type who sleeps around with anyone and everyone they come into contact with.

"Now, I *don't* agree with people who do *that*. Or when they're just feeling lonely, or just looking for a good time out of boredom. Recreational sex is *not* what I'm talking about here. Nor are either of you the leech-type of person who can't seem to exist unless they're with someone.

"Both of you are mature, responsible, very selective, and must be sure of the other first. And if you're waiting to be sure you don't hurt either yourself or my son, and he's waiting because he wants you to make the decision with a clear heart, or for the same reasons that you have, that's a lot more than the bulk of the world's population is doing. There's absolutely no rush to it.

"If you feel it best to wait, then by all means, you wait. It's no one else's decision but your own. Not even my son's. You first respect yourself as a woman, an individual who matters. Just be safe and responsible when you are ready to move forward, you understand?

"You both believe in God, and have similar goals and lifestyles from what I know. You both value friendships, giving to others, showing respect, and being loyal. And both of you adore animals. I don't trust people who don't love animals, even less if they don't even like them. I've never met a single person who didn't like animals that was a nice, trustworthy, upstanding person. There's always just something off about them! Maybe it's not true of all people like that, but I've never been proven wrong.

"Anyway, Morgan, dear. You don't do anything until you're both ready to. Sex is seen nowadays as just a thing to do on the very first date, as common as eating dinner or drinking tea or alcohol. That's wrong. I wish I could go out and talk some sense to all of the young people out there, especially the young women. I'd tell them to place a much higher value on themselves and stop putting themselves on the clearance rack! The pressure must be enormous for the dating population out there.

"For you and Josh to have been together as long as you have and not had sex yet speaks volumes because not many young people can do that. It takes a very strong person these days to be able to do it. Or rather, *not* do it. Having Val and Angie was stressful for me because I was always scared they'd come home pregnant from a deadbeat guy. Thankfully, they didn't. We tried to instill values and strength in them, but a parent can only hope!

"You and Josh are incredible role models for others, whether you know it or not. And it gives me hope that this world isn't completely in shambles yet."

Morgan nodded, tears misting her eyes. She wasn't sure if it was simply exhaustion, or the simplicity of an older and wiser woman telling her what she'd been agonizing over for a long time.

Looking down at her hands, clasped in her lap, she said softly, "Hurting your son in any way is the absolute last thing on this earth I'd ever do. He's the best person I know of, and I've known a couple of good ones. I don't want to keep him waiting forever either. Or myself, when it comes down to it." She smiled wryly, but it was still a smile. Mercedes bumped her head against Morgan's hands, so she automatically wrapped the cat up in her arms.

She looked at Annabelle for a moment, not even nervous now discussing this very personal issue with the mother of the man she was seeing. "But I need to be as sure as

I can in my own heart of why I'd be intimate with a man. *Any* man. I have to be able to look at myself in the morning, and every day after that, and know as well as I could that I wouldn't have regrets, or wake up feeling used or empty. Until then, it's better for us to wait. But I do love those times when I wake up with him there beside me, and his holding me when I fall asleep. Or the other way around."

Annabelle walked over and hugged her. "As his mother, I have to say I hope you and my son stay together. I couldn't have found a better woman for him myself. And as a woman, I agree with you. We must be as sure as we can be, and not let others dictate our lives. You stand strong on your convictions. Don't let anyone sway you. When you're ready, you'll know.

"But remember, too, Morgan, sometimes the mind gets in our way. We can get so entangled in the way society dictates the way we should live, we are apt to ignore or bypass something that may never come to us again. Love is a most precious gift, and we all need to take advantage of it and not let it slip by us. Listen to your feelings.

"The history of the world is full of changes in society, the rules of the classes, the rich and the poor. There have always been the haves and the have-nots. Sometimes we must simply follow where our hearts, our feelings, lead us. Feelings were given to us by God, so they're more real and true to me than rules written by mere men, especially by men who don't even respect women. Those men are everywhere, and they disgust me!

"We must also use wisdom. We need to think of the repercussions and consequences to anything we decide to do, or not do. You are a wise and discerning woman. You aren't the type who believes sex leads to love rather than the other way around.

"Listen to your feelings, your gut, and always stay true to yourself. In the end, you're the only one who really matters to yourself when you look back on your life. How well did you live it?" She cupped the younger woman's cheek, leaving her warmth on it when she removed her hand.

Standing up straight, Annabelle asked with a smile, "We're okay, then? Should we let him in now?" She went over to close the window and then picked up the pile of linens from the chair and prepared to open the door.

Morgan smiled back. "Of course. And thank you, Annabelle, for listening and advising me. I'm not too proud to admit I could use some advice now and then. I tend to analyze things to death so a fresher viewpoint always helps. Maybe my brain waves can relax a little now!"

She let out a breath as she put down Mercedes. "How about I go get Josh now?"

Chapter 47

AFTER MORGAN AND JOSH got settled in his old room, Annabelle made them a light snack while they talked and waited for Patrick to come home. It was barely an hour later when they heard the front door open and close.

Annabelle winked at them when her husband called out, "Annabelle! Are you entertaining some salesperson again?" They all heard the humor in his voice. Annabelle motioned for them to stay seated at the kitchen table and just let her husband walk in on them.

When he rounded the corner and walked into the kitchen looking for his wife, he stopped dead in his tracks. Surprise showed across his face then delight as it registered who was sitting at the table. Josh and Morgan stood up, smiling. Patrick walked right past his son and made a beeline for his girl.

Morgan laughed as Josh's dad gave her a bear hug, saying, "Morgan, darling! I've been waiting for the longest time to see you again. What took you so dang long?"

Josh sat back down, acting like he was resigned to the fact he now took second place to Morgan. He rested his chin on his hand as he waited for his dad to remember he was even there.

Morgan smiled at Patrick. "I tried to get here as quickly as I could. You must remember what a busy woman I am."

Patrick smiled at her before turning to his son, laughing at his resigned look. "Oh now, son. Don't be pouting. Ladies first, you know." He enveloped his son in his strong arms. Pulling back, he ruffled Josh's hair like he did when Josh was a boy.

Annabelle leaned against the counter, smiling as she watched the little reunion. "Dear, they've come to visit us for a little while. They need to leave on Tuesday, in the afternoon at the very latest, so that morning would be better so they aren't rushed. It looks like we have a few full days ahead of us!"

Patrick smiled broadly in delight. "You bring your laundry?"

Both Morgan and Josh nodded, causing him to grin. Slapping his hand on the counter, Patrick said, "I knew it. I just *knew* it! Every single time this boy came home for a visit he'd bring his dirty laundry along. And he wouldn't leave until it was done. Nothing has changed there, I see."

Josh smiled. "Well, I'd hate to break with such a time-honored tradition and disappoint you, Pops. We were deliberately going to leave our dirty laundry, but we decided to go ahead and bring it."

"Leave it where?"

"Indianapolis."

"What're you two doing in Indiana of all places? Are you at a horse show or something?"

Morgan said, "No. We're up there attending to some old family business. It's important, but being around my family is much more stressful than being around yours."

She felt bad lying to his parents since none of her actual family was even there, so she white-lied by counting Shane's family in her statement.

She looked at Josh, placing her hand on his and giving it a squeeze. Trying to keep it light, she said, "And your selfless son here volunteered to come with me to be my unfailing supporter and full-time therapist."

His parents smiled at the last.

Looking back at his parents, she added, "And I thank God every single day for Josh coming with me. He's my rock right now and has been for months now—there's no doubt about that. Thank you both for raising such a fine man. There aren't many out there like him. You have an idea of how important Ty is to me, right?"

They both nodded.

"Then you may have an inkling to how very important Josh is to me now too."

Patrick looked at his wife. "I told you she was smart, didn't I?"

Annabelle chuckled. "Yes, you did. We figured that out long ago when we first met her though. Our son wouldn't pick just anyone after all. He's smart too."

Morgan shook her head. "Thank you for not adding any kind of pressure on me."

They all smiled at her.

Holding back her own smile, she added, "But the *other* reason we came down here is because your son really just wanted to do his laundry for free. He was willing to rent a car, splurge for gas money, and drive for hours in order to do it. He said something about doing it here for free was cheaper than going to a laundry mat. I'm still trying to work out that logic myself." She sighed. "I hate to be the one to break the news to you, but your son *may* not be as smart as you think he is."

With a big grin, Josh wrapped his arms around her and hauled her against him. Her last comment and Josh's playful act with her made his parents laugh in delight.

When Josh let her go, Morgan smiled at Josh's parents. "You know, I've really only ever had two constant things throughout my life. One is my belief and faith in God, and the other is my horses. In those down moments I've had over the years, those two things kept me going and motivated—My God and my horses."

She glanced at them all before she continued, "And I hope I have the privilege of keeping all of you now as my next constants. Along with Ty, who's been there for me for a very long time now, I'd be willing to add you guys to the group."

Josh wrapped his arm around her shoulders, pulled her to his side and placed a light kiss on her head. "You've got me, darlin'. And I bet these two won't leave you either."

Patrick agreed. "You just *try* to get rid of us. The Wrights stick like cockleburs to a saddle blanket."

Josh groaned. "Those are the *worst* ones, Pops!"

"Yep, but that's why they're the best example to use here!"

Smiling, Morgan leaned against Josh. Listening to their ongoing banter, she wondered why her own family had never offered her what these people had so easily: Unconditional support, acceptance, and love. She decided she'd rather make *this* family all hers.

In that moment, she felt an unexpected weight lift from her shoulders. She was building her own family, and that was that.

Chapter 48

His parents were the perfect hosts, and the happy-go-lucky and carefree family they were seemed to resonate boundlessly. No matter what they were doing, they happily did it together.

Morgan felt welcomed and was at peace there. This break was sorely needed for her to recuperate. She also saw it as a major bonus that Josh was unexpectedly able to come home. The fact it only cost them the price of a rental car and some gas was a huge blessing.

A couple of times Josh had to do a little work with Ryan or Kristi, but for the most part, they were free to do as they pleased.

Remembering a conversation from when his parents had visited Josh, Morgan suggested he take his mom out on a long ride, just the two of them like they used to do. She was sure the two of them needed their alone time, but she wasn't sure they'd do it with her there. She figured they'd worry about offending her if they asked her to stay behind. Josh hugged her, thanking her for her thoughtfulness.

Morgan also figured she and Josh could use some time apart themselves. Just for personal space as they hadn't been apart at all in weeks.

Upon their return, Morgan saw how happy they both looked, especially Annabelle. Later when she and Josh were alone, she insisted he go riding with her every day. "Make her happy. It's so good for you too. You said yourself you're rarely ever home now.

"One day, it'll be the last ride. So get in as many as you can for the both of you. Trust me. Make your memories while you can."

They also went out on a couple of rides as a group. Morgan could barely remember the last time she rode a horse in grass. When she mentioned that, they all got into a friendly argument about whether it was correct to say *in* grass, or *on* grass.

Patrick challenged them when he pointed out, "In horse racing, it's *on* turf. So it's *on* grass. Prove me wrong."

Josh countered. "That's probably an English thing, Pops. This is America. It's *in* grass here. And we're not racing."

"It is if we're running."

Annabelle teased, "But right now, we're walking. So when walking, it's *in* grass, and when running, it's *on* grass. Sounds logical to me."

Morgan said, "Well, human runners run *on* pavement, not *in* pavement. But wait. Planes fly *in* the sky, not *on* the sky."

Josh added, "Is it walk *in* weeds, or *on* weeds? Maybe it depends if they smoked it first."

They good-naturedly argued this topic throughout the ride with no one being a clear winner.

One night, Morgan met Josh's two older sisters. Valerie and Angelina drove back to their childhood home when their mom called. Excited about seeing their brother—and meeting this woman their parents raved about—they arrived the next evening with their own families in tow.

Just as his parents expected, Morgan had no problem befriending what they hoped would one day be her sisters-in-law. Patrick noted his two sons-in-law, Jack and Dan, kept staring at Morgan when Josh's back was turned. He told them they'd better stop as someone was bound to take offense, whether it was Josh, Morgan, or their own wives. They both laughed at Patrick, knowing Val and Angie would take their obvious interest in the gorgeous woman from Arizona in stride.

But Annabelle wasn't so diplomatic. She flat-out ordered them to show some respect as she didn't want Morgan or her son offended. Annabelle wouldn't put up with these two men being the cause of future family drama between her children. Family unity was of utmost importance to them all. They meekly obeyed her without another word.

On another evening, Annabelle had Damien's mom come over for dinner. Annabelle figured she'd love to see Josh again, meet his girlfriend, and hear firsthand about her own son from his childhood friend. The five of them spent hours together, allowing Morgan to learn more not just about Josh, but Damien and Laura.

Having this time with Josh's family was both eye-opening and soothing for Morgan. Her own family was never close. She hadn't even had contact with them since she'd disappeared, and rarely before then. And Shane's family was a colossal failure in her experience.

In her mind, her families came from Lifetime movies and Dateline episodes. But Josh's family, she was certain, came straight from Hallmark.

Chapter 49

NEITHER WANTING TO LEAVE the next day, both Josh and Morgan insisted they get the most out of their visit. After they arrived back home later that night after going out for dinner, they all sat in the living room, talking and again playing a marble game they called Fast Track. Morgan got addicted to it in no time. Josh promised to make them their own board once they got home.

After some time, his parents hugged them both, wished them a good night and headed off to bed. Annabelle insisted they just get up in the morning when they wanted to and not a minute before.

Resting on the couch with a single lamp on low, Josh and Morgan simply enjoyed the quiet. After a bit, Josh laughed when he said he hadn't sat alone with a pretty girl in the dark in that living room since he was a teenager. He leaned over to steal a kiss like he said he did back then, making Morgan laugh.

After a few minutes, Morgan pushed herself off the couch and reached down for Josh's hand. "Let's go outside for a walk. I haven't seen Midwestern stars in ages. Let's compare them to ours back home."

They quietly slipped out the front door and headed toward the horse pasture where it was darkest. Looking up at the sky, so vast and never-ending, they pointed out all the constellations they knew. Basically it boiled down to just the two Dippers. Laughing and agreeing they needed to get out more, they stood there looking up, trying to find more constellations.

Pointing, Josh asked, "That's Orion's belt, isn't it?"

"It sure is," she replied matter-of-factly even though she had no clue where he was even pointing.

Both laughed at her tone. Josh moved to stand behind her, his strong arms slipping around her slim waist, pulling her toward him so her back rested against his chest. He rested his cheek on her hair. After a minute, she turned around in his arms.

On an impulse, he stepped back. "May I have this dance?" He held out his hand to her.

"You may." Deeply touched, Morgan placed her hand in his and moved closer to him as he led her into a dance. She rested her head against him as they danced in the moonlight in a horse pasture thousands of miles from home. Her heart melted as the sheer romance of the moment took her breath away.

"You follow me very well, sweetheart," he whispered in her ear as they moved through the grass.

"I'd follow you anywhere," she whispered back.

He nudged her chin up, looking into her eyes that were highlighted by the moon. Leaning down, he kissed her tenderly. Josh's heart had never felt fuller than at that moment. "I love you."

"I love you too." She leaned up, kissing him softly.

When they began to make their way back toward the house, he took a detour. Following the solar-powered lights that threw star-shaped patterns on the recently cut grass and the boarded walk, they slipped inside the gazebo's door and sat down in the swing. Letting it swing slowly, they just soaked up the quietness of the night. They tried to identify what they were hearing, mainly crickets and a frog somewhere. They heard an owl calling out from the nearby woods as the night breeze blew through the tree leaves.

It was simply a gorgeous, cool, late April night in Kentucky. Cuddled against each other for warmth and comfort in a swing in a pretty little gazebo, Josh and Morgan quietly rested, both resisting their return to the real world that was waiting for them. He used his foot to gently push the swing.

He finally asked her what he'd been wanting to for a while now. "Sweetheart? What were you and my mom talking about so long in my room the day we arrived?"

Morgan smiled because he couldn't see her face. As seriously as she could manage, she said, "She wants us to have sex."

He immediately stopped the swing with his foot and turned her around. "*What?*"

She burst into laughter at the astonished look on his face. She then explained their entire conversation to him. He was torn between amusement, sheer embarrassment—and agreeing with his mom. When he told her that, she burst into laughter again.

"I'm never going to be able to look Mom in the eyes again," he groaned.

She grinned as she leaned back against his chest. "Hey, *I* was the one who had the talk with her, not you. Imagine how I felt? But you know, it was actually one of the best conversations I think I've ever had with anyone in my life. Damien was right. Your mom is like the coolest person ever."

He was silent for a few minutes. "I do have to say it's kinda sexy and thrilling having a girl in my bed even though they know you're there. And I didn't even sneak you in through my window. Nope. You just walked right through the front door!" He heard her groan and laughed when she lightly slapped his hands that were around her waist.

"Did you ever...?"

"No." He smiled at the thought.

"I'm not sure how I feel about possibly fulfilling one of your kinky teenage boy fantasies."

"It wasn't kinky. It was completely normal."

They both laughed, knowing he was probably right. He adjusted her against him as his foot pushed off and made the swing move again. They continued to swing, each lost in their own thoughts.

"We had our own galaxy," Morgan spoke the words quietly after the long silence.

"How's that?"

"Shane and I had our own galaxy. That's what we called it. We first had our own little world, but then our world just got too small for everything. So we gradually upgraded to an entire galaxy. I'd forgotten all about it until a little while ago."

Josh kept quiet, giving her the safe space she needed to talk out her memories and emotions. Since the trial, her mind was unearthing memories she'd either long forgotten about or had blocked out entirely. Whether she'd done either from the trauma she went through, or just trying to start a new life afterward and needing to forget her past in order to do so, neither was sure.

But he felt sure it was therapeutic for her to be able to talk to him about them, so he encouraged her to when a memory resurfaced. Besides, who else did she have to talk to about them except himself and Ty? These memories also taught him more about her.

Morgan adjusted her head on his chest as memories flooded back. "I'm pretty sure it began with the moon. With his being gone on long assignments so often, we hardly seemed to see each other. One time before he left, he told me it'd be a full moon soon. If I was to get lonely, or just wanted to talk to him, I was to talk to the moon. And he'd do the same.

"So I did. The moon became one of my closest friends in no time. Then I really started noticing all those amazing stars, scattered all across the huge sky, and the North Star.

Things I'd never truly noticed before. When he finally came home that next time, we went outside one night and lay on a blanket, just looking up at the sky. I pointed out all the things I'd learned or noticed since he'd been away, which honestly wasn't a whole lot. But it all seemed different to me somehow.

"Over time, we joked about making a planet or a star the residence of a particular problem. You know, for our work, bills needing paid, different people we knew, the in-laws. You know, things that annoyed us." She smiled when she heard Josh chuckle and squeeze her hand.

"The in-laws had their own planet. You've sort of met them so you *know* they wouldn't have been satisfied with a measly little star. We tried to choose a planet even farther away than Pluto."

Morgan gasped at a sudden memory. In a voice laced with humor, she said, "I remember once Shane made me really mad about something. I can't even remember what it was now, but I yelled at him, 'What planet did you come from anyway?' Without missing a beat, he grabbed my hand, yanked me outside and pointed to the sky. '*That* one!' he shouted back. Then we started laughing and couldn't stop."

She laughed at the memory, but hot tears misted her eyes too. It helped her cope when she heard Josh laugh.

"We rarely fought, but it was so typical of him to deflate any situation with humor." She held Josh's hand in hers, stroking it with her own before she continued, "Over time, adding a planet here and a star there, we had our own galaxy. Of course, the galaxy had to be named after us."

Josh laughed. "Naturally. And a measly little star would've been too small for you too."

"Naturally," she agreed, laughing. "Our galaxy was a great place to live. But, oddly enough, thinking of life that way really is interesting. When something upset me, I'd just imagine that particular planet turning away from me and orbiting away. Then all's well, at least until it revolves *back* into my orbit as problems invariably will do.

"But I could use it for anything. Were the in-laws planning a function we were 'requested' to attend? Well, they'll soon return to their own planet.

"When a huge problem would come up, I'd think, 'Hey, universally this doesn't matter at all.' And I'd picture the whole universe, then a planet, then our continent, then the state, the county, the city, the house we lived in.

"And it would occur to me that outside of that very narrow slice of universal space, my huge problem was nothing. Literally, it was *nothing* in the big scheme of things.

That thought helped me keep things in perspective and often kept me from getting too overwhelmed.

"After Shane was killed, my world stopped turning. And I never gave it a thought until right now. I'd forgotten all about making galaxies since Shane was taken from me.

"But now I have new planets and new stars, don't I? I've had my friends, my work, and my animals with me all through these years. Then I met you. You were a star, a bright one, which somewhere along the line turned into a whole planet."

Smiling in contentment, he asked, "Wouldn't that defy evolution or something somehow?"

She chuckled. "It's *my* galaxy so it has its own unique laws." They swung slowly, listening to the quiet creaking of the chains. "And following my little storyline here, that means you have your own galaxy too. You have your own planets. Your parents live on one, Damien and Laura have one. There's your work, your play. And when I stand back in my mind and look at it all now, there's only one thing I really want to do."

Josh waited for her to tell him. When she didn't speak for a moment, he asked, "What would that be?"

"I want to change galaxies. I want to move from mine to yours. Or maybe somehow combine the two, and make an even better one. I guess we'd still be in the same universe either way, right?"

Tilting her head back, she looked at him. Filtered moonlight shone in her eyes as she studied him. "How about it, Josh? Would you like to change galaxies with me?"

"I'd love to." He smiled, adding, "But only if it's named after me."

Laughing, she looked out at the night as she thought about it. "We'll have to compromise on that one, I think."

"Why? *The Wright Galaxy* doesn't have enough of a ring to it for you?"

"Well, when you say it like that, it sounds more than perfect!"

Sitting there in the dark of the Kentucky night, Morgan sighed. It was so remote and quiet here. And in the gazebo, they were secluded.

Morgan stated with authority, "I'm sure as shootin' gonna want one."

"One what?"

"Gazebo. How long do ya think it'll take to put one up at my place?"

He laughed.

Yawning, she rubbed her face. "I'm tuckered out. It's past time to go in, I suppose. If we stay out here much longer, this is where your parents are bound to find us in the morning. You ready?"

"Yeah. But this is really hard to leave, isn't it? I've missed Kentucky. I love what I have in Arizona, but this..." He paused, saying softly, "This place is full of great memories, and it's welcomed me back home. It feels like I never left."

Morgan turned around in his arms, searching his face in the moonlight and shadows. "Do you want to return here?"

Josh shook his head. "I'd be okay with it if I ever had to, but what I have in Arizona is my new home. Like your galaxy you were talking about, I think I belong there. I have Damien, Laura, my other friends. My business.

"There are more business opportunities year-round out there due to the climate. It's one of the reasons I made the decision to move out there in the first place. I'm not overly fond of the politics out there, but that's probably true anywhere. Now I have you, and you just leaving the Center would be extremely difficult to do. And I could never leave you, so... I stay."

"I never want to stand in the way of your happiness, Josh. Never."

He looked at her and whispered back, "Sweetheart, you're the *source* of my happiness."

Morgan's heart flipped over, twisting so tightly it made it hard to breathe. "And you're mine. Thank you for finding me, Josh. Thank you a thousand times over."

Chapter 50

MORNING CAME FAR TOO early and way too soon. They ignored their alarm and slept in since they'd stayed up late.

Mercedes was sitting outside their closed door, staring at it while she patiently waited for them to open it for her. When they finally did, Morgan almost tripped over her. With a coo and a smile, Morgan bent down and scooped up the cat in her arms, rubbing her face in the soft fur. Mercedes began purring almost immediately. Smiling, Josh walked around them to head to the bathroom, rubbing his hand over the cat's head as he went by.

After their showers and packing, they hauled their suitcases down the stairs and set them by the front door. While Josh went to look for his parents, who were probably outside, Morgan went back up, stripping their bed of the linens. Getting fresh linens from the closet, she re-made the bed, folding down the top quilt as she'd seen Annabelle do that first day.

Finding cleaning supplies under the bathroom sink, she cleaned it so her hostess wouldn't have to after they left. Satisfied it was all clean, and they hadn't forgotten anything, she grabbed their towels and the bedsheets and headed downstairs to the laundry room.

Annabelle came in the back door at that moment. While appreciating Morgan's help and attitude in wanting to do the laundry, she shooed her into the kitchen, telling her she didn't need to. But Morgan insisted she did because it would've been rude if she didn't.

They compromised with a grin: Morgan would start it, and Annabelle would finish it.

Annabelle made them a brunch to remember, refusing Morgan's offer to help with the dishes afterwards. Morgan then refused her refusal, making both of Josh's parents laugh as she started the dish water in the sink. Josh agreed, telling his mom to sit down at the table while he helped do their dishes.

As they cleaned up the kitchen, they talked with his parents as the older couple sat at their table, drinking coffee. Mercedes stretched out in the sunbeam shining through the windows.

As they all ate at the large country table, Morgan had reminded his parents she'd cry when they said goodbye. And there simply wasn't anything she could do about it. Annabelle had just smiled and patted her cheek in such a sweet, motherly fashion, Morgan almost started crying early.

True to her nature, Morgan had tears in her eyes when she hugged Patrick and Annabelle goodbye. She just hated goodbyes so much, and this one seemed even harder for some reason. She felt accepted and loved here. She felt at *home* here.

Perhaps it was because she knew what they were going back to. She figured going from blessed peace and a loving family to horrific murder and spiteful in-laws was hardly an easy swap. But she knew it was more than that. After hugging them, she got in the car so Josh could have a private moment with them.

Josh tightly hugged his parents, reluctant to let them go. He knew they were getting older. And he knew one day he'd get that call that told him one had taken ill, or even died. Sometimes when he really thought about that happening, he'd cry because his love for his parents was so deep.

Annabelle cupped her son's face in her warm hands. "Thank you for coming home. I loved our rides. They will carry me over when I miss you. And it was so wonderful to see you both again!" She kissed his cheek. "I love you, Josh. You take care in your travels, all right?"

Patrick looked his son in his eyes. "We miss you. We sure loved having you both here, and we hope we can get together again soon. But if not, know we love you and your lady. Be safe going home."

"We will. I miss and love you guys so much," Josh said, stepping back but still holding onto their hands. "You take care of yourselves, all right? You let me know if you need anything too." He paused. "I really hate to leave you!"

His parents nodded in understanding and kissed his cheek again.

Josh opened his door and folded his tall frame in behind the wheel. He rolled down his window after he started the car. He knew Morgan was trying hard not to cry anymore as he sat there beside her. He heard her take deep breaths in an effort to control herself. He was trying hard to not join her, and she wasn't making it easy.

Trying to lighten the mood a bit, Patrick bent down to look his son in the eyes. He then asked him if he'd taken care of all of his laundry.

Josh smiled and replied, "Of course. You know I'd never leave if I hadn't!"

They all smiled as Josh fastened his seatbelt, and then put the car in gear.

"Love you guys!" Josh called out as he drove slowly away as Morgan waved to them from her open window.

Patrick and Annabelle, now wiping tears from their own eyes, waved back as the car drove away.

Chapter 51

WHEN THEY ARRIVED AT the courthouse early the next morning, they overheard the day would consist of the two last witnesses or experts, and then the closing arguments would begin. Now that the end of the trial was almost here, Morgan was again anxious.

Morgan sat up straighter and was alert as Attorney Wilson Andrews finally stood up to give his closing argument. He deserved his stellar reputation. He was professional, thorough, and direct. He knew his facts and had a natural gift for speaking. He also had charisma that had the jury eating out of his hands. When he finally concluded his closing statement, Judge Emerson ordered the jury members to their room to make their decision.

Many settled in the courthouse where it was cooler and prepared for a lengthy wait. Captain Sinclair had thoughtfully reserved a private room so Morgan and Josh could avoid any media hounds and Shane's relatives. Morgan gave her fake glasses to Josh so she wouldn't be tempted to tap them on the table and annoy them both as they waited.

Only three hours later, it was announced the jury had made their decision. Few seemed overly surprised at the short time it took for them to decide because of the overwhelming amount of evidence, but some thought they should've taken longer to be sure of their verdict. Morgan wanted to slug those people when she heard them talking about it in the hallway.

She watched almost in a daze as the bailiff handed the paper to the judge, who read it to himself before handing it back to the bailiff to hand back to the jury foreman. As the jury foreman stood up and read their decision, Morgan was gripping Josh's hand tightly in hers. Her heart was thudding so hard she could barely catch a breath.

Tears ran down her cheeks when she heard the one word she needed to hear. She quickly wiped them away before anyone noticed her reaction.

"Guilty."

THEY MADE IT TO their hotel room with no problem, much to their relief. They were half-expecting a throng of media personnel outside their room, waiting for them to arrive.

Once they closed their hotel door, Josh putting out the *Do Not Disturb* sign immediately, Morgan sat down heavily on the couch. The mental exhaustion she'd been fighting through suddenly hit her. She immediately kicked off her heels and removed her disguise, leaving it on the coffee table.

When she closed her eyes for a moment, Josh quietly closed all of the curtains for privacy. He removed her things, putting them in their bedroom to give her some time alone. He changed out of his dress clothes, feeling much better in his shorts and t-shirt. He walked back into the living room area and noticed she hadn't moved at all. She'd opened her eyes though.

Staring at the wall of curtains across from her, she just sat there. She didn't say anything at all.

Thinking of giving her some more time alone, Josh brought her a glass of iced tea and handed it to her. She held the glass in her hands, listening to the ice crackle. All of a sudden, she started crying silent tears, and she couldn't stop them no matter how hard she tried. When her hands began shaking, Josh quickly took the glass from her, placing it on the coffee table.

It was all sinking in now, and she was going through the first stage of healing with closure.

He quickly joined her on the couch, pulling her close and just held onto her as she let out almost nine years of emotions.

She sobbed for the loss of her husband, the lack of family, the lonely years, the struggles, and heartaches. She cried for the future they'd planned but neither one got to live. But she also cried in thankfulness for the second chance she'd been given with Josh. A second chance she never really expected to ever have.

It was a while before she was empty of tears. Josh leaned over toward the coffee table, handing her the box of Kleenex that came with the suite. After she'd blown her nose and wiped her sore eyes and her cheeks raw, she leaned back against him. She looked at the pile of used Kleenex on the table now, not wanting to do anything more except sit there, to not have to think or even feel for a while. She just felt so used up at the moment.

He pulled away in order to look directly into her eyes. Hoping this might help in some way, he cupped her face in his warm hands and said softly, "Natasha, it's over now. You and Shane got your justice."

The heartfelt and earnest look she gave him cracked his heart. She gripped his hands in hers and whispered, "Thank you for that."

He leaned over and handed her the tea again. This time she drank some before leaning over herself to put it back on the coffee table. He pulled her close to his side again and kissed the top of her head. He played with her hair, running his fingers through it.

They were quiet for a few moments before he asked her softly, "How are you feeling?"

"Numb." She was silent for a moment again as she replayed the past year in her mind. Wondering out loud, she asked thoughtfully, "Don't you think it odd how you came into my life the same time this all happened?"

Josh leaned his cheek against her soft hair. "One could say it was just pure coincidence. Some could say it was just plain luck. Others could say it was the intention and work of God. I go with the last 'others' myself."

"Me too." Morgan finally voiced her biggest fear. "But now there's you, Josh, and I'm suddenly scared of losing you. I don't know if I could bear it. What if you died on me too? You don't come back from death. I don't think I could make it through a second time."

He sighed, thinking how best to answer. "No, death is permanent."

He paused, searching for the right words to say to her. Were there any? "I, too, find it incredibly difficult to think about losing you. And losing my parents or sisters? I've never been alive without all of them being there. And what I feel for you is so... deep... that I feel my soul would be shred to pieces if I lost you.

"But I can't live with that worry, and neither can you, sweetheart. Death is a part of life. We need to cherish each other now, take our faults, and work through them in order to make the best out of what we've been given." He hugged her close, placed a kiss on her head. "I'd hope either of us could move on, not be swallowed up in the sorrow. And to have true friends there to help support the other, for as long as it was needed."

"Shane and I had a pact that we'd not live in sorrow. It was easier said than done."

"But talking about this, knowing what we want for the other to do, does that help ease any guilt for moving on? It's better than second-guessing, right? You've had to experience this while I've only heard about it. Do you think it's easier to have known what Shane wanted you to do than not?"

"Yes, it's easier in the sense of knowing he wanted me to move on, to live life, to not mourn him forever. But the pain, the shock, the disbelief, the fear of being alone? All of it can just pull one down so quickly. It's basically drowning when you can hardly pull in a breath, or see the light. You're buried so far down you don't know which way is up. It's terrifying, Josh."

He felt her trembling and rubbed his warm hands on her cool arms. "I don't know what to say. It's not easy for the survivor to move on, especially in a case as yours was. It still astounds me how you have ended up so normal. You're strong, willing to try again."

"I wasn't though. Not for years. Not until Ty began planting the seed, encouraging me to go forward. Not until you."

"As you once said, it's all in the timing. We can't control it. Time can heal hurt and wounds, but it doesn't mean they all go completely away either. We just play with the cards we've been dealt, making the best decisions we can at that time. We all make mistakes, we all struggle, and we all second-guess ourselves.

"Life's a journey, and there's an infinite amount of routes to take to navigate it. For us, we weren't ready for each other until we were."

She thought for a moment. "We just have to trust God has a plan for each of us, and make the best of it?"

"Humans don't have any other choice."

"No, I guess we don't." She adjusted her position against him before she went on. "Long ago, I remember reading somewhere that there are basically two types of people when it comes to love.

"One type consists of the people who seem to fall in love with others easily and often. They can have numerous boyfriends or girlfriends, get married time after time, and feel they were truly in love. And maybe sometimes they were. It's like every time you saw them, they were with someone new."

"And the other type?"

"The other type is like me. We don't fall in love easily, if ever. We don't mistake love and infatuation. We're strong in ourselves, so we don't need someone to love us so we can love ourselves. We're more like loners, and overall happy in that.

"But when this second type *does* fall in love, it's with every fiber of our being. Body, mind, and soul. It's deep, like to the marrow of our bones.

"If something happens to our love, the pain is horrific. We don't just snap out of it like people in the first group do because we can't. They could find a new love the next month or the next year, while my group? Possibly never. Me personally? Well, I'm going on nine years myself. If it wasn't for you, I really think I'd be alone until I died. I was also completely fine with that."

She adjusted her head on his shoulder. "But then one day last year, completely out of the blue, Ty was there making me face reality. He made me think of my future, and how I was living. He basically accused me of hiding, even using him, and Shane, as a crutch. Although I was fine being alone, he just kept making me think there *could* be another chance for me.

"Weeks later, when I was at that auction in Phoenix by myself, I made the decision to turn over yet another leaf. It was time to. It felt like it was the right time even though I couldn't tell you why.

"But I made the decision that I was going out on dates, providing I could even find some decent guy. And then just a couple of days later on the way home, I got that flat. And almost as soon as I pulled over, there you were knocking on my window.

"It has to be a part of God's plan, right? How *else* could all of this have happened like it did? I mean, seriously, Josh. *What* are the odds? None of it could've been planned to happen, especially as neatly and quickly as it did."

She said thoughtfully, "But it wasn't even so much that you were suddenly there. I mean, it *was*, but it was *more* than that. From the very start, I felt connected to you, and I found myself trusting you faster than anyone else I can think of. Even Ty.

"He'd talk to me about living life again, to be open to the mere possibility of dating someone, to go out with someone other than him—which again was always plutonic. He was preparing me for you, of course. But for me, it was still a leap of faith.

"But none of those feelings had even simmered with any of the guys I'd met since Shane, or even before him. When I met him, it was like a blast from a furnace or something. There was an instant connection, but it still took time. With you, it was more like being hit with a sledgehammer. I couldn't ignore you, or the powerful connection I instantly felt.

"The fact I felt anything at all was the greatest surprise. I had to work through *that* surprise first. Before even the idea of dating, of accepting I could maybe be happy again without Shane, could even be a possibility.

"There's heavy guilt in moving on, Josh. It's a process I hope I'm nearing the end of."

"I hope so, too, sweetheart. You deserve a life of happiness."

He paused, thinking about what she'd said earlier. "You know, I think it *was* all engineered by God. Or was it just fate?"

"What do you mean?"

"Remember where your truck got the flat? Since you now know where I live, and that I'd been in town, has it ever occurred to you that I was *nowhere* near my home? Because of that storm flooding the roads, I was forced to find another way home.

"There was absolutely no reason whatsoever for me to have been on the exact highway that led toward your place. It was the storm. It *forced* me to go there. Who controls the weather, sweetheart? And the timing of it with your flat?"

Morgan replied, "You know what? I never once thought about that! *Why* were you on my highway? You're right. It's not on the way to your house at all. Wow."

They silently thought about that scenario for a while.

She laughed. "It was so embarrassing."

"What was?"

"Soon after we started seeing each other, I'd be in the office working with Ty. And suddenly, I'd be staring off into space with a smile on my face. He'd notice and not say a word, but his grin made it worse than if he actually did!"

Picturing it, Josh laughed. "I'm sure I did the same thing except no one saw me!" After a bit, Josh said, "I've often thought, more than once as it happens, that you were *my* guardian angel. You came into my life at the perfect time and saved me too. When I look at it that way, I'd say we're even, sweetheart. We both saved the other."

Curious, Morgan tilted her head to look up at him. She wasn't sure if he was serious or not. "Really? How'd I do that?"

"You saved me from Elise."

Thinking about all of those blind dates Elise had set him up on, and how much he detested his best friend's meddling cousin, Morgan smiled broadly as she nodded her head. "Yes. I guess that *does* make us even, doesn't it?"

Josh nodded, but then said somberly, "But in truth, you *did* save me. You saved me from being alone and wondering if I'd passed on a woman who I may have grown to love.

"I have to admit that I had doubts about that. There were times I worried I may be looking for too much, too quickly. Or that I was asking for too much to just wait and wait until that woman I was looking for just came out of nowhere, and I'd just know it.

"My mom told me I'd just know. She'd told me to just be patient and not rush it. It was better to wait, you know? Maybe *that* was why I was so patient with Elise, on the slight chance her meddling was for a reason I couldn't see.

"But I was content and even happy on my own. I really was. While at the same time, I didn't want to *remain* that way forever. I'd see how happy others I know are, and at times it really made me second-guess myself.

"But it all starts with the right lady. And *you* are the right lady for me, Morgan."

"I can't argue that fact because your dad did tell me the Wright men have good taste!"

They laughed. Satisfied and content, they both savored the moment together.

Chapter 52

MORGAN WAS UP AND dressed before Josh even awoke the next morning. She gently shook him awake, letting him know she was going out for a while and taking the rental car.

He sleepily nodded his head, going back to sleep as soon as his head hit the pillow again. Morgan smiled as she leaned down to kiss his unshaven cheek, running her fingers through his soft, dark hair a few times.

She grabbed her purse, cellphone, the hotel and car keys as she walked out the door, closing it quietly. She made sure the *Do Not Disturb* sign was still on the handle.

Driving to the nearest department store, she shopped for some supplies, and then plugged the address into her GPS to a place she'd been to only once before, a lifetime ago. She drove as close as she could, getting disoriented a few times and having to backtrack. She parked the car and looked out of the windshield for a moment.

Getting out slowly, she grabbed the supplies she'd just bought. Crossing the faded gray lane of pavement, she made her way to Shane's grave.

Morgan stood in front of the large ornate granite tombstone for a moment, letting the quietness of the cemetery calm her. She felt so many emotions swirling through her. She took the time to just let herself settle down a bit as she studied the death marker of her husband.

Although he'd been cremated, his family had still put up a headstone. For her, this was far more symbolic than anything else. It just seemed the most appropriate place for her to go.

After setting down the plastic bags, she got down on her knees and traced Shane's name in the hard granite softly with her trembling index finger. In a whisper, she said, "Hi, darling." Sitting back on her heels, she wiped away the few, sudden tears that ran down her cheek.

She switched her phone to a playlist she'd made of songs she and Shane had loved.

Keeping it on low, memories filtered through her mind as she listened to the old familiar songs play. She removed from the plastic bags the green foam base and the large bundle of colorful flowers, setting them in the metal cup holder attached to the tombstone. She made sure they stood up straight. Drooping flowers would never do for her Shane.

As she worked, she began a steady one-sided conversation. "I took that CD we made of all our favorite songs with me when I left here. It's the one we'd play when we took a road trip, and sing at the top of our lungs. Remember that?" She smiled to herself with the happy memories. "I made a copy of the original as I was practically terrified I'd bust or lose the one we made all those years ago.

"Those times we had together were really great, Shane. And I miss them and you something awful.

"It's been almost a decade since you walked out our front door and drove away. I can only remember how you looked that last time we were together. You'll never age in my mind, you know. We can only remember someone as how we last saw them. Isn't that crazy? But that's how the mind works.

"And I'm thankful for that. I really am. I'll always remember you as a young, vibrant, fit, charismatic, serious, sharp, focused, loving, tender, very humorous, all-around terrific guy.

"Now, don't you go thinking I've forgotten all of your faults because we both know you had some. You weren't perfect, Shane, but I loved you so much anyway. Just like I wasn't perfect, and you loved me anyway."

She listened to the music for a minute, just being still. "I came back here just for you because they caught the man who took you away from me. They found him guilty just yesterday, and he gets his sentence soon. I came back for the trial and saw him myself. A part of me was scared he'd be someone we knew. As it turned out, I'd never seen him before.

"I could never thank enough all the men, and maybe women, for all the work they've put in over these years. It means so very much to me to know they never gave up trying to find the man who took you away.

"But mainly it's because they never forgot you. I always believed they had, and it ate at my soul. It's like I couldn't let you go because if I broke down and did that, I'd be no better than they were. How could I ever let that happen? *Someone* had to keep your memory alive. *Someone* had to remember you, and how you were. And who better than me?

"But yet, with my new life, I had no one to talk to about you. So, you lived inside of me. Knowing that they didn't forget you, and my being here now, has given me the closure I've needed for so very long."

Morgan stared for a minute at the headstone although she wasn't really seeing it. Finally, she said, "But I didn't come alone, Shane. I met a man last year where I now live in Arizona.

"Do you remember the place we always said we'd go but never got the chance to? It's more than a little ironic that of all the places I've been, I'd meet him where we meant to go ourselves. What are the odds that I'd meet the only other man I could love like I loved you in the very place we meant to go? Maybe it *is* really just all up to fate. I don't know."

She sat there, letting her old feelings come out so she could work on letting them go. As she did this, she felt better. Freer. After a time, she continued talking to her old love about her new one.

"His name is Josh Wright. He came to my rescue when I got a flat tire in the middle of a really bad thunderstorm at night. We were just discussing this last night, and how it made no sense for him to have been there at all. Except for the storm sending him that way. And that I got a flat for an unknown reason. There was no nail, no screw in it. It wasn't even a blowout. It just went flat. Right there, and only a few minutes from home.

"Anyway, we'd actually run into each other weeks before at my place at a horse show. But we didn't introduce ourselves at all. We barely even spoke with each other. Two minutes tops.

"It was like a small bomb going off for me, Shane. Somehow, we had this instantaneous and powerful connection. It seemed like we were destined to meet each other, as crazy as that sounds. There's just no other way to describe our meeting."

Morgan looked around the empty cemetery, casually taking in the cleanliness of it. Her eyes caught movement, but not what caused it. She waited, with her heart suddenly racing, to see what it was. Soon, a curious squirrel popped his head around a headstone near her, steadily looking at her for a long moment before continuing on his way. She tried to relax. She hadn't realized she was so on edge still.

The squirrel must not be around humans much, she thought, as he seemed pretty confident around her. He kept a distance, but he wasn't scared of her at all. He must've been either older, or maybe injured, as she thought his gait was a little stiff, but he looked healthy so he apparently was able to feed and take care of himself. She watched the squirrel move around the headstones for a minute before returning her attention back to why she was there.

"He's truly a wonderful person, in so many ways. And I love him, Shane." Her eyes filled with tears at her admittance of this to her deceased husband, and she fought them back. Her voice trembled as she explained, whether to him or herself, she wouldn't have been able to say with certainty. "I do, with all my heart. I didn't expect it to happen. Not with just him, but anyone. But it did. I was only trying to start a new social life. And I lucked out big time.

"And I'm not sorry, or feeling guilty, about it anymore. Me and you made that pact, remember? That if one of us died, the other was to find someone new? But I couldn't for the longest time. The guilt was just too overwhelming, Shane. How dare I try to have fun when you couldn't? How could my life go on like nothing ever happened when your life was over and gone?"

She wiped the tears from her cheeks before she admitted, "So I just stopped trying to fool myself and focused on my work with my horses. They still give me so much comfort and purpose. I wasn't looking to find anybody to replace you. I just worked.

"And then all of a sudden, out of nowhere after all these years, there was Josh. And he loves me. I don't doubt his love at all. I feel to my very bones that I can trust him. It was hard, but I finally opened up to him and told him about you. About us.

"And his coming into my life at practically the same time as they caught your murderer was beyond anything I could've planned. When I confided in him about the trial, he literally dropped everything to come with me so I wouldn't go through this alone. He's a godsend, Shane. And he's mine.

"One thing I'm absolutely sure of is that if you and Josh had ever met, you'd have liked each other. He's strong—both in body and in character. He's loyal to the bone, hardworking, and has a warped sense of humor. He has his own construction company, and he runs it very well from what I can tell. I've even met his parents—twice now. They're the absolute greatest. And his two sisters are easy to be around too. They're *nothing* like either one of our families."

Morgan listened to the birds chirping for a moment. Closing her eyes, she just listened. When she opened them, she saw a man with a cane walking among the tombstones. She looked back at Shane's.

"There's another man in my life too. Who knew I'd ever have more than one fantastic guy in my life, especially at once? He's my absolute closest and best friend. Well, long before I met Josh, I mean.

"This man you apparently know. His name is Ty. He's worked for me for many years without telling me he knew you until just a few months ago. He's been my complete, unconditional support for so long. Darling, I honestly don't know what I would've done without him over the years. Ty has been there for me at my lowest moments.

"He's helped me build my business, and he takes care of me. He guides me. He makes me laugh, and he's seen me cry. Besides you and Josh, he's hands-down one of the best people I've ever met, and I'd do anything for him. And better yet, he and Josh have become good friends, so that alone is a huge relief to me. There's no way I could choose between them since I love them both so much."

Looking up, Morgan noticed the man with the cane was looking over in her general direction. He seemed to be looking around, maybe looking for a particular gravesite. Morgan decided to be nice and raised her hand to him in a casual greeting. He looked at her a while before waving back. He stood there, his hand still in the air for a suspended moment before he slowly moved on, using his cane for support.

"I have my own horse business now, thanks to those policies you'd set up. At times, it still overwhelms me that you did all of that for me. You can be assured, my darling, that I will *never* take it for granted.

"It's my dream place, Shane. I called it Harmony Hills Equestrian Center. We give trail rides, riding lessons, train and board horses, have shows and events. We also do the horse hotel trade when needed.

"Each barn is named after something I noticed that made me feel like I should buy it when I went to look at it. Sunset Ridge, Red Rock, Quail Run, and Grand View are what I named them. The harmony of everything I saw there, and what I felt standing there, it made me feel at peace. Safe. That's where I also came up with the name Harmony Hills."

She rolled her neck around a bit when she noticed it was getting stiff. She saw the squirrel looking at her again. It flicked its bushy tail at her a few times before scampering away across the grass.

Pulling out a couple of little American flags she'd bought on impulse, she stuck them on each side of the tombstone. "And I have my German Shepherds for security and companionship as well as great people who work for me. And I have my horse for me, and all the other horses for me to share with everyone else.

"I've lost count of the number of times I've gone to the barn at night, just to pet and talk with any one of them after all my staff and customers have left. It's when the place really feels like mine, when I'm all alone with the horses. And my memories.

"I've worked very hard, and still do, to make Harmony Hills a place with hopefully a stellar reputation. And I live there in my own house. I have great friends where I live, and I feel safe and happy there. It's my home, Shane. It's where I belong. And it's all because of you."

Out of the corner of her eye, she saw the man with the cane walking closer now. She didn't see a car anywhere and wondered how he'd come to be there. Her brow furrowed as she thought about it. Casually, she looked around to see if anyone else was around, but she didn't see anybody.

She kept an eye on the man as she adjusted the little flags in the breeze. "Anyway, back to the trial. I ran into your mother, Charles, and Allen. I wasn't very nice to them, Shane. I hope you'll forgive me for that, but they left me on the street when you were taken so suddenly. And now they say they're here to support me? It was just for show, for sympathy, for publicity, and I called them out on it. It made me sick to see how disgraceful they were! They didn't even show up on the first day of the trial!

"They were making this trial about themselves when it was all about *you*. I haven't spoken with them since that day, or any of your other relatives that showed up later. Speaking of families, I haven't talked with mine in years either. But that being said, it's also safer for me if we don't communicate. I never know if I'm being watched, or if they are."

Reaching into her back pocket, Morgan pulled out a copy of a photo. It was laminated, but the corners were dog-eared from her pulling it out so many times over the years. She skimmed her fingers over it, looking at it as she did. "Shane, I have to be honest with you. I came here for a few reasons.

"One, I needed to see your marker here one more time. The last time I was here, I wasn't really here in any way but physically. And I wanted to be sure it was nice here, that it was cared for. It eases my mind that it is even though I know you're not really here.

"Two, I needed to tell you they got the man who killed you, my darling. We finally got justice. You can't know what that news did to me all those years ago. It left me in shreds, but I'm better now. It wasn't easy by a long shot, but I made it."

A single tear ran down her cheek. Morgan softly added the next reason for her visit. "And three, I've come here to say goodbye, Shane. I never, ever got to say goodbye to you.

It's haunted me that you died alone. We were never to do that, you know. But it's been a long time, and I have to move on now. I've got a great man in Josh, and I won't lose him too.

"But I think that I've known in my heart I couldn't be with him fully until I came to grips once and for all with you. It wouldn't have been fair to either me or Josh, and hurting him is the last thing I'd do if I could help it. I just needed to work out all of this other stuff by myself. And now I have. Coming here today is the last step."

She explained to him, and maybe even to herself, "He's my second chance at a fulfilling life, and I'm not going to let that chance get away from me. I'm not going to let him go. I hope you understand that. I won't *ever* forget you, but I need to let you go now.

"Josh doesn't expect me to forget you, by the way. But I don't want him to be secretly wondering if I'm thinking of you. He told me he doesn't want me to just forget about you because that'd be disrespectful. He's a remarkable man, Shane. And he's given me just incredible, unconditional love, support, patience, and understanding. He deserves all of me.

"Thank you, Shane, for being there for me, and for loving me, protecting me. I can't imagine my life without you in it all those years. You made me a better person. And you gave me the means to build my dream business.

"I would've preferred to have had *you* over all that money. But I've tried to put it to good use, in a way that'd make you proud. If it wasn't for you, I'd never been able to get it. And trust me when I say I have never, and will never, take it for granted. Or forget where it really came from.

"There were so many times I'd cry, wishing you were there beside me to share it with. And I'd cry because of all that we lost. I'd cry because I lost not only my husband, my love, but also my best friend."

She took a breath before she said softly, "And we lost our own family, the one we were building up to. I've never told anyone, not a single person, but I was pregnant when you were taken from me. I've always felt it was no one's business to know but ours. It's the *one* secret that I can hold onto that reminds me of our love. I don't know if I'll even tell Josh or not. I don't know if he needs to know unless it was medically necessary.

"But the absolute worst happened, and I lost you. Then I lost our baby. It was early in the pregnancy, and I wanted you to be the first to know so I never told a living soul. It happened at home. I got myself to a clinic as soon as I could. They made sure I'd be all right, but I lost our baby. I know it wasn't my fault. It was probably the immense stress and loneliness I was buried under when I got that call telling me you were gone.

"*How* did he find me, Shane? How could he call me at home, tell me you were gone, and how? And why? I have so many questions about that time. I recently heard the man they convicted of killing you speak in court, but it's *not* the same voice I heard on the phone years ago. I'm sure of it, so that means there are still others out there that know what happened to you."

Morgan sat there, coming to grips with her feelings, wanting so badly to purge herself of them. "I was so lost after you died, Shane. I was beyond caring about anything, even more so after I lost our baby. It was so hard to even *want* to move on.

"And I was scared, so terrified of so much for so long. But I hope I made you proud of me, Shane. I was proud of you for so many reasons. The memories we made together will be carried in my heart, but I need to move on and make new ones. I need to do that in order to heal myself completely. I pray that if you're watching me that you'll understand, and give me your blessing. I'm changing galaxies, darling."

She turned off the music from her phone. Sitting in silence now, she felt numb. Wiping away the cleansing tears now running down her cheeks, Morgan took a deep breath, letting it out slowly. She pulled a box of Kleenex from the bag, blew her runny nose, and then wiped her eyes.

"It's time for me to go, but I want to play you our song one more time. Even today, it makes me fall apart if I'm not prepared any time it plays. I remember how we danced to it outside under the stars or in our living room..." She gasped when she suddenly realized Josh had also danced with her under the stars. Was that a sign?

Reaching over to pick up her phone, she swiped the screens to their song. Morgan softly played the song that haunted her. As she played their song "How Do I Live Without You?" by Trisha Yearwood, she traced his name one more time with her fingers. She allowed herself to cry as she needed to at this last goodbye, to let her emotions go, to heal at this last stop in her personal journey.

She packed up all of her things, looking around to make sure she had everything. Wiping away the last of her tears, she looked down at the flowers and flags that now surrounded her husband's gravestone.

This was it. She was saying her last goodbye to her first love. And she was heading home with her new one with a heart that was now certain and ready.

Morgan squatted back down on impulse. She pulled an old necklace that she'd carried with her for over a decade from her pocket, lovingly wiped it down with the hem of her shirt, then placed it with the worn picture into a Ziploc bag, then put that into another bag, making sure both were sealed. Looking once more at her favorite wedding picture of Shane and herself, she felt more tears fall.

Leaning forward, she made a deep hole using the little clippers to break up the ground in the soft earth and buried the bag, covering it up with the dirt, firmly packing it down.

Standing up straight again, she bowed her head and said her final goodbye, the one she never got to say before. Her voice trembled, her lips quivered, but she forced herself to say what she knew she needed to. "Goodbye, my love. I've missed you, and I've loved you more than you could ever imagine. But I need to go now. I pray with all of my shattered, but rebuilding heart, that God blessed you and blesses you still, my darling Shane.

"And if you can see me, hear me, know that I'm going to be okay. I'll never forget you, or what you and I shared. And I'll never forget all you did for me. I won't forget our past, but I can't build a new future if I'm still stuck in it either. It's time for me to fly again, my love."

Her voice hitched as she finished softly, "Thank you, Shane, for being such a great and important part of my life. I love you."

Morgan wiped her eyes and her nose with more tissues before she picked up the bags and her phone and returned to the car. She took the time to look at her husband's tombstone one more time.

Inexplicably, she felt a deep wave of something intangible sweep over, and through, her. It almost made her dizzy in its intensity. She leaned against the car until she got her balance back and could see clearly again.

Stunned and slightly confused, she came to terms with the blinding realization she wasn't who she was just a little while ago—a minute ago, years ago. Was this what it felt like to lose one's shackles? For a key to be found and turned, releasing one from their bonds?

Morgan stared at Shane's tombstone like she was seeing it for the first time. Everything suddenly felt, looked, and sounded different. She felt *free* again for the first time in years. She blew a last kiss to Shane, wherever he was, got in the car and drove away.

AFTER MORGAN DROVE OUT of the cemetery, a lone figure made its way to the tombstone of the man known as Shane. The man stared for a moment at the bright, colorful flowers, and the two little flags fluttering in the breeze.

Seeing the little mound of dirt, he rested his cane against the headstone, carefully got down on his knees, and dug it up. He paused for a moment before he reached into the little hole and pulled out the Ziploc bags. Shaking off the dirt, he studied what he held in his hands.

The man ran a gloved finger over the worn photograph before he flipped the bag over and looked at the necklace. After a moment's hesitation, he stuck the bag in the satchel he wore slung across his body. Looking around casually, he then filled up the little hole where the bag had been, firmly patting it back down.

He then took one of the little American flags she'd left and a couple of the flower buds, slipping them in his satchel with the necklace and the photo. He slowly stood up, grabbing his cane to steady himself as he regained his balance.

Walking around the nearby headstones and the trees surrounding the gravesite the woman had just visited, the figure removed a few tiny, unnoticeable wireless microphones.

Casually looking around again, the figure then made his way over to a nearby headstone, reached down into the grass and picked up the small squirrel that was in reality a battery-powered camera device he'd invented and was still tweaking along with the others he'd created. He quickly stuffed it in the satchel.

Winding his way through the tombstones, the lone figure disappeared.

Chapter 53

Morgan could barely hold back her smile as she rode the elevator up to their hotel room. She'd stopped off at another store and bought a gift for Josh. She even bought a small gift bag to put it in, stuffing it with the leftover Kleenex she swore she'd never need again.

Both gifts were pretty symbolic to her. Picturing the look on Josh's face when she gave her gift to him, she wondered if the stairs would've been faster as the elevator kept stopping to let people on and off at their own floors.

At last, the elevator stopped on their floor. After the familiar *ding*, the doors silently opened with a whoosh of air. She made herself walk casually down the hallway, adding to the anticipation.

As she opened the door, leaving the *Do Not Disturb* sign on the handle since they weren't leaving for the courthouse today, she could hear him talking on the phone. She laid her purse, phone, and keys on the small table, carrying the gift bag at her side as she made her way toward him.

Josh heard the door open and looked up as Morgan walked into the room. He lost his train of thought as he noticed the look on her face. She was *glowing*.

"What? I'm sorry. Could you repeat that, Kristi?" Josh smiled at Morgan before trying his hardest to concentrate on what his receptionist was telling him. He forced himself to look away from her.

Morgan knew she was rattling him. Happy with the knowledge, she took the bag with her to the bedroom. She took a shower, dried her hair, added a touch of makeup before she slipped into clean clothes.

Finally, she heard Josh tell Kristi goodbye. She smiled to herself, her heart beating a little faster. Deciding she'd given him enough time, she carried the little bag with her back into the living room.

It was pretty bright in there with the sun shining in like it was, too much for her liking. She closed some of the heavier curtains to block the hot sun, while just pulling some of the lightweight curtains to still have light in the room.

Josh looked up from his papers but didn't say anything. He sat there, twirling his pen in his hand as he watched her. There was just something *different* about her.

She smiled at him, walking around behind him. He'd been working for a while, judging by the stacks of papers he had in front of him, and the emails he had pulled up on his laptop. Leaning down, she wrapped her arms around him and hugged him tightly. He leaned back against the couch, smiling as his hands reached up to hold onto her arms still wrapped around him.

Kissing his cheek, Morgan asked, "Sweetheart, you all done for a while? You look like you need a break."

Her arms still around him, her head resting on his shoulder, he sighed in contentment. "Yeah, I've been here a couple of hours at least. I'm pretty much done now. It was just clearing up some work details and ordering supplies.

"I'm just trying to take some of the office burden off Ryan a little. He said he's doing fine, but I figured to help out. He also said to tell you hi, and thanks again for the strawberries.

"Kristi has a good grip on what she's doing, so I think I'll still have a business when we get home. She also said thanks for the flowers and strawberries. And for sending them to the office instead of her house so she didn't have to share them with anybody.

"Damien also called and said to tell you hello. Laura got on and said Freeway has made herself at home there, so I'll probably need to go to the shelter when we get home and get a new cat."

He wasn't sure if his friends were serious or not, but he knew he wasn't going to give up his cat. Freeway was *his* house buddy. Damien and Laura could go get their own, he told himself.

Morgan smiled to herself as she replayed in her mind the words he'd just said: *When we get home.* Not I, but *we. When we get... home.*

"You *have* been busy! Break time." She released her arms and patted his chest before she leaned down to pick up his phone, quickly putting it on silent mode. She put it on the arm of the couch, then bent over to pick up the gift bag from the floor. Dangling it in front of him, she said, "I bought you a present. One I know you're going to love and want to use right away."

Smiling, he reached up for it, but she quickly pulled it up out of his reach.

Walking around the couch, she smiled at him.

Seeing her so carefree and so vitally alive—the only words he could think of to describe her in that moment—made his heart jump. His voice turned husky as he said, "Morgan, love, you're making my heart stop again. I can hardly breathe when I look at you sometimes. Come here."

His husky voice tripped up her heart as she walked the last couple of steps to stop in front of him. He grabbed her waist and pulled her closer, pulling her down so he could kiss her. She came willingly but pulled back after a moment. "Don't you want to see what I got you?"

"Not at the moment. Give me another kiss first." He pulled her back down, causing her to fall in his lap. Laughing, she ended up straddling him, resting her arms around his neck. Framing her face with his hands, he captured her mouth again.

This kiss wasn't a gentle, tender kiss like the first one. This one was thorough, hot, and full of passion. She heard herself moan as she leaned into him, responding to his touches. She felt his hands run firmly down her back, then her sides before they slid around to her front. Her pulse skyrocketed as she arched into his skillful hands. Her fingers slid into his hair as she kissed him back.

He finally ended the scorching kiss, brushing her hair from her face with hands that trembled just a little. His own heart was still racing as he looked into her captivating green eyes.

She was smiling at him, breathing heavily. She leaned forward to kiss his forehead then his cheeks. Holding up the bag again, she teased him, "Before you kiss me like that again, you might want to look at your present first."

He returned her smile, removing the bag from her fingers. He laughed at all of the Kleenex she'd stuffed in there. "Was the store out of tissue paper, are you recycling, or are we just getting poor?"

Still straddling him, Morgan smiled and shook her head. "Neither. I decided I just won't need them anymore."

Josh paused for a moment at the tone of her voice, catching on to her meaning almost instantly. They held each other's gaze for a long, silent moment.

When he cheerfully tossed out what he hoped was the last Kleenex onto the couch and saw what she'd bought for him, he didn't know how to react. Morgan grinned at the look on his face. It was just as she'd expected.

Josh looked stunned. As realization hit, he grinned broadly. He tried to sound nonchalant as he said, "Sweetheart, I would've hung up the phone immediately if I'd known what was in here. And isn't this a 'polar bears love to slide on snow' moment? I could be wrong, but I'm pretty sure it is."

She laughed. "You're right, of course. Silly me. If you want to talk about polar bears, we can. I suppose we *should*, per our agreement. Obviously, I'm game." She paused, caressing his shoulders as she looked into his eyes, thoughtfully asking, "So, do you want to use your gift now or later, after we talk about bears?"

Looking at her glowing face and those captivating green eyes, Josh laughed. Her humor was as warped as his, and he loved her even more for it. Morgan bought him large boxes of condoms and then innocently asked if he wanted to use them or not. Scooping up the love of his life and her much-appreciated gift, he carried them to their bedroom.

———⁂———

IT WAS MUCH LATER, as they lay there wrapped in each other's arms, that Josh was able to think again. Morgan was resting against him, her back snug against his warm chest with their legs entwined, sleeping lightly.

He'd wondered where she'd been for a good part of the morning and early afternoon, but he figured she'd tell him in her own good time. He had an idea, or rather a *hope*, but he wouldn't pry. Wherever it was that Morgan went to earlier, well, it seemed to have been the turning point for her to take their relationship one big step further. He smiled as he admitted the wait was completely worth it.

She'd stood before him in their bedroom with the curtains closed to block off the bright sun, almost shyly telling him she'd only ever been with Shane, and obviously that was a long time ago. She was nervous about disappointing him. He'd tenderly smiled at her and admitted the same.

They both promised to tell the other what they wanted, liked, or didn't like, as they went along, setting boundaries so they'd both feel comfortable at the outset. Trying to not blush, she'd laid a large towel across the sheets, worried she might bleed and didn't want to be embarrassed by soiling the bedsheets if she did. It wasn't like they were at home where she could just wash them immediately.

Josh had then wrapped his arms around her, just holding her to let the worries and insecurities fade, and for the anticipation to slowly build.

As they slowly undressed the other between tender kisses and slow touches, their passion soon ignited. He kept the pace slow, treating her like it was her first time ever. He held himself back until he was sure she was ready for him. When she saw his passion-filled eyes lock on hers, she'd reached up and kissed him, a hot kiss that scorched him. Then they took their next step forward together.

Holding her now in his arms, he knew he still needed to go slow with her and give her time to adjust. Like a virgin, she might need time for any soreness to fade. He kissed her hair, breathing in her scent. If they never left this room, that'd be just fine with him. Room service wasn't cheap, but he figured they could swing it for a while.

As he began to doze off himself, he tightened his arms around her, feeling Morgan snuggle herself even closer.

THE ROOM WAS STILL in subdued lighting from the sun being blocked by the closed curtains when Josh awoke a while later. He was still wrapped around Morgan. He just couldn't stop touching her. His hands stroked and caressed her, not knowing if she was even fully awake.

But she soon turned to him, and her own mouth and hands took over. They each took their time, feeling every curve, every inch of toned skin with hands and touches that alternated between gentleness and firmness. Their kisses transmitted in silent form their intense emotions running from ignited passion, of hurry, to tenderness, and always of love.

Later as they lay together, Morgan draped across him with her head resting on his chest, Josh smiled. His hands lazily roamed across her back and shoulders before saying, "Thank you for the gift, by the way. I don't think I've said yet how much I love and appreciate it."

Satisfied and very content, she barely heard him. When she realized what he'd said, Morgan began laughing. "You're very welcome. I'm glad you like it."

She placed kisses on his smooth, hard chest before she leaned up and kissed him, nibbling on his lips before running her tongue over them. He growled at her teasing, making her smile. Looking into his eyes, she forced herself to ask, "Was I... Was it... okay?" Even full-grown women could have doubts and insecurities, she told herself.

Josh smiled tenderly at her. "It was beyond just 'okay,' love. And it'll only get better from here. You're a natural." He kissed her to hopefully ease any insecurities. "Are *you* okay?"

"Yes." Morgan gently kissed him. "I'd have to say the same about you. But I also think we both still need to practice some more to make sure we're doing it right. I'm just not sure."

He saw the sparkle in her eyes and pulled her up against him. He grinned, saying, "Yes, dear. Whatever you say!" His mouth closed over hers, cutting off her laugh.

Long minutes later, he slipped out of bed. Returning from the bathroom, he carried a warm, damp wash cloth. Pulling back the sheets some more, he sat down beside her and once again played the gentleman and wiped her legs and most private area.

She'd never heard of a man doing this before, and she was equally slightly embarrassed and deeply touched. She had to admit, it felt really nice. More importantly, it warmed her heart and kept that hazy glow lasting longer. And it was just because he took care of her afterwards, showing her it wasn't just about the sex itself.

Josh saw the emotions on her face before he leaned down and kissed her forehead. He heard her long sigh. He looked at her and pushed her hair back from her face. "Are you sore? You need to tell me so I don't hurt you. Sweetheart, please don't be shy with me. It's just us here. We have to be honest, remember?"

She nodded before she admitted, "A little, but not too bad." She paused. "Did I... Did I bleed?"

"Only a little."

Taking his hand and lacing their fingers together, she looked at him for a long moment. "You know, having sex again was a scary thing for me to even think about for numerous reasons. But you've made it wonderful and special for me. You've lessened and taken away my fears and uncertainties. Thank you for being such a complete gentleman. It adds yet another layer for me to love."

He kissed her before he whispered, "You're welcome, sweetheart. It was very special for me too."

He took the wash cloth to the bathroom and returned to the bed. They were sitting up now, propped against the headboard. Getting herself comfortable, she trailed her fingers along his arm that held her close to him while she let her thoughts run free.

Morgan figured he wanted to know where she'd gone earlier that day. It wasn't a secret, and she knew he most likely wouldn't ask. He wouldn't want to know because he was keeping tabs on her but more from simple curiosity.

Morgan laced her fingers with his. "I don't know if I should really bring this up here and now, but I'll take the chance." She took a deep breath before saying, "This morning, I went to Shane's grave. I took some beautiful, colorful flowers there and said the goodbye I never got to say all those years ago. And when I did, when I said all I felt, well, this sense of freedom, of just being *alive*, just washed over me. I felt like a huge weight just fell off my shoulders.

"All I could think about was coming back to you and going home. But mainly, it was to come back to you because I knew with every fiber in my being, that's where I want to be."

He kissed the top of her head. "I was wondering if you were going to go to Shane's grave before we left. I wasn't even sure there was one, and if so, where it'd be. But I wanted you to. I thought you *needed* to, so I'm glad you did. It was something you needed to do on your own, and when you were ready. Are you ready to move on now?"

Morgan knew what he was asking. Could she move on with *him* now? "Yes, without a doubt. Without any reservations, Josh, yes. Over these past months, I needed to know who I was really loving, and why. I knew I loved you, and I never doubted your love for me, but something wasn't quite right. I just had to work it out in my mind and heart. The guilt, the hope, the being afraid. There was a lot I needed to work through first.

"Coming here for this trial, getting that closure, is *great* and has most undoubtedly helped me. Knowing that the criminal who killed Shane was caught, and now convicted, took a huge weight off my shoulders.

"But I stayed up last night thinking as I watched you sleeping beside me. And I wondered *what* was I doing? I love you with my whole heart, but yet I'm still somehow stuck in this other, past life. It was unfair to you, to me, to us, and it had to end. What was I waiting for?

"You've been here beside me from the very beginning, with no pretentions, no hidden agendas and motives. You never played games with me, but instead were upfront about everything from the start. No one else has done that, not even Ty when it comes down to it.

"And as I watched you sleeping last night, it all just seemed to be so crystal clear to me. It's like all of these thoughts and emotions, misgivings, whatever it all was that was bogging me down, just fell away. And everything else just fell into place.

"All I had left to do was to finish it myself by telling Shane goodbye. Let him know I was more than ready to move on—obviously it was more of a symbolic thing—because I have so much more life in me *to* live. And when I did? My world just opened up again."

Turning and now on her knees beside him, not even slightly embarrassed to be naked in the soft light thrown from the windows, she faced Josh. She needed him to see her face when she told him the rest. She needed him to see her sincerity, to know she spoke the truth.

Skimming her hands over his face, tracing it with her fingers, she smiled and looked directly into his brown eyes, those eyes that captivated her all those months ago. Knowing this was one of *those* moments a person can have, signaling a crossroads in a life, she waited a beat to savor the feeling.

Josh reached up and gently stroked her hair, pushing it back behind her shoulders. He patiently waited, allowing her the freedom to speak when she was ready. His heartbeat quickened in anticipation. In love. In hope.

Finally, she spoke again. "It became very clear to me that the most important thing in my life is you, and I wasn't going to let you go. And the only way for me to fully *live* again was to be with you." She cupped his face in her hands, leaning forward to kiss his lips tenderly. "And *only* you. I'm not thinking of anyone else, Josh. I love you to the moon and back." Looking at him, she said softly, "You're *my* Mr. Right."

He gripped her hips, moving her to straddle him so he could look into her eyes. Had he ever been this content before? Josh gently placed his hands on her cheeks for a moment before he slowly let his hands slide down her neck, her strong shoulders, her toned arms before resting them at her waist.

His heart, his entire being, felt like it was so full of love he simply couldn't hold it all in anymore. Leaning forward to tenderly kiss her, he whispered, "I love you to the moon and back, too, Morgan. You know that, right?" She nodded, seeing the love shining from his eyes. Holding back his smile, he said after a mock sigh, "So you understand when I say it took you long enough."

She blinked in surprise and then laughed as she wrapped her arms around him, hugging him close for a long moment. Pulling back, she rested her forehead against his. After a moment, she said, "Let's go home, Josh. It's time for us to go home."

"Not yet. After."

"After what?"

"After we call my mom—"

Morgan burst out laughing as Josh wrapped her in his arms and rolled her over.

Chapter 54

May

MORGAN DECIDED SHE DIDN'T need to be at the sentencing phase as she had all she needed now. They'd come and accomplished what needed to be done.

The next day, they returned their rental car and drove the original car back to the hotel. They decided to just do nothing but be tourists and have some fun and unwind. They spent their days driving far away from the city so she could just be herself. Nights and early mornings were spent making love and speaking soft words during pillow talk.

She called Captain Sinclair to let him know they weren't coming in for the sentencing. He agreed to let her know the sentence afterwards, though, for the complete closure and her peace of mind. He'd get their return flights set up, assuring her there was no rush for them to leave unless they needed to.

As it turned out, her skipping the sentencing was a wonderful stroke of luck. The media was swarming every entrance into the courthouse, hoping to get at least video of the victim's widow, even if she refused an interview and gave the noncommittal "No comment." They weren't sure if the media knew her now or not, but it was simply better to avoid the area altogether. Captain Sinclair would warn them if something came up.

Morgan left her ex-in-laws for the media to feed on like vultures. If her former relatives wanted to live in that disgusting spotlight for their own interests, she wanted no part of it whatsoever.

She couldn't understand their sick need for attention any more than she could understand the voracious appetite so-called reporters had for horrible tragedies like this. Sound bites and career moves were more important than victims and their families who all had to live in the terrible aftermath for the rest of their lives.

The stories soon die, but the pain lives on.

For her, she came not for the glory and publicity, but came only to fully support and honor her husband in death. And hopefully to gain closure so she could now freely live.

She felt satisfied and confident she'd done all three.

Chapter 55

THEIR TRIP BACK HOME to Arizona was blessedly uneventful. Both were looking forward to not looking over their shoulders anytime they went out. They both missed the simple comforts of home.

Morgan couldn't wait to see Ty and her pets. Josh couldn't wait to see if he still had one. Morgan offered to share hers with him in case Freeway decided to stay with Damien and Laura. He smiled as he took her hand as they walked off the plane and into the crowded terminal.

Finally getting to the luggage carousels, Morgan spotted Ty right away. She laughed and shrieked in delight at seeing him. Running to him, she jumped in his arms, giving him a bear hug as he swung her around. "Oh, I missed you, Ty! It's so good to see you again!"

Ty kissed her cheek as he hugged her long and hard, just holding on to his best friend. After a while, he finally put her down on her own feet. "It's great to see you too! I hardly recognized you in the get-up you're still in. Welcome home, darlin'. You seriously look better than ever!"

She was to stay in her disguise until they got to his truck, where it should be safe for her to remove it all for the final time. Since they had to use their fake IDs to return home, she had to wear her disguise one last time. But it was also for safety, in case she was being followed by anyone who could recognize her. No use botching up their efforts at the last second, after all.

Ty took in the glow on her face, her eyes still vibrant but no longer haunted in their depths. She's changed, Ty thought to himself. He could see it all over her. Truly, she was free now.

He gave Josh a manly hug instead of a handshake, saying, "You did well! You look like you're in one piece still. Did she give you a hard time?"

Morgan protested, "Me? I think it was the other way around."

Josh smiled. "Well, she was a handful all right. But it wasn't anything I couldn't handle. Wait until you see what she got you for a gift. You're gonna love it!"

Ty smiled. "Yeah? What'd she get me?"

Heading out to the parking garage and their truck for the final leg of the trip back to the Center, Morgan smiled in the bright sunlight. As she walked with the two most important people in her life, Morgan knew she was already home.

FAR AWAY FROM AN airport in Arizona, two figures were talking in a private room. The curtains were open, but the blinds were partially closed to block some of the sun coming in. The filtered sunlight highlighted the few dust particles floating lazily in the air.

One man sat in a plush chair while the other stood in front of his desk, occasionally pacing the room in agitation and uncertainty.

The seated man watched the other man begin pacing again. He asked, "Are you *sure* this is what you want to do? Are you *absolutely* sure? No doubts?"

The pacing man stopped and looked at him. "It doesn't really matter. I've no other choice, and you know it as well as I do, Solomon. She's started a new life, and she's needed to. Letting her know any more now wouldn't do her any good, none at all. I fear it'd only make things ever so much worse for her. This new knowledge would destroy all she's done. It'd also rob her of a safer future, the future she deserves.

"No, it wouldn't be right or fair to her. It's all about her, and what's best for her. It always was."

"Tomorrow could—"

"No." Sitting down in a chair opposite Solomon, he placed his cane beside his chair. "I've thought of every option out there, and there's just no way to get around the facts. It's best for everyone, so we leave things as they are.

"It's not easy. It's far from it. It's anything *but* easy. But she doesn't deserve to have her life torn apart again. Things have changed, and everything is different now. Time can't be reversed, so we just move forward. It's for the best," he repeated softly.

Both men wondered if he really believed it.

After a moment, he stood up, grabbed his cane and began walking toward the door. "It's just that the first step is always the hardest, isn't it?" He opened the door on his own question, not really expecting an answer.

"Wait up a minute, Storm," Solomon called him back, using his code name.

Storm stopped. He turned back around to face Solomon, looking at him questioningly.

"You're *not* alone even though you may feel that way. You know you can always come to me, no matter what you need, right? Whether it's just to talk, or you want the company? Anything..."

Instead of verbally answering him, Storm saluted the seated man with a small, forced smile. He left the room, using his cane to keep his balance.

Wishing he could do more, Solomon sighed as the door closed quietly behind him.

Storm slowly made his way down the brightly lit corridor. He turned into his office and shut his door, locking it. Sitting down at his desk, he unlocked and opened a thin drawer.

He pulled out a Ziploc bag that held an old photograph, necklace, and a small American flag. He also removed two dried flower buds from beside the taped recordings that had ripped his very soul in two when he'd listened to them. His anguish and despair were nearly too overwhelming to bear.

Opening the larger plastic bag, he lovingly removed the worn photograph. He looked at the two people whose lives were uprooted, and how their one life together ended so abruptly.

As he ran his finger over the two faces in the picture, a single tear slid down his cheek.

Chapter 56

The following January

"SWEETHEART, WHERE ARE YOU?" Josh called out as he walked through the wide doors of Red Rock. He smelled the sweet scents of the recently-delivered alfalfa and grass hay, and the grain in the huge bins with lockable lids. He saw the neat stack of flattened, now-empty grain bags beside the wall. "Morgan?"

"Back here!" Her voice came from behind a large stack of hay.

He walked around the stack and found her raking up loose hay and tossing it into wheelbarrows. There was hay dust floating in the air as she stirred it up, even raking and sweeping slowly with water sprinkled on it to keep it under control.

Walking up to her, he grabbed the rake, hauled her close with one arm and kissed her. She wrapped her arms around his waist and returned his kiss. After a while, he finally pulled away. With a grin, he pulled some loose hay from her hair. She ran her hands up and down his strong back a few times before stepping back.

"Hi, gorgeous!"

"Hello there, handsome!" She smiled, taking back the rake. She began cleaning again. "Have a seat. I'm almost done here." She gestured behind him at the hay bales she'd put there. "I haven't seen you much lately. It's good your business is booming, though, especially at this time of year." She glanced over at him. "Are you staying over tonight? Or are you heading back to your house?"

Helping out, he moved the wheelbarrow for her to the pile she was raking toward. He grabbed the shovel as he watched her rake together the loose hay, considering her questions.

"Well, I do have some clothes here, and I'm off tomorrow so I can stay over. I spent the morning with Freeway, cleaned her litter box, and she has lots of fresh food and water.

She still plays with that toy we got her so she's good for the night. I also left the little TV on for her, just in case." He scooped up loose hay with the shovel and dumped it in the wheelbarrow. "It'd be nice to relax for a while with you and not be rushing off for a change."

"It would."

Lately he'd been doing a lot of thinking about the two of them, and he was wondering how to ask her what he really wanted to. When he wasn't around her, he found himself truly missing her. She'd become his focus, and he'd never been happier.

Since they'd returned the previous May from attending the trial, Josh had given her the space he felt she may need or want. After almost a decade, she was now free from the haunted feeling of not having closure over her first husband. He gave her the time and space to enjoy that new feeling of freedom, to settle into her new self, and to let their relationship move along naturally and slowly. He loved her too much to push or rush her even though sometimes it was all he could do not to.

They spent as much time with the other as they could, but with them both being business owners, sometimes it was hard to do. In an effort to keep their relationship strong and solid, they both did their best to always take time out of their schedule to be with the other.

He'd watched Damien and Laura and what they did to retain their loving relationship for some time. He wasn't too proud to learn from them. His own parents did the same thing. He figured he had some great role models, and he planned to take advantage of them.

He scooped up more hay, and then watched her rake for another moment. He got the watering can and sprinkled water across the floor to help prevent more dust. When she was done with that section, he grabbed the broom, slowly swept up the finer hay into the shovel.

He asked, "Sweetheart, don't you think it'd just be easier to live together?"

Morgan glanced at him as she moved the now-full wheelbarrow out of the way and got another one. "Probably. It'll just be a longer drive for one of us. Most likely you as there needs to be someone here on property. You also know how I feel about just shacking up with someone for convenience. I don't care at all if others do it, but it's not for me."

He nodded. "You want to be married first."

"Yes."

She refused to actually live together with him just for the sake of convenience. She had her personal standards, and figured if she was good enough to live with, then she was good enough to marry too. Morgan wouldn't budge on it. Not that Josh had ever once pushed her on it.

She knew many guys would have, but not her Josh. He fully respected her and their relationship. It was one of the many reasons her heart beat for him and no other. She knew she'd hit the mother lode of gold mines in finding Josh almost two years ago, and she took care to not take him for granted. But she also wouldn't push aside her own beliefs she held as important in order to simply please him.

They compromised pretty easily on most any topic, and respected the feelings and decisions of the other on the ones they didn't. In fact, they rarely argued over anything. Simply put, neither saw the point *in* arguing.

They knew to word their opinions or positions in a more open manner to avoid an argument even beginning, knowing the best argument was *no* argument. But if they did, they worked it out like mature and respectful adults.

They knew neither was perfect. They each had their own beliefs and opinions. And they knew each had to put work into keeping their relationship good and strong. They were still very honest with each other and planned on that always being the case.

Overall, their relationship was a smooth, loving one. They were far more likely to laugh with each other than argue.

"Okay," Josh said in response to her last comment.

Morgan reached out with the rake for a small pile of hay and then froze in mid-reach. Her heart began beating thunderously in her chest, and blood roared in her ears. Slowly, she straightened up and turned to look at him. Something in his voice had stopped her.

"Okay *what?*"

Josh gave her a dazzling smile. "Let's get married, sweetheart!"

"Are you *serious?*" Morgan just stood there, gaping at him.

He propped the shovel against the wall and walked over to her. He cupped her dusty face as he poured out his heart to her. "As a heart attack, which is what I have every time I'm around you. When I look at you, think of you, kiss you, make love with you.

"Life would never be the same without you beside me. You not only complement me, you challenge me, and you complete me. And I believe I do the same to you. There are so many reasons why I want you in my life, Morgan. It'll take a lifetime to tell you.

"But what it really boils down to is I love you, Morgan O'Connell. Just you." Leaning down, he kissed her tenderly. He looked directly into her eyes for a moment, knowing *this* moment was inevitable from the moment they'd first met. "Will you marry me, Morgan?" he asked softly.

An avalanche of joy rushed through her, her smile as dazzling as he'd ever seen it. Even with the hay dust floating in the air around them, he could see the shining green of her eyes.

He caught her as she threw herself in his arms, her long legs wrapped around his waist, the rake forgotten until it clattered against the concrete floor. Her momentum nearly knocked him off his feet, but he caught his balance. She squeezed him with her arms and legs, her face buried in his neck. Josh heard her laugh and cry at the same time.

In-between her indecision on which emotion to let loose fully with, she was able to get out a joyous and exuberant, "*Yes!*"

She pulled back, looked into those brown eyes that had captured her from the very first time they met. Morgan kissed him passionately as he held her tightly to his body. When she pulled back, she decided another kiss was absolutely necessary and leaned back in to get it. Her heart was bursting with happiness.

He let her slide down his body, kissed her again. "So... We're engaged?" His smile was wide. His face full of joy. He ran his hands over her dark hair, then down to her strong shoulders.

Morgan's own face mirrored his as she nodded. Her radiant green eyes were shining with her happy tears. "What about a ring? Do you have one?" The excitement and joy in her voice made his heart swell even more in happiness.

"No."

"Why not?"

"I wasn't planning on asking you this evening in the feed barn, I guess. Sue me, sweetheart!" He grinned at her. An idea came to him. "Let me see your pocketknife." He wiggled his fingers for her to hand it over.

Reaching into her back pocket, she slipped it out and handed it to him.

Josh walked over to the cut bailing twine hanging neatly in the corner. He cut off a strand each of red, yellow and blue strings. Sitting down on some stacked hay bales, Morgan happily squeezing on beside him, he tied the ends together and handed them to her.

"Hold tight." With fingers more dexterous than she would've thought, he tightly braided the three colored strings of baling twine together. "Give me your wrist."

"Why?"

"Because I'm your future husband, and I said so." He grinned at her.

Grinning back, she held out her left arm. He wrapped the braided twine around her wrist to gauge the length he needed. Nodding to himself, he cut the strings and braided the loose ends into what he'd already done, making a small but wide loop. It wasn't exactly braiding, from what Morgan could tell, but looked sort of like macramé.

He slipped it over her wrist like a bracelet.

Holding up the leftover twine, he asked, "Which color do you like best?"

With a happy grin, she pointed to the yellow one.

"Good choice." Josh then took a piece of the yellow string and with a slip knot, made a tiny loop. With a look of seriousness mixed with humor on his face, he took hold of her left hand. As he slipped the twine ring on her finger, he said, "With this ring, I now engage thee."

Morgan's heart fell to her feet, her toes seriously tingled, and her eyes filled with tears as Josh held onto her hand and slipped the makeshift ring onto her finger. He then tenderly kissed the back of her hand and smiled at her.

"The bracelet is an engagement present. The ring is to prove we are." Looking into her eyes, he asked softly, "Satisfied?"

With tears running down her cheeks, she could only nod. Finally, she said hoarsely, "More than. I love you, Josh. So very, very much!"

She wrapped her arms around his neck and pulled him in close and held on tightly to the man who meant the world to her.

Chapter 57

EARLY THE NEXT MORNING, Ty walked into the office, letting the door close softly behind him. A bit surprised seeing Morgan there before him, he commented, "Good morning, darlin'. You're here early. Man, that coffee smells terrific!" He saw a large box in the corner. "Hey, are those fresh donuts? *This* early? Did you even go to bed last night?"

She grinned. "Sure did. I just thought I'd spoil my people this morning. And that fresh coffee is just for you. It should be done by now. The donuts are for us up here. I already took some more to Quail Run."

As Ty walked by her desk toward the donuts and coffee, he stopped in his tracks. Ty's heart stopped beating for a second, and his eyes glanced back at her face. She was glowing and happy. She'd looked happy since last May when she and Josh returned from attending the trial, but *this* was a new glow. Her beauty could still steal his breath away at times.

But this time, it was something else.

He glanced down to the yellow twine on her left ring finger and the multi-colored bracelet on her wrist. A barrage of emotions ran through him as he looked at that simple piece of yellow twine on her finger.

His eyes never left her hand as he asked quietly, "Is that a ring?"

She felt her heart skip a beat, and she looked up. Seeing the emotions on her best friend's face, she smiled a bit tremulously. Of everyone here she wanted to know first, it was Ty. It *had* to be Ty. And this was a huge step for their relationship—her marrying someone else.

She'd debated with herself last night on how to tell him about becoming engaged. She'd admitted to Josh she felt nervous about it. He understood and told her to just go with the flow. She'd know the moment when it came. They both knew Ty would be more than pleased with their engagement, but it'd also be a singularly big step away from him too.

Slowly, she nodded her head. Her eyes glistened with tears as she answered softly, "Josh asked me to marry him last night. I said yes."

Ty's heart tightened as he looked at her face. He was so proud of her he couldn't speak. *She'd done it!* he thought. Ty just looked at her, happy and sad at the same time. Fleetingly, he wondered how her marriage would affect their friendship.

Morgan walked around her desk and cupped his face tenderly. She knew the roller coaster he must be riding right now because last night when she thought about telling him, she rode it too.

"I love him, Ty. And I love you too. Josh thinks the world of you, and we in no way want our marriage to affect you and me although we all know it will in some ways."

Ty smiled at her, and she relaxed. He pulled her close to him and hugged her tightly and rocked her. Her arms wrapped around him, and she squeezed him back as she rested her head against his shoulder. They just held onto each other for a minute, no words needing to be spoken.

Finally, Ty released her and kissed her cheek. "You know I love you, too, Morgan. I'm not worried about our relationship. I'm just..." He paused as his voice cracked.

Morgan had never ever seen Ty cry, and her eyes teared up instantly at even the thought of him doing so. Not that he *was* exactly, but she heard the raw emotion in her best friend's voice and could see the expressions race across his face.

Trying to hold in his emotions, he looked at her before he forced out, "I'm just so damn happy for you, Morgan. Honest to God, I'm so happy, and so very, very proud of you. Congratulations! Josh is a terrific guy, and you know I approve of him. I just wonder what took him so long?"

Morgan grinned and hugged him again. She rested her head on his solid chest for a moment. Pulling back, she said sincerely, "You know this would *never* have happened if it weren't for you.

"*You* were the one who opened my eyes and encouraged me to live again. *You* were the one who planted the seed in my mind to date again, and *you* supported me every step of the way. And *you* were the one who put Josh through the wringer before you'd let him get near me. *You* were the one who's been watching out for me for all these years."

Ty smiled, placing his hands on her shoulders. "But *you* were the one who had to have the strength to put all those seeds I planted into play. *You* were the only one who could make them grow and get the roots planted in solid ground."

Morgan smiled and said, "*You* are the solid ground for me, Ty. You always will be. You and I have a friendship many wouldn't understand because they can't know. I'll never let that bond between us break, not so long as I can help it."

"Right back at you." Ty stepped back, his smile broad as he held her hand and closely inspected her 'ring.' He looked back up at her face as he fingered the yellow baling twine band, saying, "Well, it's certainly colorful. But seeing this ring concerns me. Is this supposed to be gold? Either our Josh is having serious financial difficulties, or he's cheap when it comes to our girl. Do I need to have a talk with him about how I expect him to take care of you?"

Laughing, Morgan replied, "He just has an incredibly romantic nature. *Our Josh*," Morgan repeated, grinning, "is doing just fine financially. He just said he hadn't *planned* on asking me in Red Rock when I asked him where the ring was. It just kinda happened.

"So, he made me one right then and there. And look! He made a matching bracelet as an engagement present too." She held out her arm so Ty could inspect her bracelet made of colorful twine.

Ty smiled broadly and nodded as he inspected it. It actually was a really nice bracelet and that impressed him. Suddenly, he asked, "Wait a second. He asked you to marry him in Red Rock, the *feed barn?*" He laughed when she happily nodded. "Classy. Very classy. I always did like him!"

WORD SPREAD LIKE WILDFIRE that Josh and Morgan were officially engaged. It seemed as if all of her workers, customers, and vendors came by, called, texted, or emailed her with their congratulations. She'd been very firm with every single person about putting anything at all on social media and absolutely no photos.

She detested social media and reminded them all it wasn't for a whole world of complete strangers to know about as it wasn't anyone's business but their own. They wanted to retain their own privacy. Once anything got online, it never got removed.

All complied with their wishes although no one knew the real reasons why. But it made sense to them, so they agreed with no arguments.

Josh's employees were about as ecstatic as hers were. Damien, Laura, and Ty got together with Ryan and Kristi and threw them a private surprise engagement party at The Neon Moon. The place was crowded with well-wishers, comprised of their employees and friends.

Patrick and Annabelle were beside themselves in excitement when they got the news.

Josh had taken a picture of the twine ring on her finger with his phone and texted it to his mom with the caption reading only: *She said yes!!!*

Morgan sent the same picture to his dad from her phone with the caption reading only: *He finally asked!!!*

Although Josh had offered to get her a real ring, Morgan declined his sincere offer with a smile and a tender kiss. She told him they just had to get married before *this* ring rotted off her finger. "I want a short engagement here. I think we've waited long enough already, don't you?"

Josh wholeheartedly agreed.

Epilogue

May

JOSH WRIGHT AND MORGAN O'Connell were married on the first Saturday in May. Kentucky Derby Day. They decided what better day for two horse people to celebrate their wedding especially when one had lived in Kentucky, and the other one from the state above it.

Besides that, for them, it was a reminder of their time together the year before when they were celebrating their new life together, moving forward, and gaining freedom from the past.

Their wedding went smoothly and the reception was just a good old Western party with some Kentucky Derby nostalgia thrown in to commemorate the day. Josh joked his personal 'run for the roses' took on a whole new meaning as that was the main flower Morgan had chosen.

Red roses and baby's breath.

Josh made sure to invite Leslie Travis. He told Morgan if it wasn't for Leslie, he never would've come to Harmony Hills that day they first ran into each other, and they never would've met. Leslie said she was sincerely honored. Josh made sure she got her discount on future work.

Josh absolutely refused to invite Elise. He refused to invite someone who did nothing but stir up trouble and drama on the most important day of his life. He was backed by his adoring fiancée, best friend (and Best Man), and his best friend's wife.

Josh built his new wife a large, screened-in gazebo for a wedding present with help from Ryan and Ty, and some minimal help from the not-so-savvy-handyman Damien. It came complete with an extra-wide overhang to provide shade inside, and electrical outlets even though the misting ceiling fan and lighting were mainly sourced by solar energy which could be stored in special batteries.

The padded bench seats inside along the screened walls doubled as storage areas, trimmed with bright interior lights that came on when the bench seats were lifted up. Morgan joked it was like lifting up a toilet seat that identified as a refrigerator door. Her new husband insisted the lights were so they didn't need to use a flashlight to see inside the darkened spaces.

She knew it was because he was afraid a snake could slither in there somehow even though he'd made it as airtight as he could. There were always scorpions and tarantulas to think about as well. Either way, she loved the idea and the effort.

He added a small fire pit to be used in the cooler winter months to chase away the chill. Her swing on one side faced the mountains to the West for the glorious sunsets, and a part of the horse paddocks. But he also made it so it could swivel around to see the other views, if so desired.

Ryan referred to it as "the fanciest and snazziest gazebo ever made."

Ty and Damien agreed. Damien was instantly worried Laura would want one too. If so, they'd have to sell their house and move somewhere that had enough space for one.

Ryan and Ty laughed—both secretly wondering how much truth there was to his concern. Josh simply offered to build him a new house to go along with it.

Morgan bought her new husband a breathtaking custom-made saddle so they could ride in fine style in her mountains and the Tucson Rodeo Parade together. Personally knowing Master Saddlemakers Loren and Lisa Skyhorse in Durango, Colorado, it was a project Morgan completely enjoyed doing with them.

She'd had the date of their wedding and their initials engraved into the leather. The other meticulous, intricate leather carvings, and the thin silver braiding and accents were a surefire hit.

Josh was speechless when he first saw it. He still thought it was too much of a work of art to sit on, let alone get dirty. He gave as much care to the saddle as some men give to a new truck or classic sportscar.

Now all they needed to do was find Josh his own horse—which they did a lot faster than either expected. A friend of one of Morgan's longtime boarders needed to sell his buckskin Quarter horse due to a job relocation. But he wouldn't sell his horse unless it was to a safe, loving, forever home.

After Morgan went out to see the horse for herself and meet the man who owned him, she thought Roman might be a good fit for her fiancé. She soon came back out with Josh to see if he and Roman clicked, and for the owner to meet Josh himself.

The owner approved of them both. He already knew the reputation of Harmony Hills, and knew his good friend had her own horse there and loved it. But it was still with a very heavy heart that he sold his horse to Josh, telling himself no one would take as good of care of his horse than these two experienced horse lovers.

It almost made both Josh and Morgan cry seeing him sell his beloved horse and hugging Roman's neck in goodbye. Josh handed him the check, and he handed over Roman's registration papers and a bill of sale. They assured him he could come visit Roman anytime he was back in the area. They'd even send him updates if he wanted them to. He hugged his horse goodbye again just before they loaded him in their trailer.

Morgan wiped tears from her eyes as she got into the passenger side as she could completely feel what the man was going through emotionally. She was torn about how Roman might feel too. He didn't understand he'd probably never see his dad again. That thought had her practically bawling for them both.

THE BOISTEROUS WEDDING RECEPTION wound down late that Saturday night. As Josh and Morgan prepared to leave on their honeymoon to tour England and Ireland for two weeks, a lone figure with a cane mingled with the large crowd.

He talked and joked with many of the others who were present, partook of the delicious catered dinner, the moist wedding cake, and drank the champagne and punch. He held his glass up for the toasts.

He also tapped his glass with a fork along with everyone else signally for the new bride and groom to kiss, which they happily did every time. He even laughed when the groom took his own fork to tap his own glass just to get another kiss from his laughing new bride.

He watched the tall man named Ty hug the bride tightly and long before kissing her cheek, his face showing genuine happiness for the couple. And he saw how she did the same to him. He watched them dance together, noticed their smiles, and sensed their strong bond.

He also watched Ty with the new groom. He studied how they interacted with each other with such ease. They seemed tight, and very much on friendly terms.

He noticed how the groom's parents happily held the bride in long hugs and more kisses on cheeks with bright, enthusiastic smiles. He watched as the groom's sisters pulled their new sister onto the dance floor, and the three danced in wild abandon and joy.

But he watched alone from a distance, standing in the deep shadows, as the bride and groom got into the decorated truck that'd take them away. He didn't bother to wipe away the few tears that ran unheeded down his cheeks. He just leaned heavily on his cane, needing its support.

After Josh and Morgan had driven away, honking their horn as they left the parking lot to begin a new life together, more tears ran freely down his face. He swiped at them now with his sleeve.

As the cheering and clapping of all those present began dying down, he continued to stand there motionless in the shadows. When he could no longer see the truck's red taillights in the distance, he wiped away the tears again with his sleeve and tried to pull himself together.

In his hand, he held the single delicate red rose and sprig of baby's breath he'd taken. He carefully slipped them into his jacket pocket.

He then slipped away from the shadows and disappeared even further into the dark.

Review Request

Thank you for reading *The Secret*.

I truly hope you enjoyed the journey of Morgan and Josh...and the others.

If so, could I humbly ask you to write an honest online review for me? What did you like best? How did it make you feel? Did it make you laugh, cry, etc.? Please give me the good stuff so I know what made you like/love it! Be honest.

If you didn't like it, please be tactful. (Surely there was *something* you liked?)

Thanks!

Please leave a review anywhere/everywhere my books are sold as reviews are not linked together for others to read.

<u>Thank you so much in advance!</u>

Stay tuned for future releases.

Happy trails,

Jordan

Acknowledgements

I'd be rude and remiss if I didn't FIRST thank fantasy author Kat Ross for her unwavering support and encouragement. We "met" under the oddest of circumstances, but I say things happen for a reason. Kat, you've been both a guiding light and a beacon of hope in this publishing journey of mine. I seriously don't know what I would've done without you. Probably nothing. (ha) I've learned more from you than you know.

And *most definitely* Dawn Hickerson with Austin DesignWorks for my website. Like a knight in shining armor, you saved the day and my sanity. It was, and is, an absolute pleasure...and relief...to work with a true professional. An experienced and helpful guru like you is hard to find. (Check your email for future mayday calls. Hi there, Crystal!)

Also a warm and heartfelt "Thank you!" to Lisa Skyhorse of Skyhorse Saddles in Durango, CO. Lisa, you said it'd be an honor to be in my book, but it's an honor to tip my hat once again to you and Loren's remarkable talents! I'm continuously blown away.

And to all of those other literary professionals out there who have been guiding me and answering all of my questions...even the ones I didn't know to ask yet. Joanna Penn in England, Robynne Alexander with Damonza in NZ, and of course, all of the Support techs in various countries at all hours. It really is a small world now.

Last, but not least, to all my readers. To the ARC Readers who read my books early: Thank you all for your unbiased reviews! And now to all of my future readers...

THANK YOU!

(I just realized most of the people who have been, and still are, guiding me on this journey are all accomplished and talented women. And global. How about that?!)

I see you all as women of strength, courage, and hope.

www.KatRossBooks.com   www.TheCreativePenn.com

www.Skyhorse.com   www.Damonza.com

www.AustinDesignWorks.com

About Jordan Standridge

An avid reader and writer since childhood, Award-Winning and Best-Selling Author Jordan Standridge is joyfully and tirelessly expanding her literary sphere. Influenced by Walter Farley and Louis L'Amour growing up, and later Julie Garwood, Jordan now creates her own stories. Weaving many of her real-life experiences with her imagination, she infuses them with her humor, love for animals, life lessons, values, and romance. And then she'll probably add a dash of mystery and suspense because she can.

A frequent traveler and mover, Jordan currently lives near Lexington, Kentucky.

Need More?

Book Club Discussion Material

"The Secret"
Book 1: The Women of Strength, Courage, and Hope Series
Also available for FREE downloads at www.JordanStandridge.com

1. What did you think of Morgan naming her new home "Harmony Hills"? And how she came up with her barn names?

2. What are some clues that Morgan still lives in fear and with caution?

3. How do you feel about animals being used as therapy in everyday living? Do you believe they can be good for that? Can humans be theirs?

4. In regards to Ty and Morgan, can males and females be that close without having a sexual relationship? Is it easier to have a best friend of the opposite sex?

5. In Chapter 8, Josh shares the story of his mom spanking him as a young boy for riding Gem. But she later apologizes to her little son. Discuss the maturity and humbleness of a parent doing this.

6. There is a correlation between Josh and the color green. Name three instances this was brought up.

7. What do you feel about Morgan's thoughts about God in Chapter 16?

8. Discuss Josh's reactions/responses to Ty and Morgan's closeness. Do you think Josh feels he's "sharing" her with Ty? Why, or why not?

9. In Chapters 17-19, we have the fateful meeting between Josh and Morgan. Discuss the safety initiatives Morgan took to protect herself from a complete

stranger.

10. From Chapter 21, discuss the ground rules that Josh and Morgan created to start a safe, mature relationship. Do you agree with the need for ground rules in any relationship? What do you think of their code for serious discussions?

11. Also in Chapter 21, Josh and Morgan discuss what qualifies as "good music." They list a few famous songwriters and singers. If you were a part of their conversation, what would you say?

12. Morgan is a woman of strength. What are some of her strengths?

13. In Chapters 16 and 46, Morgan &/or Annabelle discuss their personal beliefs and thoughts about organized religions, ministers, history, etc. How do you feel about their perspectives? How do you feel about them being able to talk about religion in a respectful and cordial manner?

14. Discuss the reasons and benefits of Morgan holding game nights at her house.

15. In chapter 24, Morgan compares adding Josh to her circle as making a recipe. Do you agree with this analogy?

16. In Chapters 31-34 especially, Morgan and Ty need to forgive each other. How do you feel about the strength of their relationship in doing this? How will their new one be affected?

17. In Chapter 40 before Josh and Morgan leave for the airport, Ty and Josh talk outside. At one point, Josh offers his unconditional friendship to Ty. This deeply touches Ty, another alpha male. They both realize how hard it is for men to be honest about needing friendship and support. Do you think this is a real issue with men? Why, or why not?

18. At the trial in Chapter 43, Clare is still judging Natasha. Ironically, Clare is judging her due to her looks and status, to the point of even practically condemning her own sons for being attracted to her by looks alone. What are the signs of Clare's hypocrisy in this?

19. Discuss the differences in family dynamics between Morgan's past family,

Shane's, and Josh's. And how she created her own. What makes a family?

20. In Chapter 44, Josh begins to truly realize what Morgan had gone through—and still was. He questions whether or not he himself could've done it... And done it completely alone. Could *you* do it?

21. In Chapter 45, Morgan worried about just showing up at Pops and Annabelle's house with no warning. She recalled her own family had demanded notice just to come over while Annabelle said family doesn't need a reservation to come home. What are your thoughts on this/the differences in attitude, culture, etc.?

22. In Chapter 46, Morgan and Annabelle also discuss relationships, sex, and women being true to themselves. They also discuss the lack of women's rights over thousands of years. Discuss these topics.

23. In Chapter 48, the scene when Josh's sisters and their husbands come over, discuss what his parents (especially Annabelle) said to Dan and Jack. Do you agree with her?

24. Also in Chapter 49, we hear Morgan sharing with Josh her old memories about her first husband. He encourages her to talk to him in order to help her heal and cope. How do you feel about Josh doing this? How do you think this affects him (hearing her talk about her first husband, and their life together)?

25. In Chapter 51, Morgan discusses two types of people, and how they love. Which type do you fit in?

26. Also in Chapter 51, Josh and Morgan discuss how God must have had a hand in getting them together. Do you believe that happens, or is everything just left up to chance?

27. In Chapter 57, Morgan tells Ty she's engaged. His emotions speak volumes. Discuss how you think he felt? How was her marriage to Josh going to affect them? Would it?

28. What patterns did you notice in how the book was written? Tying in the beginning with the end? Names that referenced real people/couples? Foreshadowing examples? How the tone/setting/feeling was built/presented?

Sneak Peek

The Witness

Book Two
The Women of Strength, Courage, and Hope Series

By courageously saving a policeman's life, she's now endangered her own.

**** SILVER MEDAL WINNER in 2025 Global Book Awards
** DOUBLE GOLD MEDAL WINNER in 2026 Next Generation Indie
Book Awards**

Be sure to visit **www.JordanStandridge.com** for more information, *and* be sure to subscribe to my FREE e-newsletter while there. You'll get a FREE character backstory when you do!